A Cloud on Sand

Alfred A. Knopf

New York

1990

A
Cloud
on
Sand

Gabriella De Ferrari

THIS IS A BORZOI BOOK
PUBLISHED BY ALFRED A. KNOPF, INC.

TITLE PAGE ILLUSTRATION: *Lewis et Irène* by
Paul Morand, Cercle Lyonnais du Livre, 1929.

Library of Congress Cataloging-in-Publication Data
De Ferrari, Gabriella.
A cloud on sand / Gabriella De Ferrari.—1st ed.
p. cm.
ISBN 0-394-55145-1
I. Title.
PS3554.E1115C5 1989   88-45767
813′.54—dc20   CIP

Manufactured in the United States of America
First Edition

A
Cloud
on
Sand

Gabriella De Ferrari

THIS IS A BORZOI BOOK
PUBLISHED BY ALFRED A. KNOPF, INC.

TITLE PAGE ILLUSTRATION: *Lewis et Irène* by
Paul Morand, Cercle Lyonnais du Livre, 1929.

Library of Congress Cataloging-in-Publication Data
De Ferrari, Gabriella.
A cloud on sand / Gabriella De Ferrari.—1st ed.
p. cm.
ISBN 0-394-55145-1
I. Title.
PS3554.E1115C5 1989   88-45767
813'.54—dc20   CIP

Manufactured in the United States of America
First Edition

Preface

BY THE TIME a cloud is reflected in the sand, the image is barely what first appeared in the sky. By the time this book was finished, the people whose stories I wanted to tell became new and very different people: Dora, Antonia, Marco, Arturo, and many others. Strong and determined individuals who not only led unconventional lives but also confronted the displacement and opportunity that comes to those who move to a different culture. It is also the story of the people whose lives they touched, of the places they lived, and of the changes they inspired. I have known many such brave people in my life, this is a story about them. I have also made a home in two different cultures and in several different cities. I love and have lived in many of the places that I write about.

A special thank you goes to my editor Carol Brown Janeway and to Robin Swados for their very many important suggestions and for their belief in this book. In particular, I wish to acknowledge the essential contributions made by Peter Walsh. My gratitude also goes to my children, Nathaniel and Bree, who have not only encouraged me to write this book, but who have always been a source of encouragement, patience, and good humour. This is also true of my friends; I am in debt to them.

And to Ray for making it all possible.

A Cloud on Sand

Prologue

WHEN THE SHIP left Buenos Aires, most of the Italian-speaking passengers were gone. Neither Antonia nor Eliana spoke much Spanish and, since Toma spoke little Italian, they felt more and more alone. The other passengers stayed in their cabins or huddled in small groups in the salon. Naturally, everyone was nervous; no one liked to talk much to strangers, not knowing exactly who the other passengers were, or if they were who they appeared to be, or said they were.

The two women were more dependent on Toma than before. This did not improve things between him and Eliana. Antonia insisted that he stay near them in case they needed an interpreter. Eliana did not approve.

"Don't sit so close to him," she said to Antonia.

"Why not?"

"He has lice."

"How do you know that?"

"He's an Indian, isn't he? He should stay below like the other servants."

And what about you? Antonia felt like saying. "But we need him to speak Spanish for us," she said instead.

"What good is that if he can't speak Italian to us?" said Eliana with a sneer. "Anyway, don't let him get you alone."

"Why not?"

"For reasons," said Eliana, "that an innocent girl like you should remain ignorant of."

"I'm not so innocent and I'm hardly a girl anymore," said Antonia. "After all, I'm a married woman."

Eliana looked at her without smiling. Her brown face was like an old orange which had dried up on the tree.

To get away from this, Antonia went on deck. She was almost always alone these days when she went outside. It was growing colder. The sun still shone out of a sky swept clean and luminous as the sky over the Mediterranean, but the blue had washed out of it as out of an old dress. The sea rolled under it in a dull, opaque gray, concealing whatever was beneath the surface.

Antonia stood by herself and stared out over the water. She listened to the water as if trying to make out Arturo's voice under the monotonous grumble of the waves and the engines. Was she a married woman after all? Her memories of her husband were growing as confused and wavering as the ocean itself; she had been on the sea, she realized, almost as long as she had known him. Had he left Genoa, was he following her over the water, as he had promised? The agent had said her ship was *l'ultimo* for South America and his word had had a cold, dry sound which had frightened her.

A couple approached her along the rail; the woman's scarf was blowing over her face in the wind. They paused, looking out. "*Banchisas,*" the man whispered in the woman's ear. "*Banchisas.*"

It was a new word. Antonia heard it often, in the babble of Spanish around her, in the next few days. *Guerra* she heard less often. *Banchisas:* Sometimes it was said lightly, with a nervous laugh, as if it were an off-color joke. Other times the speaker dropped his voice to a hush.

One night at dinner Antonia heard it again. She looked at Toma and Eliana. They were sitting in total silence, Eliana's sharp, long face staring at his round, blank one.

"*Banchisas?*" asked Antonia, turning to Toma. He said something low and unintelligible.

Eliana suddenly jumped to her feet. "Get out!" she shrieked. "Go and eat with the other animals!" To Antonia's horror, she burst into tears and ran out of the room.

"*Banchisa,*" muttered Toma, shaking his head. "*Banchisa, banchisa.*"

Next morning, when Antonia went on deck, she found a steward leaning over the rail, looking through a pair of binoculars. He turned to her, smiling. "*Banchisa,*" he said, pointing to something glittering on the horizon. He offered her the glasses.

At first she thought she was seeing another ship, but it was too big; as long as an island, as high as a continent full of mountains, it seemed to her. And it was too white, too lifeless.

"*Banchisa*," said the steward, too close to her ear. "*Ghiaccio*. Ice."

Then he gave out a cry as the glasses fell from her hand over the side. She had realized what it was, and it terrified her.

After that, she avoided leaving the salon, enduring the bickering between Toma and Eliana in silence. Then Eliana began to stay in bed, complaining of pains and palpitations in her chest. She made Antonia sit up with her, reading from the trashy romances she loved and soothing her forehead.

At night, Antonia began to dream herself on deck. She would try to turn away from the water, but found her hands stuck tight to the rail.

The seawater was silver and hazy, as if covered with a thin mist. In the distance she saw the glimmer on the horizon. Much as it terrified her, she couldn't look at anything else.

Night after night she had the same dream. Slowly, it seemed to her, the floating island drew closer to the boat. It was huge and white; the sun shining off it was dazzling. She tried to keep herself awake so she wouldn't have to see it, but it was no use. As soon as her eyes closed, those mountains of ice rose up in her mind.

In the last dream the *banchisa* was very close. Her eyes went out to it, as if through the steward's glasses. To her surprise, she saw her mother's house entirely transformed into ice. In front of it she saw her mother, walking up and down with the high, proud pace that impressed everyone who saw it. Her mother was wearing some pearls the count had given her, and Antonia's own white nurse's uniform. Her mother had hated that uniform. "Your angel of death costume," she had called it.

The *banchisa* came so close that it seemed that the ship would have to run into it. Antonia's mother turned toward her, pointing to the bow of the ship and shouting something. "*Banchisa! Banchisa!*" was what she seemed to be crying. Antonia turned her head and saw Arturo standing with his back to her. He was wearing the suit he had worn for their wedding, and pointing an enormously long boat hook toward the ice mountain.

The air filled up with white light. Her mother began to scream. The boat hook stabbed her and went right through her chest; blood flowed everywhere over the white. The house split in half and instantly sank out of sight. Only the nurse's uniform floated on the surface.

Arturo turned and began to walk toward where Antonia stood on the deck. She looked at his face and she, too, began to scream. He was made entirely out of ice and, as she watched, his features melted.

Part One

I

IN THE YEARS BEFORE the war, when Antonia was a girl, Artemisia was
one of those towns on the Italian Riviera that managed to look both
very old and very new at the same time. It was a trait foreign tourists
found disconcerting, and few of them stopped there on the way south
from Genoa to Pisa or Florence. From the highway they could see most
of what was worth seeing there. Parts of it—the broad, blue bay and
the high, green hills rising out of it—must have looked very much as
they had when the Romans came. Along the ridges of some of the hills
were piles of ancient masonry, signifying an unimaginably distant past.
Below were bands of olive and orange groves, divided here and there
by tall, yellow, leaning walls, and below these stretched the town itself.

At the center of town, at the waterfront, were the quays, the long,
gray warehouses and barracks of the naval supply station, and the harbor, which was often filled with low, flat barges taking provisions south
to the ships at Spezia. Farther inland was the tangled, congealed medieval village and its oddly lopsided church, which, behind its neo-
Baroque facade, was said to date from the time of Leo III and to have
been built on the ruins of a shrine to Venus. In front of the church was
the paved piazza, at its center a large, cast-iron fountain, representing
the *Fruits of the Sea*. This was the gift of a former Artemisian fisherman
who had made a fortune supplying Victor Emmanuel's navy. He was
the donor, too, of the improvements to the town church. The fountain
had half a dozen nude nymphs garlanded with various sorts of seafood
and holding up three enormous basins in the shape of scallop shells.

Around the piazza were several square buildings of indeterminate
age in yellow stucco and with orange tile roofs, and the hotel, small but
new, with a columned arcade along the ground floor and a *piano nobile*

graced with balconies. To the south was a modern street, lined with palms and iron benches cast in the shape of grapevines, following the edge of a promenade over a concrete breakwater. Along it was a row of pastel summer villas, built around the turn of the century by well-to-do Genoese. At the end of the street was a second hotel, the Grande Hotel Artemisia, with festoons of pink stucco shells and flower garlands under the line of the roof, and a broad, concrete veranda which, in summer, was covered by a striped awning and filled with tables. A few hundred feet behind the Artemisia Grande was the train station, a single story with a colonnade on each side copied from Brunelleschi. From the station, an untidy alley of garages and outbuildings ran behind the pastel villas back to the piazza.

To the north of the town, behind the fishing beach and squeezed up among the foothills, was a tight jumble of battered old houses, most of them belonging to the peasants who owned the olive groves and the little farming plots below the highway. In the midst of them, surrounded by its stiff, formal gardens, was the largest house in Artemisia. It was a huge white stone cube in three stories, with long, pedimented windows, and edged with pilasters. It had neat green shutters which were nearly always closed, and a high rusticated foundation which lifted the house primly above the ground. This was the house that Antonia's father had built for her mother.

The architect, a young man with ambition, nearly despaired at the site, first because it was in Artemisia, where no one of any importance would be likely to see it, and second because it was in the poorest, most cramped, and least respectable part of town, where it certainly would look ridiculous. Antonia's mother, however, had insisted, and she was not displeased with the result. From the front steps she could see the miserable hovel where she had been born, and that would remind her each day that she no longer lived there.

Antonia hated the house. It was always dark and cold, even in the brightest, hottest part of summer. It was filled with hard, heavy furniture which only her mother ever found comfortable. It did seem ridiculous, rising in such splendid ostentation above the roofs belonging to her mother's family, the family for whom the house was clearly meant as an affront. It was her mother's house, not anyone else's, not even hers, and Antonia often felt small and almost ashamed going in and out of it.

Antonia's father was a Genoese from an old family who had made his fortune in Buenos Aires. He had met Antonia's mother in the streets of Genoa and had fallen instantly and totally in love with her. His family, what was left of it, had naturally opposed a marriage to a woman from the poorest of families and of no good reputation. But there were few of them and they had less power in the world than they once had. He was already far richer than they were and lived so far away that they wouldn't even have the satisfaction of snubbing his new wife. Within a few weeks of their meeting, they set sail for South America.

What happened next Antonia learned only years later from Eliana. Eliana was their housekeeper, her mother's cousin, and the only member of her family with whom she had remained on speaking terms after her change in fortune. She was also, Antonia was convinced, the only real friend her mother had ever had.

Eliana was remarkably ugly. She had warts on her face, was nearly six feet tall, and had a figure like a bundle of sticks, though she ate like a horse. She had a high, cracked, extraordinarily irritating voice which she used to terrorize the whole household. She went about everything with a fierce, frightening energy that made everyone stay out of her way. Antonia and her brother, when they were home, spent most of their time trying to hide from her.

Eliana was the only person who really knew anything about Antonia's mother. When she returned from one of her mysterious trips to Paris, it was Eliana who was invited up to her mother's room. They would stay shut up together for hours, and Antonia would hear Eliana's penetrating laugh far into the night. Later, Eliana would dance about the house, singing Verdi arias. (One of the things Antonia never could fathom about her was how her speaking voice could be so dreadful and her singing voice so beautiful—a rich, full contralto, the only attractive thing about her.)

The story Eliana told of her mother's trip to Argentina was brief: She had taken one look at Buenos Aires, "that chicken shed of rats and savages," and had refused to get off the ship. Her husband had had no choice but to sail back to Italy to build her the villa, as she insisted, in the midst of the town where she had been born.

Much later, Antonia imagined another version of the story—not that her mother hadn't forced her father to bring her home, the truth of that was obvious, but that she had ever contemplated any other result. After

Antonia herself had seen Buenos Aires, she realized that, even then, it could hardly have been a chicken shed; at the least, it had been far grander than Artemisia. Her mother must have sailed to Argentina with the intention of returning, knowing that once she set her mind on something, it would be impossible for her husband to refuse her. Once back in Italy, she would have everything as she had planned it.

"I DON'T THINK she was beautiful, my mother," said Antonia.

"But she had so many lovers!" Marta protested.

"I don't mean she wasn't attractive to men—she was. She was very attractive. And she had a fine figure—full, in an old-fashioned way, not like beautiful women are today. But she didn't attract with her face, exactly."

"How, then?"

"I don't know. It was something about her, not something visible in her. I think it must have been something she did on purpose. I'm sure this was it. She had a power—a power she practiced and used and made better and better. It was something she knew how to use.

"She has always had a beautiful walk. It sounds odd, I know, but I think this is what attracted most men at first. Even my father, I suppose. She walks like—like a queen, or some kind of movie star, or a goddess. Everyone notices it. When she was young, she walked everywhere, in all kinds of weather and in all kinds of places. She knew how to use that walk. Even in the dirtiest, most crowded alleys, people would break step and make way for her. There was always a little space around her. In the village, no one dared come up to her until she stood still. I suppose they still don't."

"What did she look like?"

"She isn't very tall. She had a long, rather hard face as I remember it, even then. And it grew harder as she grew older. She wore incredible clothes in those days—she brought them back with her from her trips to Paris, but who knows where she got them. I never saw anyone else wear clothes anything like the clothes she wore.

"She hates bright colors; she never wore red, or blue, or yellow, or anything clear or simple. She'd wear gold gauze over aquamarine silk, or pale rose-colored lace over lavender velvet. She had a hat with a ring of feathers like an Indian princess, and a cape made entirely of silk roses. She had a dress of olive-colored crepe de Chine with ermine trimming. Unbelievable things. I think the people in the village were shocked more by her clothes than by her love affairs."

"What did she do with her time, when she wasn't having affairs?"

"Odd things. She didn't have much education—maybe three or four years at the village school. She could read and write, but didn't do much of either. She didn't pretend to be cultured—sometimes I think she pretended to be more vulgar than she really was.

"She did one thing: She collected old coins. She bought them from peasants on her walks back in the hills—or when she went to the mountains on her vacations. Coins that were two, three hundred years old—some older, some even with pictures of the Roman emperors. They are stories to her—she used to tell us all about the queens and dukes and generals who were on them. She knows all their lives, whom they loved, how they died. She particularly knows how they died."

"What was it like living with her? Did she make you miserable?"

"Miserable? Yes, I suppose she did, but I didn't think of it that way then. I was hardly even a person beside her. I didn't know what it was to be happy, or that I had some kind of right to be happy. Everything was hers, you see, and she controlled it all just as she chose.

"You know, I was in school before I learned that most people have their meals at the same time every day. She never did. Sometimes she would lie in bed all day, reading the obituaries. She threw out the rest of the paper. She'd have her meals whenever she felt like eating—at two in the afternoon, five in the morning. Huge, elaborate meals, usually. Marco and I had to eat with the cook, when there was one."

"She must have been crazy!"

"A lot of people thought so. I don't, though. She could be as charming as anyone when she felt like it—when Papa was home, for example. Soft and agreeable—even a perfect wife. The rest of the time she was completely unpredictable—but I think she always knew what she was doing. It was one of the ways she had to have things her own way.

"Sometimes she would sleep until sunset, then stay up all night with every light in the house blazing. She would have pieces of furniture—important ones like the dining table, the stove, once her own bed—taken away and wouldn't replace them for weeks or even months.

"She has little obsessions—with hiding things, for example—money, keys, cans of food, light bulbs. You know, when I last saw her she told me she'd hidden all her old coins around the house. I think she's afraid we'll sell the villa after she's dead. Why was she afraid of that, of all things?

"I told you about her clothes—another obsession. She had closetfuls when I was a little girl. She had a whole room next to her bedroom filled with nothing but hundreds of shoes. One time I remember—I must have been eight or nine—I found her in the drawing room wearing the most magnificent gown I think she ever owned. It was a long, pale blue silk embroidered with stones: amethysts or aquamarines. She had some kind of tiara in her hair—to me it looked like a cap of stars.

"I was in awe of her (I am still in awe of her). I said something like 'How beautiful you look,' and she smiled the sweetest smile and said 'Thank you, my dear.' You know, it was nearly thirty years before I saw that dress again. When we cleaned up the villa after the war, I found it stuffed in a drawer with some old newspapers. The papers were from the same year—maybe even the same week—as the time when I saw her wearing the dress. I think it was probably the only time she ever wore it.

"Some things had to be completely orderly. (It was only later that she ceased to care about such things.) Housekeeping, for example. Her bed had to be perfectly made up. Of course, it was hard to keep servants. Sometimes even Eliana would throw up her hands. She had a little room in the basement where she would lock herself up. Then I had to try to keep the place up.

"Once we had a particularly nervous housemaid. She came out from Genoa, as I remember, a cousin of our cook. She trembled the whole time she was with us—all three days. On the last night she was there, after everyone had gone to bed, Mama woke everyone up with terrible screams. We thought a robber must have been in the house. Finally, Eliana got the gardener to go into Mama's room. She was shouting, 'A wrinkle! A wrinkle in my sheets! Who left a wrinkle in my sheets?' I think that poor nervous girl ran out of the house right then. We certainly never saw anything of her again. And her cousin, the cook, left the very next day."

"Why did she do such things?" asked Marta.

"Who knows? Who knows? I don't think even she knows. And she did worse things than that. When the nuns taught us about the 'crystal vessel of the soul' I thought hers must look like a bottle of ink from all her sins. But she did it all on purpose, I'm sure of that. She had some kind of need to behave that way—a need for chaos. A 'connoisseur of chaos,' the count called her. For years I couldn't think of her behaving in any other way—as if it were her special right. She was that consistent, in her own way. It wasn't until now that I have been able to talk about it."

"Do you hate her very much?"

"What a question! No, I don't hate her. Not then—it wouldn't even have occurred to me. Not even now. She was always like—how can I say it—a fact of life. She was just there—like the mountains, or, even more, like the sea."

II

THERE WERE SOME SUNDAYS in Artemisia that Antonia dreaded more than others. These were the times her mother got up in the morning and announced that they would drive into Genoa for a visit. This meant that she and Marco, her brother, had to dress up in their fancy clothes, hers with the stiff lace cuffs and color and his with its cape and military hat, both with huge, silly bows that tickled the chin.

Donna Dora's favorite part of Genoa wasn't the docks, with the huge ships loading and unloading, or the Via Garibaldi, with its fine rows of palaces, or the Treasury of San Lorenzo, with the Holy Grail, brought back as booty from the First Crusade and broken by the French. Dora's favorite place was the Campo Santo, the City of the Dead in white Carrara marble, the most famous cemetery in all Italy.

The Campo Santo was surrounded by a high, white wall. Inside were endless marble arcades and an enormous domed building like a pagan temple. There were rows and rows of dark cypresses, Pluto's trees, which whispered in the wind as if bringing messages from the dead. After she grew up, Antonia still could never stand cypresses. Even in the hot summer sun, which glared off the marble and hurt her eyes, Antonia found the Campo Santo the gloomiest place on earth.

Their mother would go on ahead, admiring the tombs, some of them bigger than a house. Ravens would fly in and out of their latticed windows, and sometimes the stench of a recent interment would follow them. Once Antonia saw a snake crawl out from under a bronze door corroded as green as the snake's scaly skin.

"Marco! Marco!" she cried, running up to him. "Hold my hand, Marco!"

Their mother would stride on and on, looking at the marble effigies of the deceased, which stared out blankly from their pedestals. The path was full of dust and sharp stones. The figures on the tombs were stained and pitted by generations of Italian rain. Their eyes and noses were melting away; sometimes fingers, a foot, or even a whole arm or leg was missing.

When their mother found an inscription she particularly liked, she would stop and make them read it out loud. Below the figures of an old man and an old woman weeping beside an urn, the carved stone said:

Sacred to the Eternal Memory of Our Beloved
ANGELICA
Whom God in His Wisdom Has Chosen to Take from Us
In the First Sweet Flower of her Youth
We, her Mother and her Father
Pray to the Heavenly Virgin that She
Knowing Our Daughter's Grievous Suffering
With the Typhus Fever
Will Find a Place in Our Lord's Many Mansions
For Her Pure Immortal Soul
MAY SHE REST IN PEACE WITH JESUS

Below the statue of a large bald man dressed in a frock coat and seated on a Roman throne was written:

Dedicated to
GIOVANNI BAPTISTA DE LUCA
BENEFACTOR OF THE CITY
His Daughter, Sons, and Nephews
Dedicate Themselves to the Perpetuation
of His Memory and His Example
And Ask His
ETERNAL BLESSING ON THEIR SOULS

On and on she would walk until she came to her favorite spot of all. It was the figure of a praying angel, twice the size of a man, the tomb of a poor Genoese bread seller who had saved all her life to have it erected over her mortal remains.

Their mother would gaze at the angel in silent admiration. "She must have lived a good life," she said finally, "for God to have put something so beautiful on her tomb."

III

THERE WAS, AMONG a number of men besides her father who drifted through her mother's life, one who Antonia clearly understood was more important than the others. As a child she was puzzled as to how to describe his relationship to her; her mother, of course, explained nothing. Antonia knew him for many years and grew so fond of him that she took to referring to him as her "other papa." She was nearly a grown woman before she realized how accurate that description was.

One day, when she was very small, she went with her mother to the linen shop in Genoa where she bought her sheets. They were magnificent sheets that her mother bought there, of the creamiest, heaviest linen, each especially embroidered with elaborate scenes in white silk. On this particular day, however, the old woman who ran the shop took strong exception to her mother's order.

"But Signora, such a design is simply not appropriate!" the woman said.

"They are my sheets," said her mother, in the deep, full, hard voice she used when she was annoyed. "I will say what is appropriate."

"Signora, please, let me suggest something—something more traditional for you to use. If you will do me the honor of looking over these designs, I am sure you will—"

"I have no interest in your designs. You have mine in your hand. You will honor me by doing what I wish."

"Signora, Signora, such a thing is impossible! My embroiderers are good girls. What will they think if I give them such a thing to work out?"

"Signora Calvi," said a small, distinguished-looking man who moved toward the counter from the back of the shop. "If you will permit me to intrude?"

He picked up the photograph Antonia's mother had placed on the counter and peered at it. The slightest smile, an expression Antonia was soon to know well, crossed his face. The photograph was of a tomb in the Campo Santo: a marble statue of a young girl in classical drapery weeping over a sarcophagus.

"If you will allow my humble opinion, Signora Calvi, I believe you are mistaken. Surely poets from the ancient times to now have made comparisons between our nocturnal rest and the sleep of—um—more permanent nature. The signora is clearly using a metaphor of long repute, if a trifle unusual in this context, and one which should offend no one."

"Of course, Count Mora, you are right," said Signora Calvi, who, with a bow, took the photograph with her into the back of the shop.

"Pardon me," said the count. "It is not my habit to intrude on the private affairs of charming young ladies. But one so rarely encounters one with the taste and determination to be so original."

A few weeks later, the count met the woman with the funereal sheets again. It was a Wednesday. Feeling out of sorts, he left his studio at the museum early and went to visit a coin dealer he knew—Giovanni, an old Pisan—who had a shop near the Corso Europa.

Giovanni's shop was built like a conduit, very long and very narrow. The left wall was covered with mahogany cabinets full of wide, shallow drawers and was separated from customers by a long counter and grating which disappeared into the gloom and dust at the back. When the count entered the shop from the bright street, he could tell that there was a customer before him, but could see little else. His first impression was of a warm, dense, Oriental perfume. As his eyes adjusted to the light, he made out a woman wearing a pale-green silk turban decorated with seed pearls on wires and the streaming orange plumage of some tropical bird. Her dress, cut short and slit at the hem to show off her magnificent legs, was of the same soft-green silk, festooned with blue and yellow glass beads. These made a small tinkling sound as she moved. Despite the August heat, four serpentine strips of fur were pinned to her shoulder by a gold brooch in the shape of a lotus flower with a cluster of rubies at the center.

At first the count did not recognize her. She was talking with Giovanni in a brisk, staccato voice, using language the count heard more often in a fish market than in an antiquarian's shop. As he drew closer, he saw that she had a handful of coins from the old Genoese Republic; he knew well their simple designs of crosses and stylized castles which had stayed virtually the same for generations. As she talked, the woman began to sort the coins rapidly. To the count's amazement, he realized that she was sorting them by their rarity—she had set aside five extremely rare silver teston pieces, minted during the reign of Louis XII of France. Her knowledge deeply impressed him; these five coins were nearly identical in size and design to half a dozen other, much more common, coins she had.

Now began the process of bartering. Giovanni brought out trays and little velvet bags of old coins to trade for the woman's treasures. She was clearly interested only in portrait coins and seemed more concerned with the personages portrayed than with the value of the coins. At last she selected two: a silver Florentine teston of Francesco de Medici and a gold ducat of Galeazzo Maria Sforza, Duke of Milan.

"A degenerate alchemist and an assassinated tryant," remarked Giovanni. "Excellent additions to your collection, if I may say so, Donna Dora."

She gave a short nod and laugh and turned to go. As she did, the count recognized her.

"My dear Count," she said with a smile. "How nice to see you again."

In his surprise, the count could find nothing to say before she glided out the door, showing the count an alluring view of her calves under the green sweep of her dress.

"Magnificent instruments," he said under his breath, "and masterfully employed."

"Do you know Donna Dora, then?" asked Giovanni.

"Only in passing," said the count. "I was, in fact, quite surprised to see her here. Does she come often?"

"Nearly every Wednesday about this time," said Giovanni. "She is a good customer, though she drives quite a bargain. Very knowledgeable, as you may have noticed."

"Does she live nearby?"

"No, not in Genoa, at least. She drives in from somewhere down the coast—you may have seen her car, the big green one, when you came in. Obviously has money, though from where I couldn't say. You can tell from her accent she is not exactly from your circle. I really know very little about her, other than her taste in coins, which is rather peculiar—only portrait coins and, the more tragic or degenerate the life of the sitter, the better—and her style of dressing, which seems to my old eyes to be equally formidable."

"Interesting, interesting," said the count.

"You think so?" said Giovanni, giving the count a significant look. "Come back next Wednesday; she's sure to be here. I would enjoy watching you get to know each other—it would be delightful to see who ends up in whose collection."

The next Wednesday the count arrived before she did.

"Business or pleasure?" asked Giovanni. "Or perhaps you and Donna Dora will be able to have a bit of both today?"

Within a few minutes, Donna Dora entered the shop. As she walked through the doorway, she was literally dazzling: Her tall black hat and long dress were covered with large glass cabochons that caught and broke the light like tiny prisms.

"Is it the count?" she asked, offering her hand. "A pleasure once again. You are a collector, perhaps? Then perhaps you will tell me what you think of my newest treasure."

She pulled out a large silver coin from her bag. Giovanni and the count were impressed: It was a portrait by Giulio of Clement VII, one that the count knew had been designed by Benvenuto Cellini.

"My warmest congratulations," said Giovanni. "A remarkable find—one of your best. Will you deign to name your source? No? Perhaps you would care to name your price?"

"Not for this coin," said Donna Dora, looking at the count. "I will keep this one for myself. I was merely interested in your opinion."

The three of them looked through several trays of coins, but nothing struck her fancy, and she turned to leave.

"A pity you must go so soon," said the count, annoyed that he had succeeded in learning nothing new about her. "Perhaps I can accompany you somewhere?"

"Thank you, no, dear Count. I have my own car which gives me great pleasure to drive. But if you wish, perhaps we will meet here again sometime?" She smiled her small, hard smile.

The third Wednesday, they both returned and passed a few minutes in much the same way. They did so again on the fourth. Still, the count learned nothing about the woman, not even where she lived. His discreet inquiries among acquaintances in the city yielded nothing, and Giovanni's small store of knowledge about her had already been exhausted. She was clearly aware of the count's interest but betrayed little more than the fact she was aware of it and that it amused her.

On the fifth Wednesday, he impulsively presented her with a gold Genovivo. "A coin of great importance, Signora," he said, "to the history of our city."

"You are most generous, Count," she said, "though you must know I collect only coins with portraits. If you'll permit me, however, I will keep the coin. I have an idea for a way to use it that may amuse you."

The count nodded.

"In return, Count, I invite you to tea at my villa. It is in Artemisia. You must come at this time in two weeks." With that, she left.

Two weeks later, the count took the train to Artemisia. It was a hot, still day. There was no one to meet him at the station, which was almost unoccupied. The town's only cab was sitting, dusty and empty, in the shade of the station roof, its owner off helping his brother in his olive groves. The count asked the stationmaster if he knew Donna Dora's villa. The stationmaster stared, rolled his eyes, and pointed toward the center of town.

The count walked past the deserted Artemisia Grande with its veranda, past the pastel villas, abandoned except for a few small children who were listless in the heat. The humidity was terrible, even in the shade of the palm trees, and the count was not a strong walker.

He reached the piazza. A few old men were sitting outside the hotel café. They, too, rolled their eyes when the count asked for directions, and pointed up the hill where the count could see the roofline of a solitary villa.

He climbed the hill. It was not steep, but his black clothes were already stained with sweat. He reached the villa which, he noted, stood out from its surroundings as much as Donna Dora had in Giovanni's dingy shop. The house looked empty. All the shutters were closed against the heat, except for one window through which he could see the round, pale face of a small child (it was Antonia).

The gate was ajar, and he entered the stiff, formal garden. It looked as deserted as the house; there was no wind at all and the silence was ponderous. The house and garden were so relentlessly symmetrical he felt he was somehow breaking the pattern, as if he had inadvertently stumbled into a magic pentagram.

"Emilio," said a voice. It was his Christian name, but how had she learned it? Certainly not from him. He walked around the corner of the house and there was Donna Dora, seated in the shade of a large palm.

She was wearing a broad-brimmed straw hat which had been dyed or painted a delicate shade of coral; around it was a deep-blue satin ribbon with a row of delicate silver scallop shells sewn into it. Her dress was a gauzy lavender fabric that, despite the lack of a breeze, seemed to float about her. She was wearing a necklace made of silver coins, silver earrings, wide silver bracelets set with a turquoise, on each wrist, and silver shoes. The heavy scent of the Oriental perfume hung about her as it had in Giovanni's shop. The effect, the count thought, was not exactly what he was trained to see as tasteful. Yet he couldn't deny that she was as elegant a woman as he had ever known; it was as if she had invented elegance all over again just for herself.

"Please sit down," she said.

There were two high, white wicker chairs, and a wicker table set, or at least partly set, for tea. There were dainty cakes piled on white porcelain plates with wide, black borders like mourning bands and florid designs of violet flowers. There were saucers and a tall teapot to

match, but no cups. Instead there were two strangely shaped brown objects, like gourds, with silver fittings around small holes cut into the tops. Without any explanation, Dora poured hot water into both of them. A thick, musty odor came out. Then she picked up a long silver tube like a straw, with a basket of fine silver wire around one end. She plunged the basket end into the gourd and began to suck on the other.

Feeling as if he were at his first formal dinner, the count did the same. He felt exhilarated at his slight embarrassment: How remarkable, he thought, that she should make him feel at such a disadvantage! And through it all she acts as if there were nothing strange about it at all, as if there were no other way of taking tea on a hot afternoon.

The tea had a strong, exotic flavor; there was neither sugar nor milk to go with it. The count found it far more stimulating than ordinary tea; already he was forgetting the discomfort of climbing to the villa.

"Let me confess to you, Emilio," said Dora, "what I have done with the gold Genovivo you gave me. The day after we last met, I sold it to Giovanni. Then I used the money to have these made for me."

She held out a small silver tray. On it were two gold chains, each about a foot long. They had neither clasp nor pendant. Each end finished in a small, gold circle about the size and shape of a collar button.

"What are they?" the count asked, fascinated. Dora smiled but said nothing. Later he learned she had had them made to hold up her slips, which then had to be especially made with buttonholes for the gold circles, where ordinary slips had straps.

There was a noise from the back of the house.

"My children," she said, as if announcing the time.

"Marco, Antonia, come here. We have a gentleman visitor."

Two remarkably beautiful, though not particularly clean, children appeared: a girl, whom the count had seen before through the window, and a boy, a year or two older.

"Good day, Signore," they said in unison, as if they had rehearsed it. It occurred to the count that he was not the first gentleman visitor at the house.

"Hello," said the count, who was not used to children. "I am Count Mora. What are your names?"

"Antonia and Marco," said the boy. Dora said nothing. The children stared shyly at their worn shoes, and after a moment Dora waved her hand and they disappeared.

"What extraordinarily beautiful children!" said the count when they had gone.

"You think so? Other people say so, too. I am myself too aware of their shortcomings."

"Such as?"

"Oh, I suppose they are like all children—noisy, destructive, and nearly always hungry. Do you have any of your own?"

The count shook his head.

"Then you wouldn't know about it. I'm afraid I don't like children much myself. My housekeeper looks after these two."

The tea lasted another hour or so. Afterward, the count remembered more of what had not been said than what had. There was no mention, for example, of Donna Dora's husband—who he was or even whether he was still living.

After a while, Donna Dora said, "It is nearly five. You must excuse me now."

"Of course, Donna Dora," said the count, standing up. Donna Dora remained seated—she hadn't moved from her chair the entire afternoon. "An enchanting afternoon. May I call again?"

"If you wish," said Donna Dora with a smile that the count took as a dismissal. He saw himself out of the garden. The heat was breaking and the shadows were long across the piazza as he crossed it. He could hear the slow, grating sound of a single motor launch moving across the harbor.

"Not a very pleasant woman," he said to himself as he walked to the station. "Certainly not a cultured one—rather vulgar if you come to that. But there is undoubtedly something fascinating about her."

The next week he had his car brought down from the country and drove himself out to the villa in Artemisia. He had tried to call but found that Donna Dora had no phone. "An infernal nuisance," she said later. "Worse than the priest. I won't have either of them in my house."

It was still very warm, though overcast. The house looked as empty as ever, but this time the garden, and the wicker chairs and table, were empty as well. The count went up to the imposing entrance and rang the bell. After a long interval, the door was half opened by a young girl no more than fifteen and obviously only a week or two off the farm. She wore a disheveled and incomplete version of an English maid's uniform.

Was Donna Dora at home? No, was the reply, with a giggle.

Would she be back soon? The maid had no idea. She had left by train the day before yesterday. They said she sometimes stayed away for weeks.

Would it be all right if he took a walk in the garden? Yes, why not, if it suited him.

The count followed the path to the back of the house. There was a small greenhouse, a garden shed, and a garage. Donna Dora's children were playing in a patch of dirt behind the back steps, whispering to each other. They stopped and stood up when they saw him.

"Hello, children," said the count. "I am Count Mora, you may remember; I am a friend of your mother's."

"Hello," said the boy.

"Is your mother at home?" asked the count.

"No, she's gone away."

"For how long? Do you know where she went?"

"No," said the boy. "She took the train. Sometimes she does that. She goes to wherever it is going. Sometimes she is gone for a day, sometimes longer."

"Well," said the count, not knowing what to say. "How is it you're not in school? Surely you're old enough," he said to the boy.

"I went last year," said the boy without embarrassment. "I think Mama forgot about it this year."

"Well," said the count, again at a loss for words. "Perhaps you'd like to come out with me for a treat? Would that be all right, do you think?"

The children gave him such a look of delight that it reminded the count of the first time his mother had offered to take him to Paris. The boy ran up the steps. "Eliana!" he shouted, pounding on the door. "Eliana! The count has come to take us for a treat!"

A tall, sticklike woman came to the door, giving the count a grim look.

"I am Count Mora," he said, "a friend of Donna Dora's. I was here last week to tea. I came to see her today, but seeing as she is away, would it be permissible to take these children out for some cake and lemonade? My car is right here, you see. We won't be gone long."

The woman nodded without speaking, and turned away. The children looked like they wanted to jump for joy, but didn't dare.

They drove to a café in the village. Count Mora was aware that the patron and most of the handful of customers in the place were staring at them. It gave him a rather unpleasant feeling which, however, was softened by the obvious delight of the children.

They were, he reflected, no more comfortable talking to an adult than he was talking to children.

"Do you have a papa?" he asked them.

"Oh, yes," said the girl. "He is far away, though—in the place that Columbus discovered."

"Argentina," said the boy.

"That is far away. Is he away for long?"

"Oh, he lives there," said the girl. "He owns lots and lots of houses there and he has to take care of them for people. He comes home at Easter to visit us and tell us stories about the gauchos."

"And your mother—does she visit him in Argentina?"

"Oh, no, she's never been there. Or maybe only once. She says it's a savage place—not a place for children and ladies to live."

Odder and odder, thought the count. He gazed with pity at the little girl. Her dress was so old and worn it hardly held together.

That night he had dinner in his flat with his friend the monsignor. As discreetly as he could, he brought up the strange woman he had met and her beautiful, neglected children.

"I'm sorry to say the case is not all that unusual," said the monsignor after a pause. "Not everyone holds the family as sacred as the church would wish it. But the father lives in Argentina? That is a bit out of the ordinary—to leave such a house and such a family so far behind on a permanent basis. What kind of a man could he be, I wonder?"

"Couldn't anything be done for them, the children, I mean?" said the count. "Perhaps a boarding school of some kind? The children seem bright; I hate to think of them cast adrift like that."

"There are such places in Italy," said the monsignor. "They are run by good Catholics, some from my own order. But in our country, at least, they are not always the pleasantest of places. Fortunately, we do not have much need for them here—we are not, God forbid, like the English. Mostly such schools are for children like these two—children with parents who are too bored, or too rich, or too busy, to take care of them. This does not make for a happy or healthy upbringing, and a school with some discipline, order, and Catholic principles can help in some cases. But the best of such schools are no substitute for a good home."

"But still, if the home is not satisfactory . . ."

"Enough," said the monsignor, waving a hand. "I get your point. Tomorrow I will suggest one or two alternatives if you think that will be useful to your, um, friend. Now tell me about this new coin you have acquired."

WHEN THE COUNT next saw Donna Dora, it was at Giovanni's. He invited her out to a café he knew nearby, and she accepted. She smiled when he asked about her trip, but refused to say where she had been or what she had done.

"Perhaps you would like to come with me on the next one," she said. "Then you would know everything I do."

The count, who thought of himself as a man of the world, nevertheless blushed.

"I visited with your children while you were away," he said, to change the subject.

"So they told me."

"They must be a burden to you, with your husband away most of the year. Have you thought of putting them in school—in a boarding school? Then they would be out of your way."

"No, I have thought of nothing of the kind. I don't see what good school would do for them, or for me, for that matter. Besides, it must be expensive."

"I could help with that, if it is a problem," said the count, noticing a gold and emerald bracelet she was wearing that day. "Please consider it for my sake, at least. It might"—he cleared his throat—"give us more time alone together."

When Donna Dora next left Artemisia, it was to take Marco to school. The count went with her.

IV

THIS IS HOW the count came into Antonia's life. He was soon as "natural" a part of the house at Artemisia as Eliana, or Donna Dora's peculiar whims. For Antonia, he was like a window opening onto an ancient garden, full of flowers which she had never known had existed. Almost everything about the count, she thought, came from the past, a distant past like a great jewel wrapped in layers and layers of faded years.

The count was from an old, wealthy family that had made its fortune so long ago that no one was quite sure how it had done it. Such fortunes give one the aura of the highest respectability. Even in Genoa, wealth like the count's seemed to come directly from God.

The count was a painting restorer in the Museo di Genoa, and had a flat in an ancient palazzo near the Via Garibaldi which had been in his family, he said, for four hundred years. The flat was very dark and filled with wonderful, mysterious things: old manuscripts written in Latin, Greek, and Arabic and full of strange signs and pictures; fossil fish, all bones, in glass boxes; delicate moths encased in globes of amber; an Egyptian mummy, still wrapped, in its painted case. There were ormolu clocks and bronze tigers on the mantelpieces, Greek vases, and hands and feet from Roman statues. In a glass case he had three majolica plates, two vases of Venetian glass, an Etruscan helmet, a miniature porcelain bust of Napoléon as first consul, and a silver-gilt Venus attributed to Cellini. The only new things were some odd-looking paintings of disturbing subjects—empty streets and hollow cathedrals like stage sets, peculiar little still-lifes of bottles and cans, which seemed to twist and bend like living things, and odd conglomerations of what looked like machinery and bits of old shop mannequins.

Dora disapproved of the paintings. "How unfortunate," said the count, pretending to be disappointed. "They remind me so much of you!"

Antonia's favorite room was a large salon at the back of the flat. It had four long windows opening onto balconies over a quiet garden full of the smell of orange blossoms and roses. In the middle of the room was a magnificent inlaid piano.

When she first saw that piano, Antonia stood still in front of it in pure awe. "Does she play?" asked the count. When Dora shook her head, the count smiled his half-smile.

A week or two later, a huge crate arrived at the house in Artemisia. It contained a fine, black grand piano. The count also sent an old friend, Madame de Cranne, a thin, stiff, gray French lady, to Artemisia every week to give Antonia lessons. Neither Donna Dora nor Eliana could stand Madame de Cranne. Eliana made a particular point of cleaning the drawing room, where the piano was installed, loudly, during all of Antonia's lessons. But Madame de Cranne pretended not to notice. The lessons went on, and soon the piano was the most important thing in Antonia's life.

Marco's favorite in the count's flat was his collection of coins. He kept them in an oak cabinet with wide, shallow drawers. He had hundreds of them in gold, silver, and bronze, many with pictures of the Roman emperors. "This one tried to overthrow the Church of Rome and revive the old pagan religions," said the count, turning a coin in his fingers. "He died in Persia. This one married his aunt, who murdered him. This one defeated the Queen of Palmyra, who had great beauty and great ambitions, and brought her to Rome in golden chains."

The count's mother was a Parisian woman who was still living. She lived with the count's wife in his country villa in the mountains. Antonia never saw either of them. The count said they were both invalids. "The sea air would not agree with them," he explained.

The count's grandfather had been a *carbonaro* when he was very young, and later a friend of Piscane and Garibaldi. He had watched the Red Shirts leave Genoa for Sicily. "More than once the great Mazzini hid in these very rooms on his secret trips to Italy," the count said. "Those were historical times."

The count was neither tall, nor young, nor handsome, but, like Antonia's mother, he nonetheless managed to look impressive. He wore a monocle, and wing collars, and a decoration in his buttonhole, and a gold chain across his broad, silk vests. He had almost no hair, and his face was like a round, pink sea with delicate features like tiny islands. This ocean and its little continents were usually still; most emotions— anger, irritation, sadness—did not register there. Only amusement moved them: first in small tremors, the pursing of lips, the lifting of an eyebrow, then in great earthquakes as his eyes squeezed shut and his mouth opened wide in a loud, almost terrifying, laugh.

If Dora's *magnificente* was in the way she moved, the count's was in the way he stood still. Antonia would watch them in their twilight walks along the avenue of the pastel villas. First they would walk together, then her mother would move ahead. Then the count would stand still, spreading his arms so his broad, black cape flapped in the breeze. With his wide-brimmed hat and silver-headed cane he looked as grand as Napoléon or Mephistopheles himself.

V

"YOUR MOTHER and the count had a real passion, then?" asked Marta.

"Yes, I suppose. For the first year or so, anyway. 'Passion' may not be the word, though. It wasn't an 'affair' like in the movies. Even then (I couldn't have been more than eight or nine) it seemed very strange to me, their being together. He was the most educated, the most cultured man I had ever known—I think he still is, in fact. What could he see in the crude, vulgar daughter of a poor peasant, one who could hardly read? What had they in common? What could they talk about?"

"Yet he was devoted to her?"

"In a way, in his own strange way. They spent a great deal of time together. At first, he visited us almost every week—or we went up to Genoa. He liked to show her off—in shops, in restaurants, at the opera, always the best, most conspicuous places. He seemed to particularly enjoy taking her to places where they would see his friends. Mama would make scenes—you know, commotions—so that everyone had to notice."

"And he liked that?"

"Oh, it delighted him. Absolutely delighted him! He used to call Mama his 'little anarchist.' 'Caserio and Bresci were nothing compared to you,' he would say."

"Caserio and Bresci?"

"Famous anarchists from the nineteenth century—I looked them up in the encyclopedia years later. Bresci assassinated King Humbert. For some reason, they were the count's particular heroes."

"The count thought your mother was an assassin?"

"Not exactly. It was something about the way she made scenes, how she made respectable people look ridiculous.

"One time the count took us all to dinner in the Corso Europa, at a place that, before the war, was supposed to be one of the finest restaurants in Genoa. Very dark, very elegant, with dark-red velvet curtains and old paintings of the harbor. The count insisted on taking Marco and me along—so you could imagine. Everyone else there was at least as old as the count—even Mama looked much too young. They all seemed to be old acquaintances of his family—I could feel them staring at us when we came in, but of course they were too polite to turn their heads.

"Mama was in high form that night. I think it was one of the times the cook left—this gave the count his excuse and Mama had done nothing but fuss about food for days.

"The maître d' came in all smiles—Mama did nothing but glare at him and she refused to check her coat—some outrageous fur—and wore it to the table. There were red roses on the table and she made the waiter take them away because 'she was allergic'—of course, the garden at home was full of roses, though she wouldn't have red ones. Then she said there was a draft—'I will become ill!' she said so loud that everyone must have heard her. She made the waiter move us and take away another bowl of roses. I was afraid to look, but I'm sure people were turning around to glare at us by this time.

"Mama ordered three kinds of pasta and no main course. Can you imagine? In a restaurant like that! I thought the waiter would truly choke, but he couldn't say anything because of the count. Then she ordered chicken soup for Marco and me. 'A double portion.' We hated chicken soup. But the count wouldn't let her, and ordered our favorites.

"The count asked Mama if she would like champagne before dinner. 'No,' she said. 'I detest French wine' (an outrageous lie!). 'The French know nothing about wine. Bring me the house wine—a good red, Italian wine for my pasta!'

"The count didn't bat an eye, but I could see his lips twitching. The waiter went away looking whiter than the tablecloth. Then Mama began to look around the room. 'The food can't be so bad here,' she said as loud as anything. 'The customers look well preserved. Nevertheless, it is much too cold in this room. It could give you pneumonia!'

"Oh, she was a demon when she was like that! She knew exactly what she was doing! Exactly! And the count knew she knew! They were like two bad children sitting there, tormenting the adults.

"When the waiter came back with her first elegant little dish of pasta—spaghetti alla Carbonara, I think it was—Mama took one look at it and said, 'Bring back the menu!' Then she looked up the price and said, 'This portion is too small. For the price, you should bring me a decent amount, on a real plate.' The waiter looked at the count, but the count just nodded as if it were the most natural thing in the world. The poor waiter! What could he do? The count had probably been coming there for fifty years at least. He went back to the kitchen and brought a big dinner plate full of pasta.

"Mama took one, tiny, tiny bite. Everyone watched as she brought it to her mouth, as if she were a queen or an empress. She did everything very, very slowly as if in a pantomime. She paused. Then she spat out the bite onto her plate.

" 'This is revolting!' she shouted. 'How dare you serve me such food! Take it away, take it away before I become ill!'

"Marco was starting to laugh. I wanted to hide under the table; no one even pretended not to be staring anymore. I looked up at the count and he was as calm as ever, but I could see his lips twitching more and more.

"When the waiter brought the second pasta, Mama looked very bored. She gave out that long, loud, almost musical sigh she used when she was tired of something or someone. 'Well,' she said, in her sweetest, sweetest voice. 'I find that, after all, I have no appetite tonight. You may take this away as well.' The waiter was redder than the tomato sauce—he was so old I thought he was having a stroke. But he went away without saying a word.

"Mama spent the whole time with her hands in her lap, staring at Marco and me. It took away my appetite, but the count made me eat up."

"Did the count say anything?" asked Marta.

"Nothing. Nothing at all. When we were finished, he left a big tip, and when we were in the street he broke into that huge grin he had just for Mama (it used to scare me half to death) and said to her: 'You were magnificent, my dear. You have made me very happy.' And as a special treat, he took us straight to the opera. *La Bohème*, I think it was."

"And they were always like that together?"

"Yes, that first year they were. Just like that."

VI

THE COUNT'S "ADVENTURE" with Donna Dora, as he called it, went on for a year and part of the next. His old friends—even Giovanni—thought he had gone mad. The calm, regular, predictable, and utterly respectable life he had lived for fifty years had been disposed of. He got rid of his sedate black car and bought a new, faster one painted a bright green. He took to wearing silk scarves to the museum instead of ties, and was often seen in public without a proper coat. He would break off in the middle of conversation to say he had to meet "his lady" and made clear, with a look, that he didn't mean his wife.

"It's in the blood," his friends said. "With his grandfather, it happened even earlier."

In the spring of their second year together, the count noticed certain disturbing changes in Dora. She would miss their appointments and would take long trips without him. She offered no explanations. "I am going away for a few days," she would say. "But do come out and stay with the children. They like your company."

What was worse, she began to be nice to him. She was slowly becoming the most charming, agreeable woman he knew. She never raised her voice or refused him anything when they were together. When they went out for an evening, he couldn't imagine anyone behaving more respectably.

The count began to have suspicions. They worried him, mostly because he had never taken their relationship very seriously. "Just a little adventure for my old age," he told himself. But the pleasanter Dora became, the more he began to suspect her motives. To his horror, he found he was jealous of the time she spent somewhere—and no doubt with someone—else.

He began to be quarrelsome, to lose his temper with her. He demanded to know why she spent so little time with him.

"But my dear Count," she said in her sweetest voice. "You are speaking of obligations. I don't recall that we ever promised obligations to each other."

"Obligations!" said the count. "No, I suppose we didn't speak of that. I suppose I should be grateful for the time we do spend together, then!"

"Well, why not?" said Dora.

"And your husband," said the count in an evil tone. "Does your husband feel this way about obligations?"

That put an end to the conversation, though the count was far from satisfied. Hoping to get some response from her, even a mercenary one, he began to shower her with gifts. He took his grandmother's jewelry— which by right belonged to his mother or wife—out of the bank and gave it to her piece by piece. If she admired anything in his flat, he gave it to her instantly; he even presented her with some of his finest coins—ones collected by his father. But, though she always thanked him politely, her attitude didn't change.

Finally, he grew so irritable that Dora, to placate him, suggested a holiday in the mountains. She had a favorite resort in the Dolomites, a nice, quiet place. They could spend most of August there, just the two of them.

Even this didn't please the count. He couldn't get rid of the idea that she must have gone to this place first with another lover. Still, he agreed.

A few days before they were supposed to leave, something unpleasant happened in Genoa. The Socialists called a national strike. Out of nowhere, it seemed to the count, bands of black-shirted young hoodlums set upon the strikers, smashing their newspaper equipment and offices and beating them up in the streets. In Genoa, where there were many Socialists, the fighting went on for two days. Giovanni the coin dealer went out to investigate a disturbance outside his shop, was grabbed by the mob, searched, and when found to be carrying "subversive literature" had his shop looted, was force-fed castor oil, and was given such a crack on the head that he wound up in the hospital.

The count, for whom all politics had long since receded into a distant and dimly annoying noise, was perplexed. He was only vaguely aware of the new party and its flamboyant leader, a former radical out of Milan, who commanded in some unclear way these black-shirted toughs. But when he had dinner with the monsignor a few days later, he found his clerical friend in a state of ecstasy.

"At last someone has found the courage to put those hooligans in their place," said the monsignor.

"Someone has done something about the castor-oil merchants with the funereal wardrobes?"

"No, I mean the Socialists, of course, that Bolshevik rabble that's been dragging Italy down since before Caporetto. Thank God someone is taking the responsibility at last!"

"Responsibility for what?"

"For restoring peace and order, of course."

"I don't follow politics much, as you know," said the count. "But as one who has led, by and large, a peaceful and orderly life, I am rather well aware of the disadvantages of peace and order."

"Disadvantages! My dear Count, you have spent too long tucked away in your museum! The world of the twentieth century is slipping out of your grasp. I suppose you consider defeatism, national humiliation, lawlessness, agnosticism, inflation, and the babbling chaos called Parliament the advantages of modern Italian life! Do you know how many so-called governments we have been cursed with since the war? Do you think the rest of Europe is not laughing up its sleeve at us? Or perhaps you are one of those sentimentalists who cling to the lost dreams of the *risorgimento?*"

The count was thoroughly taken aback by this outburst. The monsignor was usually one of the most circumspect men he knew.

"Think of the future," the monsignor went on, without waiting for the count to reply. "Think of the possibilities once we are rid of these ridiculous, outmoded ideas about how to run a modern nation. Haven't we been disappointed enough? We need to return to the ideas of our Roman ancestors. Then Italy will again be able to hold up its head among nations, and surely, soon, the church will take its rightful place in the new Italian state!"

"But I thought their leader was an atheist?"

"Merely a ruse, a ruse to gain the confidence of the godless masses! I have it on good authority that he is a deeply devout friend of the church and just awaits the consolidation of his power (which surely will come soon) before declaring his true allegiances! Oh, he is clever, very clever. True leaders always are. Everything is being carefully planned, let me assure you. Nothing will be left to chance."

The count began to color. "I doubt very much if our friend Giovanni would agree with your favorable projection."

"A mere casualty, Count, a necessary martyrdom to a larger cause. Giovanni should have known enough to stay clear of the course of history! Besides, one can deplore the roughness of their methods while still admiring the nobility of their cause."

"What cause? What nobility, may I be so bold to ask. I fail to see how attacking innocent people in the streets can—"

"But they are men of action! Action! Don't you see? Don't you feel how inspiring that is, after all these years of useless bickering? Men who can cut through to the heart of the thing without endless quavering. Action, not words! Didn't I once hear you praising d'Annunzio (that debaser of the Italian language) for trading words for action? Of course, I deplore this use of violence, however necessary it may be. To be sure, many, if not most, of these people are vulgar, uneducated, even crude. Their methods are not what one would call refined. But then, as I say, one must stand aside for history. Certain things must be done if our destiny is to be worked out. One must bow to the inevitability of power."

"Forgive me, Father," said the count. "You know I am not a devout man. But I think that if the disciple of our Lord had followed your advice you would not be dressed as you are but as a priest of Jupiter!''

The monsignor turned very red indeed. He was about to reply when the housekeeper entered with the next course. The count deftly changed the subject, but the conversation lagged. After dinner, the count sent the monsignor home early, complaining that he was very tired and had to get up early the next day.

He couldn't sleep, however. He was too disturbed by the monsignor's outburst. The count liked to take a stand of bemused detachment from what he called the ''misfortunes'' of modern life, into which he classed all politics and all human and natural disasters, including the recent war. But he prided himself that he was always in touch, that nothing important ever escaped his attention. Now, it seemed, events had gotten ahead of him.

THE TRIP to Mónte di Sangue did little to distract him from his irritation at being forced to think about what was going on in the streets. Dora insisted that he drive his new car, and complained the whole way that he was driving too slowly. She refused to have anything to do with politics, so he couldn't speak about what was on his mind. Worse, the car broke down past Bergamo, and they had to spend two days in a miserable village hostel waiting for the car to be repaired.

As they entered the new Dolomite Road, Dora's chief reason for wanting to drive, his mood worsened. Long before they reached Monte di Sangue, he had developed an intense dislike for the Dolomites. They were, it seemed to him, a distasteful combination of the bucolic and the sinister; cunningly picturesque green alpine valleys with little fantasy chalets and farmhouses set among oddly shaped pinkish massifs that turned violet or mauve with changes in the light. There were also lugubrious alpine lakes, looking very cold and deep, typically ringed with a dark band of conifers like a noose. Nor could he abide the unintelligible patois that the natives spoke, or the pretentiously archaic costumes they sometimes wore. They all seemed to eye him with an icy suspicion; recently, too recently, they had been Austrian, and they made him think of barbarian hordes pouring down from the north.

Their hotel was new: half-timbered alpine confection on the outside, dark wood and green leather, in imitation of a British club, on the inside. The dining room overlooked the lake, which was dark and greenish in color, and, when the weather was clear and calm, reflected the twin peaks known locally as Dante's Gates, though whether they led to Paradise or the Inferno was not clear. Behind the hotel rose the strangely formed pile of limestone, stepped like a Mexican pyramid, that gave the village its name. Its lurid color at sunset was a celebrated attraction.

The count didn't care for the hotel, its setting, or, least of all, its patrons. He took particular exception to a group of elderly widows from Ferrara who wore long, white frocks of a prewar style and flitted about the ground to the accompaniment of little arias of giggles like, the count thought, a chorus of geese.

Dora, on the other hand, seemed entirely in her element. She had brought a trunkful of frilly dresses, all in shades just short of white, which were just stylish enough to impress without startling. To the count's disgust, she even carried a parasol. She adopted a light, singsong voice, several octaves higher than the one she used at home, and took great delight in dancing among the guests, bowing to each and greeting her favorites from past years with uncharacteristically charming smiles. She was very popular, and for once seemed perfectly at home. The count, on the other hand, felt like an ancient thoroughbred gelding sent out to the stable of a widows' riding academy.

The count began to have bouts of indigestion. He would wake in the night and then sleep until noon. One morning at six he staggered into the bathroom to find Dora's door ajar. Pushing it open, he found her bed empty. Putting on a robe, he went downstairs to see if she was having an early breakfast. The lobby was empty, except for a glassy-eyed clerk. There were the sounds of clattering crockery and female laughter coming from the kitchen, but the dining room seemed empty as well.

"Ah, Count Mora! You will be looking for your lady?" said a voice with a strong, oddly clipped accent.

The count turned to find a long, bent, very old-looking man seated by himself in the corner next to the door. He was very thin, very pale, and very wrinkled. He had huge, round, watery eyes and was holding a glass of clear liquid.

"Have we met, sir? How did you know my name?" Thinking the man must be German-speaking, the count spoke in that language.

"No, Count, we haven't been introduced," answered the man, also in German. "Idle sorts like me notice many things that busy men miss. But then, even a very busy man could hardly miss a woman like Donna Dora, or her consort. I am an incurable insomniac. I am to be found, nursing my affliction all of most any night, at the post where you see me now. And the last three mornings (including this one) I have seen your Donna Dora leave this hotel before first light, dressed, I would say, for a long walk."

The man paused; his wide, thin, and slightly bluish lips parted in half a smile. The count, thoroughly annoyed, said nothing.

"But I am not German," the man went on, in Italian. "I am Aleksei Nagarin—a Russian, which signifies nothing. Also a prince, which signifies less. Also a general, which signifies least of all. But please forgive me for being so rude. Surely you can indulge someone in my state of decrepitude? Do sit down. Perhaps you will join me in a drink?"

The prince held out his glass. The count took a step backward.

"Oh, don't worry, my dear Count. It isn't vodka. A vile, vulgar drink, vodka—never touch it. This is a fine English gin. I have my own supply, which follows me everywhere I wander. Do join me. One gets so little company this hour of the morning. No? Perhaps it is too early for you. Of course, for me, it is still the night before." The prince's laugh sounded like a rusty knife scraping a stone.

The count muttered and went back up to bed. He awoke five hours later with a fierce headache. He found Dora in the lobby, in animated conversation with two of the Ferrarese widows. He had never seen her look more natural; he felt his stomach tighten as he watched her.

The count said nothing about Dora's early-morning excursions, but he thought about them all day. What the devil was she up to? He felt his jealousy shift inside like a tapeworm.

The next morning the count woke up at five and went down to the lobby. The same clerk was at the desk. The count sat down to wait for Dora.

"Missed her, my dear Count," said the prince from the door to the dining room. He walked into the lobby with a gait that made it look as if all his joints had been detached. "Missed her by a good half hour."

The prince grinned with delight as he sat down opposite the count. He was wearing a heavy, sweet cologne that nearly made the count gag.

"I can see that our Dora is a difficult woman to get the best of. A man has to be quick and perhaps a few years younger than we are, Count, to stay ahead of her."

The count said nothing.

"You are from Genoa, I believe?" the prince went on without stopping. "A marvelous city, Genoa. All the other Italian cities are museums for American virgins and sentimental homosexual English lords. Only Genoa is still alive. I make my home—such as it is—in San Remo now, which is crawling with well-heeled countrymen of mine. When the heat and the twanging of those damned Slavic syllables (why do we speak Russian so much in exile when we hardly ever spoke it at home?) gets too much for me—for some reason, this always happens about this time of year—I come up here for a little rest. So peaceful, don't you think? I have cousins in Berlin and cousins in Paris and a nephew in New York, and an ancient great aunt in a flat in Belgrade. So you can't say that we Nagarins are not men of the world, eh?

"Have you been to my country, Count? No, no, of course not—I can see you are a man of taste. Miserable place—damp and bitter cold in winter; hot, dry, and windy in summer. I was raised in Petersburg—forgive me, Petrograd (this last war has muddled up so many things), and I swear my health has never recovered. My dear parents used to take me to Baden, for my heart, you know, and I never wanted to go back home. Such healthy people, the Germans.

"But Russia! Oh, a miserable place!—I'm old, I can say such things. There are two kinds of rocks in Russia, eh? The ones in the wheat fields and the ones in people's heads. Like our late lamented Nicholas, czar of all the Russias. Finest stone-head in Europe, good, solid, Russian basalt. I knew him as a boy—a fine-looking lad, but never could tell a whip from a lace handkerchief. And that Hessian hussy he married! *Quelle méphitique!* If you ask me, they got exactly what they deserved. Those who can't break the beast get thrown, eh?"

The count, who wasn't listening, was silent.

"Listen, Count," said the prince, moving over to the couch where the count was sitting. "I don't know where your fine lady goes so early in the morning. But I do know how to find out."

The count got up to leave, but the prince grabbed his arm. "No,

my dear Count, I am quite serious. Listen—the local lads are quite
amenable to financial considerations, and they aren't nearly as stupid
as they look. And they're early risers, not like certain old gents. I can
arrange to have one—for a modest fee—follow your sweet Dora and
solve the mystery! He'll report back to me and, in the evening, I can
impart to you the precious information—in what will appear to all eyes
to be no more than a casual conversation. What do you say?"

The count pulled away from him.

"Consider it, Count," insisted the prince. "You know where to find
me."

That afternoon, Dora wanted to go out on the lake. A sullen-looking
boy rowed them from a boathouse surrounded by hundred-foot-tall
pines. The air was very still. They could hear a slight rustle in the trees
and girlish laughter from a boatful of widows near the shore. The water
was very smooth and black, as if it were frozen solid.

"Where have you been walking to in the mornings?" the count
asked.

Dora laughed; a bit too lightly, it seemed to the count. "Why, Count,
you have found me out!" she said. "I'm not deceiving you. It was for
your sake I went out so early. You know how much I like to walk, and
these mountains are so perfect for it. It was out of consideration for
your poor feet that I went out while you were asleep."

The count looked up at a hawk circling above Monte di Sangue—
the bare rock was almost yellow in this light—and down at the tip of
Dora's parasol where it touched the surface of the water, slicing open
the perfect surface. If one drowned in this lake, the count thought, it
would be years, if ever, before the body came back to the surface.

That night, at dinner, the prince caught the count's eye. The count
stared back, nodded twice, then stared at his plate. He didn't want to
see the prince's grin.

The next day it rained. Dora played bridge with the widows while
the count tried to read the papers. The prince was nowhere to be seen.

He turned up after dinner. It had stopped raining, and Dora had
gone out to watch the moon rise over the Gates of Dante—a splendid
sight, according to the headwaiter.

"The mystery grows deeper and deeper," said the prince, with a
sympathetic smile. "We didn't, on account of the rain, expect to catch
our quarry this morning. But just at a quarter past five, she appeared.

It seems a little damp wouldn't keep our Dora from her secret wandering.

"Our young agent followed at a safe distance—had some trouble keeping up with her pace, he tells me. She went off to a little farming village about two miles west of here. There are about half-a-dozen cottages in a clutter. She stopped at two of them for just a moment. Then she entered the third and stayed the better part of an hour. Then she walked straight back to the hotel. I saw her come in. She was drenched to the skin, but had a look of absolute triumph, a look I saw on the face of Lenin once just after the October Revolution.

"Now, whatever was she up to? Logic suggests it was not an assignation. If so, why the visits to the first two cottages, and why so short a visit there? Also, on the previous morning, I definitely saw her set out in an easterly direction. Does she have a movable lover? Do they play hide and seek? Was this the source of the look of triumph, success at some sort of erotic game? Such a remarkable expression for someone returning from the pleasures of the bed! In what state did she leave this lover, if there is indeed such a lover, that would be cause for such an expression! Come, Count, tell me your interpretation."

The count shook his head. Whatever it was, it was more than a simple walk in the mountains.

That night, Dora came into his room. "I have a surprise for you," she said.

She held out her hand. In it was a fine bronze *dupondius* with a head of Faustina the Younger.

"I made an excellent bargain for it this morning and I want you to have it."

The count began to laugh. So this was the source of Dora's famous finds! She bilked them out of innocent peasants! No wonder she was so fond of solitary walks. He was about to confess his silly suspicions of her when she stopped him.

"No, don't thank me," she said. "It isn't a gift, it's a bribe. I want you to let me leave you a few days earlier than we had planned. I've made arrangements to meet someone—it doesn't matter who—in Venice. We're such good friends, I was sure you'd understand."

She paused. The count stood with his mouth open, frozen at the start of his laugh.

"Please come to see us when you're back in Genoa. I am sorry about this little vacation. It was probably a mistake—we seem like an old married couple and I hate that. I'm sure you do, too. But come and visit the children. They're very attached to you, you know, more than they are to me, in fact, though I've never pretended to enjoy being a mother."

She smiled. She knew the children were important to him.

The count sighed and lay back in bed. He closed his eyes. "Of course, you know I agree to everything. Of course you are right, my dear. And, of course, I will come visit the children. Now, if you will leave me, I will go to bed. I am most extraordinarily tired tonight."

That night, the count slept very well. In the morning he was delighted to find that his stomach ailment had vanished, and he celebrated with an enormous breakfast followed by a quantity of champagne.

Dora came down with her bags. She smiled at the count without coming over. He smiled back and blew her a kiss without getting up. She went out. He went to look for the prince, to whom he felt he owed an explanation of some sort. But the prince's table was empty.

"Have you seen the prince?" he asked the headwaiter, who was checking the luncheon settings.

"The prince? Forgive me, Signore, I don't know to whom you refer. There is no prince registered at the hotel, at present, so far as I know."

"Prince Nagarin. The old Russian gentleman."

"Oh, him!" said the headwaiter, his face dropping its formal expression. "You mean the old 'insomniac' who likes to sit in the corner with his glass of gin? No—he left late last night—no doubt without settling his bill. He isn't, you know."

"Isn't what? Russian?"

"Yes, Russian, but prince? No. Only an old inebriate—though I'm told he's less than half as old as he looks. I've heard he was some minor official in the old government before the war, then he did something— supplies or the like—for the White Russian Army. Came south, with a tidy little fortune from somewhere or other, after the Whites packed it in. He spends a lot of time at Monte Carlo, they say, trying to turn his little fortune into a big one. Imagine him telling you he was a prince! The prince of fools, more like. But look here, he didn't try to make any—ah—business deals with you, did he?"

"Not exactly. Why do you ask?"

"Only because there was a commotion last year, when he was here, on account of one he made. Apparently he attached himself to an old American gentleman who was afraid his young wife was, you know, secretly seeking fresher companionship. The 'prince' as you called him offered to set his 'agents' on her for a fee, but just made up a bundle of lies about what she was up to that led the old American on quite a dance. I don't think he did it for the money he got out of it—more for the pleasure of it, I'd say. It created quite a stir at the time, though the 'prince' slipped away before anything serious came of it. I don't suppose they would have let him come back, except that he's an old compatriot of the owner."

"Well," the count thought to himself, "at least I'm a genuine count, though what else I am at this point I'd rather not think about."

As he drove back to Genoa the next morning, the count found himself thinking, not of the prince's fake title, or of his possible other swindles, or even what he had said about Dora. Instead, he thought of what the prince had said about Russia and about what had happened to the czar, who had once seemed to be the most powerful man in Europe. It was as if the czar had been a great rock on the edge of the river, ignoring the water eating away the bank until, too late, the undermined rock fell into the water. The fate of the czar made him think of the Black Shirts. Were they the river or the rock, he wondered. And which was Dora? And which was he?

When he got home, the count began to look up the speeches of the Black Shirts' leader. The style was so bombastic he couldn't help but like it. Such audacity! he thought. At one moment he talks like a Socialist, the next he babbles about Mare Nostrum and the glories of Rome! To think that people actually swallow this! One has to admire someone who gets away with such outrageous nonsense.

He read how statesmen, eminent professors and philosophers, even symphony conductors, men whom he knew and admired, had praised this strange man with the inflated chest and chin like the prow of a battleship. Rome said he was a necessary evil, some said he was the savior of Italy. Those who can't break the beast are thrown, thought the count.

He ran into the monsignor right after the March on Rome. He nodded and smiled to show his approval and the monsignor, delighted at the count's conversion, smiled back. The count continued to approve until the murder of Mapteotti put some doubts in his head. But soon his doubts were of no significance.

VII

"WHY DID YOU GO to South America?" Marta asked.

"Well, your Uncle Arturo lived there. I didn't have that much choice after we married. I didn't fancy a life like Mama's, with a husband thousands of miles away. And the war was coming to Europe. Nobody knew if there'd be any way of leaving Italy for years.

"But there was more to it than that, I suppose. Marco and I always dreamed of going to South America—because of Papa. We loved him so much, and it seemed that South America must be the land of dreams. He always promised to take us with him one time, but he never did. I think Mama was against it, but she never said anything in front of us. She was so funny about Papa—always used 'voi' with him. I hardly ever remember her disagreeing with him or even raising her voice when he was staying with us. She wasn't like that with anyone else I can remember.

"Anyway, when Marco and I were very miserable—when he was having trouble at school, for example (this happened often)—we would make plans to run away to South America. Once we even hid in Papa's big steamer trunk, but the porter dumped it upside down. I fell on top of Marco—and we both started to howl. Mama was furious about the whole thing—wouldn't let us out of the house for weeks.

"It was a year or two after that, when we were both home for the summer, that Marco built the boat. He was like that—more resourceful about things. He was always able to wriggle around situations, not like me at that age. I could only endure them. He made up all our games, found places in the garden where we could hide from Eliana. He figured out how to sneak into my room at night, and we would hide under the covers for hours, planning our escape to Papa. When I was at school, I used to say three whole rosaries for Marco every night.

"Anyway, the summer I was ten and he was thirteen, he built the boat. It was wonderful how he did it—like everything he did. One day when Eliana and Mama were away in Genoa, he stole the key to the closet in the cellar where they kept the wine. He filed his pocket knife into a copy, and put the key back so no one would notice. He would sneak down early in the morning, before it was light, and steal one or two bottles at a time. He took only the most expensive ones—the ones with the French labels that were only for Mama's 'particular friends.' He traded the bottles at the grocery for cigarettes. They must have known how he got them, but I think they felt sorry for us. And, of course, nobody in town much cared for Mama.

"Marco made friends with a carpenter down at the naval depot, and traded cigarettes with him for wood. He also bribed our gardener to let him use the back of the garden shed (neither Mama nor Eliana ever went in there) to hide his work.

"You should have seen it when it was finished! It was barely big enough to hold the two of us, it tended to turn to the right and to take on water, but Marco painted it a bright blue and to us it was the most magnificent boat in the whole world, finer than the white liners that brought Papa from South America.

"Marco hid the boat on the fishing beach above the Navy docks—in our Uncle Roberto's fishing nets. (This would have been the worst thing if Mama had found out about it—we were forbidden to talk to Uncle Roberto.) When Mama took one of her trips to Paris, Eliana would spend the whole morning—most of the day, even—in bed. This gave us our chance. We would sneak out of the house before dawn, and when Uncle Roberto took his fishing boat out into the harbor, he would tow us to the Piglets—he called them the 'Islands of Bad Children'—they were just rocks, really, covered with a little brush and beach grass. We'd spend the whole day out there. Oh, it was wonderful! Only children can be as happy as we were with our little boat and our little cluster of rocks."

"What did you do there?"

"Nothing. Children's things. You could see the whole town from out there, shrunk down to the size of toys. The Navy docks were just little gray boxes and our house a white doll's cap dropped on the green hillside. We could see the boats leaving Genoa for Africa and, through the Pillars of Hercules, for America.

" 'Someday,' Marco would say, 'I will sail on one of those ships to Argentina and become a gaucho like Papa.'

" 'But Papa isn't a gaucho!' I would answer.

" 'He wears gaucho clothes, doesn't he? And he lives in the land of the gauchos?'

" 'Well, I suppose . . .'

" 'Well, if he was in the land of the gauchos and he wore gaucho clothes and the gauchos saw him and he wasn't a gaucho, then they would take out their knives and slice him to ribbons for their girlfriends.'

"When the tide was low, we would climb around the rocks, looking for crabs and breaking open mussels for pearls. The crabs—if we found any—we'd roast over a driftwood fire. If they didn't get too burned, we would even eat a few. We'd pick up things the sea had left—broken nets and cork floats, bits of rope and rusty chain—other rubbish, particularly pieces of packing cases with foreign words on them.

"We would play out the things they taught us in school—you know, Queen Isabella and Columbus—and we'd sail off to find the New World. Or Marco would row out toward the open sea and he would be Lamba Doria and I would be Marco Polo, his captive.

" 'Tell me about Kublai Khan or I will pinch you to death,' he would say.

" 'Kublai Khan lives in a great palace of gold and crystal, and has a thousand virgins to sing his praises by day and two thousand to sing them by night.'

" 'Lies, you damned Venetian. Tell the truth or it will not be well with you,' and he would start to pinch.

" 'Kublai Khan lives in a hovel of mud and sticks, and he has six wives who curse him by day and twelve who beat him with thorn branches by night.'

"And Marco would pretend to curse me for a liar and would pinch and pinch until I pushed him out of the boat.

"Or we would row back to one of the Piglets, which would be Sicily, and he would be Garibaldi with the Red Shirts and I would be the queen of Naples, begging for my life. And after he had run my husband through with his sword, he would gallantly offer to marry me.

"Sometimes a young couple would row out from the villas, both all in white and with a picnic basket. Marco would spy on them when they lay half-undressed in the hot sun behind the bushes.

" 'Marco, Marco, don't look!' I would whisper. 'Marco, it's a sin to look at them!' (The nuns at our school said that looking on a naked body, even our own, was a sin. We had to take our showers in little tents.)

" 'Shhh! They'll hear you,' Marco would hiss at me.

" 'Marco!' I would shout almost on purpose, and there would be a commotion behind the bushes, and the sound of rustling clothes.

"In the late afternoon, when the air was most intense, we would lie on our backs on separate rocks and stare up into the sky. It was the most wonderful, wonderful blue, as blue as the Virgin's dress in the statue in our chapel at school. 'What a beautiful home God has!' I would think to myself.

"At sunset, Uncle Roberto would come back for us. His boat would be full of smelly fish that made flopping noises all the way back to shore.

" 'Just wait till your mother comes back,' Eliana would say when we got home. 'When I tell her how you hid from me all day, she'll beat you until you can't even stand up.' But she never breathed a word to Mama, and she never found out that all summer we used that little boat. It is in the gardener's shed to this day.

"In a way, that was our last summer together as children. The next spring, when Marco came back from school, he was changed. He looked sullen and frightened. He refused to take out the boat, and hardly said a word, even to me. He used to sit in the gardener's shed alone, smoking and reading magazines, and he stole Mama's wine to drink himself.

"I asked him what was wrong, but he wouldn't say. Something had happened at school, with one of the priests—I think one of them had—you know, bothered him. He was such a beautiful boy in those days.

"One morning, in the garden, he took out the rosary they had given him at school and smashed it to bits with a rock. 'I'm not going back to that school!' he said. 'I'm never going back to that school!'

"He was wrong, of course. Mama took us to a fancy hotel in the mountains; then, at the end of the season, she sent us back to school. Marco was in tears and shaking, but he went. I don't think he spoke voluntarily to a priest again."

AFTER MARCO WENT off to school, Antonia was left with Dora at home. Until she, too, went away to boarding school, Antonia took the train every morning to a convent school two towns away. It was a lonely time for her. She never dared bring her friends home with her, and few of them invited her. She always heard whispers around her; Dora's notoriety was such that it had spread to the town where the convent was and to the families of the girls who went to the school. So the girls stood a little apart from her, and gave her looks of pity, of condescension, and of mystery and awe. It was almost as if she were the daughter of a great sorceress. None of the girls taunted her, they didn't dare. But, although some of them were kind to her, they all were distant. Antonia never had any close friends, the kind she could tell her secrets and fears to.

Her life at home wasn't much better. She kept up her piano lessons, and two or three times a month she saw the count, who sometimes took her to concerts or matinees at the opera. But Dora was often away in those days, on her mysterious trips to Paris or in the company of gentlemen who seemed to be younger and less affluent each year.

Antonia saw little of her mother's "friends" after Donna Dora and the count drew apart. Eliana, who gave Antonia her meals and looked after her in a desultory way, made sure she was in bed before Donna Dora returned from her expeditions to Genoa. Only one, a young tenor who sang in the chorus of the opera, became more than an evening shadow to her, and this only because he would burst into song sometimes in the middle of the night. Several times, waking to the sound of her piano and the tenor's voice, Antonia crept down the stairs to where she could see the drawing room reflected in one of the hall mirrors. The scene was always the same: the tenor standing at the piano, tears streaming down his face, while Donna Dora sat, stiff and silent, with her back to the door.

The tenor must have seen Antonia's reflection because, a year or two later, when he began to get bigger parts at the opera, he recognized her sitting in the count's box. He had flowers and mysterious packages

sent to her. The packages came with notes written in the most sentimental tones, urging her to take his "offerings" to the "great queen of
love and beauty, your mother." The notes deeply embarrassed Antonia,
and she asked the count to deposit the "offerings" near the stage door,
where the tenor was likely to see them so abandoned. In time, he was
called away to La Scala, and his entreaties ceased.

Aside from this, Antonia and Donna Dora lived almost totally separate lives. Later, Antonia could remember few times from her girlhood
when she felt close to her mother. They were memories she nourished
in her heart.

One such memory was of a conversation with her mother when
Antonia was fifteen. Dora had returned from a long trip in an unusually
happy mood. It was one of the times when there were no servants.
Marco was at school and Eliana had gone to stay with a sick relative
in Genoa so mother and daughter were alone together for two days.

On the first evening Antonia, not knowing whether to expect her
mother, cooked dinner. Dora did come down for dinner. She was
dressed in a shiny silk robe with purple flowers on a soft yellow background. She had her hair piled on her head and held in place with a
Chinese lacquered comb.

They ate on the little table in the kitchen. "The food smells good,"
Dora said as they sat down. "You must have a talent for it. Serve me
a large portion; I'm very hungry tonight."

"What did you do while I was away?" Dora asked as they began
to eat. Antonia was surprised. Dora almost never asked such a question,
even when she had been away for weeks.

Antonia described what had gone on in her classes, the history she
had been taught, the piece she was learning for the piano. Dora listened
quietly, following with her eyes and making no remarks as she usually
did.

"Then there was the day I was sent home," Antonia went on.

"Sent home? What for?"

"There was something—wrong with me," Antonia said, gazing into
her cup. "I had what—Eliana called it 'the curse.' " She looked up.
"Mama, it scares me. Eliana says it will happen over and over."

Dora touched Antonia's cheek. "Don't blush, I will explain it to
you," she said gently. "You are young for it, and it is too bad Eliana

told you that. It is not the *curse* of woman; it is a price one pays for being a woman."

Dora, in a soft, calming voice, gave her a long, very detailed and accurate description of the entire process and its meaning. It took all of dinner.

"Men try to make us think there is something evil in it," Dora said as Antonia was cleaning up. "They do this because it frightens them; it shows them there are things about women they can never fully understand and control. Remember what it means to be a woman. It's the men, the poor bastards, who have to do the work. We can arrange our lives so that we can get what we want by using these things about women that men don't understand. Don't forget that. The man builds the house, but the woman dreams it to life."

Antonia did not forget, but she had a hard time understanding exactly what Dora had meant. She thought about it for years. One day, years later, sitting in her own house two thousand miles away, it came to her.

VIII

ANTONIA'S FATHER WAS named Rodolfo di Credi. As a young man, he had gone to Argentina and made a fortune. He had not set out to do this—in fact, his first successes had been almost by accident. But once he began to make money, he found it hard to stop; soon he realized that he was meant to be a rich man.

Rodolfo was from an obscure branch of an old Genoese merchant family. They were comfortable but no longer rich. To them money was not important; they had lost interest in making more of it. They looked on money as something that helped them maintain their position in society as a reasonably respectable, well-off family, known to what they called the "better" circles, with a certain degree of respectability. Although Rodolfo never said so, he found their attitude immoral and, what was worse, excruciatingly boring.

When Rodolfo was twenty, his parents both died. A friend of his father's offered him a job in Buenos Aires as an agent in a meat-exporting firm. Rodolfo accepted the job for no reason he could name. He cared nothing about meatpacking and knew next to nothing about South America other than that poor Genoese often went there to seek their fortunes and sometimes came back poorer than ever.

The steamer he boarded was a slow one—it took him nearly two months to reach Buenos Aires. His first stop on the continent—Rio—perked up his interest. Here was a city with a setting more magnificent than that of Genoa. His second stop, Montevideo, reassured him. It was a pleasant, sleepy little place with little clusters of whitewashed houses like those in any Mediterranean village.

Buenos Aires was like neither of them. From the boat it looked like a city of mud. The thick, brown, lazy water of the Río de la Plata surrounded the ship like a rancid sauce and the city itself barely rose above it on the horizon. All Rodolfo could make out beyond the water were a few steeples and the dome of the cathedral. For the first time in his life he felt a pang of regret—that he had made a bad decision he would somehow have to overcome.

He was wrong. As Rodolfo soon discovered, Buenos Aires was anything but a dull place. It grew like some rank, mutant mold on the river's edge: It pulsated at its edges with a kind of furious vegetable life. You could almost watch it spreading out, becoming wider and taller in the humid sunlight of each new day. In Buenos Aires everything turned old in an afternoon, in a matter of hours, like an iridescent dragonfly or a tropical flower that blooms for only a day.

For the first few days, Rodolfo didn't stop to see his new employer but stayed in a sagging old hotel near the wharves. He walked through the city trying to find out which sort of place he had come to. Starting at the muddy, flat, odorous banks of the river, the streets set out in a timid, provincial way, making neat, square blocks up and down the waterfront. But these streets already looked out of date, like the stuffy old Spaniards who had built them. As the city edged back from the water, the streets slipped away like a wild boy running from his mother, racing away, faster and faster, toward the flat, open land in the west.

Even the older blocks were full of the noise and confusion of change. Rodolfo walked past huge puddles where the pavement had been torn away, and negotiated planks over the mud where the pavement had yet to be laid. He touched the cracked walls of shy, low-built Spanish mansions, plain and secretive along the older streets, abandoned by the rich and given over to the poor and the hoards of immigrants who were swarming into the city from all over Europe.

A few blocks to the west, Rodolfo found where the rich had gone: to the new palaces of the city, standing tall and portly along the new boulevards like modern men of substance, spaced with gardens, vacant lots, and new foundations waiting for the construction crews. These houses were built in a solid, confident style, more French than Spanish. They bristled with balconies, turrets, and chimneys. Their smooth stone walls were heavily weighted with pilasters and pediments adorned with garlands of flowers and sometimes with the faces of nymphs and bearded old river gods. The steep slate roofs were edged by intricate iron tendrils reaching into the sky. When Rodolfo passed these houses at night, their tall windows blazed forth into the darkness, revealing richly furnished rooms through long lace curtains. In these streets of the rich, the modesty of the old Spanish mansions, which hid everything private from the street, had disappeared.

In the heart of the city the *intendente* had razed the rotting shops dividing two muddy Spanish plazas and built of them one great square, the Plaza de Mayo, with green lawns and neat beds of bright flowers, benches and elegant lampposts, a triple-tiered fountain, and sturdy monuments to the Day of Independence. Along the river side of the plaza had stood the old fort of the colonials; now, behind a new pink facade of sandstone, it was the Casa Rosada where the ministries and the president had their offices. On another corner rose the tall, awkward dome of the cathedral above the Roman pediment and columns. Next to it was the great mass of the Teatro Colón, where Sarah Bernhardt had performed.

From the Plaza de Mayo to the west, workmen were slowly cutting through old buildings and paving over back patios to make the city's greatest boulevard, the Avenida de Mayo. Rodolfo liked to walk there on his free afternoons, dressed in his best clothes, listening to the work-men's shouts and the thunder of bricks as another wall fell to dust, moving the vista another dozen yards toward the pampas.

In the streets near the Avenida de Mayo, new shops were opening, their gleaming plate-glass windows full of the richest goods from Europe: linens and oil paintings, fragile china and great brass candelabra. But to Rodolfo, as he walked through the streets among the people of Buenos Aires, it had an air of the temporary, of the experimental. Even the people who, it seemed, were as likely to have been born in Madrid, or Naples, or even Kiev, as in Argentina, were blending and melting, co-agulating into some unimaginable race of beings. A new city was de-vouring the old, even as the old was being born.

Rodolfo found a room in a *conventillo* a few blocks southwest of the Casa Rosada. It was a crumbling, adobe mansion built forty years be-fore, already a relic—two stories of cramped little rooms opening onto galleries around three filthy, roofless patios. The other tenants told him the house had been evacuated twice in epidemics—once for cholera and once for yellow fever—but the last outbreak had been nearly a generation ago and there was, they assured him, no danger now. Still, the street tended to be full of potholes and garbage and, during the heavy rains, often flooded up to the raised sidewalks that hugged the buildings' walls.

During the day, the *conventillo*'s patios were filled with pools of water, the smells of twenty kinds of cooking, and with dozens of chil-dren. When he stopped to listen to their high, shrill voices, Rodolfo could make out half a dozen Italian dialects and Spanish. More than a hundred people lived in the house, most of them immigrants like him. The other tenants thought he was rich and extravagant to take a whole room to himself.

The packinghouse where he worked was run by an old Genoese. Like most of the Italian-born in the city, he distrusted criollos, so most of the men Rodolfo worked with were Italian. They worked hard during the day and pretended to look down on the "lazy, shiftless" criollos whose drunkenness and indigence would surely lose them their place in their own country. But at night it was to the criollo bars and cafés along the waterfront that Rodolfo and his compatriots went to drink and to watch, at least, the strange, feral life of the most deranged city they had ever known.

These were low haunts, and not especially safe, particularly for gringos. Yet Rodolfo, who was not one to take risks, and his sober Genoese friends were fascinated by them. They were frequented by *compadritos* in high-heeled boots, slouch hats, and silk scarves; gauchos, real or imaginary, wearing bright, fringed ponchos; mulatto women who laughed at the Italians' "gringo" accents. Sometimes there would be a gang of *indiada*, spoiled rich brats who liked to pick fights with the *compadritos*, or even a contingent of British merchant sailors who liked to shout in bad Spanish and break furniture. There was always a sense of tension and danger that Rodolfo found exciting. And it was true that many of these men carried revolvers or knives, and there were often fights where fists or weapons were sometimes used. Once he had seen a man bleed to death on the floor before being dragged away like a broken chair by the owner.

But mostly, for Rodolfo, it was a great spectacle, like Podesta's famous gaucho circus show. He would sit quietly in the shadows listening to a *payada*—long duels of melancholy song and guitar music— totally bewitched, though he knew that some of these "gauchos" had fathers born in Naples and had never earned a living off the distant pampas they sang about. On hot, humid nights in February he would find the *compadritos* at their forbidden dances—consisting of sudden, threatening movements and slow, voluptuous gestures done to harsh instrumental music with whores or other men. To Rodolfo, these evenings were seductive and exuded unspoken sins in the world. He sensed something fleeting, something phantasmagorical about these characters he watched, as if they drifted out of their own lives into someone else's dreams.

The part Rodolfo liked best about his work were the trips to the harbor, which were frequent, sometimes several times a day. Although it was less than a mile from the warehouse to the docks, the trip could take several hours by the antiquated carts that the company used. The beef carcasses were in constant danger of rotting before they reached safety in refrigerated steamers.

The harbor was in a state of frenzy from dawn to past sunset, the maddest part of the entire city. The ships—mostly steamers with a few decaying sailing vessels—jammed every inch of dock space. More ships were constantly waiting in the basins, so close together that they nearly crushed the towboats between them. The wharves were invisible beneath the swarm of carters, peons, Neapolitan stevedores, horses, and carts—everyone and everything making as much noise as possible. A handful of officials from the customs house tried to keep track of the mountains of goods moving on and off the ships, while a small army of agents like Rodolfo made sure that the wagonloads in their care got to the right boats. Nothing, Rodolfo thought, was more representative of the bustling city than this.

Rodolfo had a criollo friend whose name was Esteban. Esteban had grown up on an *estancia* in the country, and claimed to be as good with a horse and bolas as the best of the gauchos—a claim that unfortunately he never had the opportunity to demonstrate while Rodolfo knew him. Esteban's grandfather had been an important landowner who moved in political circles, and Esteban liked to brag that he had "connections" that would one day make him rich.

"I am the patron of your patron," he would boast to the Italians. "It's my real job to look after all you poor gringos."

It was true that he always had more money than any of his friends, and was a flashy dresser.

"He is one boy with real *viveza*," said Esteban's criollo friends of his vitality.

Rodolfo understood that what attracted the garrulous, flamboyant criollo to the quiet, sober gringo was the need for an appreciative audience. Rodolfo was always along to admire Esteban's exploits: as when he would insult a *compañero* and get away with it with a joke; or get the most beautiful whores to sleep with him "for love," or swindle some poor Turkish laborer out of his hard-earned cash. He even taught Rodolfo how to help him cheat at cards.

"You look like such a sweet, dumb, innocent little gringo," said Esteban, when Rodolfo protested. "No one will suspect you of anything." And he was right.

Rodolfo had a little money hidden away, a legacy from his parents. Esteban was always suggesting ways for him to spend it.

"You will bring back the most beautiful whores in Paris," he'd say, "and set them up in the most magnificent house on the Avenida de Mayo. And we'll charge admission to see all the *gente decente* in indecent positions." When Rodolfo would smile, Esteban would say, "Just you wait, little gringo, someday I will make you richer than you can imagine."

aps of rubbish and a few squatters' huts of corrugated iron,
these looked abandoned. What was worse, it had started to
olfo shook his head. Was his friend trying to swindle him?

end, Rodolfo realized his friendship with Esteban was more
to him than the money, so he gave Esteban what he asked.
his bets, he bought a lot near the suburb of Belgrano, where
decente were building summer villas. And that was the end of
s' legacy.

course, Rodolfo's new property was surveyed and broken up
narrow lots. Feeling sick to his stomach, Rodolfo went with
o the big tent set up for the land auction. The auctioneers had
s in all the papers and had hired wagons to bring hundreds
erks and city workers out from the heart of Buenos Aires. The
of the company made a speech about the new electric cars
d whisk them back and forth from their jobs for a few centa-

e your *conventillos,*" he urged them. "Take your families and
r money-grubbing landlords forever. We offer you here the
pportunity of your lives—to own your own land to have and
 to your children and your children's children. We offer you
, and the city of the future, a future of free, independent men.
ou can manage in sixty small, monthly payments. Can you
hance at the future itself?"

htfall, nearly every lot had been sold. Esteban was in ecstasy.
d I tell you? What did I tell you, little gringo? You're rich.
romise you I'd make you rich?"

o was thunderstruck. While Esteban literally danced in the
walked in total silence. Could it be all so easy, so ridiculously
 rich?

the Tramways Eléctricos Metropolitanos laid its track and
wires from the Plaza de Mayo out to the western district. In
shower of sparks, the little horseless cars spun out the line at
hing speed of eight miles per hour, nearly three times the rate
horsecars. The trip to the end of the line took less than twenty
nd, as Esteban was promised, the fare was several centavos
an any other line in the city. The owners of the older lines
holding mostly to the horsecars, and the new company found
 attracting their customers. When the company's second line

One day Esteban came up to him
gringo," he said. "Here's where you w
work." The pamphlet was in German, a

"What's that?" Esteban asked him
cover.

"It's a streetcar."

"Wrong, little gringo, it's an electric

Rodolfo started to smile, but Esteba
knew some people who had obtained a
streetcar line and were looking for inve
slower than a three-legged mule," he s
that even people richer than us can't r
we will be able to charge half as mucl
and make twice as much money as the

Rodolfo was still skeptical, but Estel
gave him half his money to put into
Eléctricos Metropolitanos.

A few weeks later Esteban showed h
district. It had a red line running across
the path of a new line.

"Interesting," said Rodolfo.

"And?" said Esteban.

"And nothing. Thank you for show

"Little gringo," said Esteban with i
what this is? Do you think I showed
'Interesting, interesting' like an old bull

"Well, what then?" asked Rodolfo.

"You stupid-ass gringo," said Este
with you? Here's what you do, brainles
map. "All this land here is empty, wort
in, it won't be worthless—in fact, it v
you've ever seen. You must give me tl
much of this worthless land as we can!

Rodolfo was even more skeptical tl
day afternoon walking out to the place
map. He was right about it being emp
let alone trees: just an endless, flat wast
the muddy track where the tramway w

it but h
and eve
rain. Ro

In th
importa
To hedg
the *gent*
his pare

In d
into long
Esteban
placed a
of shop
presiden
that wou
vos.

"Lea
leave yo
greatest
to pass o
the futur
A future
refuse a

By ni
"What d
Didn't I

Rodo
street, he
easy, to

Soon
strung its
a hissing
the aston
of the ol
minutes
cheaper
hesitated.
it was so

was planned, Esteban and Rodolfo repeated the transaction and looked for other investors. Soon Rodolfo was selling four hundred or five hundred lots at a single auction. He owned part of a bank that gave out mortgages. With Esteban, he set up a construction company that built one-room houses on the new lots, about forty feet from the street. Then, as the years passed and their owners saved the money, he would add more rooms for them. As the children came and grew up, the houses would creep, room by room, toward the street, until they finished them off with a *sala*, a parlor, opening right on the sidewalk. So the useless muddy fields around the old Buenos Aires streets grew up into the endless barrios of the city.

Rodolfo himself bought a smart little chalet in Belgrano. He had a cook and a housekeeper. He acquired a fine victoria and two horses to pull it. His neighbors in Belgrano, many of them rich criollos of the *gente decente*, would nod to him on the street, though they never spoke to him, much less invited him into their summer villas nearby or to their *palacios* in town.

He was made a member of the Circolo Italiano and often took his meals there after a day in his office. Its members, well-off immigrants who had been born in Italy like himself, sometimes invited him to their houses for dinner. There he would meet their unmarried sisters or daughters, mostly old maids in their late twenties, but their shy, demure manners did not attract him.

He owned nearly half a block on the street called Florida. He liked to collect the rents from the merchants in the shops there himself, pausing to admire the rich, imported goods—Italian silks and French champagne, but he continued to live rather simply, even austerely, by the standards of the city. Sometimes he went to the theater, and sometimes to the opera, which reminded him of home, but he spent most of his evenings in the house in Belgrano, reading.

YEARS PASSED. After a time he became aware of a certain uneasiness in himself, a feeling he had never had before. He had grown rich and, to some degree, respected, but his life reminded him of nothing so much as of his own family, whose ways he had despised so much when he was young. In fact, it was worse. He was no longer a real Italian. His only close relative in Italy, a brother who ran a factory in Milan, was now a stranger to him. Yet Rodolfo wasn't an Argentine, either. At night he would walk past the lighted windows on his street, knowing that the curtains hid whole families—busy living a life in which he had no part.

Buenos Aires had changed more than he thought possible. It was certainly a magnificent city, the "Paris of the South," as the *porteños* or natives liked to call it, but he missed the warm evenings of his *conventillo* days. Esteban was gone. He had gotten himself into a situation he couldn't joke his way out of and had turned up in an empty lot in Nuevo Chicago with three deep knife wounds in his back. Rodolfo missed him terribly, and no one came to take his place. The *compadritos* and even the *indiada* were gone, too—they became no more than legends in the fading memories of old-timers like himself. The wild dances he had watched had been stolen away to Paris and had come back some years later as something called the Tango, a tame, elegant performance suitable for English Lords. Because the dance came from France, even the *gente decente* embraced it as the national dance.

There were still many gauchos around, but these were mainly the pretend kind, middle-class sons of immigrants who dedicated them-selves to the "preservation of the gaucho tradition," dressed up on weekends and belonged to clubs such as the Desert Bandits and the Cubs of the Pampas. He wanted nothing to do with their silly gaucho newspapers and their silly picnics and steak roasts.

ONE NIGHT, at the Circolo Italiano, when he had had too much to drink, he launched into a diatribe against the Jesuits. A few days later some members, who were also Masons, approached him to join their group in battling the "evil influence of the clergy." In considerable confusion, he turned them down and, out of embarrassment, stopped going to the club.

He grew more restless. He would walk the streets of the endless dark barrios, listening for music, looking for lighted rooms which he never found. Thin young men leaned out of doorways, staring without smiling. Sometimes a dog barked in the distance, or a door slammed, or a child cried. None of it had anything to do with him. He had built these streets but they no longer belonged to him.

One winter, without knowing why any more than he had known why he had first come to Buenos Aires, he set sail for Genoa. On the afternoon of his third day there, he met Dora.

IX

RODOLFO ARRIVED in Genoa in May. He checked into a hotel off the Corso Europa and spent several days without talking to anyone, without even contacting his family. He felt very strange: The city where he had spent half his life was now part of a foreign country.

He spent the second and third afternoons sitting in a café watching the people pass by. They seemed strange to him; Genoa was strange to him. It seemed old, old and very slow, like an aging gentleman stiff in the joints. He sat at his table and wondered why he had come.

Then he noticed a young woman—-she was no more than seventeen or eighteen, he thought—walking slowly down the street. It was very late in the day and the shadows were already filling the sidewalk. She wore a simple muslin dress with a high collar; her dark hair was piled on her head. She walked along aimlessly. She looked in windows without entering any of the shops. She did not stop or speak to anyone.

What fascinated him was the way she walked: slow, casual, without particular direction or force, but full of some unimaginable energy beneath the surface. He thought of things to compare it to—a cat? a tiger? Neither fit exactly. It was a walk all her own.

The wind blew her thin dress against her legs. No one paid any particular attention to her; they all seemed too busy going about their business. But they stepped out of her way as she passed, as if they sensed that strange, pent-up power behind her movements.

He stared at her. She seemed unaware of him, unaware of everything. He watched her until she disappeared into the shadows at the end of the street.

A few days later he saw her again, a little earlier in the day. She was on his side of the street, this time, wearing the same clothes, and walking toward his café. As she passed his table he caught her eye. She stopped and he shivered. There was something deeply luxurious about the way motion slowly slipped out of her body. Her skirts blew gently in the wind. She smiled. It was an oddly out-of-focus smile which seemed to mean nothing.

Rodolfo jumped up. "Signorina," he said. "Will you join me? Would you like some lemonade, perhaps?"

She smiled again. "If you wish," she said.

They sat down. He asked her name. "Dora," she said, still smiling. He couldn't place her at all, not from her voice, not from her oddly severe way of dressing. She might have been a duchess or a prostitute. Her face, her expression, her manner were indecipherable to him, written in a foreign language, or perhaps one he had forgotten. Had he been away so long? he thought to himself.

The waiter brought two glasses of lemonade. She picked up her glass without saying anything. The afternoon sun shone on her hair, making it golden. He noticed that she wore no jewelry. Her dress was very plain but beautifully made.

She said nothing but met his gaze evenly, keeping her smile gently in place. Was it proper, he thought, for a young woman like this to be sitting with a strange man in the middle of the afternoon in Genoa? Again, he felt like a foreigner. He looked at her hands, searching for a clue. They looked strong, not delicate, but not ruined by work.

He told her his name. "From Argentina," he said. Her look showed neither interest nor boredom. He went on, suddenly garrulous after so many days of silence. He told her how he had gone to Buenos Aires. He told her about the docks, about Esteban, about the land he had bought and sold. He told her about his little house in Belgrano, about his housekeeper who was an old woman now. He told her how he spent his days, how he walked the empty streets at night. He went on and on; it seemed like hours as he spilled his whole life on the table in front of her. Through it all she said almost nothing. She kept her smile. She looked into his face calmly, as if taking everything in, but he could see no sign of what she made of him.

At last, when the night began to engulf the street, he stopped. "I must go now," she said softly.

"Of course," he said, standing up quickly. "Forgive me for keeping you so long." She stood up. Once again he was struck by the sense of hidden power beneath her movements. She hesitated, then gave him her hand, and broadened her smile which, it seemed to him, filled with a sudden warmth.

"Will I see you again?" he said, hastily. "Perhaps here, tomorrow?"

"If you wish," she said, and was gone.

Dora, he thought. It was all he knew about her.

X

NO ONE KNEW how long the Merisi family had lived in Artemisia. "Time beyond memory," they said in the village. They said it when Napoléon took the iron crown of Lombardy and, for all anyone knew, they might have said the same in Charlemagne's time.

Old Merisi had had one son and six daughters. "What a misfortune," they said in the village.

They lived in a two-room old house on the hill overlooking the piazza. The house was low and dark and made of stucco-covered stone. They had a plot and a few olive trees behind the road and—their great pride—the "hill field," which was only a few feet from their door.

Long, long ago the Merisi had been well off, even prosperous, by village standards. In the first years of the Ligurian Republic they owned patches of land all over Artemisia, including a large hay field where, much later, the pastel villas stood. But slices of their land went for dowries, other slices went to pay off the debts from the bad years, and several sizable chunks were drunk away by the two generations after the Congress of Vienna. By old Merisi's time, only scraps of land remained. But—though the land was hard and rocky and worn out from generations of use—they held on to the hill field.

The hill field, it was said, was part of a grant to the Merisi from the emperor of Italy, but whether this was Charlemagne or Constantine the Great was a source of some disagreement. The land was also said to have been the site of a great battle, fertilized with the blood and bones of hundreds of soldiers. When the foundations of the house were dug (who knew how long ago that was?) bronze weapons and armor were supposed to have been found. So said the legends, though the decree of the emperor and the old bits of bronze had been lost long ago, as had whatever special fertility the land had had. Still, the hill field had been theirs, as far as anyone knew, as long as there had been a Merisi in Artemisia.

If hard times had fallen on the peasants of Artemisia, the hardest times had fallen on the Merisi. Besides the misfortune of having only one son to balance all those daughters, old Merisi had fallen into a strange, unexplained stupor. A doctor in the village examined him but found nothing; he could only conclude that it was the effect of an old head wound from old Merisi's army days in East Africa. Maria, the oldest daughter, had married a sailor and moved away; Anna, the second, was as strong as a man and did most of the work in the fields, but the three youngest were still too small to help much.

The handful of ancient olive trees in the foothills provided the only cash crop. The olives were sold to the naval depot at a fixed price. The other two fields no longer provided enough to feed the family, so Signora Merisi took in washing, and Roberto, the only son, went to work for the docks in Genoa, taking the third-class carriage on the train every day.

Then there was Dora, the third daughter. Her mother called her "the silent one"—she couldn't understand her. If she spoke to anyone it was to her cousin Eliana. Dora never cried, even as an infant, and hardly ever laughed when she was around her family. She refused to play with her sisters. She also refused to help in the fields. She didn't say anything; she just wouldn't. Signora Merisi could beat her but it would have done no good; Dora wouldn't let out a cry. She'd just stare at her mother with a determined, icy look that unnerved her.

She set Dora the task of looking after her three younger sisters. Once again, Dora neither refused nor accepted; she said nothing. Once again, she didn't need to.

One evening Signora Merisi came back from helping Anna in the upper field to find the younger ones howling because Dora had fed their dinner to a passing dog. Another time no one greeted her return. She found Dora sitting on the chest at the foot of the big bed, calmly braiding her hair, while her two smallest sisters screamed and pounded and kicked to be let out of the other room.

Late one afternoon, the village priest brought the youngest of all, who had barely learned how to walk, up to the field. She was soaking wet and babbling something about "ladies" and "pretty shells." She had wandered into the catch basin of the fountain and it was "an act of mercy," the priest said, that some old pensioners in the piazza had pulled her out before she drowned. He had found the other two dragging the day's laundry out into the street and had found Dora nowhere.

"You lazy, selfish, hateful good-for-nothing!" Signora Merisi screamed at Dora when she found her. "You will go straight to the Devil! You will wind up in the gutter next to that whore of a cousin of yours!" Dora, as usual, said nothing at all.

Finally, in desperation, Signora Merisi told Dora to help her fold the washing when it was dry, and kept her eye on her the whole time she was at it. To her surprise, Dora did it; in fact, she did it beautifully. She made an art out of it. Her hands moved quickly and smoothly over the cloth, gently and expertly folding and tucking everything in place. Even Signora Merisi's customers noticed.

This gave Signora Merisi an idea. Dora was as silent as ever, but, if she showed no sign of pleasure at this work, she didn't seem to detest it, either. She was clearly good with her hands—she even made things, though they were useless, frivolous things like flower crowns. Signora Merisi scraped together the money and bought Dora an apprenticeship with a seamstress in Genoa, more in the way of a paid education than she had been able to give any of her other children.

Dora was as close-mouthed about this scheme as about everything else. Still, she went in to Genoa with Roberto every day and came home every night to supper. Dora said nothing about her work, but Signora Merisi received reports from time to time from the seamstress. She said that Dora refused to gossip with the other women in the shop and, in fact, seemed to want to have as little as possible to do with them, but that she was a steady worker and showed great promise. "One of the neatest apprentices I have ever had," she said. "Almost none of her work has had to be ripped out."

Signora Merisi took heart at this. Perhaps there was hope for the silent one after all.

Dora wasn't the only silent one in the family but, because the other one was her son, Roberto, Signora Merisi didn't think of him that way. This may have been fair, because Roberto's silence was different. He was a thinker; he spent his time going over ideas in his mind again and again until they were worn smooth like an old stone.

Roberto was a Socialist. When he had gone to the docks to work, a huge, smiling bearded man about ten years older than him had shown him the ropes. They had become friends. The older man's name was also Roberto, and the other workers took to calling him "Big Roberto," and Roberto Merisi, who was hardly a small man, "Little Roberto." Little Roberto grew heated hearing this, but Big Roberto told him not to mind. "There are more important things in the world to get angry at," he said.

It was Big Roberto who introduced him to the Socialists; he had been a member of the party since he was a boy. At first Little Roberto had known nothing about it; he'd joined only because he admired Big Roberto in everything. Big Roberto had lent him his battered translations of Marx and his copy of Labriola's commentary on the *Manifesto*. Little Roberto struggled over these hour after hour in the evenings, cursing his third-grade education, but with Big Roberto's help, he gradually worked the great ideas free from the pages.

Great ideas! Little Roberto, who had hardly known what an idea was before, was enraptured with them. Nothing he had known in church, with its mumbled Latin over a distant altar, its plaster and gilt saints whose perfect lives seemed so remote from his, could compare with the fiery passion of those ideas. The story of the class struggle was better than that of Moses, and, more exciting still, men like him, instead of being on the ragged edges of things, were right in the middle, the central force of modern history! Their triumph was preordained, written into the ineluctable script of human events with ink, as scientifically inevitable as the rise and fall of the tide on the beach at Artemisia.

Big Roberto had a friend from the party named Giulio, a student at the university. Together they would go to the Piazza Ponti to listen to the harangues, or would spend hours talking in the working-class cafés. Little Roberto felt too ignorant to contribute much to these discussions, but he was a passionate listener, and the ideas in their argument would sound in his brain like trumpets. With astonishing ease the names fell from his friends' lips: Croce, Sorel, Labriola, Juarez, Ferri, Turati, Bernstein. He knew that his friends looked on these names with varying degrees of hate or admiration, but to him they were the names of high priests with the knowledge and the privilege of interpreting the words of Marx. It made him proud to be in Genoa and to listen to them; after all, wasn't it in Genoa that the party had been founded?

Sometimes an idea would seize his imagination—the labor theory of value, for example. He had first felt grateful for whatever the bosses of the docks would condescend to pay him. They did not have to provide him with work, after all. But from Big Roberto and Giulio, he learned that these bosses were thieves, that their wealth, their huge reserves of capital and power, were really the fruits of his and his fellow workers' labor which the capitalist bourgeois had expropriated from them.

"You should consider yourself lucky," Giulio said to him. "Your family owns its land; it's practically bourgeois. Think where you'd be if you were a poor *braccianti* in the south, not knowing from day to day if you'd be working the next. The future of the party lies in the south; Turati is a fool for not realizing that."

"But the industry, the proletariat is in the north," said Big Roberto. The north is the home of the workers who will make the revolution."

"The misery and the oppression are in the south, and the party must follow these two. Let that be our little Italian 'revision.' Don't get distracted by your northern prejudices."

The talk turned to the return of Giolitti from one of his little "vacations" from power. Big Roberto and Giulio agreed that he was the "minister of gangsters," but Big Roberto had been a boy of seventeen on the docks during the strike of 1900, when the government had outlawed the Socialist Party and very nearly all organizations of labor. He had grateful memories of Giolitti's passionate defense of the rights of labor before Parliament.

"Keep in mind," said Giulio, "that he spoke of the rights of labor but of the advantages of capital. You can see how his mind works—he uses logic to confuse, to blur, not to clarify. He plays to everyone's reason—he's very careful to make everyone see the reasonableness and the advantages of his position. Sometimes I think he is more dangerous than the king himself.

"Yet the saber-rattler Bissolati has turned down his offer to join his den of thieves!" he went on. "One would have thought he had crossed the threshold already: What Socialist could propose an Italian marriage with Russia, the rotting carcass of degenerate reaction itself? Even Turati could see that, but then Turati turned down the minister of gangsters when he was tapped to join. Even he could see that a Socialist minister in a bourgeois government is a contradiction in terms. Since the government would not have stopped being bourgeois to suit his conscience, he would have had to stop calling himself a Socialist."

Big Roberto asked him what he thought about Libya. "Yes, indeed, another example. The 'reasonable' Giolitti now talks of the advantage to Italy of an overseas empire! One would have thought the last African disaster would have shattered that little illusion. If that doesn't make Turati apprehend the truth, nothing will."

The conversation went on to the threat of Austria, the Triple Alliance, the possibility of war, the Social Democrats.

"It is Fraulein Luxembourg's opinion," said Giulio, who had been to the Stuttgart congress of the International, "that capitalism will collapse from the rivalries of imperialists. Being a member of the largest and most 'successful' Socialist party in Europe, I suppose she should know. Yet I sometimes wonder, should this last war of imperialism break out, whether these well-organized Social Democrats will side with the workers of France and Russia, or with the Kaiser."

At points like this, Big Roberto would take exception to Giulio's cynicism and would launch into long counterarguments that could last for hours. Little Roberto could follow only part of them, but these were, for him, hours of sheer delight.

When Dora began her apprenticeship, Roberto's afternoons were, much to his chagrin, altered. Since she finished her work more than an hour before he did, he had to rush to the Piazza Acquaverde, where he would meet her in the shadow of the Columbus monument. The long delicious hours of discussion and argument were over for him; naturally, he half-blamed Dora for this. People in the village said they were alike; he couldn't see the resemblance at all. She was as much an enigma to him as she was to Signora Merisi, though he thought he detected much more than their mother did a strong strain of selfishness in her and, in the way she showed a budding love of luxury, of bourgeois attitudes. On their trips home together he would sometimes try to point out their class position, the reasons for their poverty.

"Poor people are stupid people," she would say in reply. "Stupidity is the only excuse for poverty."

Recently he had had to wait for her at the Piazza Acquaverde; once she had been more than an hour late. What was she up to? He was not at all sure it was a good idea to send her into Genoa, a city full of strangers, every day. She had far too much imagination, far too much love of capitalist pleasures, and far too little self-restraint. He said so, in an offhand way, to his mother. She only sighed.

"What am I to do? The apprenticeship is the only thing she has taken to. You know as well as I that I can't afford to keep her here in idleness just so we can keep an eye on her."

XI

DORA HAD BEEN meeting Rodolfo two or three times a week. They took short walks through the city, to the Via Garibaldi to look at the palaces, or to San Lorenzo where, for a fee, the ciceroni brought them before the precious Sacro Catino, won in the plunder of Caesarea during the Crusades, said to have been a gift of the Queen of Sheba to King Solomon, or to have been the vessel in which Joseph of Arimathea received the sacred blood of the Savior, or to have held the head of John the Baptist, or to have been given to Herod by Caesar Augustus, or to have been used by Judas at the Last Supper. Its green glass shimmered like seawater in the dim light, imitating emeralds.

Outside, the cicerone showed them the facade, with its cut black and tan stone like a patchwork of lace and columns of colored marble, pointing out the bits of Roman carving, the chunks of sarcophagi and old buildings set in the walls. A stone lion with a sad patient expression watched them, as if waiting for a new race of scavengers to pull out the stones and use them again in a new cathedral of some as yet uninvented religion.

Dora liked walking through the old town best. She strode ahead along the steep, narrow streets, up the little flights of steps, through the tunnels cut in the hills, under the raised shutters and the iron lanterns and the little bridges of electric wires hanging over them.

One day they went down to the waterfront and climbed the Lanterna, the ancient lighthouse famous down the coast. You could see France from there, and Artemisia to the south. Rodolfo pointed to the west. "Columbus went that way to find the gold of the New World," he said. "And so did I." They looked down on the boats leaving the harbor, carrying cargoes of immigrants. "Such a long way to travel to grow rich," said Dora, half to herself.

All this time Rodolfo deliberately refused to define their relationship. He no longer thought much about its propriety or its direction. Sometimes he reached out a hand to caress Dora's waist and felt his fingers twitch from the desire to tear through the cloth to the smooth flesh he imagined beneath. But she showed no sign that she was aware of his touch, no sign at all. He loved to contemplate her indifference. Deep inside him, an infatuation was warming. His heart was paper; Dora was the sun, and her detachment a lens focused on the paper of Rodolfo's heart.

He had learned that she was a seamstress's apprentice and that she lived in a village south of the city. Now he recognized her accent as that of a landowning peasant family. These were no more than simple facts. Her character remained as opaque as on the day he met her.

He had never felt more at ease with a woman. Her manner toward him was simple, unaffected, with just a shade of deference. On the surface she seemed very passive; it was always he who suggested their walks; she never offered an objection or an opinion. "If you wish," was all she said. No one had listened to his talk with more patience and less comment. He found himself telling her his most intimate thoughts, things he had told no one before.

Yet beneath this placid, unmoving surface he continued to sense some great power, some enormous, unformed will at work. He saw this, as he had the first time they met, in the way she walked, in the almost innocent manner in which she shifted her clothes, so that they revealed every line of her full figure. Although her face and voice suggested passivity and obedience, her body promised a great deal more than that. Her body seemed fully aware of something her mind had not yet grasped.

He noticed that she wore the same dress every time he saw her and that she never wore jewelry, though she was always neat and clean. One day he handed her two boxes, a small one and a large one. The small box held a gold necklace; the large one, a dress in golden silk.

"Now you are really Dora d'oro," he said, "Dora the Golden."

She dropped her eyes; her thanks was softer than a whisper.

She is too shy to show her delight, he thought.

The next afternoon, when she left work, she was wearing the dress. She walked quickly to the Corso Europa, searched the shop windows for a sign and, finding what she was looking for, stepped inside.

The shop belonged to a famous jeweler, the best in Genoa. The shop clerks stared at her—the dress she was wearing was designed for evening wear—but she didn't seem to mind. She glanced at the gleaming cases of plate glass and bronze and paused in front of one of them. She asked the clerk to bring out one of the velvet boxes that lay inside. It contained a necklace identical to the one Rodolfo had given her.

She glanced at the price tag and smiled. She handed the box back to the clerk and walked out of the store.

Signora Merisi began to get more worried about her daughter. She not only had her son's reports on Dora's mysterious lateness, she had also noticed that Dora spent more time with her cousin Eliana. They would walk over to the hill field in the early evening and talk in whispers for hours. Eliana's raspy, high-pitched giggles would drift back to the house.

Signora Merisi realized she had rejoiced too soon at Dora's compliance with the apprenticeship. She suspected that the silent one had cooked up some scheme even before she had begun working in Genoa. Yet Signora Merisi had no real evidence yet. She had checked with the seamstress, who said that Dora showed up regularly every day. Her work was still improving, the seamstress said. One day soon she would make a handsome living from her craft.

Then Signora Merisi found the necklace. It fell out of the pocket of

Dora's dress when she went to wash it. It was such a ridiculously obvious hiding place that Signora Merisi couldn't believe at first that Dora
had left it there.

"Is this yours?" she asked, holding up the necklace. Dora nodded
calmly. "Then where did you get it?"

Dora started to smile her infuriating, silent smile. Her mother slapped
her. "Don't smile at me like that! Where did you get it? Where did you
get this necklace?"

"A rich man gave it to me," Dora said, as cool as ever. "A rich
man who gives me many presents."

Her mother let out a scream. "How long," she cried, "how long
have you known this 'rich man'?"

"About two months," said Dora. "More than two months, I think."

Signora Merisi sat down. She knew there was no point in scolding,
or shouting, or beating her daughter. There was only one thing she
could do.

She waited until Roberto came in again, then she showed him the
necklace.

"I found it in Dora's dress," she said, beginning to cry. "She said
a rich man gave it to her! A rich man! That's where she's been while
you've been waiting for her! And you can be sure that even a very rich
man doesn't give away such a thing without getting something in return!"

Roberto said nothing. In truth, he wasn't particularly surprised.

"It's up to you, my son," she went on, wiping her eyes. "You know
your papa is beyond doing anything about the family honor. I can only
turn to you. You must find this rich man, whoever he is, and you must
force him to marry our Dora. There is no other way; it's all up to you.
I pray to the Virgin that we're not too late."

Roberto was not at all pleased at this. He was inclined to let Dora
go to the Devil, if that was what she wanted. Yet he supposed he had
no choice. He shook his head in anger. At least if she were married
they'd be rid of her once and for all. If, that is, the rich man could be
found, and would consent to marriage without putting up a fight, which
he doubted.

The following day he took a bottle of mustard water to work and
gulped it down just after lunch. In full view of the foreman he emptied
his stomach over the side of the quay.

"Get out of here, you drunken bastard!" shouted the foreman. "Sleep it off on your own time and we'll take off a day's pay. You sure as hell better show up bright and sober tomorrow if you plan to work here through Saturday."

A waste of a good meal, thought Roberto.

He walked up to the street where Dora worked and stood in a doorway across the crooked alley from the seamstress's shop. When Dora came out, he was almost sure she saw him. She didn't turn around or stop, however; she just walked briskly up the street to the Corso Europa.

He followed her at a discreet distance. Sure enough, soon after she turned into the Corso, she stopped at a café. There a middle-aged man greeted her. He looked prosperous, though his way of dressing was a little odd. He might be foreign, Roberto thought.

He watched them for about an hour from the shadows across the street. All they did was talk. The man did not appear to be particularly lascivious; he didn't even touch her. Once or twice Dora looked in Roberto's direction but showed no sign of seeing him.

After a while, Dora got up. The gentleman stood up to say goodbye, and Dora walked off toward the Piazza Acquaverde. The gentleman sat down to another coffee and smoked a cigar. When he got up to leave, Roberto followed him.

The gentleman walked a few blocks up the street and turned into a fine-looking hotel. Roberto heard the doorman greet him as "Signor di Credi." A rich man, to be sure, thought Roberto. He waited a few moments then walked into the lobby: a grand, marble room with potted palms and elaborate velvet settees. He felt very out of place in his workman's clothing.

He asked the polished-looking clerk at the desk to see Signor di Credi "about an urgent family matter." The clerk eyed him with some suspicion, but rang Signor di Credi's room.

In a minute or two, a pleasant-looking, rather small man with thick, graying hair walked into the lobby. The clerk indicated Roberto with a short gesture.

"I am Rodolfo di Credi," he said, walking over to Roberto. "May I ask what this is about?"

"Can we go somewhere quiet?" asked Roberto a little nervously. "I have a few words to say to you."

Signor di Credi shrugged as if he were tired. Roberto noticed that his shirt and suit were new and of the finest quality. The two of them went to a corner of the hotel dining room, which was being set for dinner. "Please sit down," Rodolfo said, "Signor—?"

"My name is Roberto Merisi," said Roberto.

Signor di Credi smiled. The name seemed to mean nothing to him.

"I am Dora's brother," Roberto went on, twisting a napkin with his left hand. "I take it she's a friend of yours?"

Signor di Credi nodded slowly, beginning to frown a little.

"I have come, Signore, to ask your intentions."

"My intentions?" said Signor di Credi, apparently surprised.

"Your intentions regarding my sister," Roberto persisted.

"Forgive me, Signor Merisi. Please explain what you mean."

"I mean to ask," said Roberto, turning very red, "if you intend to marry her."

To Roberto's surprise, Signor di Credi laughed. It wasn't a cynical or insulting laugh, but a light, simple one, a laugh of pure delight.

"Marry Dora?" said Signor di Credi. "Marry her? Yes, of course I intend to marry her! Of course! Only I didn't realize it until just this moment!" Seeing Roberto's mouth drop open, Rodolfo grasped his arm and shook it over the table. "Forgive me, you must think I'm a little crazy, and perhaps you're a little right. I've been living in some kind of dream—not thinking clearly. But of course I'll marry your sister. As soon as you say, Roberto—did you say that was your name? Please call me Rodolfo, since we'll soon be brothers. Please, Roberto, let me buy you a drink! Champagne! Please, a little celebration! Thank the saints you came by! I might have gone on in my little dream forever but for that!"

So Roberto found himself sitting in the hotel bar with its beautifully polished wood and brass and cut glass, drinking with a man who insisted he was his "future brother-in-law." Rodolfo went on and on about his business interests in Buenos Aires, about his bank shares and apartment blocks, about how well he was prepared to provide for his sister. Roberto drank more than he should have on an empty stomach. He felt dizzy—something was very wrong about this, nothing had gone as he had expected. Something was not right, but he couldn't put his finger on it.

An hour later he staggered off to the Piazza Acquaverde. Dora was waiting for him in the shadows of the Columbus monument. The nude Indian princess at the explorer's feet looked down on Roberto with a mocking glance. "La Patria," the inscription read. He'd never noticed that before. What did it mean about Argentina?

Dora said nothing about his being late and drunk. She only smiled.

"I've been to see your gentleman friend," said Roberto. "The gentleman who gave you the necklace."

Dora smiled calmly. "I suppose you told him," she said, "that he had to marry me."

Roberto was suddenly furious. "No," he said with a hiss. "No, I didn't tell him that. I told him that if he ever saw you again, I'd break off his head. And I'm telling you the same thing now."

Dora began to scream; the sound hurt his head. Her fists beat his chest; she tried to reach his face to scratch it. People were beginning to stare. Two men near the station started to walk toward them.

"Be still!" he hissed in her ear as he grabbed her hands. "Be still or I swear by the saints I'll tear your arm off!"

She calmed down. Her dark eyes darted from side to side, then up to his face. Her mouth twisted slightly to one side. He held on to her arm firmly, held it as they got onto the train, held it all the way back to Artemisia.

His mother looked at them with alarm when they came into the house. "I've resolved your little problem," Roberto said to her. Dora stared at them both in silence.

He watched her all evening. After dark, Eliana came by. He nodded to Dora, but he followed them when they went out. He sat in front of the house, keeping an eye on them as they whispered together. They talked briefly, then Eliana went off alone. As Dora came into the house, she flashed him her insolent, silent smile.

"WHEN YOU LEAVE work tonight," he said as they took the train to Genoa the next day, "I will be waiting for you. I will be waiting for you every day from now on. So you'd better give up any thought of seeing that rich bastard again." Dora looked out the window as if she were bored.

When Roberto met her that evening, she still had the same slightly bored expression, her mouth tilted to one side in what could either have been a frown or a smile. They walked in silence to the station and rode in silence all the way to Artemisia. But when they approached the house, his mother and all his sisters rushed out to greet them.

"Dora! My dear, my darling Dora!" said Signora Merisi, embracing her. "The Virgin has blessed you! I'm so happy! Eliana brought him to us this morning! It's better than I could have hoped! Such a respectable, polite, distinguished man! And rich! Who could have thought that my daughter would marry a rich man! We went to see the priest together. In spite of everything, you have made me happy! So happy!"

So it was settled. The ceremony took place in early October in the village church. Most of the town was there. Rodolfo had insisted on buying new clothes for the entire family. Roberto sat through the ceremony in his stiff suit, swearing he'd never wear it again. And he never did.

XII

AFTER THE WEDDING, Rodolfo took Dora to Nice for two weeks. The season hadn't really started yet, and most of the hotels and casinos were still closed. The people in the cafés and on the Promenade des Anglais were mostly year-round residents and people from the north— Englishmen and Russians.

Dora complained that the place was expensive, particularly since the beach had more stones than the one at Artemisia, but he already knew her too well to believe her.

On their wedding night, Dora stood in front of him and took off every piece of the clothing he had bought for her, until all she had on was her gold necklace and a half-innocent, half-worldly smile which wouldn't have looked out of place on a plaster statue of the Virgin in a village church. The sight of her golden skin, the curve of her thighs where they joined her torso, hit his chest like an explosion. In the back of his mind was the annoying thought that her behavior reminded him a bit too much of certain "easy" women he had known in Buenos Aires, women whose company he had enjoyed but whom he would never have married. But the sight of her breasts rising and falling slightly with her breathing put the thought out of his mind.

"Would you like to come to bed?" he asked.

"If you like," she answered.

In the daytime, they walked on the Promenade. He loved to watch her as, it seemed to him, she drank in her surroundings, savoring every drop. Each day she seemed more of a woman, more of a mystery to him. She drew stares which delighted him. They are wondering who she is, he imagined, just as I used to do.

He bought her clothes. Her unerring taste never ceased to amaze him. Her sophistication, her sense of style, soon outstripped his; soon he would be asking her what he should wear.

Now that his future was settled, he began to worry about his business affairs. It had been months since he had left Buenos Aires. Already in Nice he began to make plans for their return. One night in their hotel Dora asked him if she could take Eliana with her as her maid. He didn't like the idea but he could think of no reason for refusing.

The three of them set sail for Argentina in early November. The voyage was without incident. Dora created the same effect on the decks of the steamer as she had in Nice; she seemed to be perfecting her technique. From a distance, no one would have guessed that she had grown up in a peasant cottage. Her style seemed very exotic—she might have been an Estonian princess—but it was a style all her own.

Eliana was discreet enough to leave them alone together most of the time. But sometimes Rodolfo would come upon them whispering together. It made him uneasy, but he couldn't tell why.

Toward the end of the month they reached Montevideo. Rodolfo was already planning out their new life in Buenos Aires. Perhaps he would buy a new house, a larger one closer to town. Other lonely men would walk outside, he thought, thinking of the life going on behind his lighted windows.

As the ship sailed up the Río de la Plata, he noticed a change in

Dora. She seemed nervous and no longer went on deck. She and Eliana spent more and more time together. When the boat docked at Buenos Aires, she refused to leave the cabin.

"I feel sick," she said. And she did look very pale. Rodolfo sent the ship's doctor to examine her.

"No need for concern, Signor di Credi," the doctor said afterward. "I don't believe she's ill, exactly. It appears she's going to have a child."

Rodolfo was overjoyed. Dora, however, refused to get off the ship.

"I can't, Rodolfo, not here," she said. "I can't have my baby in a strange country. Let me go home—to Italy, to my family."

"What did you think when we got on the ship?" said Rodolfo. "Was this something you couldn't anticipate? Why didn't you say something before?"

Dora smiled weakly. But she still refused to leave her cabin.

Rodolfo was getting more and more concerned about his business affairs. He felt like a man who had discovered his tobacco had been secretly and regularly laced with opium: furious and panicked, but with a horror that he was about to lose something that he could no longer do without.

Finally, he had his luggage moved off the boat, and left his wife in Eliana's care. He would visit Dora each day as if the ship were a hospital, alternately cajoling, pleading, and demanding. Nothing moved her.

The other passengers had all disembarked and the ship was reloading for the return voyage. Rodolfo's sense of panic increased. His wife's intransigence both infuriated and embarrassed him. After months of easily giving way to his every wish, she suddenly stood firm.

"Don't worry about me," she said. "Tend to your business. Eliana can look after me on the way back. After the baby is born, you can come over for us. Then we can decide how to settle our life together."

Through all his visits to the ship, Rodolfo got to know the captain, a pleasant Englishman who seemed half sympathetic and half bemused by Rodolfo's plight. Occasionally he would invite Rodolfo into his stateroom for tea.

"There's no accounting for the mind of women," the captain told him in his accented Spanish. "Believe me, I have good reason to appreciate your predicament. One minute they're soft as eiderdown, the next tough as steel. There's no way known to man to change the one into the other. Still, we'd hate like hell to have to do without them, eh?" He gave Rodolfo a wink that sent his heart plunging.

Days stretched into weeks. The captain began to hint that something would have to be resolved soon.

"Short of knocking her on the head and dragging her over the gangplank, I don't see too many ways around it," the captain said. "If she's bound and determined to go back, what can you do? And with the child coming on! I don't envy you your position, that's God's truth."

Rodolfo was near despair. He no longer tried to argue with Dora. He asked Eliana to intercede for him, but she only held up her hands. Dora was as pleasant as ever as long as he didn't talk about her leaving the ship. She seemed to be thriving now; she was eating better and walked around the cabin, speaking of how she would prepare her lying-in back in Artemisia. Rodolfo thought she had never looked more desirable.

"There's always what they did in the old days," said the captain over tea one day.

Rodolfo looked up.

"In the old days—the days of the viceroy, the Spanish colonials, before Bolívar and all that." He smiled.

Rodolfo said nothing.

"Well, you must know what I mean, you've lived in the damn country," he went on. "The old conquistadors, the better sort, couldn't bring their families to this savage country. So they set them up in the old country in a fine house, visited them every other year or so, had their children and all that. That would be what they called the 'big family.' Back here they'd take up with some native woman and raise their 'little family,' house and all. Made enough in those days, I understand, to support both families in grand style. Quite a nice arrangement all around, I'd say." He smiled again.

The very next day Rodolfo arranged passage to Italy for Dora and Eliana.

DORA'S SUDDEN return to Artemisia naturally raised a few eyebrows. Dora established herself and Eliana in the finest suite in the Artemisia Grande. She let it be known that she was soon to bear Rodolfo's child, and that Rodolfo would shortly return to build a house for his wife and family. In the meantime, she delighted in showing off her new wardrobe by walking down the avenue of pastel villas each evening.

She had had little to do with her family since her marriage, so her mother was a bit surprised to see her climbing up the hill to the house by herself one afternoon when Roberto was at work. Dora embraced her and asked to go inside. "I have something important to discuss with you and Papa," she said.

Signor Merisi shuffled out of the dark corner where he always sat, and the three of them gathered around the table.

"Now that I have married a wealthy man," Dora began, "I have the ability to help you a little. I know I haven't always been the most obedient daughter, but I want to make up for it now.

"You know that my husband and I, when he returns from Argentina, will be looking for a place to build our house. I'll make sure he offers you a good price for the hill field—you know it's no longer good for growing things. With the money you can buy a fine fishing boat for Roberto. You can make a good living from a fishing boat, a very good living."

WHEN THEY DUG the foundation for Dora's villa, the workmen made a discovery. They unearthed a large quantity of human bones and, mixed in with them, bits of green metal that looked as if they might once have been weapons or some sort of armor. The village priest came up to look at them and he brought a gentleman with him from one of the pink villas. They looked over the objects that had been unearthed, which included a handful of ancient, corroded bronze coins, with great interest. They wanted to call in an archaeologist from the university, but Dora wouldn't hear of it. She was in too much of a hurry to have the house completed.

XIII

ANTONIA LOVED her father's visits. He came only once or twice a year, but, because he never came twice on the same date, she could keep his visits clear and separate in her memory. There was "the time he came in June, the time he came in Easter, the time he came and it snowed, the time he came during Lent and we ate flounder until he couldn't stand it and bought us all steaks."

When her father came, everything changed. It was a miracle that never ceased to delight her. If she was at school, someone (usually a new, disgruntled driver—they never lasted long) came to fetch her.

At home her mother would be in a fury. She would fuss with everything: rehang the curtains, move the chairs around, have the poor servants beat the rugs over and over again. The changes she made were tiny—so tiny no one else could even see the difference—and as the date approached; they grew tinier and tinier. She would pick up a speck of plaster from the top of a door frame, a hair from underneath a hassock, would wipe off a fingerprint from beside a keyhole.

Donna Dora was never more disagreeable than at the preparation for these visits. By the time Rodolfo was due, she was lucky to have a servant left besides Eliana, and even she would go into a sulk and disappear for most of the visit. Dora was particularly unpleasant to Antonia: She concentrated on pointing out flaws in her anatomy. As Antonia grew older, Dora grew particularly displeased with her legs, which Dora always said were fat and ugly. "Lower your skirts, Antonia. Haven't I told you before? Your dresses are much too short for someone with your legs."

Antonia never really minded such criticisms. For one thing, it was the one time of the year when she would get new clothes. For another,

Marco was at home with her. Most important, she knew what would always come next.

Suddenly, everything would grow calm. Dora would drive off alone to Genoa and would return with Rodolfo. For a month or so, there would be order in the world. They would have three meals together every day at exactly the same time: breakfast, lunch, and a big dinner. Dora seemed to be a different person. She never raised her voice; she did everything Rodolfo asked without a murmur, and even addressed him with a respectful *"voi."* The four of them would sit together in the evenings. Antonia would play the piano, and her mother wouldn't cough or frown or leave the room as she usually did. Sometimes Antonia was so happy she'd close her eyes.

"Are you sleepy, little gringa?" her father would ask. He always called her La Gringa but never explained why.

"No," Antonia would answer. She would hope that her real life was a dream and that this, her imaginary life, would go on forever.

When her father came on his visits, he would wear special clothes that looked like holiday outfits. His children never knew they were costumes; they thought he dressed that way all the time. He would wear a white shirt, a bright silk scarf tied around his neck, a round black hat with a narrow brim, and boots with high heels. It was how a gaucho dressed, he told them.

This, he knew, was not strictly true. Although he sometimes owned an *estancia* or two, usually through foreclosures, he rarely visited them, and left them in the hands of one of his agents until he could sell them. He wasn't sure he had ever seen a real gaucho.

One reason he wore the costumes was so Marco and Antonia would ask him about gauchos. He would tell them about the gauchos he did know, the gauchos out of books.

He told them of Santos Vega, the greatest *payador* and greatest lover among the gauchos. No man could defeat him in song, just as no woman could resist him in love. One day a strange gaucho challenged him to a *payada*. The contest lasted for three nights and two days. But at the dawn of the third day, Santos Vega was defeated. The unknown man vanished in a flash of flame and the odor of sulfur, and Santos Vega died on the spot of shame. At night the gauchos say they can see his ghost riding the pampas, and they sometimes hear his famous songs in the early morning breezes.

"And who do you think the strange man was?" asked Rodolfo.

"The Devil!" said Marco.

"Some gauchos say that he was," said Rodolfo. "But others think that if there is a devil, he is a lazy fellow who doesn't walk among men. They say that there are enough temptations in the world, particularly for gauchos, without his having to lift a finger."

"Was it our Lord?" asked Antonia. "Did he want to punish Santos Vega for his sins?"

"Our Lord knew that Santos Vega had already been punished for his sins in this life."

"Well, who was he, then?" asked Marco.

"Nobody knows for sure," said Rodolfo. "But I think he was Santos Vega himself."

"But one man can't be in two places at once!" said Marco.

"You're wrong there, little one. A gaucho like Santos Vega can be in many places at once. Right here, for example," said Rodolfo, putting his hat on Marco's head.

Rodolfo's favorite gaucho was Martín Fierro. Rodolfo would tell them the stories and would recite bits of Hernández's poem from memory. The stories were so sad, they nearly always made Antonia cry. Yet she begged to hear them over and over.

"A gaucho's life is hard, very hard," Rodolfo would begin. "No one is more free than he is, yet no one is more abused. He has the whole wide pampas on which to roam, yet he has not house of his own:

> *Sin punto ni rumbo fijo*
> *en aquella inmesidad*
> *entre tanta escurida*
> *anda el gaucho como duende;*

"He lives by his horse; he breaks his horse's will with cruelty, but he can't live without it. Everyone mistreats him: the law, the government, Martín Fierro says, is for rich men, not gauchos:

> *la ley es como el cuchillo:*
> *no ofende a quién lo maneja*

"But a gaucho does not complain. He carries a knife, but his songs are his real weapons. With them he makes love and war against sadness":

> *el que por gusto navega*
> *no debe temerle al mar.*

Rodolfo told them how Martín Fierro was tricked into the army, had to endure hunger and want until his clothes wore off his back, and then was tricked out of his pay by the authorities. When he went home, his house was empty. His wife, his children, and his cattle were gone. Martín Fierro wept at this. What had happened to his wife?

> *Me dicen que se voló*
> *con no se que gavilán*

What would happen to his children?

> *Como hijitos de la cuna*
> *andaban por ahí sin madre*
> *Ya se quedaron sin padre.*

Martín Fierro went off to look for them. He met a Negro, fought with him, and killed him:

> *Nunca me puedo olvidar*
> *de la agonía de aquel negro*

More gauchos, tools of the police, came to capture him. They caught up to Martín Fierro, but he fought them; he fought them all night. Finally, one of them, Cruz, became a turncoat and helped him. Together they killed half the police and scared off the rest.

Martín Fierro and Cruz rode off together across the pampas. Cruz told Martín about his life, which was hard, like Fierro's. He had had a woman, too, who was stolen by his commandant:

> *Es triste a no poder más*
> *el hombre en su padecer*
> *si no tiene una mujer*
> *que lo ampare y lo consuele:*
> *más pa que otre se la pele*
> *lo mejor es no tener.*

Rodolfo looked at Dora when he said this. She didn't understand Spanish.

Martín and Cruz were captured by the Indians, who were cruel, savage people. Cruz died of the plague; Martín killed an Indian who had butchered a captive white woman's baby, and then escaped. After a long time, he found his sons.

They, too had suffered cruelly. They told him of their hardship:

> *ni casa tenía, ni madre*
> *ni parentela, ni hermanos;*
> *y todos limpian sus manos*
> *en el que vive sin padre.*

At the end of the story, Martín encountered a Negro who challenged him to a *payada*. The Negro sang the songs of the sky. He sang of the sea, of the earth, and of the night:

> *Son los secretos misterios*
> *que las tinieblas esconden;*
> *son los ecos que responden*
> *a la voz del que da un grito*
> *como un lamento infinito*
> *que viene no se de donde.*

The Negro was the brother of the Negro Martín killed long ago. But Martín didn't fight with him. He went off with his sons into the pampas.

"And that's the end," said Rodolfo.

"There's nothing else?" asked Antonia.

"Only that Martín Fierro asks his countrymen to remember him."

"Why did he want that?" asked Marco.

"So that children, when they asked, would know what a gaucho was."

After Rodolfo went back to Argentina, Marco and Antonia would play gaucho in the yard of the villa. The pampas of their imagination was a beautiful, smooth, green immensity, more perfect than the best-tended lawn in Artemisia. There were also certain additions to Rodolfo's stories: There were castles in the pampas and even an enchanted mountain. And Antonia insisted that the stories all be changed to have happy endings.

XIV

ON ONE OF HIS TRIPS to Italy, favorable winds brought Rodolfo's ship to Genoa two days earlier than expected. He hired a car and, as a surprise, drove out to Antonia's school.

The mother superior, a small, agitated woman with a thin, hatchet-shaped nose, received him in her study.

"Signor di Credi, how delighted Antonia will be to see you so soon," she said. "She speaks of your trips so often! And how she looks forward to them! I think these visits must be more important to her than holy days."

"Thank you, Mother," said Rodolfo. "I only wish I could come as often."

"Oh, I am sure you do!" said the mother superior, and paused. "But it must, of course, be difficult, living so far away as you do. And of course, children do need to spend time with their natural parents. We cannot offer everything here, as I'm sure you know."

"I'm sure you do your best to . . ."

"But of course," the mother superior went on, "of course, I don't mean to imply that we have any difficulties with Antonia. She is quite an angel, quite an angel, I assure you. I wish, I only wish that all pupils could manage to follow her example. Our life here would be much calmer, I assure you!"

"Does Antonia need anything? New clothes? Perhaps some spending money? I could provide—"

"Of course, our work here will always need the support of good men such as yourself, Signor di Credi. But as for Antonia, her fees are paid through the end of the year and I believe Count Mora has provided for all her personal needs as well. I'm sure of it, in fact."

"Count Mora?"

"Why yes, Count Mora," said the mother superior. "Count Emilio Mora. I was given to believe—to believe he is a relative of yours? Such a dignified man, if I might be permitted to say such a thing—a very, very dignified man, certainly of a very good family and with excellent manners. I can't remember meeting anyone with better manners. He pays all Antonia's fees—all Antonia's fees—well in advance as well."

She paused. Her glasses had slipped down on her nose, and her hand flitted around her face as if she wanted to adjust them but didn't dare to. The silence lasted for several seconds. The mother superior dropped her eyes and looked a bit pale.

"Yes, of course," said Rodolfo abruptly. "My late mother's brother. Forgive me, Mother, I was thinking of his Christian name."

"Yes, well, of course," said the mother superior, rising from her chair. "You will—you will come with me now? I'm sure Antonia must be ready for you, or nearly so."

In the car on the way to Marco's school, he turned to Antonia on the seat beside him.

"Little gringa," he said, "who is Count Mora?"

Antonia looked horrified. "Is it permitted to say?" she asked. "I'm sure Mama wouldn't like me to say."

"It is permitted to say, little gringa. I hear he's a great friend of yours?"

"Oh, yes, and of Marco, too. He has done so many kind things for us, and, I'm sure, for Mama too. You would like him, if you met him."

"Does he live in Artemisia?"

"No, in Genoa, near the Via Garibaldi. He has a beautiful flat full of wonderful things. He gave us the piano, and Madame de Cranne, and so many other things."

Rodolfo frowned. At Marco's school he asked the priest in charge, "Has Count Mora paid all the fees for this term?"

"Oh, yes," answered the priest. "Through the end of the year, in fact. And a little extra for the order besides. A most generous and devout man. A cousin of yours, I believe?"

A few days later, Rodolfo took the train to Genoa and walked to the street Antonia had mentioned, searching until he found the brass plate with the count's name.

A tall, thin, gray-haired woman in black answered the doorbell. He gave his name. "The count's cousin from Argentina," he said.

The woman gave him a long look. "I will see if the count is free," she said, and left him in a small square reception room off the hall.

The room had no carpet and only two worn, green velvet chairs for furniture. The stained satin covering the walls had light shapes on it where pictures or mirrors had clearly hung for many years. A carton of old books sat where a bookcase had apparently once stood. The bare marble mantel was covered with dust.

After a long time, the woman in black returned. "The count will be ready to see you in a moment," she said.

"Signora," Rodolfo asked. "Is the count preparing to move?"

She gave him another long look. "Alas, no," she said, deliberately. "I'm afraid your—cousin—has been obliged to part with a number of his beautiful things in the last few years. A great pity—they were in the family for generations—but old money, as they say, one day wears as thin as old shoes. And as I am old," she said, glancing at the mantel, "and all alone here now, we can't keep the house as well as we'd like."

Rodolfo was almost relieved to see that the count's study, when he was taken there, was still packed full of "beautiful things."

The count got up from his chair, smiling. "Cousin Rodolfo," he said. "How good to see you after so many years! Please sit down."

Rodolfo remained standing. He couldn't think of anything to say, so he stared into the count's face for some moments in silence. The count's face, as usual, was expressionless.

"I understand you have been paying my children's school fees," he said at last.

"Why yes," answered the count. "It gives me great pleasure to look after them. I have no children of my own to care for, you see."

"I am not a poor man," said Rodolfo. "I can easily provide for my own children. You must tell me what you have spent and I will repay you."

"Please, no," said the count. "Really, it isn't necessary. I'm very fond of them, and, as I told you, it gives me great—"

"Count, I must insist that you—"

"Please, enough," said the count. "Let me suggest a compromise. If you will accept my past generosity as a gift to your children, I will be pleased to allow you to pay the fees in the future. You must do this through me, you understand. Charming as she is, I'm sure you realize their mother has a somewhat thin grasp of the importance of money."

Rodolfo was silent again. The count continued to smile patiently. At last Rodolfo sat down.

"Well, yes, that sounds reasonable. Of course it's reasonable. I should be thanking you."

"Not at all. Please. Not at all. But I do think I should emphasize that it might be unwise to let Donna Dora know of this arrangement. You do understand?"

"Of course, of course."

"Good. I'm glad we don't need to talk of this any further. Are you at all interested in old coins, Signor di Credi? If it wouldn't bore you, I'd like to show you part of my collection. An indulgence, but I'm very proud of it. Alicia could bring us something to drink, if you have the time."

Rodolfo took the time. Over many years, and as many visits, Rodolfo grew as fond of the collection as Marco.

XV

THE LAST TIME Rodolfo went to visit the count, he found him in bed. He had never seen the count's bedroom before. It was a dark room with a low ceiling crossed with black beams and with gilded designs on the spaces between. In Chinese cabinets along the walls were Oriental vases and a row of green terra-cotta elephants and a muddle of smaller

objects Rodolfo couldn't make out in the gloom. The room had a bad smell, as if it hadn't been aired out in a long time, and the count's bedclothes didn't look very clean.

The count was sitting up in bed, wearing a red silk dressing gown. The bed was set up as a kind of couch; a cloth embroidered with Chinese dragons was thrown across it, and books and papers were strewn everywhere.

"I do apologize for letting you see me like this," said the count. He seemed thinner than Rodolfo remembered, and his bright eyes were nearly buried in heavy folds of loose skin. "There is a decent chair somewhere in this mess. Frightful, isn't it? Alicia has gotten so forgetful these days. Sometimes I'm afraid she'll forget to feed me! I haven't the heart to send her to my wife so I can get someone younger. But this is really all too much for her old age."

Rodolfo found a chair at the edge of the room.

"Do come closer so I can see you properly," said the count, putting on his glasses. "Don't worry, I don't have anything contagious—just that illness 'for which there is only one cure,' you know. I find that a day or two in bed now and then helps me get about better the rest of the time. If nothing else," the count went on, looking at Rodolfo out of the corner of his eyes, "it reminds me to make good use of the time I have out of bed. Time is always passing, as you well know, my friend.

"Did you know that my mother, just before she died, refused to go to bed? She said she was afraid she'd never get up again. She died in her chair reading a book—I think it was Shelley. She was ninety-six."

Rodolfo coughed slightly.

"Sorry to be so morbid," said the count. "Has something to do with what one reads in the papers these days. Horrible, horrible. I don't know what is worse—reading them and being horrified or not reading them and worrying about what you don't know.

"I'm reading one of my favorite books today," the count went on, holding up an ancient leather-bound volume. "It is a Latin translation of one of the most important books by the greatest Arab astrologer— Abu Ma'shar, Albumassar to our medieval ancestors. Are you at all interested in astrology?"

"I don't know anything about it, Count," said Rodolfo, who was feeling very uncomfortable.

"Oh, I don't mean the trash one reads about nowadays—the babblings of fatuous charlatans. For Abu Ma'shar, astrology was a science—the highest science; in fact, the very study of the workings of the cosmos. He was a student of the philosopher al-Kindi, and his great achievement was to unite the wisdom of the ancient Greeks with the astrological methods of the Sassanian Persians, which, they, in turn, had borrowed from the Indians. This book made a great impression when it reached Europe. Albertus Magnus ranked Albumassar higher than Aristotle.

"The Arab astronomers of the ninth century (that was when Abu Ma'shar lived) practiced cathartic astrology. They called it *ahkam al-nujum:* the Judgment of the Stars. If you wanted to get married, say, or start on a long journey, the astrologer would consult the heavenly signs for you and choose a propitious moment. They also wrote out long astrological histories—not histories of the past, necessarily, though they also did this, but histories of the future. Since the astronomers could predict the movements of the heavenly bodies, the astrologers could predict the events on earth they controlled—a simple procedure of natural history, as Abu Ma'shar would have put it.

"Abu Ma'shar once made an unpleasant prediction that came to pass and the Caliph Mutuwakkil (a very nasty man) was so incensed that he had him beaten to within an inch of his life. The prediction was for something rather unpleasant, I imagine.

"What would Abu Ma'shar predict for our future, do you think? War? Madness? Destruction? Who knows—certainly not anything pleasant or settled in the short term. Well, what can one do? We are all victims of the judgments of the stars.

"And how are your children?" said the count, suddenly looking up from his book. "Well, I hope? It has been quite a while since I have seen them."

"They are both well, Count," answered Rodolfo, surprised by the count's sudden change of subject. "Marco will be finishing school soon, thanks to you. It seems hard to imagine."

"Indeed," said the count. "Time keeps moving, that much we can count on. And what will Marco be doing after school?"

"I'm not sure he's thought much about it. He hasn't spoken of anything in particular."

"My dear Rodolfo," said the count, sitting up and reaching for

Rodolfo's hand. "That is exactly what I was afraid of. This is a problem, is it not? 'Anything in particular,' alas, is not sufficient for this moment in history. Have you spoken to him about it?"

"No, I haven't. I haven't even thought about it. It seems to me that there's time—"

"No! No, my old friend, there is no time! No time at all! What have we been talking about since you came in? War! And if there's a war, what good will 'anything in particular' do? Are you so rich that your money can fly over guns and destruction to protect your children?"

Rodolfo sat with his mouth open. The count sank back on the bed.

"Forgive me," said the count, losing the strength in his voice. "Forgive my fears, my old friend. But your children—they are still your children, of course—are very dear to me. We are not young. We are— need I say it?—old men, and won't be here always to look after them. And their mother is not very wise when it comes to looking after people other than herself. They must be given the means to look after themselves when we are gone. Do you understand me?"

Rodolfo was deeply shocked. "Yes, Count," he said slowly. "Yes, I do understand. You make me ashamed—"

"Don't worry about that—it is not the point I am trying to make. The point is what is to be done, is it not? For example, have you thought about taking the boy back to Argentina with you? To train him in your business, I mean? Might that be a solution, in his case, at least?"

"Yes, I suppose I could do that. I would like having him with me."

"Good! Good, I am glad for that. Think about it—make plans, make plans starting today, starting this moment. There is no time for doing anything else."

Rodolfo was very upset when he left the count. He had said that they were old men, and Rodolfo's mind couldn't get past those words. He had always thought of the count as being much older than he was, though the difference was perhaps only ten years, and ten years at their stage of life was not as much as when they were younger. He looked at his hands. They seemed to have grown very long and were beginning to be covered with spots. The flesh was sinking between the bones, and the veins and tendons were very clear through the pale skin.

He watched Marco when he was home. Marco had grown tall and handsome, and seemed to have far more energy and enthusiasm than Rodolfo had had at his age. But it was a kind of unfocused energy moving in all directions like a litter of puppies. Marco spoke only of the next day or the next week, not of the next month or the next year. Perhaps it was difficult in this time and country, and in this house, which Dora seemed to be determined to keep away from the rest of the world.

But Rodolfo couldn't bring himself to talk to the boy about the count's suggestion. There would be time for that on the next visit; he could talk to the count again, work things out in greater detail. He could prepare the ground at home, make a place for his son in his business. Then, on the next visit, he could bring it up—carefully—with Dora.

But there wasn't another visit.

XVI

WHEN RODOLFO RETURNED to Buenos Aires, he found himself immediately immersed in his business. His chief agent—a quiet, patient man from a fine (though ruined) criollo family—was trying to get him to sell some land he owned in the north. The land was worthless, the agent said, overworked, and Rodolfo had paid more for it than it was worth.

Rodolfo ignored this suggestion at first; when he had bought the land, an *estancia* near Rosario, he had prided himself on the bargain he had struck. But the agent kept bringing the matter up, showing him balance sheets with year after year of losses. Finally, Rodolfo grew so annoyed at this he decided to investigate it for himself.

Without telling his agent, he took the train north to look over the land. He got out in the town nearest the *estancia*—half a dozen decrepit adobe buildings near the station which had been whitewashed some time around the turn of the century. In a fit of madness, he hired a horse and rode the ten miles out to the *estancia* the same day he arrived.

He had never been much of a rider and was thoroughly exhausted when he reached the gates to the *estancia* headquarters.

He had bought the land from the heirs of an English railway engineer who had been born near Birmingham. The engineer had built a fine house there, an enormous imitation of a Tudor country seat, had spent a few summer weeks out of half a dozen years there, and then retired to the south of France.

Rodolfo turned his horse into the drive, which skirted a broad open field that had once been a manicured lawn and was now returning to pampas. The four front gables of the house peered at a stand of ragged-looking eucalyptus trees. The windows were clouded with either dust or chalk, and several panes were broken. Some of the iron-bound shutters were closed, others hung loose from their rusted hinges. The shingles had blown off one of the gable roofs, revealing the planking below.

A dog was barking somewhere behind the trees. From its choked cries, Rodolfo guessed it was tied up. There was no other sound besides the wind, which was whipping up a bank of dark clouds over the house. Not wanting to encounter the estate foreman, Rodolfo turned left, away from the house and off the drive.

He passed through the eucalyptus and through a tangle of rose bushes gone wild. The horse's hooves struck something smooth and hard; looking down, Rodolfo saw they were crossing the ruins of a tennis court.

He moved through another stand of trees and came into a field that looked as if it had once grown corn. He stopped to take a soil sample. The ground looked fertile enough, though there was no sign of recent cultivation.

In fact, he found no evidence that anything was being grown on the land at all. He crossed field after empty field, broken only by the occasional empty shell of a tenant farmer's hut. The only living thing he encountered was a solitary, filthy sheep which gazed blankly at his horse for a moment before bounding off.

Rodolfo was enraged. Was his agent a swindler or a fool? No wonder the land had shown such big losses. It didn't look like anything had been raised there in years.

It started to rain. Thunder rolled out of the blackened distance. The horse shook its head, began to trot, then gallop. Rodolfo pulled ineffectually on the reins. The horse stumbled in a gully and threw him into the mud. Then it ran off toward town.

Rodolfo had hurt his ankle. He lay on his back and let the rain wash the mud off his face, then he found his hat and hobbled painfully in what he thought was the direction of the estate house.

He came upon another farmer's house. Peering at it through the downpour, he thought at first it was abandoned like the others. It sagged so badly that one end of the rusted iron roof nearly touched the ground, and the mud-plastered walls seemed to melt back into the ground.

A torn, dirty piece of canvas hung across the door opening. He pushed it aside and started to go in. There was a short cry of surprise and a shuffling sound. Somebody lit a kerosene lamp, and when he turned to look he saw an old man dressed in cotton rags, his skin so darkened and wrinkled by the sun, old age, and dirt that Rodolfo couldn't tell if he was an Indian, mestizo, Negro, or mulatto. The old man held the lamp in one hand and a bare knife in the other.

Rodolfo held up his hands to show he had no weapon. He pointed to his injured foot and hopped a step into the room. The man's expression softened, and he began to make cooing, inarticulate sounds of sympathy. He helped Rodolfo to a heap of old sheepskin, blankets, and rubbish that evidently served him as a chair. The dirt floor was covered with bits of leather, iron, and fur, bundles of rags, and jars and bottles containing indeterminate substances. The smell was extraordinary.

The old man helped him settle his foot and covered him with a filthy blanket full of holes. Everything must be full of lice, Rodolfo thought, but he was too tired to care.

His host crawled through a hole in the back wall and Rodolfo could hear him starting a fire in the lean-to. He looked around. The mud was crumbling off the twigs and straw that made up the walls. All over them were pasted pages from magazines—Rodolfo couldn't tell if they were there to fill the cracks or for decoration: they were pictures mostly of Mexican movie stars and American cars. There were some chickens in the room. Rodolfo couldn't see them, but he could see their droppings and hear them clucking and scratching somewhere in the rafters. From time to time a bit of down would drift past his eyes.

The old man returned with a bit of very tough, dried beef and some excellent maté. Then he began to talk—mutter, really—Rodolfo couldn't tell if it was to him or to himself. In his exhausted state, he was perfectly glad not to answer, and sipped his maté while half listening to the old man's monologue.

He was saying something about the *estancia*—about the Englishman tearing down the old hacienda and putting up the big house, about the English and other gringos who came there in big, American cars. There was something about his wife and his sons. He had had two sons. "Gone—all gone," he was saying. "What happened to him? Some say he drowned in a ditch." Did he mean the Englishman, or one of his sons?

There was something about a foreman "drunk all the time." Something about sheep in the house—the estate house? Rodolfo wondered. More about his wife—some sort of disagreement. Something about the the town, people moving away. "Left all alone." Something about someone named Guido. His son? The foreman?

Rodolfo was so sleepy he couldn't make out all the words, only a general tone of loneliness, self-pity, and a kind of resigned, repressed anger. It was as if the man were setting out random, indecipherable bits of his life, like the murky jars on the floor of the hut. Finally, Rodolfo fell completely asleep. Just before he did, he realized the old man was speaking Italian.

When Rodolfo woke up, the old man was sitting on his haunches, staring at him.

"Town. I need to get into town," said Rodolfo. "I need to get to the train station." He started to reach for his wallet, then thought better of it.

The old man looked at him blankly. Then Rodolfo remembered his speech from the night before, and repeated his words in Italian.

The man's face brightened. "Italian?" he asked.

"Yes."

"Me, also. From Cremona. Fifty years, now. You have done well—in Argentina?"

"Reasonably well, yes."

"Me—not so well." He laughed, opening his toothless mouth very wide. "So goes life, no?" He laughed again.

The old man helped Rodolfo to a rickety cart which he hitched to an ancient ox. The ox, which turned out to be Guido, was obviously the old man's prized possession. He stopped the cart every few hundred feet to whisper something in the animal's ear. In this way it took them most of the day to reach town. The old man twice refused Rodolfo's money, but accepted on the third offer. "For Italy, eh?" he said, and laughed again.

Rodolfo bought a new set of clothes at the *pulpería* and paid a little extra for the owner to let him wash in a tub out back. He bound up his foot as best he could and caught the train in the early evening. Though his foot kept him in agony, he couldn't keep his mind off his chief agent. Was the man trying to cheat him? Or was he just being stupid?

Rodolfo reached home with a cold in addition to his sore foot. He stubbornly refused to stay home and went to Buenos Aires to send off his soil samples and to check up on his agent. The papers on the *estancia* were perplexing—incomplete and vague. He couldn't even determine the name of the foreman. Rodolfo was annoyed with himself: How could his affairs be in such a state? Was he getting too old and forgetful to look after them properly?

A few days later Rodolfo got out of bed with a pain in his chest and collapsed at breakfast. His housekeeper put him to bed and sent for the doctor. The doctor examined him, spoke lightly of "a touch of pneumonia," prescribed some pills, and told Rodolfo to stay in bed. He did, but he did not improve. The doctor returned a second time and a third. He still spoke cheerfully of the benefits of a little bed rest, but his face was grave. When the housekeeper brought Rodolfo his meals, she would burst into tears.

"I must be dying!" thought Rodolfo. "How ridiculous! My whole life I have fallen into things without expecting them, and now I am dying that way!" He thought of all the things he needed to do and grew very annoyed.

He sent for his lawyer. After the lawyer left, he couldn't remember if he had told him what he meant to or not; he seemed to have been asleep during the whole meeting.

There seemed to be strangers in his room: it was as if his eyes had sunk into the back of his skull and he couldn't quite peer out. He began to be very aware of certain sensations but could no longer describe them to himself. "I have a pain in my—leg, is that it?" he thought. It was very odd—the pain was still there but was no longer something close and bothersome. It was something far away, almost an object that he could turn around in his hands and set aside.

His vision grew blurred and he closed his eyes. Perhaps he was asleep for a while. Someone was singing but he couldn't understand the song. He opened his eyes. He could see that the person singing was a man—at first he thought it was the old man from the *estancia*, then he thought he recognized Esteban.

"Esteban!" he said. The man went on singing and he couldn't make out the words. It must have been a very amusing song, for the singer stopped after every line to laugh. He looked straight at Rodolfo and laughed and laughed.

The room began to fill up with something. Blue butterflies, it looked like. There were more and more of them until they became the sky. Dora was there, dressed as she was the first time he saw her. She looked down on him—he seemed to be on the ground looking up at the blue sky behind her head. She was smiling. There also seemed to be a house, perhaps the house on the *estancia*, but it had been repaired. He saw Dora standing on the lawn. She had a little boy in her left hand and a little girl in her right hand. "I ought to know who those children are," Rodolfo thought. They were dressed in white like a first-communion outfit. They seemed to be laughing. They pulled Dora's arms behind her and crossed to the other side. Now there were two of each of them; they crossed again and there were four of each, then eight. Soon there were dozens, dancing in a circle around Dora. And they were singing. Rodolfo strained to make out the words.

"Rivadia, Victoria, Potos, Moreno," the children sang. Those were the names of streets in Buenos Aires, Rodolfo thought. Perhaps he owned property in those streets. He couldn't remember. He couldn't remember where any of his property was. "Rivadia, Victoria, Potos, Moreno," they sang.

There was a crack like thunder, but it wasn't thunder. The house and the people fell flat as if they were made of cardboard. Rodolfo could see into the blurry distance. There was a rushing like wind, but it wasn't wind.

"This is it," he thought. "This is death." And it was.

Part Two

I

"IT WAS SO STRANGE when Papa died," said Antonia. "So strange. Somehow I don't think I've ever really believed he did. It was so sudden in a way, though he was an old man by then. It wasn't as if he was with us all the time—there was just a telegram—and we never saw him again. His visits were always so irregular. It was as if he had just put off coming over for an extra-long time. Mama didn't have the body brought back; she just had a miserable mass said in town. Nobody came, of course. Nobody knew him. I've never seen his grave. When I went to Buenos Aires, I almost expected to meet him there.

"Mama was terrible about the whole thing. Not happy or sad but angry—very angry. Papa had less money, I think, than she thought, and then there was his will."

"You mean about your brother?" Marta asked.

"Yes—the codicil that said Marco had to go to Buenos Aires to help run the business. Mama was furious about that. (Marco, of course, was delighted—it was the answer to his prayers.) But Mama—she never spoke of it. After Marco left, she never even mentioned the fact that he was in Argentina. I've never understood the will, really. I guess Mama had expected everything to come to her without any strings and this was what upset her so. It really affected the way she felt about Marco. You would have thought it was all his fault—right up to the day she died."

"How did you feel about it?"

"I don't really know. As I said, I didn't really understand what had happened. I'm not sure I really had feelings of my own then. I knew Papa was dead, of course, but it wasn't at all the way I had imagined it—as children do, of course. I had always thought he would die at home, in a big bed, with Mama weeping at his side and begging him not to leave her—all those things, with angel choirs and so on. And after we buried him Mama would be very changed and would always wear black and weep on his tomb. Of course, she was just the same; worse, really, particularly since she didn't have to be a 'good wife' for his visits anymore.

"I imagine it was then that I began to think she was really evil, you know, bad all the way through, with nothing soft or noble about her. I thought she had never cared about Papa or Marco or me at all, that all she cared about was herself. In one way, I suppose, that was true. But there was more to it—I know that now, but not then."

II

WHEN SHE THOUGHT about it later, Antonia felt she had spent the year after her father's death shut off somewhere. It was as if she were a goldfish in a bowl. The world went on around her—she could see it, but she was somehow separated from it, floating in a separate space. Something—she wasn't sure what—had ended or was coming to an end. Something else was due to begin, but hadn't. It perplexed her, but not deeply. Few things touched her deeply that year.

Marco, on the other hand, knew exactly what was ending and what was to begin. He drifted through his last year of school. He still hated it, but the hatred was dulled by the fact he would soon be free of everything. He was more bored than anything else.

Antonia would visit him, sometimes with the count, sometimes by herself. Her behavior was so good at school that the sisters gave her special permission, and their schools were only an hour or so apart that year. When she came she would smuggle cigarettes or even liquor to him. They pretended he was in prison, waiting for the end of his sentence, or, sometimes, for the king to die or the revolution to overthrow him.

She had a beautiful old copy of *I Promessi Sposi* that the count had given her. That year she read it over and over. She was fascinated by the strange troubles and adventures that drew Renzo and Lucia further and further apart, then, miraculously, sorted themselves out.

Marco was like Renzo, she thought. He made sense of it all—he drew practical morals from his adventures. "I've learned," Renzo said, "not to meddle in disturbances, not to make speeches in the street, not to drink more than I want, not to hold the knocker of a door when crazy-headed people are about."

Lucia, she thought, was more like her. "What ought I to have learned?" Lucia said at the end of the book. "I did not go to look for troubles: They came to look for me." Antonia's troubles were much smaller than those of Lucia and Renzo, but she didn't look for them, either. What should she learn from them?

The count came to see her often that year. He took her to the museum with him, or to the opera or theater. She admired him more than anyone. He could point out a line in a painting or in a piece of music so that she could instantly see to the heart of it. When she played a new piece or showed him a new dress, he would point out the detail needed to make it perfect.

Still, there were things about the count she did not understand, things that even frightened her. The more she learned from him, the more she realized how peculiar her own life and her mother's life was. Her mother's behavior, which she as a child had taken more or less for granted, she now knew was bizarre, outrageous. She understood now why she had no friends in the village, why the nuns sighed and looked at her with an air of self-righteous pity when vacations came. She understood the smirks, giggles, and the allusions to her "trials" and "difficulties." Her troubles were, she knew now, her mother.

She could not understand why the count seemed to tolerate her mother, how her outlandish clothes and her scenes seemed to please— even delight—him. "What ought I to have learned?" she wondered. It was a mystery.

III

RIGHT AFTER MARCO graduated, the count took both of them to Venice. Dora refused to acknowledge the invitation and then, two days before they were to leave, went off to Paris. Perhaps she thought the count wouldn't dare take Marco and Antonia without her. But she was wrong.

Venice wasn't at all what Antonia expected. She had been there twice as a girl with her mother, but remembered little. It wasn't the way things looked that surprised her. Although the city was dirtier and shabbier than in the guidebooks, the buildings and canals were more or less the same.

It was the experience that she hadn't expected. Something very strange happened to her; it was as if she had been asleep. She expected Venice to be brown and vague and soft at the edges, like the photographs. Instead, everything was suddenly, even alarmingly, vivid. The colors hurt her eyes; shapes were bizarre and almost menacing; ordinary noises seemed enormous and unusually intricate.

It wasn't the magnificence of Venice that overwhelmed her. In vain did the count drag her in front of endless Tintorettos and Titians and Veroneses, through interminable palazzos full of gilt, frescoes, and marble. She couldn't concentrate on them. Instead she was fascinated by minute things—a crack in a yellow wall, a pool of azure and gold, soft rustlings of the pigeons over a plaza. At night she would lie awake in her room listening to the lapping of the water and the strange cries of nameless Venetians in the dark.

She was hypnotized by the light reflected by the water, by the meaningless, constantly changing patterns it threw over columns and balconies. She would gaze at insignificant details—a stained stone saint's broken finger, a crumbling funnel-shaped chimney, the color of a patch

of pavement. The count and Marco would drift farther and farther from her. Years afterward, a scent in the wind, or a shade in a sunset, would press something inside her and one of these little bits of Venice would come back to her.

Venice, it seemed to her, was full of lovers. She had never been so aware of the young couples moving through her days like living instruments, each with its own melody of desire, sometimes in harmony, often in a kind of harsh, insistent dissonance. Her head ached from watching them, whose every touch, every motion, set off a powerful resonance, too high-pitched for most to hear. She watched how their bodies swelled to fill their light summer clothing, how the breasts and thighs of the women pressed upward, how the bare arms of the men rounded and tensed as they grasped their lover's arm or waist. The air of Venice was full of a music she had never played on her piano and whose echoes filled her sleepless nights.

One day the count took them to a palazzo belonging to an old lady with a famous collection of pictures. She received them in a large room full of overgrown plants and savage, garishly colored paintings of nude women. The room was scented with rosewater which failed to cover a strong odor of cat.

The old lady wore a white lace dress, and her skin was so pale and so wrinkled it was difficult to tell what was cloth and what was flesh. She spoke in a husky, rather monotonous voice, catching her r's and cc's high in her throat. She told them about her days as a young woman in Paris, of the artists she had known and the pictures they had painted of her.

A black cane rested on either side of the lady's high wicker chair. A servant came and went, bringing small glasses of a thick liqueur and rich little cakes. Antonia felt herself going into a stupor. She watched the lady's hand out of the corner of her eyes. She wore a large, fascinating ring, set with a huge black opal surrounded by diamonds. The deep blue surface of the stone washed over depths that flashed red and green and gold.

At last the lady reached for one of her canes and rapped on the floor. A servant appeared.

"Eduardo will take you to see my pictures," she said to the count. "You will forgive me if I don't accompany you myself? I have seen them so often. Your young lady will, I am sure," she smiled at Antonia, "stay to keep me company. What use does a girl of her age have for pictures?"

The lady leaned back and closed her eyes as Marco and the count left with Eduardo. They popped open suddenly as soon as she and Antonia were alone. For several moments, they stared at each other without speaking or moving.

Then, with a quick jerk, the lady leaned forward and grasped Antonia's chin with her long, sharp nails. She pressed Antonia's face away from her so she could examine her profile. Her soft breath was the only sound. At last she let go and drew her arm back into the shelter of her chair.

"You are very beautiful, my dear," she said in her high, dry voice. "Why do you act as if you were hideous?"

"Is it so important to be beautiful?" said Antonia without flinching.

"Important? Of course it is, my dear. Why would anyone think otherwise?"

"Because it doesn't last," said Antonia, looking straight into the lady's faded eyes.

"Last?" squeaked the lady. "Nothing lasts! Does that make it any less important? What could be more important than beauty?"

Antonia thought for a moment. "Love," she said.

"Love?" croaked the lady. "My dear, what do you know about love?"

"Nothing," said Antonia, with the slightest hint of a sigh. "What do you know about love?"

The lady sat back in her chair. She laughed a dusty little laugh. "What do I know about love?" she repeated to herself. Her eyes gazed up at the ceiling, which was covered with stained frescoes of nymphs and satyrs. "Love. To be in love is—well, very exciting, very intoxicating—also very dangerous. All of a sudden, everything becomes so simple, so small. Love is everything then, love is the whole world. Because you love, you want the whole world, to swallow it up. You feel as if you will burst any minute with it, you are so full, and then the world is full of pins, the sharpest pins. Love—oh, that kind of love is a kind of disease. It doesn't last either, thank God—such fires usually burn themselves out.

"Being loved, however, can be quite useful. Yes, my dear, being loved is much more useful than being in love.

"But we shouldn't talk in generalities. Tell me about your experience of love."

Antonia blushed and said nothing.

"So, you really do know nothing," said the lady, smiling. "But you will, my dear, I am quite sure of that." She reached down for her cane and cracked it on the floor with such force that Antonia jumped. A servant came into the room. The lady whispered something in his ear and then he went away.

"Do you think there will be another war?" she said, turning back to Antonia.

"I don't know. The count thinks so."

"Does he? My friends say there won't be. It's all so strange. War is a total mystery, don't you agree?"

"I suppose. I really know nothing about it."

"You know, I've survived two wars already. They both were very odd, they seemed like such distant things. Though I imagine it would have been different if I was a man and had to fight in them, don't you think?

"The first time we were living in Paris. It was more than sixty years ago. I was just a little girl, a very little girl. You know, we weren't French; we were supposed to go away to London or somewhere. But my father—well, he was the sort of man who had trouble dressing in time to hear the overture at the opera. So we were still there after the empress left and when the Prussians were all around and it was too late.

"Things didn't seem to change much at first. You could hear the guns sometimes, like thunder in the distance, but the cafés and restaurants were open. We even went to the theater. Later on the animals in the zoo began to disappear, and the dogs and cats. Papa said people were starving, though we seemed to have enough to eat. I remember walking through the Champs-Elysées with Papa and watching them cut down the trees. Then the bombardments began at night. Later there was terrible fighting in the streets; one night we stood on the balcony and watched the Tuileries burning. I never did understand what it was about.

"The second time I was living in Vienna with my husband. It was much the same—no battles, except in the newspapers. Just not enough food, and trouble in the streets. Then the emperor died. We stood with the crowds along the Ringstrasse. I remember the great black plumes on the heads of the horses leading the hearse. And I remember thinking, 'This is the end of it—the last of them.'

"And one day the war was over and the empire had vanished—just this tiny little country you could hardly find on the map was left. My husband was broken-hearted. He died of the influenza not long after, and I came here to live. We had many friends in Vienna, but I never really liked the place. Too heavy somehow, like their pastry, and somehow too dreary after the war. I always preferred the south.

"There was another thing about that war. There was an artist, a painter we knew. He painted that picture," she pointed to a canvas of three blue horses prancing in a yellow landscape. "He was a beautiful boy; if I had been younger, we might have been lovers. A beautiful boy; art meant everything to him. You know, the sort who would starve to buy paint. I've always thought that's why he died in the war."

Antonia said nothing. After a moment, the lady asked, "Are you a patriot, my dear?"

"What do you mean?"

"I mean, if there was a war, what would you do?"

"I would try to help."

"Help? Whom would you help? The leader, the government?"

"No, I would try to help those left behind."

"What could you do? What do you do well enough to help?"

"Nothing. Well, I can play the piano. I suppose that wouldn't help much, would it?"

"It might. It might. I've been told people do extraordinary things in time of war."

A huge Persian cat walked into the room. It jumped up onto the lady's lap.

"Cats," said the lady as she stroked it. "I imagine cats know more about love and war than any of us. Don't you think so, my dear?"

Marco and the count returned. So did the servant the lady had sent away. He handed the lady a small, oblong box. As they were leaving, the lady pressed the box into Antonia's hand. "For your wedding night, my dear," she whispered into her ear. The box contained a fine, gold chain with a tiny gold cross, elaborately made, set with rubies and diamonds.

IV

THE COUNT HAD good days, when he was full of energy, and took Marco and Antonia through galleries and churches, and bad days, when he stayed in bed. On the bad days, Antonia and Marco would wander off by themselves, sometimes losing themselves in the cramped, dimly lighted alleys, sometimes spending hours in an obscure café. They would talk—or rather Marco talked—about the future, about Argentina. Antonia began to grow tired of his enthusiasm; for the first time in their lives, he began to seem immature to her.

"How do you know what it will be like in Buenos Aires?" she said one day. "We hardly know what Papa did. Maybe he had a hundred mistresses and all their children over there. Maybe he ran a great big house and when you get there the fat madam will come downstairs in her red gown to meet you. Just when you thought you'd gotten away from Mama!" She laughed; Marco blushed and looked rather shocked, but he laughed, too.

"Marco," she said. "Remember when we used to stay up at night and talk in whispers so Mama or Eliana wouldn't hear us? Remember the stories we told each other about the future, about how much happier we'd be? Now I sometimes wonder if that wasn't the happiest part of our lives."

"No, Antonia, how can you say that? Soon I will be living on my own—that's bound to be better. And when I am, I can send for you. There are plenty of rich, handsome men in Buenos Aires looking for beautiful wives."

"You mean like Papa?" Antonia said.

Marco lost his smile. "What's wrong with you, Antonia?" he said. "You've never been like this before."

"I don't know," she answered. "I feel so strange. I don't know what I feel. I feel as if I will do something incredible, something outrageous. But I don't know what, or when."

Antonia's moods were, in fact, beginning to disturb her. It was an odd, distant kind of concern, as if she were worried about an acquaintance instead of herself.

Most of the time she was restless. She would stay up in her room at night for hours, with the lights burning bright. She would stare at herself in the mirror, combing her hair in different ways. She thought about what the old lady with the paintings had said. Was she really beautiful? Did she really act as if she were hideous? She took the little necklace the lady had given her out of its box and put it on. The precious stones glinted at her out of the mirror.

Sometimes, long after the count and Marco were asleep, she would slip out of the hotel on her own. She would walk alone along the canals. Mist came off the water, coating the walks and the stones of the houses with moisture. The floodlights along the Grand Canal glowed yellow and ominous.

She spoke to no one. Sometimes a solitary man would follow her. She was amazed to find she wasn't afraid. She didn't quicken her step or look back. Soon the man, somehow sensing something dangerous and unapproachable about her, would turn away.

When she came back into the empty lobby, the brilliant light would hurt her eyes. The night clerk would glare at her with disapproval.

At times she felt other, very different moods. In a gondola, for example, with Marco and the count, on a golden afternoon, she felt the deepest, most complete contentment she ever had. She leaned back, stretched like a cat, and let her eyelids drift down until they were half closed. She lay absolutely still, thinking of nothing. She felt time stretching over her like a wave, a golden wave that would last forever, sealing her in this moment as if it were amber.

One day, in the gloom of San Marco, while the count was explaining the origins of the peculiar architecture, she began to cry.

"What's wrong, what's wrong?" asked the count, alarmed.

Antonia shook her head, gasping. She could hardly speak. "It's too much, too much. I can't take it in. It won't come together."

Marco and the count, who could only conclude that she was tired, took her outside to a café table in the shade. She sat quietly over lemonade for a while, while the count continued to talk about the square, about the legends of the bronze horses and about the pigeons and other bits and pieces of Venetian history.

There was a pause. Antonia stared over the water, watching the little waves catch the sun.

"If Mama was here," she said to the count finally, "would you be saying all this?"

The count looked surprised. "I expect not," he said. "Why do you ask?"

"Because," said Antonia, "because you make me realize how horrible and vulgar she is. I don't understand it. I don't understand what you say to her when you are alone. I don't understand how you, of all people, can even stand being with her."

Both Marco and the count stared at her. She colored a little, as if she hadn't quite realized what she was saying.

The count cleared his throat. "I can give you a kind of answer to that, though I don't think you'll understand it. It has more to do with me, I suppose, than with your mother.

"You can't choose your family, you know. Let me tell you about mine.

"My grandfather was a republican, a revolutionary. When I was a boy, he was already an old, old man—a ghost really, a silent, bitter, ghost.

"He had worked all his life for a united Italy, for a republic. He thought that once this had happened, when the Austrians were pushed back over the Alps again, that a new era would begin. He believed people were, at heart, good and reasonable, that once the oppression of their situation was swept away, they would live in harmony. He thought Italy would become great again, greater than it had been under the Romans.

"But Italy united under a king, not a republic. Soon my grandfather found that his new nation was weak and backward, that men still murdered and cheated and stole. That little, in short, had changed. It was a great, great disappointment, of course. It broke him; I think it tore up his soul like an old piece of paper.

"My father had little sympathy for him. Sometimes I think he blamed my grandfather for the failures of Italy. Anyway, he came to the conclusion that it was all over for Italy, perhaps for the whole human race.

Most people were beneath his contempt; every year he talked to fewer and fewer of them.

"He became a connoisseur; this was his profession in life. It is a French word; it means 'one who knows' or, in my father's case, one who thinks he knows, or, worse, one who thinks he knows all that is worth knowing.

"He became a great lover of art. He collected beautiful paintings, ate off only the finest, thinnest china. All his books were old and rare. His carpets were silk and Persian. He had nothing to do with the everyday world; he even made my mother convey his wishes to the servants; he refused to talk to them himself.

"He had a small group of friends who thought like he did: stiff, dried-up rich people like himself. They were his companions right up to the day he died; he saw no need for any others; he didn't want any disturbing new faces around him.

"I am sorry to say that I idolized my father and shared his contempt for my grandfather. I was my father's son. My house is his house; most of what is in it was his, even the coins and the stories that go with them. Even my profession—trying to make paintings, whose painters have been dust for four hundred or five hundred years, look new again—was one he chose for me.

"I had his friends, or rather, the children of his friends, which was the same thing. When I married, I chose one of those friends. For years and years I lived as he had—quietly, correctly, surrounded by beautiful things, going to elegant dinners in the same houses, reading the same books, watching the same operas.

"You will think this is not such a bad thing, but you will be wrong. You are wrong—you don't understand the unendurable boredom that creeps into your soul after years and years of this kind of life. One day I woke up and realized I had been in a coffin for thirty, forty years.

"The beautiful, delicate culture of my father was no culture at all. A civilization of the past, without change, without life, without danger of some kind, is no civilization at all. It is no more than that," he gestured toward San Marco, "an enameled box for some stolen bones.

"But it was too late for me. I was far too old to change my ways. I thought, so, then, this is my life; there is no more, just turning the same pages over and over again until I can no longer read them and they fade into the darkness.

"Then, by some bizarre chance, I met your mother. She embarrassed me, shocked me: I who had not lost my composure, even laughed out loud, for more than half a century! She was extraordinary: the first person I have ever met who had totally invented herself, who had risen out of the sea like some shivering Venus. She was like a storm at sea, a typhoon, a force of nature itself. You may not like the typhoon: It may frighten you; it may, of course, even kill you. But you are never more alive than when you are in it.

"She made me realize something very important—that all my life I had been a different person inside from the one I thought I was. She was a kind of awakening for me. It wasn't so much what she was as what she represented to me. I thought I was in love with order, with dignity—what she was was a breaking away from that. She fascinated me because she changes all the time—not that she has a philosophy but that she always does what comes into her head without trying to fit it into a pattern.

"I've never told you about the countess, my wife. She is a woman always concerned about being correct—doing the thing expected of her. It was one of the reasons why we married: Our families had been connected for years and years, and it was the correct thing for both of us to do.

"Her mission was to raise children. When no children came, she stopped thinking, because there was nothing else for her to do.

"She is a thin woman dressed in black who worries always about the linen, about drafts, about indigestion. She has boxes full of beautiful old jewelry which she never wears. She drinks camomile tea. She crochets. She reads Dante over and over. She goes through the motions of religion without passion or guilt, without really believing in anything at all, I think. She visits an orphanage once a week. She makes up packages of food for the poor. She plans our meals. From time to time, someone will come and do her hair. She has a migraine, and will spend a day or two in the dark.

"It's been years since we've had anything to say to each other, and I think both of us are relieved. When my mother was alive and lived with us, they complained about each other. Now that is over. When I come home, I will ask about her life, and she will tell me about the visits to the orphanage, the crocheting, the packets of food, the new young woman who comes to do her hair. She never asks me about my life. A peaceful life, the kind of life that drives you mad sooner or later.

"Think, my dear children, what your mother might have been. She might have been a poor seamstress all her life, poor as her family had been for centuries. Then chance picked her up from near the bottom and left her somewhere near the top, all in an instant. If she had been different, what might she have done?

"She might have gone to Argentina; she might have learned how to fold her hands; where to put her feet. She might have learned to talk sweetly and say nothing, to serve a proper English tea, how to buy fine clothes that were elegant but not too elegant; to pay compliments but not to praise. She might have learned not to notice their smiles when she used the wrong word, took up the wrong fork, to overlook her husband's lovers, how to raise her children to behave, to be respectable, to play the piano and bridge, to go to mass on Sundays.

"She might have grown, as women do, smaller and smaller each year so that in the end, you'd hardly notice her at all. And what would have been her reward for her work, for this sacrifice of herself? When she was an old, old lady in the corner, an old lady beyond caring, beyond knowing even, they would say of her: 'She seems quite nice, quite respectable. One would almost never guess that her father was a peasant.' And when she died, they'd write that on her tomb: 'One would almost never guess.'

"No, children, I don't always like your mother. I certainly don't understand why she does what she does, why she wants what she wants. Perhaps she doesn't understand, either; perhaps that is her special tragedy.

"She is a kind of lover of chaos; you might even say a connoisseur of chaos. Nothing is calmer, more orderly, than death. Chaos is not very nice; loving chaos is dangerous, very, very dangerous. You can see that even in the streets these days; it might be the end of us all, this love of chaos. But then life is always more frightening, more dangerous, than death is."

V

THE ODD EFFECTS of Venice, if that was what they were, lingered with Antonia for more than a month. The sensations were less intense and intermittent, but she still had the same impression of seeing things for the first time, as if she were a newborn. The flaws in things stood out with a particular vividness. When she played the piano, the gaps between the notes overwhelmed the music; it was as if she could no longer play the melodies but only a disjointed series of tones.

She began to imagine herself as a child, examining her memories one by one, as if wrapping them up to save them for the future. She went over her memories of her mother, of the count. They made her feel very old. How could she have taken so much, and understood so little?

One memory of the count came back very vividly to her. It was not long after she had first met him, while she was still a very little girl, frightened of everything, and particularly of this strange new man who had come into her mother's life. Marco had gone off to school and she was alone in Artemisia with her mother for the first time.

The count had driven out to visit her mother, but as she was not feeling well and stayed in bed, he suggested to Antonia that they take a walk by the water. The count was still a solemn, distant figure to her, but she was too afraid to refuse.

Not long after they reached the beach in front of the pastel villas, they heard a distant roll of thunder from over the water. The count stood still, staring out to sea. Dark clouds began to roll up over the horizon, and the count's black cape flapped in the rising wind. The thunder grew louder and came more often as the sunlight disappeared.

"Please, Signore," said Antonia, tugging at his hand. "Please, Signore, it will begin raining soon. We must go back."

The count said nothing. The monocle had fallen out of his eye and he stared at the waves without any expression on his face at all.

Antonia stood with her hand in his, too frightened to do anything else. The sky grew darker and darker, the thunder, louder and louder. The wind blew sand and bits of straw into her eyes. Still the count didn't move.

Lightning flashed. Antonia let out a cry and buried her face in his coat. She could hear the rain beating across the waves, coming closer and closer. "Please," she said in a small voice, starting to cry. "Please, please, Signore."

Suddenly, she felt herself being lifted up. The black cape wrapped around her small body. She began to feel warmer and almost safe. The count began to joggle her in his arms. He was running! This strange old man was running with her!

Then he stopped. He pulled the cape away from her face. They were on the veranda of the Artemisia Grande and the rain was pouring down on the awning over their heads. She looked up into his face and he was laughing, laughing an enormous laugh that drowned out even the thunder. It was the first time she had heard him laugh, and it surprised her so much that she held herself very still. I should be afraid of such a laugh, she thought. But somehow she wasn't afraid. She wasn't even afraid of the storm anymore. The laugh filled up the space around them and wrapped her up, tighter and warmer than the count's own cape had.

VI

MARCO LEFT FOR Buenos Aires on a hot, cloudy day in late August. The count made the arrangements and Eliana did the packing, but Dora said nothing about it. On the day of his departure, she was nowhere to be seen. The count came with his car and driver, who loaded Marco's trunks and drove them to the docks in Genoa.

As they unloaded the car in Genoa, Dora's car pulled up behind them. It was a long, silver convertible with a red leather interior. Dora was driving. A slick-looking blond young man, no older than Marco, was at her side.

Dora, with her companion, came over to them. She was smiling her most charming smile. She was wearing a cream-colored dress, simple and unornamented except for an elaborate series of pleats, and a wide straw hat. Antonia, with a shock, noticed she was wearing makeup. Dora had always been so proud of her complexion and had nothing but contempt for "paint." But now Antonia could see the deep lines around her eyes and mouth, cracking the surface of the powder, which had been laid on thickly and evenly like whitewash over an old wall.

Dora was carrying a small parcel in brown paper, which she handed to Marco, giving him a kiss on the cheek. She chatted with the count, who didn't seem at all surprised to see her. They walked with Marco onto the boat. Dora admired its size and the elegance of Marco's cabin. It compared most favorably, she said, to the boat that she had taken to Buenos Aires. Dora's young man brought some flowers for Antonia. They stood at the rail for a while looking at the people on the pier while the count described how the Atlantic had looked to Columbus and his sailors.

At the bell, the visitors got off. Marco stood on deck looking out over the crowd. Antonia and the count waved at him as the boat pulled away; he had lost sight of Dora. The houses of Genoa, crowding up the hill behind the harbor, fell behind him. Looking down the coast toward Artemisia, he imagined he could just make out the Piglets.

Several weeks later Antonia received a letter from him.

"Everything is even more exciting than I imagined," Marco's letter said. "It's hard to describe what it's like. It's as if the games we played when we were children have come to life.

"Buenos Aires is a big, modern city. Not at all how Mama and Eliana used to describe it. No gauchos, either, except in the theater. It's more like New York, I think, than Genoa—really part of the New World.

"At first I thought I'd live in Papa's old house. But Señor Parodi, Papa's chief agent, said it was too far out from town. He said Papa was a bit of a recluse and liked to be away from things. He said it wouldn't do for me. He said he was sure I'd want to be in the thick of it all and close to the business so I could keep an eye on things. He was right, of course; he fixed me up in a flat in one of our buildings in town, and we've put Papa's house up for sale.

"I've got so much to learn. Señor Parodi is more like a friend or a teacher than our employee. Naturally, he knows a lot about the business because he was Papa's right-hand man for fifteen years. He took me to see Papa's buildings all over the city. You wouldn't believe what we own! Apartment buildings and shops, even a bakery (or rather a building that a bakery leases). Also land and *estancias* out in the province that I haven't seen yet.

"Señor Parodi speaks good Italian and helps me with my Spanish. He has also been showing me around, introducing me. Sometimes we go out together at night—there are a lot more clubs and entertainment spots than in Genoa, and Señor Parodi knows all the prettiest dancers and singers. He's been useful to me in all sorts of ways.

"We've been going over the books the last few days. I think he knows I can't make head or tail of them, really, but he's pointing things out. He says the business needs work, that it had really fallen into a rut before Papa died. He said Papa made his money in real-estate specu-lation, but that now it was more a question of real-estate management, which was a lot more difficult, particularly with the problems from the Depression.

"But I am learning. I can't ever remember being more excited about anything. The only bad thing about it is thinking about you left behind."

VII

"How DID YOU happen to become a nurse?" Marta asked.

"I didn't, actually," Antonia answered. "I was only six months into the training when I married your uncle. But it was Alberich who suggested it at first."

"Alberich?"

"Signor Ravecca, president of our bank in Artemisia. He always countersigned Mama's checks when we brought them in. After the count took us to see *Das Rheingold*, Marco and I started to call him Alberich— just to each other, of course. We used to joke about the gold he had at the bottom of his vault.

"He was a good man, though. Very proper; he had a very old-fashioned idea about money—that it was part of being respectable, like a good education and manners and wearing evening clothes at dinner, and that it should be treated with dignity and even with honor. I think he despised Mama—no doubt for the way she mistreated money—but he seemed to care about Marco and me. He knew more about Papa's money than any of us, I'm sure."

"And he suggested that you become a nurse?"

"Yes—though I think it was a last resort, really. At first he tried to marry me off. After Marco went to Argentina, he began to hint that there was something wrong with Papa's money. He used to ask me about Señor Parodi, Papa's agent in Buenos Aires. I could only repeat what Marco wrote in his letters. Marco had nothing but the highest praise for him, but Alberich didn't seem satisfied at all; he would only frown and shake his head.

"He used to offer to introduce me to various respectable unmarried men he knew—mostly lawyers and officials of a certain age, some of them widowers. But we both knew it was hopeless. Anyone he knew was almost sure to know about Mama—and Mama was too much of a mother-in-law for anyone, even an out-and-out golddigger.

"Finally, he began to hint very strongly that I needed to find a way of making my own living. After Papa died, Mama became even more extravagant than ever. She was beginning to feel old and used money to make up for it, I think—particularly with the younger men she was seeing in those days. Alberich was trying to tell me that Papa's money wouldn't last forever (he was right about that, of course). Also, the war was coming, and nobody knew what would happen then. The count was hinting at the same thing, though in a different way.

"I was in a terrible state at the time, though I didn't really know it. I was finished with school. All my friends were married or had become nuns. Marco was in Argentina. I hardly knew anyone. No one my age in the village would talk to me because of Mama. The count, too, was no longer well. We saw him less often, and when we did, he seemed so sad and tired I could hardly stand it. I was terrified that he would die and leave me, too."

"What did you do with your time?"

"Nothing, really. I stayed at home. I knew Mama didn't want me to work—it meant something degrading to her, probably because she had been so poor and had to work herself. And she was really a snob when it came to certain things, even though she pretended to care nothing for social conventions. On the other hand, she chased off any man who showed any interest at all in me—wouldn't give me any money for clothes—didn't seem to want me to have any life of my own. She even sent me away when she had gentlemen callers."

"What did she want you to do?"

"Take care of her, I guess. We had no servants besides Eliana by then—if you can count her as a servant. She was even more cranky and useless than Mama. I did most of the cleaning and cooking myself, and with Mama you can imagine how awful that was. The rest of the time I would shut myself up in the drawing room and play the piano eight or ten hours a day. My playing was the only thing that was mine, really, the only thing I could control.

"I played Chopin, Schumann, Schubert. There was something about this music—how can I describe it?—a sense of refuge, of order, of a complete world, a locked garden. All the shades of emotion were here, protected, like beautiful exotic flowers. Inside the music I felt safe and yet free, as if it were only there that I owned my own life. Does that sound strange to you?"

"Not at all."

"There was one Schubert minuet that I played over and over. It was the way I wanted to be. A delicate dance in form, but it was as hard as steel inside. It had a force to it like a march that wouldn't be stopped by anything. That was what I wanted to be like, but of course it was such a dream then, I had no life to live for myself.

"Then, one day, Signor Ravecca invited me to tea at his house. This was quite out of the blue—something he'd never done before. As it turned out, both Mama and Eliana were away somewhere (maybe he knew this) so there were no awkward questions. He said he had someone important for me to meet."

VIII

THE SOMEONE IMPORTANT turned out to be Dr. Gassendi. He was head surgeon at one of the largest hospitals in Genoa, and his family spent the summers in one of the pastel villas. This is how Signor Ravecca happened to know him.

Dr. Gassendi was a tall, broad man who wore his pince nez on the very end of his thin nose (Antonia wondered how he could see anything through them at that distance) and kept his thin, black hair brushed back from his forehead. He had a large, unlined face which managed to look pompous and kindly at the same time—a great advantage in his profession. He had a tiny beard and mustache that were much too small for his chin, which was beginning to double.

Antonia had hardly been introduced when Dr. Gassendi began to talk about the nursing profession. Although his words were carefully chosen and sounded like a speech at a physicians' convention, she could tell that the lecture was for her benefit. Signor Ravecca would nod and smile at her whenever the doctor made a point about "young women of good breeding and intelligence."

Nurses, the doctor said, were at the new frontier of the medical profession. "Here in Italy," he said, "we are behind the times. England and America have made much more progress than we. There, nurses are no longer the scullery maids of medicine! In these enlightened countries, nursing is a respectable profession, one that attracts young women of good breeding and intelligence. Young women of modern science— this is the future they are joining!

"My hospital will be the first in Italy with the new training. Young women—young nurses—should know as much about the human body, about anatomy, about medical science, as do young doctors. And why not? Are we living in the superstitious past? Are we still bound by the foolish prudery of our grandmothers? Why should young women of today pretend to be slow and ignorant and weak-minded? In the future we will regard the idle, China-doll woman as an archaic luxury, as an amusing relic of the dark past!

"Our nurses will become the envy of other women. Their work will become respectable, intellectual, and of great benefit to mankind! My own daughter (who unfortunately was unable to be with us today) will soon be one of those young nurses. And, who knows, if she shows herself capable and diligent, she may even enter the hallowed profession of physicians someday. And why not, if she proves worthy?"

Signora Ravecca was frowning. Antonia could see that she did not approve of the doctor's ideas. But Signor Ravecca was beaming.

Three days later, Antonia wrote a letter to Marco.

"Dear Marco," the letter said, "you will never guess! For once I have news about something really good. I have a profession! (No, don't be shocked, it isn't that.) Actually, like you, I am going to learn a profession. I am going to become a nurse! I know you'll think that nurses are the scullery maids of the medical profession, but I won't be that kind of nurse at all. I've been asked to join the training program at the most modern hospital in Genoa, where they treat the nurses like true women of science. Alberich introduced me to an important doctor there (Alberich, imagine! I guess he's given up trying to marry me off to his lawyer friends), and he said they were truly seeking 'women of good breeding and intelligence.' I have an interview with the matron tomorrow. Dr. Gassendi says it is just a formality, but of course I'm very nervous. Fortunately, Mama is away. Wish me luck, Marco!"

THE INTERVIEW took place in a bare, high-ceilinged room painted a blinding white. The matron had a broad body and a thin, sour-looking face. On Dr. Gassendi's advice, Antonia wore a plain cotton dress, but she could see that the matron still did not approve of her.

"What makes a young woman such as yourself want to be a nurse?" she asked in a low-pitched, cutting voice.

Antonia tried to explain what the doctor had told her about the new kind of nurse.

"Yes, the doctor has some wonderful ideas," said the matron, cutting her off. "I assure you I know all about them, signorina. But the doctor has never been a nurse. Let me see your hands."

Antonia, surprised, held them up to her. She was glad she had taken off her rings.

"Beautiful," pronounced the matron, almost pleasantly. "They are beautiful hands. You play the piano, perhaps?"

Antonia said that she did.

"Look at these hands," said the matron, holding up two reddened palms attached to wrinkled, painfully knotted fingers.

"These are a nurse's hands. Do you think you could play your piano with these? Would you like to have hands like these?"

Antonia said nothing and looked down at her delicate fingers where they lay in her lap.

The matron got up from her chair. She was tall as well as large. She came around her desk, keeping her eyes fixed on Antonia all the time. She walked behind her, and, when she reached the other side of Antonia's chair, she stopped.

"Signorina!" she said with a hint of triumph in her voice. "Where did you get such beautiful shoes?"

Antonia blushed. She had forgotten she had worn her new shoes, an elegant pair the count had bought her in Milan.

"Such beautiful shoes!" said the matron, pacing heavily back to her desk. "Not the shoes of a poor girl, surely. What would make a rich signorina with such beautiful shoes want to be a nurse?"

Antonia opened her mouth, but the matron wouldn't let her speak.

"Most nurses are poor girls," said the matron, with acid. "Poor girls who work in order to eat. Why would a rich girl like you want to take food out of their mouths?"

Antonia kept still for a moment, trying not to cry. Then, suddenly, she burst out.

"How do you know I'm a rich girl?" she said, speaking rapidly. "What makes you think I don't need to work in order to eat? What do you know about me? What gives you the right to imply I am not hard enough to be a nurse? Give me a chance, you will see! I can be hard. I can be as hard as anyone, as hard as you even! Let me be a nurse and I will show you how hard I can be!"

The matron looked surprised. She opened her mouth and closed it again.

"Very well, very well," she said with an air of indifference. "Since your heart is set on it, you will be a nurse, at least for a while. You will never make it through the first two weeks, of course. You will find us all as unpleasant and boring as I am. None of us plays the piano here, you know. I would tell you to go and find a husband, since there is more future for you as a rich man's wife. But try it for a while, you will see for yourself.

"Show up in two weeks, and don't wear those shoes. You don't want instant hate from your classmates, do you?"

Antonia walked out feeling a mixture of relief, humiliation, and dread.

"MAMA MADE a terrible fuss about the whole thing when I told her. She ranted and raved and asked why she had spent all that money on school and piano lessons (and of course the count had done all that, not her).

" 'You've never had to grovel to eat,' she told me. 'Why do you want to start now?'

"That made me angry. 'What choice do I have?' I said. 'What do you give me? Only what you don't want yourself. I have to work like most people work—in order to live.'

" 'Go live somewhere else, if that's what you want,' she said. 'If you want to live your own life, you won't live it in my house!'

" 'Your house!' I said. 'This is Papa's house. But if that's what you want, I'll leave gladly. I'll go stay with the count. He cares about me, you never have!'

"She shut up after that—for a while, anyway. She made a point of seeing me off every morning so she could tell me how ugly I looked in my uniform. 'Do your patients like those bread-loaf legs?' she would say. I wonder if she knew that was the main reason I stuck to it—if I stopped, it would have looked like giving in."

"And did you like nursing?" asked Marta.

"Oh, it was horrible, worse than the matron said! It was awful! A dozen times a day I wanted to run away. Dr. Gassendi must have been having trouble finding his 'women of intelligence and good breeding' because most of the girls in the training were as crude and ignorant as any I have ever known. They hated me almost at once: called me 'the principessina' and played nasty tricks on me. The matron and the older nurses were cold and unfair. I think they deliberately assigned me to the worst, the most hopeless cases in the charity wards. I never knew people could be in such a condition and still be breathing!"

"DEAR MARCO," Antonia wrote. "I think I will be a good nurse, though it's harder than I thought. Not physically, though it is very tiring, or intellectually, because it's actually rather easy. Spiritually, though, it's hard—harder than being with Mama in some ways. I have to learn to be a strong woman.

"Perhaps I will be the kind of nurse who works for surgeons, the kind who takes the really difficult tasks. I like anatomy. Dr. Gassendi teaches the classes himself. The body is so complicated. Dr. Gassendi makes it so different from the way the nuns talked about it. 'A perfect work of art,' he calls it: like a great city with highways and telephone lines and magnificent factories. I love his colored charts and diagrams. I could study them for hours, but I'm not sure how I will like looking at the dead bodies when that comes, all cut up by the medical students.

"I don't talk much to most of the other nurses, but I have made a new friend. Her name is Elsa—Dr. Gassendi's daughter. She wants to be a doctor, too, but her family wants her to go to nursing school for a year before they decide. She thinks her father really wants her to be a doctor. Her brother became a lawyer and disappointed the whole family. If she does well, next year she'll go to the medical college at the university, so she works very hard like I do. She's ahead of me in the training, but she got herself transferred to my ward so we can help each other.

"It is nice to have a friend. I haven't ever had a friend like Elsa, even in school, where nearly everyone was a brat or a mouse like I was. Elsa is always laughing and making jokes. We take the train together— her family has a summer villa in Artemisia. She says that the last three days a very handsome man has been looking at me. I did not notice it, but today he tried to talk to us. She was friendly, but I felt so shy talking to a stranger. She says it is me he really wants to talk to.

"I find it funny. I suppose with Mama and all that I don't even know that a man could ever find me attractive. Remember when she used to say that I walk as if on eggs, that I should learn to step firmly? I wonder if I really walk differently? I asked Elsa and she laughed and laughed. She said, 'Don't worry how you walk—*perche sei bella.*' Imagine that—me—*bella!*"

IX

"Is it true you met Uncle Arturo on the train?" asked Marta.

"Yes, it is true," said Antonia, laughing. "He followed me for days. I was terrified."

"And you married him three weeks later?"

"Two weeks. Yes, that's also true."

"And you went to Yayaku right after the wedding, without him?"

"Yes. He needed to settle a few things. He was worried about the war and said it would be easier for a single man to get out later than for a man and a woman."

"He came back to Italy because of Grandmama?"

"Yes, she was dying. He wanted to see her again. But he had to leave before she died."

"But married in two weeks! How romantic."

"It might seem that way. It didn't feel that way at the time."

"Are you going to tell me about how it went?"

"No, I don't think I will."

Dearest,

The American shipment is off. Not a moment too soon: There's talk of another strike on the docks. Please don't give me another of your lectures on the "blind self-interest of the capitalists." Remember, dearest, how useful you find the proceeds.

Could you come here next week instead of my going there? I know you'll say it's inconvenient, but I've persuaded Aunt Antonia to stay another few days and I don't want to leave her alone.

I wish you were here now so I could get your opinion. Such a strange person she is! Not that you notice that right away. Remember what you said about Nadia Bregendahl? That she was only real on the screen, that all her beauty and glamour vanished in real life, that you wouldn't even notice her on the street? Aunt Antonia's strangeness is like that, in a way, but all inside. Outside she could be any bourgeois Genoese signora, but inside there is something quite different. Like a fire inside a mountain.

She's been here four days. Did you know she was staying in a hotel? My wonderful relations hardly spoke to her when they found she buried Uncle Arturo in Pica. They thought she should have brought his body back for a proper burial. All the time I was growing up she was always "that woman who married Arturo"—we children weren't allowed to call her "aunt" at home.

Her strangeness—it's like—what?—an aura of some kind, but an inside aura, one that changes color all the time. Am I making any sense? Let me describe it.

The first day: She comes with two small bags. She says she had so much else to carry back to Italy that she couldn't bear to bring much luggage. She is very reserved, speaks slowly, as if not used to Italian, though they must have spoken it at home back in Yayaku. She has a very clear voice, not loud, but firm, with all the vowels set in their places like pearls on a string.

She is still very attractive, but doesn't project it. Her beauty stays very close to her, so that you aren't really aware of it until you watch her for some time. At first she looked not dowdy, really, just a bit out of date. Her clothes, it turned out.

She's about my height but looks taller somehow. Her face is very strong. From the lines you can see she's used to having a firm expression. Her walk, on the other hand, is very light and delicate, very graceful, the walk of a very young girl.

We come home. She admires the flat. "Everything so modern!" she says. She says it's still hard to get things in Yayaku. When she first lived there, during the war, everyone had to buy almost everything from traveling merchants and make do with what they had. The same red silk would turn up in one lady's dress and another lady's parlor curtains. "Everything so old-fashioned," she says with a sigh.

She goes to bed at eight, without making apologies. I stay up late, thinking of Uncle Arturo.

The second day: She's up long before me, of course. She seems in a more cheerful mood. "I'm going out shopping," she says. "I really need more clothes if I'm going to stay longer than I thought." I offer to go with her if she waits until afternoon. "No, I'd rather go by myself," she says.

About four o'clock she appears at the office. She has armloads of boxes and is nearly laughing. "Can I take you out to eat tonight?" she asks. "I want to try my new dress." I'm surprised, but agree.

At seven-thirty she appears wearing a truly stunning dark blue silk dress. She looks extraordinarily chic, very elegant without being over-stated. "What a lovely dress," I say. "Yes," she says, "I'll have to make use of it while I'm here. At home no one will care."

I invite Franco to come with us. I think he's about her age. Antonia surprises me again by being absolutely charming, also intellectual! She and Franco talk about Jack London! Also Darwin! It's quite over my head but Franco seems taken with her. She also tells a very funny story about her mother—the infamous Donna Dora—eating in the same restaurant before the war. (There are more of these stories, as I'll tell you.) The party goes on until quite late.

The third day: I come home and somehow the house seems changed. A sense of order has fallen over everything. the flat is not only clean but all the odds and ends seem to have found an appropriate place. I am nonplussed! You know how hopeless Angelica has become. I think she's been spending all her time reading movie magazines while I'm at work, if she hasn't been entertaining her boyfriends in the house. I've been waiting for you to come home to sack her. I can't bear her excuses and arguments.

When I ask Antonia who put the house in order she says it was Angelica. I can't believe it, but when I go into the kitchen Angelica is busy making dinner and humming to herself. (The kitchen, by the way, hasn't been so clean in a year.) The meal is good, too, and Angelica serves it perfectly without any of her usual snide remarks.

This gives me a very odd feeling, as if I've been turned into the guest. Another of Aunt Antonia's auras—this aura of order—it seems to spread around her like an organizing cloud, not entirely benevolent. During dinner she tells me about her garden in Yayaku. Everyone laughed at her when she started it because it was so dry there no one expected the flowers to grow. "I willed that they grow," she says. Now I believe her.

After dinner, she suddenly begins to talk on and on for hours and hours, about her mother, her childhood, growing up before the war. I am fascinated! We go on until almost two!

One thing she stops at—her meeting with Uncle Arturo. I know that he met her on the train only two weeks before they were married. He had a little house of his own at Nervi, and I gather they met there a few times. What do you suppose happened? What do you think he told her? Do you know he sent her off to Yayaku alone, and this was 1939! My family always said that she seduced him (there was also a story that her mother tried to seduce him away from her!). Arturo was supposed to marry my mother's sister, you see, Aunt Lisette (he was lucky to be out of that one, wasn't he!).

Somehow I can't imagine her seducing him, particularly because she described herself as such a mouse at that age. Maybe he raped her at that little house? Doesn't it pique your curiosity?

It's the evening of the fourth night and she's gone to the opera with Franco. I'm busy writing down everything I can remember about what she's told me. Perhaps you can interest one of your literary friends in it! Don't you think it would be a wonderful film for Niccolo?

Be sure to let me know about next week—it's impossible for me to come to Milan while Antonia's still here.

Love,
Marta

• • •

ARTURO HAD been known as a cynical and restless young man, even at a time when Italy was full of cynical and restless young men. There had been bad times with his family, troubles that eventually sent him to Yayaku. But in recent years people had noticed a change in him.

"He's not so rude," his father said after one of his visits home. "He doesn't seem to be laughing at us all the time. Nor does he disagree with everything I say before I say it."

"He seems so dignified, so correct," said an aunt. "Who would have thought Arturo would turn out like that?"

"He seems a bit melancholy to me," said another, "a bit lonely. I wonder why he's never married."

"Arturo?" laughed the aunt. "He's never thought much of wives or of families. Remember all those horrible things he used to say to his father? So unnatural he was. Thank the saints he is no longer like that, but he can't have changed so much."

On his previous visit, Arturo had built himself a house, on a hill overlooking Nervi, just south of the city. It was small—just three rooms—very modern, very elegant, but it never looked finished. There were no rugs, no curtains, and hardly any furniture. When he wanted to sit, he bought a chair. When he wanted to eat, he bought a table. His little cot was lost in the enormous bedroom.

To tell the truth, the house had become an annoyance to him. Why had he built it? He had no intention of leaving Yayaku; his business, though profitable, was too precarious to leave and, with the war coming, would be difficult to sell.

His mother, Signora Rontella, was a cheerful, generous woman known to her neighbors and friends as a saint. She was very weak and lay in her bed, wheezing and coughing in a way that Arturo found intolerable. The doctors said that she might last this way for a very long time.

The Rontella flat was darkened and still as if Signora Rontella were already dead. Arturo's father paced the house nervously, and walked back and forth from his office several times a day. He would visit with his wife a few minutes each time he came in, but wouldn't stay with her for long. Instead he would sit in the kitchen and talk about his business (it was wine-exporting) with Arturo and would worry aloud about how bad things would be if there was another war.

To get away from the claustrophobia of the flat in Genoa, Arturo spent most of his evenings in the house at Nervi, taking an afternoon train from the station. Toma, a half-Indian servant he brought with him from Yayaku, looked after him, sleeping in a tiny space off the kitchen. Arturo would watch the sunset over the orange roofs and cypresses of Nervi; at night he would sleep with the windows open, listening to the oleanders bending in the sea breeze.

Marta:

Impossible for me to come to Genoa next week! You know this, why do you ask? It's just as well. Niccolo has asked me to help with the research on his new film and I wouldn't be able to spend much time with you. You know how much you hate moping about on your own.

Besides, with the troubles at the newspaper, I haven't been in a very good mood. Our good editors seem to have forgotten that our leader died twenty years ago, and we grow restless under his dead hand.

I have read your notes about your aunt. There are some good things here—the count and Dora are marvelous characters. Trouble is, everything else is pale and rather dull in comparison. I don't find your aunt interesting at all. As for her escape to Yayaku, what is remarkable about that? Your uncle was rich and probably not bad looking. It certainly didn't take brains or imagination to leap at a chance to leave Italy in 1939! And there's certainly nothing interesting about your uncle. Sounds like a typical Genoese bourgeois to me.

What can I say? Leave the filmmaking to Niccolo; I find your current work far more useful.

> *Guido*

• • •

Guido:

You disappoint me! You doubly disappoint me! I haven't seen you for almost a month, and the last three times I came to Milan. That can't be any easier for me than for you!

Also, you're very wrong about Aunt Antonia. Can't you see how she's the center of everything? Her mother may have been more flamboyant, but Antonia is the one who triumphed over her. Can't you see that?

Think of all the things she's done. Yesterday, for example, she asked if she could come to work with me. I asked her why. She said she needed to learn more about business for when she went back to Yayaku and had to run Uncle Arturo's business.

"But that's not possible," I told her. "You can't learn how to run a business by visiting someone else's for a day."

She said she hoped to spend several days and that she didn't have any other way to learn what she needed to know.

"Antonia," I said, "it's absurd to take all this on. There must be someone else who can manage it for you."

She said there was no one she trusted to take it on.

"Sell it, then," I said. "Come back and live in Italy. Surely that's what everyone expects you to do."

She gave me a little smile. "Yes," she said. "That's exactly what they expect me to do. That's why I'm going back to run it myself."

I started out by showing her the books. She drew everything in. It was eerie, as if she were a witch. I could see the figures reflected in her dark eyes. After she had listened for a while, she began to ask questions. Such questions! She seemed to understand what I had told her better than I did myself. She would ask, "Why do you do this?" or, "Wouldn't it be better if you did it this way?" and I wouldn't know how to answer her.

Later, she asked me how I had come to run Grandpapa's business. I explained how Papa and my brothers were all lawyers and not interested so they had turned it over to me. "And do they share in the profits?" she asked. I told her that they did. "Why should they if they do nothing for them?" she asked. Again, I didn't know what to answer.

Do you understand what I am trying to tell you about her? She's like a cat; she doesn't explain, but goes right to the heart of things. She's so quiet, so that you almost forget her sometimes, but then she pounces, and always lands in exactly the right place.

What I can't figure out is whether she is good or evil. No, that sounds silly. What I'm after is subtler than that.

With Uncle Arturo, for example. Why won't she talk about him? She has told me so much about herself, but she is still such a mystery. And the question I keep asking is, which one was the seducer?

Love,
Marta

"WHAT DO YOU think your husband will look like?" Elsa asked one day, after Antonia had known her for about a month. Antonia frowned; she didn't like this game. When the girls at school played it she had always drawn a blank; the best she could do was think of her father, who came closest to being a real husband than any other man she had known, and this wasn't very close. The movie stars and opera singers and other heartthrobs her friends dreamed about Antonia instinctively took to be frauds. The few boys her own age she met seemed silly and childish.

The other girls, even at twelve or thirteen, could describe their future mates down to the shape of their toenails. They looked like the pictures in magazines or in advertisements or like the handsome friends of their brothers or cousins. Antonia couldn't even come up with the color of his hair. Her mother had "friends" with locks of every shade; the count was bald.

Antonia knew through her mother a great deal more about life than most women her age, certainly more than Elsa. Antonia didn't really grasp this about herself, and Elsa was not the last of her friends to misunderstand it entirely.

Elsa took it on herself to teach Antonia about the world, particularly about the relationships between men and women. She gave many pointers on dress and grooming, which Antonia appreciated not, as Elsa imagined, because she wished to be more appealing to the opposite sex, but because Elsa provided a convenient medium between the extremes of Dora and the count on the one hand, and that of the nuns on the other. Antonia was delighted to learn how to be merely "fashionable," that is to say, inconspicuous, in the way ordinary girls were.

Some of Elsa's other advice was less welcome. Through her mother's affairs, Antonia had learned a good deal about the true intentions of men. So when Elsa said to her, "That boy is smiling at you. He thinks you're pretty," Antonia was more annoyed than flattered. Worse were Elsa's pointers on how to stand, how to look out of the corners of her eyes at boys and lead them on without going too far. "Pretend I'm the boy," Elsa would say. "Now look at me without looking at me. No. Don't stand like that! You look like a prostitute, Antonia. You want to draw him on, but keep his respect." Antonia was amused that Elsa thought there was a distinction.

This is not to say she didn't like Elsa. She felt Elsa was totally harmless, nearly always cheerful and full of energy. Antonia was starved for this kind of brightness, particularly from other women. She laughed with Elsa at her stories and gossip, at her imitations of the matron and the other nurses. And she tried to share, without much success, in Elsa's fantasies about men and marriage.

In the end, Antonia and Elsa came closest to falling out over boys, not out of jealousy or competition, but from Elsa's well-meaning attempts to match Antonia with her male friends. Antonia felt insulted by Elsa's taste. Thinking Antonia needed someone to bring her out of herself, Elsa always introduced her to the liveliest and most gregarious boys she knew. Antonia was mortified that Elsa thought this was what she wanted—these breezy, empty-headed show-offs who could talk for hours about themselves without apparently wanting to know a thing about her. Not one of them could sit still; Elsa's outings were always half on the run, tennis parties and bicycle trips, buffet suppers and dances. They exhausted Antonia, who found nursing tiring enough.

Then there was the man on the train.

X

You asked me to write about Uncle Arturo. This isn't easy, not just because I didn't know him all that well. After all, he was living in Yayaku before I was even born.

I was brought up to find it hard to talk about Uncle Arturo. This sounds peculiar, but he was one of those relatives whom one's family has difficulty coming to terms with. It took me years to figure out why he had left Italy. (I wonder if Antonia knows. She's never mentioned it.)

He always did the wrong thing. I don't mean just that he did things his family didn't like, which he did, but that he got away with them. When he refused to go to the university, he was supposed to wind up a failure. Instead, he made more money than anyone else. When he went to Yayaku to work for his uncle, he was supposed to be "taught how to behave." Instead, his uncle died within a year and left him the business. When he married Antonia, she was supposed to make him miserable and leave him in a matter of months. Instead, she gave him a fine family.

Because he didn't fit in with them, they said he would never fit in anywhere. Instead, he became the hero of the town where he lived, honored and respected, with an impeccable life. The president of Yayaku came to visit him, and when Arturo died, Antonia told me, they turned off the lights all over the little city in his memory.

He was contrary, he was arrogant in a smug, secret way that you sensed rather than noticed. He believed himself more than he believed anyone else, and he didn't pretend otherwise. My family hated that. It didn't fit into their way of seeing the world, and it made them uncomfortable. That's why they couldn't talk about him.

This is how I first remember him: in a beautiful white linen suit with sharp creases and a straw hat. He wasn't a tall man, but he had that presence. He wasn't much of an intellectual, but he had a way of making you think he was very wise, that he knew everything. My aunts said he was like that when he was quite young. They said he was a very rude young man when he was twenty, but at forty he was polite and polished in a way that was even more exasperating.

He would come back from Yayaku and somehow the whole family revolved around him, the black sheep. He had a little smile he used in family gatherings, a smile of triumph. He had a way of sitting in a room, without saying anything, and dominating the conversation. I re-member that my grandfather, who was a very proud man and who had disapproved of him bitterly when he was young, always asked his advice.

He was so handsome! All my cousins were in love with him. So was I. After it turned out that everyone had been wrong and he'd turned out all right despite their predictions, they wanted him to marry my mother's younger sister. They had it all arranged, but he did the wrong thing again. That's why they've always been so nasty to Antonia—they blame it on her. But of course they should have known he would never do what they expected of him.

We used to wonder, my cousins and I, if he was lonely in Yayaku, away from his family. I always said he wasn't. He didn't seem like the type of man who could be lonely, he was so complete in himself. But perhaps I was wrong. After all, he married Antonia.

ANTONIA FOUND herself thinking about the man on the train a great deal. She told herself that he frightened her, but another part of her knew this wasn't all there was to it. When the train went through a tunnel, she'd study his reflection in the window.

His face was just right, she thought. What did she mean by that? That she found him handsome, that his features were regular? She thought about that. His fine, straight nose rose past his even gray eyes and broadened into a high forehead with just the right number of lines. His mouth was just full enough to suggest laughter and tenderness.

It was not a face that tried to be handsome, it just was. It was a face that seemed calm, but that contained power, like the sea on a cloudy day. He would look at her—almost stare, but not quite—and she would feel that hidden power, a warmth that spread through thin air.

Elsa, sitting beside her, giggled. To her, it was all some kind of silly game, a flirtation that meant nothing. That is the difference between us, Antonia thought. She doesn't look beyond the games, doesn't see the deep, indecipherable patterns in the rules. To Elsa, the stranger was already a potential husband for her friend. She didn't see that marriage would be the beginning, not the end, of the mystery of such a man.

Arturo watched, and the special smile he used with his family crept despite himself across his face. Elsa was just the type of girl who had delighted him when he was young—pretty, ripe, delectable, open. Her face was like a lamp switched on in a dark room, one that would not understand or tolerate the darkness, or anything suggesting death or decay.

It was the contrast between Antonia and her friend that fascinated him. Antonia was taller, darker, less pretty, and, to his mind, far more beautiful. Her hair was long and dark, her skin very pale and clear. She was anything but eager; she drew herself in, as if afraid of touching life even at the edges. While her friend babbled on, she only smiled gently and sadly, and often turned away to look out the window toward the sea. They always sat on the seaward side of the train; the dark-haired girl by the window, her friend on the aisle.

The girl seemed shy, but not in a naive way. There was something very odd, a kind of hidden asymmetry, about her, Arturo thought. Even her beauty was strange—not something in her features or her figure, which were handsome enough, but beneath the surface, something that revealed itself slowly, in flashes, like the glowing coals beneath the ash of a fire. There was something exquisite about the way she held herself: cautious, hesitant, but suggesting power and experience. Her uniform was hardly becoming, yet she wore it with a sense of grace and style that he hadn't noticed at first. This was the asymmetry—the shyness, the constraint, that she showed to the world at large, that didn't match the spark that he saw when he looked again. She was clearly not a woman who could be taken in at a glance, he thought. Or did he only imagine this other side of her?

His first attempts to talk to her failed. Her vivacious friend got in the way, answering all his questions for her, trying to be charming and flirtatious for her friend. She was clever enough to realize immediately where his interests lay, but evidently thought her friend was too shy to make an impression on her own. Consequently, he and Antonia hadn't managed to speak a word to each other and she seemed deeply embarrassed by her friend's transparent attempts at matchmaking.

To avoid appearing too obvious, and attracting the unwanted attention of the friend while scaring off the object of his desire, he took an earlier train for a few days. Then, one Sunday afternoon, he saw her again and, to his delight, she was alone. Antonia had been to visit the count and was not wearing her uniform.

He went up to her seat and asked if he could join her. She looked at him with a start of recognition, but said yes, and he slipped into the seat usually occupied by her friend.

They rode in silence for a few miles. She was staring fixedly out the window. Finally, he made some remark about the scenery.

"Yes," she said. "I like looking at the sea. It reminds me of my father."

"Is he a sailor?"

"No, he's dead now. But he used to live in Argentina. He came across the sea to visit us."

"How interesting," said Arturo. "I have recently come across the sea myself. Most of the time, I live in Yayaku."

Antonia turned to look at him for the first time. She saw a broad, handsome face, with pleasing lines around the eyes and mouth, lines that looked sympathetic to her, as if he were used to listening calmly but seriously to other people's troubles. Suddenly, something in her relaxed. She no longer felt shy at all; she felt she could tell this strange man anything without seeming odd or ridiculous. At the same time, her chest tightened with an excited sensation she had never felt before.

"Do you miss your children," she asked, "when you are in Yayaku?"

"I don't have any children. I've never been married. And as for the rest of my family, I first went to Yayaku to get away from them. But, yes, I miss them sometimes now."

"Why did you want to get away from your family?"

"Oh, there were problems, difficulties with some of them."

"I can understand that. There are some people in my family I would like to cross the ocean to escape. Does that sound wrong to you?"

"Not necessarily."

"It's my mother I would like to get away from."

"That can happen sometimes, with many mothers."

"My mother is not like any other mother. If you knew her, you would understand. But perhaps not," she said, looking at him. "Most men seem to like her."

"Oh?" said Arturo.

"Yes," said Antonia, with a sigh. "She is a very powerful woman that way."

They said little more until they came to Nervi. Arturo stood up to leave, and said, with a bow, that he hoped he would see her again.

"Yes," said Antonia, and smiled for the first time.

He saw her several times in the next week. She was always with her friend, so he did no more than smile and nod at her. Then, one evening, he saw her alone again.

"Where is your friend tonight?" he asked as he took the seat beside her.

"She had work to do for her father," answered Antonia. She turned and smiled at him. "Usually, I wait for her. But tonight I said I had to go home early."

"How lucky for me."

"Perhaps. Elsa is my best friend. I like having her to talk to on the way home."

"She is a nurse also?"

"No, neither of us is. We are merely studying to be."

"And do you like that?"

She sighed. "No, not particularly."

"Then why do you do it?"

"I feel I have to do it. Aren't there many things like that that you must do but would rather not?"

"I suppose. I don't like to think that way."

"Did you want to go to Yayaku? Or did you feel you had to do it?"

Arturo laughed. "Some of each, in a way. I made a choice—this unknown over that evil."

"Did you make the right choice, I wonder? Do you think you did?"

"Who knows, I'm not sure it really matters now."

"Oh? Don't you think it was important for you to go to Yayaku? Do you think it's your home?"

"Well, at first I didn't, but that was more because I didn't want to have a home. But yes, now I do. I think it's important to belong somewhere, so now I belong there."

"What's it like there?"

"I'd have to take you there," he said.

"Yes, I suppose you would," said Antonia.

They saw each other several times after that—always on the train. Antonia grew adept at making excuses for avoiding Elsa. Their talks grew less serious, more relaxed, but somehow very private. It was as if they set a space around the two of them when they were together, a space in which the rules of the rest of the world did not apply.

One night he surprised himself as he was getting up to leave by asking her to visit his house.

"Not tonight," she said simply. "I might be missed at home. Tomorrow I will try to come earlier. Wait for me at the station."

The next evening they walked up the hill from the station of Nervi. It was a beautiful clear day. Antonia stopped several times to admire the view. She seemed to be in a cheerful mood, but still was veiled with that mysterious melancholy, Arturo thought. There was a slight tension between them, one that was more exciting, inviting, than disturbing. Neither one of them had chosen to think about what would happen when they reached the top of the hill.

"But it's so bare!" said Antonia when they entered the house. "There's hardly any furniture!"

"There's more than there was," said Arturo. He had bought a second chair.

"But it could be so charming! You should have flowers or something, at least. And there aren't even any curtains."

"The house is too high for people to see in. Besides, there's been nothing to hide."

"It would depress me to live in a house this empty."

"You must tell me what to put in it."

"Don't be ridiculous. I could never do that. You should decide for yourself."

"I suppose you're right."

The door to the bedroom was ajar. Antonia glanced in and saw the cot, then moved away. When her back was turned, Arturo silently closed the door. It seemed somehow to interfere with his mood. Already, the house had become part of their private space.

They sat and watched the sunset through the plate-glass window. Toma brought them maté.

"My father used to drink this," Antonia said.

"Many things seem to remind you of your father," said Arturo.

"Yes," she said, and then laughed.

"What is it?"

"I was thinking how silly you both were, to go so far away, and then to build houses back here which you hardly ever see. So wasteful!"

She was silent for a while, then she said, "I should go. It will be dark soon."

Arturo walked her to the station. He stood in the shadow of the platform staring at her face, which was partly turned away from him.

A ray of twilight struck her right profile, coloring it a deep red; the left side, lit by the bare bulb of the platform fixture, was sallow. A strand of hair slid down her forehead, dividing the two; her eyes were in deep shadow. The effect was arresting, like an expressionist painting, mysterious and alarming. Yet the clarity of her beauty shone through the vivid coloring. Was it an accident, he wondered, as he saw the red slowly fade from her skin, or some sign put there, as what? A warning?

The train arrived. At this hour, it paused only a moment to discharge and take on passengers. He took her hand to help her up to the car. In the last instant, he pulled her toward him, kissed her on the mouth, then gave her up to the train, which was already pulling away from him.

XI

ANTONIA TOLD NO ONE about Arturo, not even Elsa, not even Marco in her letters. This wasn't difficult at first; their encounters were so brief. After her first visit to the house at Nervi, she spent time with him every day. She told Eliana she would be home late, then told Elsa she had to be home early.

No one suspected. They had come to think of her as such a shy, nervous girl that they simply thought she wanted to be alone. "You're such a recluse, Tonia," Elsa complained. "You really should have become a nun."

Arturo and Antonia's meetings were still short, no more than a few hours, and of a kind of enchanted simplicity. They did little together, so little that the sparseness of his house seemed the perfect setting for them. But it was a sparseness, an emptiness, of the subtlest shades and colors, as fleeting as the patterns of light that washed across the bare light-gray walls.

Mostly they sat together and talked about their families and the details of their lives. Sometimes they laughed together, but they rarely raised their voices either in excitement or anger. There were disagreements, but because the terms of their relationship were so uncomplicated, there were no quarrels.

Toma, discreet to the point of invisibility, served their meals if they were hungry. If they went out, they never went far. Occasionally they would walk down to the ocean. Once they rented a small boat and rowed out into the harbor. Antonia told Arturo about the boat Marco had made and their visits to the Piglets.

Often they watched the sunset, usually without speaking, as an old couple listens to a favorite piece of music, no longer needing to express in words its qualities. Each was still mysterious and unworldly to the other, and this was a large part of their attraction for each other. But as they grew used to these meetings they began without realizing it to depend on them, as one grows to depend on a drug which at first seems innocent and harmless. In this there was a trap: so much of their desire for each other's company grew out of its very lack of focus; as the desire grew stronger, so would the purpose of their meetings and their need for them. In the end the need to name this purpose seemed to gather like a cloud. It was six days from the first time they had come to Nervi together.

The visits began to disturb Antonia first. Not out of any feeling of guilt—Arturo, perhaps sensing the depth of their separation, never pressed her and touched her only in isolated moments. Besides, for her Arturo was not connected to the everyday world, which included the world of morality; he was part of her own world, as private to her as her thoughts.

It was late summer. The sea breezes were welcome in the little house which grew warm in the afternoon. With the heat came these disturbing thoughts. Who was this man, really? Where were these meetings going to lead? She could see nothing beyond them—there were too many entanglements, too many dark passages to be crossed.

She and Arturo would spread the newspapers across the bare table. Their huge headlines were terrifying, as if the whole world were tottering in the lines of type. This, she knew, could not be kept away forever.

"I must go back to Yayaku soon," Arturo said one evening.

"Why?"

"I can't leave my business forever and, if the war comes, it will be difficult to travel."

"How is your mother?"

"No different."

"Do you find it very painful, the fact that she is dying?"

"Yes, I do. It's odd how such a good woman could cause me so much pain."

"How could that be, if she is so good?"

"By being so. It can be like that if, like me, you're not very good yourself."

"Why do you say that?"

"Because it's true. You didn't know me when I was young. She used to make me go to confession—not by saying anything, but just by looking at me. And I went, even after I'd stopped believing in the church. Her look said she knew my sins more thoroughly than any God could. Even today I still go, and I always think of her. I hated that for years—the way I couldn't be away from her even after going thousands of miles."

"My mother hates the church," Antonia said. "I think she watches me too, though, the way your mother watched you, waiting for me to sin."

"And has she been satisfied?"

"Never; either way I might have gone she wouldn't have been. I think it is my victory over her."

"What will you do if there's another war?" Arturo asked her one evening.

"I don't know. If I'm a nurse, I suppose I'll be an army nurse."

"Is that what you want to do?"

"No. I don't even like being a nurse, and I'm sure I wouldn't like being with soldiers."

Arturo frowned. He didn't like the idea of her being with soldiers either.

"Isn't there something else for you to do?"

"What? Stay with Mama? That would be even worse."

"You could come to Yayaku. You could marry me."

"No," she said quickly. She caught her breath and had the odd sensation of taking the whole world into herself. It was as if a million voices were chattering away inside her head.

"Why?"

"Because of everything: because of the way I am, because of Mama. It would be impossible."

"Don't you even want to talk about it?"

"No. I don't want to talk about it."

It was what she had been dreading. As long as there was no purpose to their meetings, she felt safe from thinking about them. It was this protection she craved, being with Arturo, and having no meanings beyond that. It was this she had loved.

Arturo put his hand over hers. It was warm, but something more than heat passed from his hand into her body. She looked up into his face. He had a gentle, serious smile; it was such a good face. She flattened her hand slightly under his grasp. Something almost electric was surging into her. It was power, some sort of feeling of control. The buzzing in her head cleared away, and a part of her very deep in her mind started to speak to her. Her eyes opened very wide. Could it be like that? she thought.

"What's wrong?" he asked.

"Nothing. I was only thinking how little time we have left to be together." She got up to leave for the station.

"You don't really know anything about me," she said on the next evening. "How could you marry someone you don't even know?"

"Why?" said Arturo. "What else is there to know?"

"My mother, for example. You haven't even met her. She always ends up by scaring everyone off."

"I'm not so timid as that. Besides, we'll be living far from her. The distance has advantages. From what you tell me, I don't think she'll visit us often."

"But I have no idea how to be a wife. I've never had a normal family. I've told you about that—everything was chaotic. How could I manage your family?"

"You could learn."

"How could I learn? I don't know the first thing."

"I could teach you."

"How could you? You've been alone yourself all these years. You've got your habits, your business, your home, your life. I have nothing to offer in exchange."

"That's not true at all."

"Two babes, innocent of the world," she said, laughing. "Who could teach us how to be man and wife?"

"We could find people to teach us. There are good people, good families, in my home. They could teach us."

Antonia only smiled at him.

Later, she said, "But I don't really know you."

"Don't you? I think you know me better than anyone."

"No, that's not what I mean. We've never even been introduced. How could I tell someone I wanted to marry a man I've never actually met? How could I explain I've been coming to your house for weeks alone? What would people think of that?"

"We'd think of something," Arturo answered, and touched her hand. He noticed her eyes widen again, as if she had seen something remarkable in the distance.

XII

AFTER ANTONIA HAD GONE, Arturo sat down to write a letter to Dora. He explained the situation as best he could: that he was in love with her daughter and had asked her to marry him, that she seemed willing but had reservations. Could he come to Artemisia to discuss it with her? Perhaps she had some thoughts on the matter. Toma mailed the letter that same night.

Two days later, the reply came back. The envelope was a rich, heavy cream color, very dignified, with a strange device, not quite a monogram, on the flap. The letter was written in a small, tight, old-fashioned script.

"My dear Signor Rontella," the letter said. "I have received your surprising letter. Or, rather, I should not say surprising as I am not unaware that my daughter is now a grown woman, and grown women are attractive to grown men. I can also sympathize with your impatience with my daughter. Her tendency to have 'reservations,' as you put it, is well known to me.

"I can see by your letter that you are an honest and direct man, one with whom I can discuss things openly and frankly. And I do wish to discuss this matter with you further.

"Will you do me the honor of coming to visit me on Thursday evening? I am sure in an hour or two we can settle on what is to be done."

As Arturo was reading this letter, Antonia was having lunch with the count. They ate at his flat, since the count said he was not feeling well enough to go out.

Antonia thought he looked awful. He had grown thin, and the skin on his face was blotchy and hung in loose folds over his jaws. His hands shook slightly as he ate his food.

The count wanted to know about her work at the hospital. He was paying her fees there, since Dora had refused to have anything to do with it. Antonia patiently explained the things she was learning, trying to sound more enthusiastic than she really was.

The count looked at her. "And this is what you really want? To be a nurse? Is this the future you choose for yourself?"

Antonia's head was full of Arturo and his proposal. What other future is there for me? Antonia wanted to say. Instead, she only nodded.

"And how is your mother?" asked the count, changing the subject. "Is she the same?"

Antonia said she supposed she was. Since the training began they hadn't had much to do with each other.

"Your mother is a remarkable woman," said the count with an odd sigh. "A truly remarkable woman, although putting it that way doesn't do her justice. I know you don't agree with me on this. But perhaps, in time, you will come to appreciate her more remarkable qualities. Perhaps, when you are away from her, you will find ways to make use of her example."

Antonia looked horrified. "I don't think, Count," she said, "that I will ever have the opportunity to be away from her. But if I ever did, I certainly wouldn't follow her example if I could help it."

The count coughed into his napkin, then looked up at her, his eyes slightly watering. He made a slight move with his lips, which Antonia took to mean "you are not telling me everything."

So she told him everything; he was the only person besides Arturo to know about their secret meetings at Nervi.

"So," said the count when she finished. "Are you in love with this Arturo?"

"Love?" said Antonia. She thought for several moments while the count waited. She was remembering the feeling of power she had had when Arturo placed his hand over hers. "Yes," she answered.

"But you have reservations about marrying him. Why is that?"

"I don't really know anything about him. I've only known him for two weeks. And I've heard so many stories about how men live on their own in South America. What if he already has a wife in Yayaku, or several wives? How could I find out?"

"I've heard of the family," said the count. "Very respectable, if unremarkable. I could make some inquiries."

"He hasn't met Mama yet."

"I might be able to help with that, too, when the time comes."

Antonia left the count, thinking of the times when her father and mother were together in Artemisia, how peaceful and orderly those times were, how safe she had felt. Perhaps her marriage could be like that. "It will be like that," she thought to herself. "I will make sure it's like that."

Arturo went out to Artemisia in the early evening. He hadn't said anything to Antonia, and, in fact, knew she would be working at the hospital that night.

The sun was just beginning to set as he climbed up the hill. The front of the house was golden, and the light bounced off the panes, making it look as if a fire were raging inside.

"If nothing else can be said of her," Arturo thought, "she didn't bring her daughter up in a hovel."

The door was ajar when he reached the top of the steps. He knocked on the door frame, and a voice from inside told him to come in.

The huge entry hall, with its black-and-white marble floor, was empty. A clear-glass vase of brilliant crimson flowers of a variety he didn't recognize stood on a small black table near the door. There were no other furnishings.

He heard a sound from the room to the right, which could be entered through a marble arch flanked by long mirrors in silver frames. He walked toward the sound without speaking.

In the middle of the bare marble floor was Dora, sitting in a large, high-backed couch covered in a violet velvet so dark it was nearly black. On her right was a candelabra holding eight candles, though only five of them were lit. On her left was another vase of the strange crimson flowers. Dora was wearing a silk dress of exactly the same color. It was loose and draped around her like a toga, revealing the tops of her ample breasts. Over her heart was large brooch made of a huge, pink baroque pearl in a jeweled setting which made it look like the body of a fish wearing a high, ruby-studded crown. The brooch was so placed as to suggest that, if it was removed, her dress would immediately slip off. More gemstones glittered from her hair, which lay in folds over her bare shoulders.

Arturo suddenly grasped the effect Dora was attempting to create and, at the same instant, knew she had failed. "Messalina," he thought to himself.

For a moment, neither of them moved or spoke. Then Dora turned her head slightly to look up at Arturo.

"Come in, Signor Rontella," she said in an even, full voice that was neither loud nor soft. "I am so pleased that you have come."

Arturo came forward a few steps. Though it was dark, he could see enough of the room to observe that it was extraordinary—nearly as bare as his house at Nervi but somehow almost frighteningly elegant. The candlelight combined with the last of the sunset to give the bare walls a rich, warm color, which, despite the size of the room and its starkness, gave it a feeling of intimacy. In the shadows he detected a grand piano.

"Please sit down, Signore," said Dora, indicating a small, dark chair beside her couch. "Would you like something to drink? I want you to feel at home in my house." She had a strange expression on her face, not quite a smile. It was inviting and threatening at the same time.

"No, thank you, Signora di Credi. I can't stay long. I'm very honored to meet you and hope I'm not inconveniencing you in any way."

"No, not at all, not at all." At this she really did smile.

There was a long pause. Dora's expression did not change. "Signora di Credi," Arturo began finally. "You are, I'm sure, aware of why I wished to see you."

"Am I?" said Dora.

"Remember my letter, my wish to marry your daughter."

"Your letter mentioned that you had thought of it. May I ask how long you have known Antonia?"

"Only a few days, actually, but I'm sure you understand that a man of my age is not prey to sudden impulses when it comes to marriage."

"Indeed?" said Dora.

"That is, I want to assure you that there is nothing foolish or hasty about my feelings toward Antonia."

"Yes, well, *she* is very young, don't you think?"

"Younger than I am, if that's what you mean, but she is certainly a mature woman. She is training to be a nurse, for example."

"Is that what you mean by maturity?"

"Well, yes, it is difficult work, surely, and requires a certain steadiness of character. What I mean to say is that Antonia is certainly wise enough, I'm sure, to know what she really wants."

"What *she* wants," said Dora, a bit sharply. "I thought we were talking about what *you* want."

"Of course, but I wanted to assure you that I'm not trying to take advantage of her in any way, because I'm sure she could see through me if I did."

"Is *that* what you mean by maturity?"

"To be sure. Is there some other meaning?"

"I think so. I think there are reasons to think that there are more mature women than my daughter."

"Well, there are women who are older, but that is not maturity."

"Certainly not. I had something else in mind."

"What, may I ask?" said Arturo, beginning to be annoyed.

"I mean, Signor Rontella, that my daughter has had little experience of the world, that she has had no time—and, I expect, has no inclination—to acquire certain skills that are essential to any wife, to any woman, if it comes to that, who wants to please a man."

"I don't know what you mean," Arturo said.

"I mean that, should you make the enormous mistake of marrying my daughter," said Dora, lowering her voice, "you are likely to be very disappointed. You will find that she lacks imagination, finesse. You will tire of her before you even reach Yayaku."

Arturo said nothing.

"You are a man of the world," said Dora, looking straight into his face. "You need a woman of the world to make you happy. I am the only woman of the world in my family."

Arturo cleared his throat.

"It's nonsense to pretend we don't know what I'm talking about," Dora went on, that smile coming onto her face again. "I could see it in your eyes when you came in. I can make you far more happy in a week than she could in a lifetime of marriage."

"With all due respect, Signora, I don't believe so."

"What nonsense, that naive girl, that *nun*, keep you happy for thirty or forty years? You'd be sleeping in separate rooms before the end of the first month. Come, don't make yourself ridiculous. Spend a few days in Paris with me and I'll cure you of this silly infatuation with my daughter."

"My dear Signora," said Arturo, beginning to smile. "I am flattered

by your offer, but I thought I made it clear that I am attracted by younger women, not older ones. Your daughter lacks nothing in experience that I won't be happy to teach her. You will forgive me if I say that I doubt I could teach you much of anything."

Dora stood up slowly and abruptly began to scream. Arturo stood back, hesitating for a moment. He expected someone to come rushing into the room and didn't want to seem to be running away.

No one came. Dora stood in one place, continuing to scream, apparently without taking a breath. Arturo stood watching her, half with fascination and half with the fear that he had killed her, for what seemed to him like a long time. Then he turned around and left the house.

It was nearly dark outside. He could still hear Dora's screams as he left the garden. He turned his head, expecting to be chased. A few people came out to the street to watch him, but they only shook their heads and turned away after he had passed.

Arturo tried to reach Antonia at the hospital to warn her, but failed. She went home the next morning knowing nothing about his meeting with Dora.

She wanted to go to Elsa's house instead of her own. But Elsa was in Genoa, and only the servants were in the villa at Artemisia. She walked up the hill.

When she got to the house she noticed the door was wide open. Through it she could see that something was strewn over the hallway. On the doorstep, she picked up a shoe. She recognized it as one of her own.

Antonia came into the hall. At first, what she saw did not make any sense to her. Strewn all over the stairs were vast quantities of things—heaps of clothes, books, papers, jewelry, and other odds and ends. She thought, "How odd of Mama to allow such a mess in her house." Then she saw a shell Marco had collected for her when they were children; the broken binding of one of her favorite books was tangled with her spare nurse's uniform; hanging from the balustrade was a gold and amethyst necklace the count had given her for her sixteenth birthday. Everything she owned had been thrown down the stairs.

She closed her eyes. Feelings of despair and anger were flailing around her mind like whips. She grasped the shoe in her hand, then threw it at the mirror next to the foot of the stairs. The mirror broke, shattering into a heap of dresses. For the first time she noticed Eliana sitting on the landing.

"She's gone to Paris," said Eliana, with no discernible emotion in her voice. "She said that since you're such a mature woman, with a rich fiancé, you can find your own place to live. She said to take your things away before she got back."

Antonia turned around and ran out of the house. At the gate she ran into Signor Ravecca and Arturo. Arturo caught her in his arms.

"You're coming back to Genoa with me—to stay with Elsa," Arturo said. "Signor Ravecca and Eliana will tend to your things. Don't even go back into the house."

"What happened? What made Mama do this? How did you know?" Antonia asked in a rush.

"I went to see your mother last night—"

"My mother? Why did you see my mother? You didn't say anything to me about it."

"I wanted to talk about our marriage."

"Our marriage!" said Antonia, glancing at Signor Ravecca. "We don't have any marriage. And why is Signor Ravecca here? What does this have to do with him?"

"Antonia, please, he's a friend of an old friend. I thought he might help. He knows the Gassendis, too. They've already offered to put you up if—if there's a problem with your mother."

"My mother's thrown me out of the house. My own mother! I don't understand it."

"Antonia, we had a little disagreement—a little disagreement over you. I think she just got upset over losing you—"

"A disagreement! What did you say to her? What did she say to you?"

"I just said I loved you and wanted to marry you. She—she didn't quite believe me, and now I think—"

"You think she's a monster like everyone else! So now you know, now you understand why we can't get married."

"Don't be ridiculous, Antonia. It doesn't matter. It really doesn't. Does anyone have the family he would choose? I don't."

"And you still want to marry me, then?"

"Yes, yes, of course! Of course I do!"

Antonia walked over to him, tears streaming down her face. She stopped in front of him. As he reached out to embrace her, she slapped him hard across the face. He stared at her, astonished.

"That's for coming into my life," she said, breathing hard. "That's for wanting to marry me. That's for talking to my mother. Yes, I will marry you. And you'll make up for all of it, for this and for everything that came before."

She walked away toward the sea. After a moment, Arturo ran after her. He matched his step with hers, and after a moment he put his arm around her.

"My life has never been my own," Antonia said. "You might as well have it as anyone."

"You'll have mine as well," he said, smiling. "That should be some compensation."

"It had better be," said Antonia. She took his hand and felt that surge of power again.

Antonia went to live at the Gassendis' flat in Genoa. Everyone tried to be very kind, very efficient, and did everything for her without being asked. The count and Elsa's family made the arrangements for the wedding in the chapel of the hospital. Signora Gassendi set about ordering things for the dinner, complaining bitterly how hard it was getting to find decent things in the shops. Arturo took her to the steamship agent to choose cabins for the trip to South America. The little squares on the plan of the ship meant nothing to her—she couldn't imagine them as volumes of space which she would soon occupy.

Antonia insisted on going back to Artemisia to pack her things, however. "It's not necessary," said Arturo.

"Signor Ravecca can hire a truck to take them away," said Antonia. "But I will pack them myself."

She did let Elsa come with her to help. When they arrived at Dora's villa, they found the front door unlocked. Inside, everything was as Antonia had seen it when she was last there.

Almost without talking, Elsa helped her carry her big school trunks down from the attic. Then they began to sort out her things into piles to fold and pack away.

They had been working for about an hour when Eliana came in.

"So it's true, Signorina," Eliana said. "You are leaving."

"Yes, it's true," Antonia answered.

"Your mother was very displeased about your marriage. She said your fiancé was a fortune hunter."

"He's not," said Antonia. "Besides, what my mother thinks doesn't matter to me now."

Eliana was silent for a moment.

"So you will marry him," said Eliana, finally, "even though your family doesn't approve of it."

"My mother is not my whole family. But yes, I would marry him anyway, once I decided that myself."

Eliana said nothing more. She watched Elsa and Antonia at work for a few minutes, then she walked away.

A few days later, Signora Gassendi took Antonia to choose her wedding dress. The shop was a large and fashionable one, painted white, with molded ceilings as lacy as the gowns. It was full of giggling young girls. It put Antonia in a testy mood.

She turned down all the white frilly gowns they showed her. Then she saw a smooth golden silk dress with a short, tight skirt and a matching turban.

Signora Gassendi frowned. So did the shop lady. "This is not intended for a first marriage," she said quietly, looking at Antonia oddly.

"It is the count's gift to me," said Antonia. "I am sure he would want me to have the dress I chose for myself."

Antonia left the hospital without completing the training. In spite of everything, her departure caused her some regrets. The matron didn't say anything about her marriage or her leaving, but her superior smile said that she knew she had triumphed. "She was right," Antonia thought. "The only thing I could manage to do was get married."

The Gassendis' house was in a flurry. Signora Gassendi seemed to enjoy making a fuss over everything. Elsa often disagreed with her plans for the wedding. "This is *Antonia*'s wedding," she would say, and would tell her mother how Antonia wanted things done.

Hardest of all for Antonia was meeting Arturo's family. A large contingent of them had been hoping Arturo would marry his brother's wife's sister, and they made it clear, in subtle, genteel ways, that they considered her an interloper. Antonia, for her part, took an instant dislike to them. She found the Rontellas' flat, crowded with overstuffed furniture and lace, a perfectly ordinary setting of a middle-class Genoese family and not so different from the Gassendis' home, stuffy and vulgar. For the first time she began to appreciate the stark elegance of her own home.

She couldn't abide their conversation. Arturo's father brought up the possibility of war only in terms of the harm it would do to exports. "What about the people who will die?" Antonia wanted to say. "What will the price of wine mean to them?" But she kept her peace.

Arturo's mother, however, seemed to like her. When Arturo introduced them, his mother looked up from her bed and said, "But she is so beautiful, Arturo! And she looks so kind! You will need a kind wife." In spite of herself, Antonia felt flattered.

Watching him in the midst of his hateful family, Antonia found the idea of marriage seemed even more impossible than ever. "Either he is really like them," she thought, "in which case I could never stand living with him. Or he is a fraud. If he is a fraud, what is he? What is he really when he is home in Yayaku?"

XIII

MEANWHILE, THE COUNT was making discreet inquiries into Arturo's background. He enlisted Signor Ravecca to help. Together they located some old friends of the family and some Genoese businessmen who had known Arturo in Yayaku.

"At least," said Signor Ravecca with a sigh when he and the count met, "at least there are no children. And no legal complications I can think of."

"Yes," said the count. "In a way, I'm glad he's not too respectable. Antonia has more of her mother in her than she thinks. I wouldn't want her to get bored. But this business with his brother! That's a bit more disturbing."

"But that was a long time ago," said Signor Ravecca. "There's been no sign of trouble since."

"True. Still, I wonder about that."

"So do I. But what alternative does she have, really?"

So the two of them gave Antonia their approval.

Not long after this, Antonia brought Arturo to have lunch with the count. It was the first time they had met.

"Tell me about your home," said the count.

"You mean Yayaku? That's a difficult subject. Any way I seem to approach it seems wrong to me. Yayaku is extraordinary; my town is perhaps not so very remarkable, but I've grown very fond of it."

"I imagine you've grown very attached to the people there?" said the count.

"Yes, I have. It is not difficult to do in such a place."

"But not too attached?" said the count. "Not so attached as to leave them at a distance, if necessary?"

Arturo stopped for a moment. "No, not that attached," he said with a small smile. "I will soon have a wife who will be the first person in my life."

The count seemed pleased at this. The conversation moved on to other topics. Antonia spoke little; the count and Arturo seemed to be warming to each other's company, and this was enough for her.

They discovered a common interest in Roman history.

"And what do you think," asked the count, "of our leader's plans to revive the Roman empire?"

"I think that if he had your memory of Roman history," answered Arturo, "he might think more about how the last empire came to an end."

"You fear he will bring us another Ricimer?"

"No, I fear he will bring us worse. Italy has some reason to distrust friends from the north."

"Forgive me, but are you calling our leader a fool?" said the count.

"Not exactly. He is a statesman who has lost track of his illusions."

"What do you mean?"

"I mean that because there is no such thing as a state, really, then a great statesman is an illusionist."

"I recall," said the count, "that my father said Italy was a cartographer's trick."

"When I first came to Pica, my home," Arturo went on, "Chile had the illusion that Pica was part of Chile. Unfortunately, most of the people had the illusion that they were Yayakuan. The Chileans were not particularly clever; instead of making the Yayakuans realize that they were really Chilean, they started to take away their property to give it to Chileans. As an Italian, I could see the absurdity of this. Of course, the Yayakuans became more Yayakuan than ever."

"What happened?" asked the count.

"We created another illusion: that the Yayakuan property belonged to an Italian—myself."

"Your Chileans must have been rather credulous."

"Oh, it was perfectly legal. People simply signed things over to me for safekeeping. When Pica became part of Yayaku again (through another remarkable piece of illusion-making) I simply signed them back."

"That must have been a difficult illusion to let go of."

"Not really. I think it would have been more difficult to convert to reality, and I never lost track of that. Besides, something stuck with me that, though it couldn't be seen or felt, made my fortune for me."

"And our leader? Where did he go wrong? Did he start to hold too hard to his illusions?"

"Yes, that was part of it, but not the fatal part. As long as everything stayed on the level of an illusion, he was safe: Illusions of armies fight illusions of wars better than real men."

"But you're afraid the wars will turn real?"

"Exactly. I'm sure of it. And everyone will sleep until it is too late."

"It will take more than geese to wake us this time?"

"Yes. And more than the goose step."

Antonia was smiling to herself.

ONE DAY Elsa came down to the flat very red in the face. "You have a visitor," she said, looking as if she were about to burst out laughing.

"A visitor?" asked Antonia. "Who is it? Not Arturo?"

"You'd never guess," said Elsa. "You must come and see."

Sitting in the middle of the parlor, wearing her best dress and coat and surrounded with boxes and bags, was Eliana.

"Eliana!" said Antonia, astonished. "What are you doing here?"

"I've come to take care of you, of course," said Eliana.

"But I'm leaving for Yayaku right after the wedding."

"I know that," said Eliana. "I'm coming with you."

"What do you mean? What about Mama?"

"I've left your mother to herself and come to look after you. Please show me where I am to sleep until the boat leaves for Yayaku."

Signora Gassendi found Eliana a room. "It will only be a few days," said Antonia. "Then she will see how ridiculous this is."

She tried to laugh when she told Arturo about it. They were walking near the harbor. He stopped short and didn't smile.

"It might be a good idea if she went with you," he said.

"A good idea! That's like saying it would be a good idea if Mama came along! How can you have such an absurd idea?"

"It's not an absurd idea," said Arturo, looking down. "You may need her with you, if I'm not there."

"What are you talking about?"

"I'm not sure I'll be able to leave with you right after the wedding."

"Why not?"

"My mother, mostly. She needs me now and I won't see her again after this visit. And there is business to attend to. It may be years before we can return to Italy."

"Then I'll wait with you. We can come on a later boat."

"No. Things are too precarious. There might not be many other boats. A single man can travel more easily in difficult times than a woman. You go on ahead. Take Toma and Eliana with you. I'll follow and meet you in Yayaku."

Antonia turned her head and looked out to sea. "My mother," she said. "At least my mother went on the same boat as my father. She didn't stay, but she went with him."

"What has this to do with your mother? Am I like your mother?"

"No, that's not the point. It's the pattern I'm talking about."

"Pattern? I don't know what you mean."

"I mean the pattern. A man goes from Italy to a new land—South America. He comes back, meets a woman, and marries her. But they are separated—one stays in Italy, one in South America. Don't you see it?"

"Yes, but not in the way you mean. That has nothing to do with us."

Antonia turned back to him. She was crying. "I don't believe it.

I'm trapped. I can't do anything. I am nothing. What do I have besides you? And you're a stranger. What else do I have besides you and this pattern?"

"You have yourself."

"That's nothing."

"Don't talk like that."

"I will. I will talk like that! If you don't want me to talk like that, then don't send me to Yayaku alone!"

Arturo held up his hands and sighed.

"If I go to Yayaku alone," said Antonia, "how will I know that I will ever see you again?"

"You won't know. You never will. No one ever does. But I'll swear I'll do my best to follow you as soon as I can. And to do my best to make you happy there."

"And you'll never leave me alone again?"

"I can't promise that. I can promise to try."

"It's not enough. No, it's not enough. I must have more than that. I will have more than that. I say that I will, and I will have it."

"Then you will," said Arturo, putting his arms around her. "Promise yourself, then."

XIV

AFTER THAT, THINGS went very quickly. Arturo booked passage on an earlier ship, one that sailed to Valparaiso by way of Buenos Aires and the straits. Then he moved the wedding date to the day before the departure. Italy was "nonbelligerent," but no one believed the official pronouncements anymore. "When the illusion fails," said Arturo, "it turns into fraud."

The news was dreadful. Two days before the wedding, an English steamer was sunk in the Atlantic on its way to America. Antonia could hardly sleep; she felt as if she had iron bands around her head and an army of spiders in her stomach. Now she was glad other people were making the decisions.

The Gassendis were very agitated, and not just over the wedding. Dr. Gassendi had lost all his good humor. At night, Antonia could hear him pacing up and down the hallways of the flat.

Antonia had heard from Signor Ravecca that Dora had returned from Paris. The afternoon before the wedding, when everyone was out, Antonia left Genoa and took the train to Artemisia.

It was hot and still when she climbed the hill up to Dora's villa. The fluttering in her stomach was agonizing. The house looked deserted; all the shutters were closed and the door was locked when she tried it. She rang the bell and could hear it sound through the empty halls. She looked up at the windows, not knowing what to do. She imagined her mother watching her from behind the shutters. Or perhaps she was not really home at all.

She turned around to leave. As she passed through the plaza, someone called her name.

"Signorina! Signorina Antonia!" It was Angelina, the woman who sold flowers, one of the few people in town who got along with Dora, perhaps because she was such a good customer.

"Signorina! Your mother told me about your wedding and I wanted to congratulate you! Here, let me give you these!"

She pressed a huge bouquet of orange blossoms into Antonia's hands.

"My mother told you about my marriage?" Antonia asked.

"Oh, yes! She was so proud! She said you had found a rich, handsome husband who was really in love with you! She said she had never imagined you were so clever!"

Antonia thought for a moment, then she smiled. On the train back to Genoa, she slept.

"THE WEDDING was a horrible rush," said Antonia. "I don't remember much about it."

"I remember everything," said Marta. "It was the first wedding I ever went to, and I've always thought it was beautiful."

"How old were you?"

"I must have been five or six. It was extraordinary how much confusion it caused at home. It seemed much more important than the war. Mama didn't want us to go at first. She was furious with Papa because he hadn't done more to stop it. But Uncle Arturo had promised I could hold your flowers, and I cried and screamed until Mama gave in. Then of course they all had to go. How clever Uncle Arturo was, really."

"Yes, he was."

"Mama didn't like your dress."

"No. She said 'She's just like her mother, she'll be back in a year with all of Arturo's money.' I don't think I was supposed to hear her, but that's what she said."

"I thought your dress was beautiful. I thought you were the most beautiful girl I had ever seen, and I told Mama I wanted to have a wedding just like yours."

"You did? How ridiculous!"

"That's what Mama thought. You should have seen her face. Then your mother showed up."

"Yes, I nearly fainted."

"You needn't have worried. Nobody realized who she was until it was all over. She looked too respectable, really elegant. Even Mama said so. Of course, because she came with the count, Mama thought she was the countess."

"Really?"

"Yes. The count introduced her as 'my dearest companion.' It wasn't until after she left that we realized who she was."

"She never said a word to me. Or to Arturo, of course. The appearance was entirely for the benefit of your family. The count came back alone after she'd gone."

"I thought it was a wonderful wedding! I don't think I was so happy again until after the war. Didn't you think it was wonderful?"

"Yes, I suppose, but I also thought it was sad. In some ways it was a funeral, you know. The funeral of my old self."

Arturo had originally arranged for them to spend their wedding night in a grand hotel in Portovenere.

"No," said Antonia. "Let's spend it at the house in Nervi. No one will know where we are, and it's been so long since we've been there."

So they got off the train at Nervi. Only Toma knew. He had set up the house for them and arranged for a meal to be left. Then he had gone back to Genoa to make the final arrangements for the passage.

Dinner was almost like the times when they first got to know each other. It was dark when they finished. The empty dishes sat patiently on the table. A single candle burned, lighting up their faces. Antonia moved to clear the table. Arturo grasped her hand.

"No," he said gently. "Don't touch anything."

Antonia turned away from him briefly. "I was thinking," she said, "about how we only have this one night before I have to leave you."

"A night can last a long time," said Arturo, smiling.

He took her hand and led her to the bedroom. It was the first time she had ever been inside. By the light of the candle she saw he had replaced the little cot with a full-size bed covered by cream-colored sheets.

Sometime before dawn, Antonia woke up.

"He was right about the time," she thought to herself in the dark. "We could have been immortal."

She drifted halfway back into sleep. "On the other hand," she thought, "could it always be like that to be married?"

She smiled for a moment, then frowned. "Perhaps Mama was right about that, after all."

She thought about her mother for a moment. Then she fell asleep.

They got up and dressed not long after sunrise. There was a chill in the house and a film of clouds in the sky.

Arturo wouldn't let her touch anything in the house. "Leave it as it is," he said. They said nothing else as they got ready to leave.

Arturo locked the door with the shiny brass key that was almost new. He looked at it in his hand for a moment, then suddenly threw it up in the air so that it flew out over the rim of the hill and was lost among the rooftops and orange trees below.

Antonia looked horrified. "It's nothing," he said hastily, catching her gaze. "Just a gesture. I have another key back in Genoa."

IT WAS MORE than a year before anyone entered the little house at Nervi again. A young soldier, with a young woman whom he didn't love and would never see again, forced the lock.

The lovers stared in awe at the remains of the wedding dinner on the table, at the candle that had burned itself out on the floor by the bed. It made their lovemaking more sober than it might otherwise have been, and in the morning the soldier secured the door carefully and kissed the girl gently before he left.

Three more years and part of another passed. It was spring. An American bomber, lost on the way to Genoa, passed overhead and dropped a single shell. It landed just east of the house, and leveled it to the ground. After the war, Arturo, knowing the house had been destroyed, sold the land without revisiting the site. A block of vacation flats stands there now.

Years later, after Arturo was dead, his daughter sorted through the odds and ends in his desk and came across a key. A battered tag attached to it said "key to the house at Nervi."

Part Three

I

WHEN ANTONIA FIRST saw Yayaku, it looked like a long, brown line. Toma stood with her on the deck of the boat, looking over the turquoise water. Along the edge of the horizon ran a thin, tan stripe, and above it a slightly wider one. "This Chile," said Toma, pointing to the south, then to the north. "This Yayaku."

There were other lines on the water, brown, with sometimes a crust of white. They were islands. A peculiar smell hung over them, sour, like wine gone bad. "Birds," said Toma, pointing toward the islands. "Guano. Much money to be made from them in the old days."

Eliana refused to leave her cabin. She stayed in bed with her pains and palpitations. The ship's doctor looked at her again. "Her heart," he said to Antonia, but he didn't seem to think it was very serious. Antonia did not have much sympathy for her. "She wanted to come," she said to herself. "I didn't ask for her to come." She remembered that Eliana's illness had begun about the time that Toma became more useful than she was. "It's out of spite for him that she's sick now," she thought.

In the afternoon the ship pulled toward the shore. Toma was busy with the baggage. The group of passengers for Casilda gathered on the deck. An old woman who was coming back from burying her husband in the old country was weeping, and a handful of others clustered around her. Antonia was the only first-class passenger going ashore.

The steamer stopped, shuddering a little as it cut its engines. A flotilla of little white and blue boats was on its way out to the ship. One of them picked up the guy lines of the ship and moored them to steamship buoys.

The sun was very bright over the water, and the sky was an even, pale blue. Antonia strained her eyes toward the shore, but could make out only a few low adobe buildings near the water. The clear water was choppy; sea lions were swimming among the towboats, peeking up out of the water like shy children. A sharp smell of salt and seaweed blended with the odor of the guano islands.

The little boats were clustered around the sides of the ship, bobbing on the surface of the ocean like leaves at the bottom of a well. Porters were carrying the luggage down a long, fragile gangway rigged against the side of the ship. When a swell came by, the gangway would swing out a little and then bounce the men clinging to the railing. Someone's suitcase burst open, spilling garter belts and girdles over the water. They quickly grew soggy and sank, looking like strange, white jellyfish beneath the surface.

Two sailors lowered Eliana in a sling over the side. Her black dress fluttered in the wind, and she moaned and crossed herself all the way down.

At last it was Antonia's turn. "Hold tight to the railing and close your eyes, Señorita," the porter advised as he helped her onto the gangway. "Señora," she answered, but closed her eyes anyway.

Halfway down, she opened them again. "If I'm going to live in this place," she said to herself, "I'll have to look at it." She looked down at the boat bounding under her, held her breath for a moment, and then climbed the rest of the way down.

Eliana was huddled in a corner of the little boat, her eyes half closed, moaning and muttering to herself. "I didn't ask for you to come," Antonia said, but not loud enough for Eliana to hear.

On the shore, the whole town watched them arrive. She mostly saw children with patient, unsmiling expressions she soon came to know very well on their broad faces. Casilda, a shabby collection of one-story huts painted in dull, pale colors, looked as if it had just been washed up by the sea. It was strangely quiet; the people watching her did so in silence. She noticed a smell of dried fish. The sun was hot, very white, and cruel. It hid nothing. Once they moved away from the water, the dryness seemed to settle over everything. Antonia felt her skin shrivel and tighten. "Is Pica like this?" she asked Toma.

"Oh, no, Señora," he answered. "This is Chile. Yayaku is much better than this," he said, gesturing with his hand.

At the customs house, all her bags were opened. The customs officers went through her things as if examining a forbidden treasure, as if they had never seen such beautiful garments. A small, murmuring crowd had gathered to look at her possessions, as the officers held them up to the light and turned out the sleeves and pockets.

A thin, nervous-looking man in a wrinkled tan suit was talking animatedly to Toma at one side of the room. It was one of Arturo's agents who had come to meet Antonia's boat.

"Signor Rontella not in Pica," said Toma, coming over to her. "No one knows where he is gone. No one hears anything. Señor Prado wants to know, what do you wish to do?"

Antonia looked over to where Eliana was sitting on a battered wooden bench. She was gasping and leaning backward and forward on the seat.

"Tell Señor Prado that we will not go to Pica today," Antonia said to Toma. "We are too tired. We will go to the hotel and rest. Tell him we will go to Pica tomorrow."

The hotel was called the Bolívar. It had been built twenty years earlier for the great international conference that concluded the war of the Pacific and was the grandest thing by far in Casilda. But Antonia noticed that the white columns of the porch were no longer straight and that huge cracks were creeping across the terrazzo floor. Sawdust gathered in the corners of the stairs and corridors.

In the room, the beds sagged and the sheets had a sweet, spicy smell of citronella that, however, did not appear to discourage the insects. Antonia sat in a wooden chair and listened to Eliana's heavy breathing as she lay on the bed. Through the window Antonia could see over the low flat roofs to the sea, and the smoke from the steamship disappearing to the north.

She watched a fly settle on Eliana's lips, fly up an inch or two when she breathed out, then settle again. "Eliana," called Antonia. "Eliana, are you asleep?"

Antonia went down to the lobby. Toma was there, managing her luggage. "Go, find a doctor for Eliana," she told him.

HOURS PASSED. Antonia sat in the room, watching the sun go down over the silver-gray Pacific. Gradually, her breaths lengthened to match Eliana's long, slow sighs. It was as if she were trying to keep Eliana alive by breathing for her.

Toma returned. It was almost dark in the room, and Antonia stood up and switched on the electric light when he knocked. Like the Casilda sunshine, it was white and unkind and hid nothing.

"No doctor," said Toma. "They say he drunk, or perhaps gone out in the desert. Nobody knows."

In the morning, Eliana was dead.

So Antonia first came to Pica accompanied not by her husband but by a coffin.

II

"I THINK THAT WEEK in Casilda was the most depressing one I ever had in my life," said Antonia to the count. "I felt caught at the edge of the world. I could understand why Columbus's sailors wanted to mutiny. If this was the New World, I thought, why leave the Old?

"There were all sort of problems with Eliana's death. There was something wrong with her papers and about the death certificate. Nobody could find the doctor, though a sour-looking priest finally arrived for the last rites. We sat together, Eliana and I, for a whole day after she died. Finally Carlo, Arturo's agent, came out from Pica to straighten things out. They took Eliana's body to the undertaker to be embalmed.

"There was still no word about Arturo. Nothing. I was so upset I could hardly move. Finally I asked Toma to tell me about Pica.

"Such a picture he painted! It is an oasis, he said. I imagined something out of Arabia, palm trees and houses covered with blue tiles. He said Arturo had the most beautiful house in town, the second biggest; the envy of everyone. He gave me such a false impression. What would I have done, I wonder, if he had told me the truth?

"Then Carlo's wife, Lina, came out to help me. I began to wonder about Toma's stories when I saw her. She was a big, fat woman and I could tell she had done her best to dress up for me. Nothing quite matched in her features or in her clothes. Her dress was new and looked American, her hat came from Paris, but at least twenty years before. She gave me such a warm hug that I couldn't help liking her. It was so good to hear her speak Italian!

"She went with me to the customs house to see about getting Eliana's body out of Chile to Yayaku. She and the customs officer spoke Spanish, so fast and continuously that I couldn't hope to follow what they said. At last the officer threw up his hands and signed the papers—I think he just wanted to get rid of her.

"Lina and Carlo took me in their car, an old black American one, brown from the dust all over it, and Toma came behind in an open-bed truck with the luggage and Eliana's coffin. The dust was from the road. There was nothing but a brown truck driving through the flat desert with not one green thing to be seen on either side of the road. The Andes were in front of us in the distance—three huge jagged peaks and many smaller ones. You could see them very clearly though they were very far away. They were purple and pink with snow all along the peaks. They were so huge, so much grander and more remote than the ones at home. They seemed to me to be eerie that day as if they were watching over us—they looked flat and not quite real. Toma told me later that the Indians think the tallest peak is a volcano that will one day destroy the town.

"In the middle of nowhere, we came to a cluster of little huts and two sets of barriers across the road. It was the border between Chile and Yayaku. We had to get out and open all our bags again. They went through everything, even though they had already done it at the customs house. I think, also, that Carlo had to slip some money to them on account of the coffin. Then they let us through the barrier and we had to go through the whole thing all over again on the Yayakuan side.

"Then we saw some green on the horizon. It was the palm trees of Pica, their great shapes reaching above the housetops. I was so relieved that everything wasn't gray or brown in Pica. It sort of spilled out over the desert, as if it were a pool of gray-green water. I remember thinking how different it was from Artemisia, which was packed right up into the hills with no space wasted and the houses right on top of each other.

"I remember driving down the Alameda, under a row of tall palms, and then down the main street, with its old-looking adobe buildings, stores on the first floor, balconies and long, shuttered windows on the second where people lived. The jacarandas were in full bloom and the flowers gave a soft, purple tint to the pastel buildings.

"It was noon, I think, and all the stores were closed. The people who were out stood and waved; it was like a little parade. They smiled and looked so friendly! I felt reassured for the first time since leaving Italy. Lina stopped a few times to introduce me as *"la bonita"* who finally drove Arturo Rontella to the altar.

"Lina took me to their house. It was a huge, low place of adobe facing the main street. Like all those old houses in Pica, it seemed to ramble on forever. We sat in their parlor, a big, musty room that they didn't use very much. I remember thinking how odd it was, how nothing in it seemed to belong there or with one another. The curtains and the upholstery were all new, bright red brocade. There were little lace doilies on all the tables (the ladies in town spent half their time crocheting them) and big silver trays and dishes set around. The chairs were large and heavy, made of dark wood. They squeaked; the joints were all working loose because it was so dry. There was a mirror in a heavy, gold-leaf frame, and a huge radio covered with a black lace mantilla and big vases full of dusty, faded, paper flowers.

"The furniture was spaced so widely apart that it was hard to talk. We spoke mostly about the war, if it was coming. Nobody said anything about Arturo or about Pica. It was as if I had been in town forever.

"I remember looking around and wondering why everything looked so strange and ordinary at the same time. Some of the furniture looked French, some Spanish; some even looked modern and American. But there was something wrong about them; the arms were too heavy, or the legs too thin. I found out later that almost everything had been copied by the carpenter from pictures in magazines from Europe and America, and he never quite understood how they were supposed to be.

"Carlo kept on standing while we talked. He was dressed in white, with suspenders that pulled his pants well above the waistline. He reminded me a little of Arturo, though he was older and heavier and much more ordinary. His Italian had an odd, flat sound to it, as if it had dried out from so many years in Pica.

"Finally, a maid came in and said lunch was ready. We ate under a grape arbor in a courtyard at the back of the house. The table was too big for only three people! It looked as if it had been made for banquets, and we were spread out so that the conversation became even slower.

"Lina called the lunch a *'piqueo.'* There was an endless number of small courses: barbecued cow's heart, tamales, rice with seafood, spicy dishes with chicken, a kind of corn pie, and all kinds of dessert with coffee. My head was so full I could hardly concentrate on eating, but later I found out that it was the choicest foods, a real honor for Arturo's wife. But it was odd about Arturo, because they never mentioned him.

"Lina offered to put me up in her house. I thanked her but said I'd rather stay in the hotel until I could move into Arturo's house. Carlo frowned, as if to say that might be a long time. But they said yes, of course, they could understand.

"It was late in the afternoon when we arrived at the hotel, a small, two-story building much like the others on the main street. I had only one bag. Toma had taken the other things, including Eliana's body, to Arturo's warehouse. They told me there were only five rooms in the hotel, and that they had given me the nicest, the bridal room. The nicest! I pitied those who stayed in the worst! The poor old bed sagged, and I could hear the insects scuttling over the floor all night, even though the smell of citronella was overpowering.

"I couldn't sleep. I spent that whole night in a chair by the window, looking out to the Alameda. Between the rows of palms were masses of geraniums and other flowers I had never seen. The sky was so black and deep, the deepest and clearest I had ever seen, and the stars were all wrong. I don't know why I hadn't noticed that on the ship, but of course the night sky is different south of the equator.

"There was no one in the street until the sun rose, and then the women came, wrapped up in long cloaks and leading their burros down the street to the marketplace. Some carried fruits, others vegetables or brown jugs of milk. Some had their babies with them, wrapped in colorful blankets.

"I remember thinking how beautiful their faces were, not like European faces at all. They reminded me of the bronze statuette of a Chinese goddess you had in your flat; these women had the same round, coppery faces, the same wide, sloping eyes; and the same look of infinite patience. Like the goddess, their faces were almost, but not quite, peaceful, as if they knew a bit too much about the troubles of the world. Of course they did.

"I had so many things in my head! What would happen to me in this strange world? I hadn't even begun to think, until then, about what I would do there. I felt bad about Eliana, but I was both relieved and frightened that she had died. I liked being alone for a change, even if everything was so uncertain. I felt myself swelling up inside. My arms and head and legs felt light, as if I had been bound up in a cellar for years and years. Even though nobody knew where Arturo was, or would even talk about him, I felt sure he would come. I could feel his strength reaching out to me from wherever he was. I think that that morning, sitting by the window and looking out into the sunshine, I actually laughed.

"Not long after the sun rose, the hotel owner's wife knocked at my door. Of course the Señora would not want to have breakfast in the dining room, where only the traveling salesmen ate, she said. Would I like breakfast brought to my room? I was too curious, so I said I would go to the dining room.

"The dining room turned out to be a dark, unaired place with five tables, covered with green linoleum. There were two men eating there who both stood up and stared at me when I came in. The hotel owner's wife grabbed me by the arm and led me to a table in the corner, where breakfast was already laid out. She obviously wanted to make me as inconspicuous as possible. I sat down to eat, but the two men were still standing and staring as if I were some sort of apparition.

"Toma appeared at the door, and he and the hotel owner's wife had a heated conversation in low tones. He told me later that the only women who usually ate alone in a public place at that hour were "available women" on their morning rounds. He had assured the hotel owner's wife that he had seen me having breakfast that way on the ship, and that in my own country this was customary and respectable.

"I didn't mind all this attention. I even liked it a little. I had more trouble with the food. The coffee was all right, but the cup was not very clean, the bread was hard, and the jam was surrounded by flies. I asked for some fruit, but was told they did not have any."

A FEW DAYS after she arrived in Pica, Antonia told Toma to get the keys for Arturo's house. He hesitated for a moment, but did as he was told.

The house was an old one, one of the oldest and largest in Pica. It was built in the time of the guano fortunes. It was two stories tall, built of warm, brown stones instead of adobe, and stood on the corner of the Alameda facing the Plaza de Armas. It was part Spanish and part French on the outside. The windows on the first floor were short and arched, those on the second were long, topped with classical cornices like the house in Artemisia. There were shutters inside and outside the second-floor windows, and iron balconies.

The house had been empty for ten years. The previous owner had been a mining operator from Nancy who had come to Pica because, they said, of "some unpleasantness" at home. Arturo had bought the house, along with the man's other interests in town, from his widow, who wanted to go back to Marseilles, where she came from. Arturo said later that the house had been a "real bargain" but that he felt strange about living there by himself, so he stayed in the flat above his office. He rented the business rooms on the first floor to a grocer, and left the rest of the house empty.

Toma showed her up the back stairs (the front ones were riddled with dry rot). He bounded ahead from room to room, opening doors and throwing back shutters to let in the dusty sunlight.

Inside, behind the shop, the rooms were arranged around two large courtyards; in the second of this was a small fountain (not working) and a cluster of flowering shrubs. The house smelled of dust and jasmine blossoms.

There were a number of large, very tall rooms, shadowy and shuttered against the heat. The furniture was heavy and sparse and spread along the walls like shy people at a party; it wasn't quite as peculiar-looking as the furniture in Carlos and Lina's house, because most of it had been brought over from France. The wallpapers had light patches where the Frenchwoman had hung her family portraits. There were no books—only a glass-fronted bookcase containing two seashells and a silver inkwell—and no piano.

There were old-fashioned electric lights with frosted-glass shades. Antonia tried to turn one on, but nothing happened. Toma shook his head. "No power now," he said, "only at night."

The best room was the big salon at the front of the house. The windows came to the floor and faced north, across the plaza, so the shutters when open let the clear, white light into the room. The mining operator had been a student in Paris and had decorated the room to remind him of those years. Outside the windows was a broad, iron balcony that Arturo said had been salvaged from the ruins of the Tuileries. Antonia thought it was unsafe and never used it, but the cook, who was fat and hated climbing stairs, used to infuriate her by pulling sacks of groceries over the railing with a rope.

There was a marble mantel with a rococo arch and a set of Louis XV chairs covered in a faded blue-striped silk. These were so dried out that they split into ribbons immediately. The walls were hung in yellow silk and had a set of watercolor views of Versailles. Looking at these made Antonia sigh; faded as they were, they were greener than the landscape outside. There was a brass sconce on either side of the fireplace and a small crystal chandelier hanging from the ceiling that broke up the light.

Later, Antonia used to spend a great deal of time in this room. She learned a lot about the town by looking out those windows.

Right across the plaza stood the cathedral—a big brown building with a tower on each side. Eiffel was commissioned to design it at the turn of the century, but it had never been finished. French things had gone out of fashion.

The Plaza de Armas was wedge-shape and lined with dusty-looking palm trees. It had a large, three-tiered fountain at its center, copied from one in the Place de la Concorde and painted in bright green. Because there was so little water, they turned it on only on national holidays. There were cheerful-looking beds of geraniums and benches painted to match the fountain. There was a statue of Columbus, too. It made him look fatter, older, and shorter than the statue Antonia remembered in Genoa. How odd, she thought to herself, to come all that way to find Columbus waiting.

"We obviously can't live in this house the way it is," she said to Toma. "Take me to my husband's office so I can talk to them about ordering repairs."

Toma looked very hesitant, but they went out and crossed the plaza to Arturo's office. It was a big stone building on the corner, with a huge open door right at the curve of the street. They walked inside.

There was a big room with an aisle down the middle and counters on each side. Behind the counters were dozens of desks for the different agencies—insurance, airline, tires, gasoline, cars—with little signs to indicate what they were. At the end of the room was a big glass wall behind which was Arturo's office. A big portrait of an elderly gentleman was on the wall over Arturo's desk. It was Arturo's uncle, who had left him the business. Arturo had had the portrait painted in Italy from a photograph. He used to say the mustache was the only part that looked like his uncle.

It was very busy inside. Many men stood at the counters talking with the agents. A great hush fell when Antonia came in. She realized she was the only woman there.

Toma took her up to Carlo's desk at the head of the room beside Arturo's glass box. Carlo stood up.

"Signora, I am surprised to see you here!" he said. "If there's anything you need, I would be happy to come over to your hotel to talk with you."

"That's very kind of you, Signore," she said, "but I am in a bit of a hurry and, besides, I wanted to see my husband's place of business."

"Of course, Signora. Won't you come with me, please?"

He took her quickly into Arturo's office where there were some sturdy wooden chairs and a table. They sat down.

"What is it that you need, Signora?"

"I need some help getting our house ready. It needs a good deal of work and I'd like to start right away. And I'll need some money to begin." She told him a sum in soles, not really knowing what a sol was worth. The amount made him blush.

"Signora, what would you do with this amount of money, may I ask? You may not know that household goods can only be purchased when the traveling salesmen arrive."

"I am not interested in the things the traveling salesmen sell," she said.

"Very well," said Carlo. "If you'll excuse me for a moment, I'll see what I can do."

He went out into the main room and spoke to some agents who had their desks near his. They consulted for what seemed to Antonia to be a long time. Then one of the agents left the building. Carlo spoke to Toma, who was waiting below, and Toma also went outside. Then Carlo came back into Arturo's office. He was blushing again and his forehead was wet with sweat.

"You'll forgive us, Signora, there are a few formalities because your husband is absent," he said. "I have taken the liberty of sending Toma to your hotel for some papers we need."

The papers turned out to be her passport, marriage certificate, and Eliana's death certificate. When Toma brought them in, he looked as embarrassed as Carlo. Carlo spread them out on his desk and examined them. Then he said a few words to Toma in Spanish which she couldn't catch. Toma nodded his head vigorously.

"Please forgive this delay," Carlo said, smiling and wincing slightly because he could see how angry she was. "Everything seems to be in order." He gestured to an agent outside, who came in and handed her an envelope with the money she had asked for. "If there is anything else you need, Signora," Carlo concluded, backing them gently out of the office, "please send for me and I'll be happy to do whatever you require."

Antonia was furious. "Why did he need those papers?" she asked Toma as they walked back across the plaza.

He turned away from her and took a couple of quick skips to the right. "It is difficult to say, Signora," he answered.

"Toma, I want an explanation! How dare you get those papers for that man! He has no right! He is only my husband's agent, and I am his wife!"

"Well, Signora," he said, moving even farther away, "many people noticed you did not come with your husband. They noticed you came with a coffin instead. They think you act a bit—well, not like a married lady. Some people say, 'Signor Rontella is dead! She is coming to take away his money!' Other people say, 'She is an impostor! Signor Rontella is caught across the sea and won't be able to unmask her.' It is very confusing for people, but now I tell them, they will know."

Antonia felt almost like laughing, it was so ridiculous! After all she had gone through getting there! And it was some time before these rumors went away altogether.

III

DURING THOSE FIRST DAYS, Antonia went everywhere and showed herself everywhere. For the first time in her life, she was unknown, as free of history as a mysterious flower blooming in the desert. At the same time, Pica was fresh and new to her, brighter and more fascinating than it would ever be again.

She ignored, with a boldness that surprised her, all the little hints she received, shrugging away all the bounds of "propriety" that were pointed out to her. She insisted on doing the shopping herself, accompanied only by Toma, despite the efforts of Arturo's business partners to keep her safely at home.

Toma walked with her always, either a few steps in front of her when she did not know the way, or a few steps behind when she did. Toma carried two baskets tied to his back. He had gone back to his old habit of going barefoot, and he shed the European-style clothes he had worn in Italy. He now had on loose pants held by a colorful woven belt and a shirt made of rows of rough cotton sewn together. Even his walk had changed; he moved in little steps as if jumping from one cobblestone to another, looking for the most comfortable place to land.

They went to the stone market building, noisy with vendors' shouts and infested with flies, and to the dusty little shops of the Alameda, with their meager stock of imported goods. They took long walks through the streets while the women peeked out from the shadows of the upper stories of the houses.

One night, Lina and Carlo took her to the little theater, a miniature version of the Lyons opera house, gift of a wealthy French family half a century in the past. Amid the threadbare velvet seats with the now-familiar odor of citronella, below the fogged-over mirrors and peeling plaster cornices, Antonia watched an incomprehensible Spanish melodrama. Lina, in a dress made of the same bright red brocade as the curtains in her parlor, pointed out the notables in the audience with terse comments on each: "Drinks too much." "Hasn't a penny to her name, *pobrecita.*" "A devil of a woman."

"WHERE DOES ONE buy cloth?" Antonia asked Toma one morning as they left the house for the market.

"Nowhere, Signora," he answered. "The traveling salesmen bring it to town."

"I don't want that kind of cloth," she said, thinking of Lina's red brocade. "I want cloth like that." She pointed to the skirt of an Indian woman in the street.

"That cloth made in the mountains, isn't sold here. Nobody wants that kind of cloth."

"I do. Do you think I could buy some?"

"Possible, Signora. I go to the other market on Sunday to see what can be found."

"The other market?"

"The market for the Indians, Signora, where they sell to each other."

"And where is this market?"

"Is only on Sundays—out there," he pointed to the edge of town.

"We will go there on Sunday, then," she said.

The Indian market was in a big field on the outskirts of town. The peddlers had spread their merchandise on blankets on the ground and the trading was by barter.

Antonia walked through the disorganized rows of people and objects and, when she saw something she liked, offered money. The women stared up at her in amazement, hiding their smiles behind their hands. She was the only European there. Toma explained what she wanted and Antonia simply paid what they asked, with no idea whether she paid too much or too little. She bought some woven shawls and some bowls and spoons carved in wood. She asked if she could buy more cloth, and made arrangements to have fabric brought down from the mountains where it was made.

The Indians looked at Antonia even more intently than the people in town did. Sometimes they spoke to Toma in their own language, and pointed at her. *"Virgencita,"* they said, meaning not the Little Virgin but the beauty of the Virgin of Macarena, patron saint of Pica, whose image stood in the cathedral.

Word of the strange foreign lady spread through the market, and later, back to the mountain villages from which the Indians had come. After that, all kinds of visitors found Antonia's house in town, bringing woven blankets and cloth, old wooden saints with brightly painted clothes and wide dark eyes, silver bowls and boxes from the colonial days, and, sometimes, ancient painted bowls and beads and fragments of thousand-year-old textiles as dry and fragile as old leaves. They came at all times, sometimes well into the night, but she always let them in and looked at what they had to show her. She never went to the Indian market again, but she never lacked suppliers.

Meanwhile, Arturo's house was being cleaned and repaired. Toma had hired a cook and some cousins of his to help. Sometimes a small crowd would gather in front of the house, hoping to catch a glimpse of the signora who was behaving so strangely and didn't care what people in town thought of her.

Antonia was busy obliterating all trace of the Frenchwoman. She had the rooms painted in pale, flat colors, using paint made for the outside walls of the adobe houses. She fashioned the Indian cloth into curtains to replace the faded silk and velvet ones, re-covered the chairs, and took down the views of Versailles. Gradually, the rooms filled up with light and the colors that most delighted her about Pica.

A letter arrived from Arturo. He wrote from the American hospital in Panama. He had been taken sick on the trip over from Italy, but was recuperating. "I will be leaving from here soon," he wrote. "But I don't know when I will be able to reach Pica. Travel is not easy these days. Don't bother to write me here; I will be gone long before the letter arrives. Keep well and be patient. If there is anything you need, ask Carlo. I have written to him to tell him to look after you. We will be together soon, despite everything."

The letter was very short and said little beyond what was essential. When Antonia finished it, she felt like crying. She wasn't sure why. It could have been from relief, or from Arturo's words, which seemed so cold to her, as if they were the words of a stranger and not the words of the man who had taken her to the empty house at Nervi.

The letter left Antonia with an uneasy feeling that lingered. She and

Arturo had been apart for ten weeks, and to her it seemed so long that she wasn't sure she could really remember him. People she didn't know nodded politely to her in the street, but she thought she saw questions in their eyes. Single men came up behind her, muttering flirtations to the air around her. Sometimes thay would walk beside her. *"Virgencita,"* they would say. "Where you walk, flowers grow. You are the sun of my life." She smiled at these compliments—*piropos*, she found out they were called. Later, she learned she was supposed to blush and be very annoyed with them, and then repeat them to her women friends with a sigh and a mysterious smile.

But the unvoiced questions bothered her. Are you really Signora Rontella? she saw in their eyes. Why are you so strange? Don't you understand that there are rules, customs, certain ways of doing things? Why don't you learn them? What will your husband say when, and if, he gets back? What indeed, thought Antonia, reading Arturo's letter.

IV

ARTURO ARRIVED IN LATE JULY as the heat of spring was coming on. Despite Arturo's request, Antonia had written to him, telling him she had "moved into his house" and told him to expect "many surprises" when he came.

"If we are dealing in surprises," he thought with a smile, "I'll give her one of my own." So he told no one that he would arrive, and took the little train from Casilda on his own.

When he reached Pica, it was just after sunset. The last rays of the sun were coloring the tops of the palms golden along the Alameda and a bird, whose name he had never bothered to learn, was making long, mournful calls. His head ached and, although the sun was gone and it had cooled down, he felt hot and very tired.

He went to his "home"—the flat over the office. The windows were dark, and when he opened the door, he saw that no one had been there for a long time. Dust lay over everything; the bare mattresses lay on the beds, turned over themselves like broken reeds.

He looked out a window across the plaza and saw lights in the apartment over the grocer's, the place he had never spent a night in. He went out and walked across the plaza. He was surprised to find the door locked. Toma came to let him in.

"Don't say anything," he said to Toma's delighted face. "This is my surprise."

He went upstairs. He found Antonia in a room full of rich colors; Indian tapestries hung from the walls, and the furniture was covered with a thick, dark orange fabric. Antonia was sitting in a chair with her back to him, reading a book.

"Antonia," he said.

She started, stood up, and turned around. In the dim light, she didn't recognize him at first. Then she saw his face, paler and thinner than she remembered. She walked over to him and reached out her hand to touch the lines on his face.

"Welcome," she said. "Welcome home, Arturo."

He smiled. "Is this my home?" he asked. "I don't recognize it!" Seeing her frown, he quickly took her hand and said, "It is a wonderful surprise you have made for me. I'm proud of you."

"Are you?" asked Antonia softly. "I was afraid—afraid you'd find a stranger when you came home."

"I did, in a way," said Arturo, smiling again. "But a stranger I would very much like to know."

Antonia said nothing but only pressed his hand, which felt warm and damp. He nodded to her and his smile narrowed slightly. Without speaking, she led him to the bedroom and helped him undress.

Once in bed, he fell asleep instantly. For two hours, perhaps three, Antonia sat in a chair watching him by the light of a single candle, which she shielded with her hand to keep from waking him. His breathing was very deep and low, as if with each breath he sank to the bottom of the sea, and then slowly rose again to the surface. She shivered and shook her head. She wondered how Arturo felt to be back. Had he found her changed? Or was it he who had changed? Was he really ill? She hugged herself, listening to the sounds a silent house makes in the dark. What was she afraid of? This half-strange man in her bed? His strength? His weakness?

Around midnight, she undressed and crawled into bed beside her husband. Responding to her weight on the mattress, he half turned, muttered something in Spanish without opening his eyes, and settled again beside her. When she slept at last, she dreamed of her father as he was the last time she saw him.

In the morning, Arturo had trouble getting up. He looked so pale that Antonia was alarmed.

"Stay in bed and rest," she said. "You tired yourself out coming here all alone after being so sick."

Arturo looked at her with very wide, bright eyes and a half smile that seemed to say, "All right, but I'm only doing this to please you. I should be back at work."

"Go back to sleep," Antonia said. "Later I'll bring Carlo over so you can yell at him for making a mess of things while you were gone. And for asking to see all my papers before he would let me be your wife."

Arturo smiled again and closed his eyes.

Later, when she looked in on him, he was awake. "There's a crowd of people outside," she said. "They've been there since first thing this morning, just standing there and looking up at the house."

"I'll have to get up," he said, pushing his legs out of bed.

"Don't be ridiculous! You are resting. Why should you bother with them?"

"I'll have to show myself," he said. "Don't worry, it'll only take a moment." He winked at her. "If I don't, they'll say you have me bewitched, and they'll be gossiping about when you'll be out in widow's weeds."

He put on a coat and went out to the salon. Antonia gasped as he opened one of the long windows and went out onto the balcony. There were shouts and cheers. He gestured to her.

Wincing at every creak of the rusty balcony and at every shout from the crowd, she went out and stood beside him. He put one arm around her and raised the other.

There were more shouts and cheers. It looked like half the town standing down there and smiling at them. Some of the women threw white flowers at them. "*Caramba*, old man, the little flower has you tired out already!" shouted a male voice. "*Mierda*, Rontella, you've really put a leg in the stew this time!" shouted another. Several of the women crossed themselves at this.

Everyone seemed to be clapping and cheering, except for one woman Antonia noticed in the back of the crowd. She stood a little by herself. She had a dark, frowning face with lines around her mouth and eyes, and wore European clothes that were quite fashionable. "Perhaps she is a mestiza," Antonia thought, "that's why she looks so dark and angry." She was staring up at the balcony with a very fierce expression in her dark eyes, eyes that Antonia had difficulty forgetting.

"What does it mean," Antonia asked when they went inside, "put your leg in the stew?"

"It means, little flower," said Arturo, putting his arms around her waist, "to make a mess of things."

"It's a good expression," said Antonia. "I'll have to learn how to use it."

"I'm sure you'll be good at that," said Arturo, smiling.

V

DURING THEIR FIRST WEEKS together in Pica, Arturo and Antonia were strangely stiff with each other. Unlike the little house at Nervi, their house in Pica was filled, filled with rooms and things and other people. They each had to make room for the other, to find space in their habits and their thoughts that had been so solitary for so long.

They found themselves falling silent at meals, staring at each other across the Frenchwoman's big, mahogany table, as if they were two strangers sitting on opposite sides of a train compartment. It was not that they had nothing they wanted to say, but that they were uncertain what they could say. When they did speak, they were formal and polite, as if looking for a sign from the other for how to act, for what kind of person to be. Antonia even found herself using the *"voi"* with him as her mother had with her father.

Arturo was gentle with her, as he had always been. He was careful to ask each morning before he left the house if there was anything she needed. There never was, and she preferred to buy things for herself, but she tried always to think of something for him to bring home for her. He always remembered, and often brought small, useless gifts for her as well—a painted comb, a Chinese scarf. She thanked him politely for these and put them away. Sometimes she felt like a poor orphan girl that some kindly, rich man had taken into his house to care for. Only at night, when they made love, wordlessly and with an intensity that often frightened both of them, did they become again the lovers they had been in Italy.

Arturo was still weak. After his return, he spent two long days at his office and came back on the second day exhausted. Though he protested, she put him to bed, brought him his dinner there, and sat with him until he went to sleep. She spoke about her plans for the house, of what the servants were doing. He nodded in agreement, but added little. She hoped he would talk about his life away from her, but his conversation stopped at their door. What happened to him in the streets of Pica, in his offices and warehouses, was not part of their world.

Gradually, he grew stronger, and their life together began to fall into a pattern. They awoke early in the mornings, not long after dawn. Antonia cooked their breakfast herself, and they ate together in the little room near the kitchen. Then he would walk off across the plaza to work.

In the mornings she looked after things in the house. As if trying hard not to be like her mother, she arranged everything to be regular, predictable. She gave long lists to the servants, telling them in rudimentary Spanish exactly when and how everything was to be done. She told the cook where to buy food and when to serve the meals. She made the maids learn how to clean all over again, demonstrating the new brushes she bought and explaining to them how to use the new soaps and disinfectants. She even put on one of the new uniforms she bought for them to show how it was to be worn.

At first they laughed at her for trying to make them change the way they had done things for years. But after she shouted at them, and even pulled the youngest maid's hair once or twice, they were obedient and silent, respectfully opening their wide, dark eyes when she spoke. She found a soft but firm way of speaking to them. And once she had said something, she never changed her mind. Arguments only made her short-tempered.

She was always fair to them, and they grew to like the regularity of her ways, but, apart from Toma, none of them loved her. It became known among the Indians and the shopkeepers that Señora Rontella was not to be trifled with, or to be cheated with tough cuts of meat or overripe vegetables. When she came into a store, the laughter stopped and the voices grew low and respectful. She gathered none of the town gossip the other women brought home with their groceries.

At one, Arturo returned for lunch. Unless the weather was bad, they ate in the front courtyard. As at breakfast, she cooked the meal: Italian food, simple and lightly spiced, because Arturo still complained about his digestion.

They ate alone, without servants or guests. They liked this time together. But they were still mostly silent.

Over the coffee, they opened and read the mail, which Arturo picked up himself at the post office. Usually, they were letters for Arturo, mostly having to do with his business and contacts outside Pica. But one day, a month or so after Arturo's return, there were two letters from Italy— one for him, and one for her, and a letter from Buenos Aires.

My Dear Antonia (began the count's letter),

I was very glad to hear from you, and to hear that Arturo has reached you at last. I knew that things would work out for the two of you in the end, and I wish you all the best in future years.

This will seem a very short letter. I don't mean to be brusque: There are things I would like to tell you, but cannot; there are things I can tell you, but don't wish to. Words seem weak and dangerous in these times, which I can't describe as either peace or war, and in which everything hangs by a thread.

It was enough for me to hear you are happy. It must be enough for you to know you are cherished in my thoughts.

With love, as always,
Emilio

· · ·

Dear Antonia,

It was so good to hear from you! And that your husband has arrived at last! You see, things can turn out well for you if you have faith! I am well. Business is not as good as it could be, however. Señor Parodi says it is a temporary slump because of the war, but it is awkward. Mama keeps writing for more money and asks if I intend to cut her off because of the war and let her starve to death. She is still the same, isn't she? I am trying to oblige her, but it has meant giving up the house and moving into one of our empty flats—not one of the best, unfortunately, facing a smelly alley. But as Señor Parodi says, it is only temporary.

The old house—well, it was very grand, but a lot of trouble, like some other things here, the women, for example. Why is it so many bright and shiny things turn out to be black and ugly inside? I am well rid of them!! Keeping you always in my thoughts.

Marco

Antonia put down the letters. The last of the jacaranda petals blew across them. "Like lavender tears," Antonia thought, but her eyes were dry. It was very, very still in the courtyard under the afternoon sun. She watched Arturo as he finished reading his letter.

"Good news?" he asked, looking up.

"No," she said, "and yours?"

"Not very. My mother has died."

Now Antonia's eyes filled with tears. "Oh Arturo!" she said. "I am so sorry." She reached for his hand.

As if in reflex, he started to move his hand away, but then left it where it lay on the table, and Antonia's hand closed over it. He looked up into her face, and she saw eyes close, open, and close again.

"It's not as if I wasn't expecting it," he said. "It was only a matter of—"

He stopped. Antonia pulled his hand toward her and held it in both of hers, rubbing it as if she could draw the pain out of him. It seemed to her that years came down over his face like the curtain at the end of a play. His jaw sagged slightly, and his eyes seemed to grow deeper.

"Oh, Arturo," she said. "Is there anything I can do?"

"No, nothing. Everything has been taken care of. I made all the arrangements before I left. By now she will be buried."

"How is your father?"

"He seems well enough. My sister-in-law stayed with him for a while. He sometimes calls her by my mother's name, and he wakes up in the middle of the night thinking that he and my mother are newly married again, that she is in the next room with the babies. Once he got up and wandered around the house looking for her, but all the rooms were empty. He says the hardest thing is finding his own clothes in the morning."

Antonia was thinking of the sea, of all the empty water between Pica and Italy. Their house seemed like a boat, with just two passengers.

They sat together quietly for a while longer, until a wind came up and blew one of the napkins off the table. Antonia let go of Arturo's hand to pick it up, and he stood up to go.

"Is there anything you want? Anything I can bring home for you?" Arturo asked.

"No, nothing."

And Arturo walked back to his office across the plaza, thinking of how his mother had looked when he was very small, when all of her hair was black, as Antonia's was now.

One night, a few days later, when Arturo came home, he found Antonia sitting in the little sunroom surrounded by old, leathery looking books. She was reading so intensely that she did not hear Arturo as he approached her. He sat beside her and drew her close. "What is it that you're reading?" asked Arturo.

Antonia's eyes lit up. "I found these wonderful histories of the Inca and the Indians of Yayaku in the Frenchwoman's attic," she explained. "They tell how the Mayu, the Indians who lived in Pica, were the dispossessed, the 'thrice-betrayed.' They were conquered three times: first by the Ayaru, then by the Incas, finally by the conquistadores. They even lost their language and now speak Quechua, the Inca tongue."

"I know little about the Mayu," said Arturo, "but I do know that Corequenque—just under the mountains where the ruins are—was their city. Some say it was the oldest on earth, the mother of cities."

"They have wise men—soothsayers—who still know the secrets of the ancient times, Arturo. According to one of the books, the Indians only pretend to go along with things as they are. They think that everything in Yayaku is really theirs, and are still waiting to push us all into the sea!"

"They are a mystery," Arturo responded. "They all have their villages in the mountains and do not really think of Pica as their home. Even Toma at times will vanish, and after a few weeks will come back without an explanation, acting as if he has not gone at all. They always look so patient, as if they were ready to wait for a thousand years.

"It is their patience," he added, "that frightens me about them."

Arturo smiled at Antonia. "One day soon we will drive to the mountains to visit the Corequenque," he said.

VI

SHORTLY AFTER HE LEARNED of his mother's death Arturo set up a small room in the back of the house as a study. He brought some boxes, books, and papers from his old rooms over the office. The most important was a flat, wooden box, painted black and containing, among other things, the deeds to the property he owned in the capital. This property was not the most important or valuable he owned, but he liked to keep the deeds near him, rather than in his office safe with his other business papers. He sometimes took this box down from the shelf and spread the deeds on his desk, reading them again to himself before he went to bed.

At other times, he wrote letters to men, important men he knew in the north. The content of the letters again was not important; they dealt with small things, favors he had done, suggestions he had. But he was careful to keep copies, which he filed away with the deeds in the box.

He had an old leather chair in his study that had been his uncle's in which he sat for an hour or two some evenings before dinner. He did nothing as he sat (unusual for a man who was so active), but simply thought. After his mother's death, his thoughts were mostly about time.

As a young man, he had bothered little about his future or the past. His early years in Pica had been a series of games, played with unwitting opponents, among them his uncle. The games were a year or so in duration, and when he won them, as he nearly always did, he looked for more. There was no larger scheme or plan to his life.

In a way, he thought, Antonia was the last of these games. It had been quickly taken up but, he realized, would take a long time to play out. It would need a score to come out right.

Arturo was not a man to fantasize, but in these evenings he began to indulge in thoughts of bits of old dreams, half-formed plans, and vague fears, with schemes he had before he went back to Italy and met Antonia. And as he pieced them together in his mind, he saw that Antonia had a place in them, that she had always had a place. He began to think of ways to make her feel that place.

As the number of these evenings grew, he began to calculate, as he had never done before, how much time he had to work out the game. He knew, somehow, that the illness had not entirely left him. He had always tried not to be sentimental about death, about his own death, at least. But now he felt as he hadn't before that his life would not always roll on as it had, that at a point ahead there was a signpost marking the end of it. He wanted to put the rest of the distance to good use.

Meanwhile, as Arturo knew, Antonia was restless. As she grew to know Pica better, the place shrank. It became Arturo's town in which she lived as a part of his life. She felt Pica's narrow streets tighten around her, its increasingly familiar places press in on her, its eyes watching her every move. Although she was in Yayaku by day, at night she dreamed of Italy. Sometimes she woke in the morning thinking she had to get ready to catch the train to Genoa. Then she realized where she was, and that the train ran only to Casilda.

In Pica, she had "obligations," as Arturo put it. It was strange how obligations gave form to her life, which had had no form at all before. She was like a stream that had meandered without force or direction on an empty plain. Now that someone tried to channel and dam the water, she strained against the banks. Where the channel moved north, she pushed to the south. Quietly, without being noticed, the water built up toward the bank, straining to burst out in sudden flood.

It was so dry in Pica. Day after day she looked out on the endless sunshine, slowly turning the palm fronds gray with dust. Everything seemed to grow brittle—the furniture, her skin, most of all her temper.

One morning she looked to see a cloud blowing up from the ocean. It was dark gray at the center, and as it passed over the plaza a few drops began to fall from it. "Rain," Antonia said out loud.

She ran to her room, and, from one of her Genoa trunks, pulled out an umbrella. Grasping it in her hand as an old soldier grasps a sword, she ran into the plaza.

The umbrella split in several places when she opened it, and the rain stopped so quickly that the cloth was hardly wet when she went back inside. Still, she patted the handle with love as she set the umbrella in the corner to dry.

A few moments later, she heard the street door bang open and footsteps running up the stairs. "Antonia," she heard Arturo shout.

She went out into the hall. "What's wrong?" she asked. "Why are you home in the middle of the morning?"

"Are you all right?" he asked, grabbing her hand.

"Of course! Why wouldn't I be? And don't squeeze my hand like that," she said, pulling away.

"Weren't you out in the plaza just now?" he asked, without letting go.

"Yes, but nothing bad happened. I didn't even get wet, it hardly rained at all."

Arturo looked at the umbrella in the corner. "So that's it," he said, and began to laugh.

"What, the umbrella? What are you laughing about, Arturo?"

"A moment ago," said Arturo, sitting down and pulling Antonia into his lap, "one of the street sweepers came right into my office in hysterics. She was shouting to everyone that my new wife had gone mad, that she was standing in the plaza in the rain with a little roof over her head."

"My umbrella!" said Antonia. "You can't mean that she'd never seen an umbrella."

"No, she hadn't. I know it seems ridiculous, but the story's probably all over town by now."

"All over town? What? I didn't do anything wrong! Can I help it if an ignorant old woman got frightened by an umbrella?"

Arturo frowned slightly and patted her hands. "No, it's not your fault, that's not what I meant," he said gently. "But you have to be careful. These people aren't very sophisticated, and the ladies have almost nothing better to do than gossip."

"But what has that got to do with me?" Antonia said, raising her voice.

"Hush, Antonia. Remember you are married now. In a way, you are part of me. And people watch me and you because we are important people here. I know it doesn't seem fair, but you have to care about what these people think of you."

"But I didn't come all this way to be spied on by fools! This is worse than at home! What kind of nonsense will I—"

Arturo grasped her hand and gave her a look. His face was very serious and sad, but it also seemed to be warning her that he might get angry in a moment.

"Oh, have it your way," said Antonia. "No more umbrellas. From what I see, I won't need one anyway."

She stood up, moving out of his reach and grabbing the umbrella with her left hand. She stood still for a moment, then shook the handle in the air. "Why do you side with them? Why do you put me under those stupid people? I am your wife! Not a silly, fat goose like the wives of your agents. Why did you bring me all this way to humiliate me like this?"

Her face was very red. Arturo moved toward her, but she pulled away and ran to her room. He heard the door slam behind her, and the key trunk turn in the lock. He thought of following her, but turned instead to go out.

As he crossed the front courtyard, something flew past his ear. It was the umbrella, which fell to the pavement with a smack like a slap on the face. He picked it up and looked up to the balcony, but no one was there.

"Antonia!" he called out, with anger in his voice. There wasn't a sound. He set the umbrella, whose point was bent from the fall, against the door and went out. When he came back home that night, the umbrella had gone, and he didn't see it again.

Antonia greeted him with a kiss, a delightful smile, and a magnificent dinner. Neither of them spoke of the afternoon adventure. That night their lovemaking was deep and enfolding and took them to the bottom of the sea.

THAT WAS the first of the battles; there were a few more in those first few weeks.

Although neither of them was particularly devout, Arturo and Antonia went to mass each Sunday. It was an "obligation," Arturo said, if not a holy one, then a practical one. Mass hadn't been a habit for Antonia since school, and because of this, she was not pleased to renew it. But in time she came almost to like Sundays, though she didn't really admit it to herself.

She would watch the plaza from the room with the balcony at the front of the house. It turned into a kind of stage as people gathered. The well-off people of the town, those who ran businesses or worked for the government, took the entire area around the fountain for themselves. Each family walked slowly up and down, showing off their best clothes. The young women of marriageable age were prominently displayed; each family seemed to have its own place. At the center was the bench where the prefect and the comandante of the garrison would discuss the events of the week.

Around the edge, the poorer families did their best with the scraps of land between the geranium beds. Beyond them sat a group of people—soldiers from the garrison, traveling strangers, sometimes workers from the mines and smelting plants from the north, mestizos, servants and other Indians who had taken up European ways. There was an anxious, restless air about these people; they took no particular place, but moved back and forth as if looking for a gap in the flower beds.

At the outer edge, almost in the street, huddled the Indians. They alone did not look in toward the fountain, but outward, toward the cathedral, the desert, the mountains beyond, and their city of Corequenque.

At noon, everyone went to mass. Antonia and Arturo passed through a long line of smiling, nodding heads; it reminded her of the little parade on her first day in Pica. The women put on their lace mantillas—white for the girls, black for the adults. Inside, they sat in the front and the men in the back. During the sermon, Antonia noticed, they would slip outside for cigarettes.

But the bishop was someone Antonia never grew to like. He was a large, round man who seemed to swell into his vestments as if he were a balloon. His head tipped back slightly when he spoke (as if casting a sidelong glance at heaven, Antonia thought later), but his small, dark eyes rested almost always on a tiny woman in black sitting in the front row.

The bishop reminded Antonia of a baritone she had once heard sing in Genoa, a baritone who, as the count pointed out, had made up for the thinness of his talent with his gestures. Like the baritone, the bishop moved slowly, as if the air were thick and heavy. There was a deliberateness, a calculation, in the slightest tremor of his face or hands. When he raised his arms, each finger found its separate place, like the petals of a flower slowly opening. Antonia was fascinated but, because of the baritone, distrustful. The gestures seemed not to echo the truth in his words, the rich sincerity of his voice, but to betray them. They were exquisite, beautiful, almost as fine as the movement of a dancer, but they seemed to her not to speak for God but instead of God.

"This man is a shell," Antonia thought to herself, "an emptiness who draws everything from that strange little woman he keeps his eyes on."

"Who is that little woman the bishop kept looking at?" she asked Arturo, when they came home on the first Sunday.

"That was his mother. She lives with him here in the bishop's palace and is always with him." He paused. "There are some people here who call her the 'anaconda's grandmother.' "

"Why do they call her that?"

"Partly because she comes from the east, from an hacienda beyond the mountains, just above the jungles where the anaconda lives. And partly because she reminds them of the anaconda that squeezes its victims to death before it swallows them."

Another "obligation" was the Ladies' Social Club, the chief function of which was a canasta party held every second and fourth Friday of the month. Although it was held in the houses of its members on a rotating basis, everyone knew that canasta was the particular property of the prefect's wife. It was she who had brought the game from the capital where, she said, she had learned it from the wife of the Argentine ambassador. For a long time, before there were official rules, she was the arbiter of the game.

The routine was always the same. The first time Antonia went, the game was moved specially to the prefect's house in her honor. The prefect's house was an old one, out on the edge of town. Over the years, it had been added to many times, expanding out toward the desert like a creeping plant. Most of the additions were made to fit the house with the latest fashions from the capital; when the fashions faded, the rooms were no longer used much and, since they were never refurbished, the house grew on and on. There was a detached ballroom now used for storage, and a neglected library with books all a generation old.

The prefect had eight daughters ranging in age from twenty to three. The prefect's wife was a tall woman, not so much plump as large and strong-looking. She smiled and laughed a good deal, and waved her hands in the air, but when she grabbed Antonia's arm to move her to her seat, her grip was so powerful it hurt. When one of the daughters embraced her, as they did often, she pressed the daughter to her so that the girl almost disappeared into her flesh. This is a woman who gets what she wants, Antonia thought.

The canasta routine was always the same. The guests arrived at four; tea was served with a profusion of sweets: elaborate pastries, homemade chocolates. No men ever appeared; the serious players often stayed on until ten in the evening, and the men in those families usually went out to dinner. These were definitely ladies' holidays.

The gossip started: Antonia, with her poor Spanish, could follow only some of it. The ladies began with the affairs of movie stars and the latest episode of *The Right to Be Born*, the radio soap opera from the capital. They slowly moved onto topics closer to home.

"Did you hear about María Sánchez? She's thrown Señor Belunda's wife out of the house!"

"*Mamacita!* You'd think she was his wife!"

"Perhaps soon. I hear she's been ordering a trousseau for that second daughter of theirs. Isabella—that's the one."

"True. She has eyes on that new lieutenant from the barracks. The one from Santa Victoria. She's sure to want her daughter to be legitimate."

"*Pobrecita!* Legitimate she might become, but happy with that one? Never. Such an *hijo de puta* (if you'll forgive me) that one is! He'll break every little heart in Pica before he's finished, with his big brown eyes and heart of stone. They say he has two mulatto mistresses already who want nothing better than to scratch each other's eyes out. Watch out for your little ones when he's around!"

"Ah, but who's to know? Ask the Virgin?"

"*Jesusito!* Is my seam crooked? Quick, check my stockings before the prefect's wife comes back."

"You're Arturo's wife, aren't you?" said an elderly little lady in pink sitting next to Antonia. "Ah, yes, they have said what a beauty you are! So many went to bed to cry into their pillows when you came to town! Ah! Such an enchanter your Arturo was! So many years he kept us guessing who he'd marry in the end! Ask anyone, they'll tell you! But, I can see he chose well. Isn't she a regular *Virgencita*, Tanta?"

"To be sure! To be sure! It's been years since we've had such a beauty in town. But look, my dear, doesn't she seem a little pale? A bit thin?"

"Yes, now that you mention it, she is. You should eat more, my pretty one. A man likes a sweet fish, but not all bones, eh!"

"It's the liver, you know? It's always the liver with you Italians. Listen, my dear, I will lend you my prescription. It's the latest cure from the capital. I can't tell you what agony it has delivered me from; twenty years of praying to the Virgin didn't help me much! You know, I have such a delicate constitution, quite a disadvantage in this climate. I was born and raised in the capital, you know, my dear. I'll bring some of my own supply by your house tomorrow. It will put you right soon. The liver is a thing that wants watching—don't let it go too long."

"Ah, no, Tanta. The little señora just needs a little careful feeding. Try one of these. The prefect's wife always seems to have the daintiest things, but then she must, mustn't she? You must tell me about your dress. Is it from Paris? You make us seem very out of date here."

The conversation went on. Antonia smiled and nodded, excusing herself for her lack of Spanish. Such a narrow world these ladies seemed to have. There was no talk of men, except in relation to marriage or affairs, or of the world of men. The only mention of the war, Antonia noticed, was to question its effect on fashions.

At five-thirty, lots were drawn and teams set up for bidding. The prefect's wife made a few adjustments, moving Antonia to her own table to "help explain the rules."

"No, no, my dear, only three wild cards are permitted. Just take these back, we won't notice," she said. "No, no, my dear, you mustn't take from the bottom of the pile. You really must pay attention to play well, Antonia dear."

There were giggles from the hall. "My daughters," the prefect's wife explained. "They are dying for a look at you, Antonia. May I call them in?"

Antonia nodded.

Half a dozen girls in pastel dresses lined up at the edge of the room, laughing at one another and covering their faces. The next Sunday, at mass, Antonia noticed they all had trimmed their hair to match hers.

Two of the older girls lingered by the windows overlooking the street. "Dolores, Celeste, what are you doing there?" the prefect's wife asked.

"Mama, it's Captain Martín!"

"Well, *por Dios*, come away from the window! What if he should see you staring at him like that?"

"That Captain Martín!" said the woman to Antonia's left, who wore a bracelet dripping with gold coins. "So young, so handsome! He's only a mestizo from a poor family, yet he is already just under the comandante. Some say"—she lowered her voice—"could it be true? Some say he's General Salas's son by an Indian woman!"

"Nonsense," said the prefect's wife. "I don't wish to hear any more foolishness about Captain Martín."

Antonia wanted to hear more, but something in the prefect's wife's frown made her think better of asking.

At the other tables, Antonia noticed, they were playing for money. From time to time, cries broke out, with loud accusations of cheating. "You drew too many!" "I did not!" "Count your cards!" "I did not draw too many!" Otherwise, the conversation grew sparse as the social players gradually departed and the serious players were drawn into their game, and Antonia thought of Count Mora's wife, of all things.

"When is the next meeting?" Arturo asked when Antonia came home.

"For me, never."

"What happened? Didn't they offer to make you a member?"

"I declined."

Arturo looked up from his chair. "Declined? This is not good."

"I don't care. I was bored there. All they did was gossip about everyone else in town."

Arturo frowned. "Come over here, Antonia." Antonia slowly did as she was told. Arturo put his arms around her waist and tried to pull her toward him.

"Antonia, my love," he said, "you are a much finer and more intelligent woman than any of them, but you worry me. Won't you be lonely with no one to talk to?"

"Why should I be lonely? And don't try to make me sit in your lap as if I were a little girl."

"My ill-tempered little girl," said Arturo, squeezing her tight and trying to kiss her neck.

"Oh! Let me go, Arturo."

"Come," said Arturo, standing and picking up Antonia in his arms. "Since you've decided to make enemies of everyone in town, come to the bedroom. We will have a council of war."

"AFTER THAT, he used to make little bargains with me," Antonia explained to the count. "We called them 'the business of home.' I wouldn't have to do certain things, but for everything I refused to do, Arturo could suggest something else I would have to do. I didn't have to go to the ladies' canasta parties, but I did have to go to mass; I didn't have to bake cakes for the bishop, but I did have to invite him to our Sunday lunches. We made a joke out of it, but I knew he still felt uneasy. I think it made us both uneasy that first year, as if we were somehow under siege."

VII

"In Pica, there were so few of us, really, who could be friends—maybe a dozen families in those days, the aristocracy of Pica. Only there weren't any real aristocrats there, the landowning kind like in the capital. Just the businessmen and some of their managers and the prefect and some of the officers from the garrison. We were in another world entirely, even with the Indians living under our own roofs.

"We gave one another lunches. They were so important; it's hard to imagine the importance of such a thing in any other town. We planned them carefully so we could all arrange to go. They took place after the noon mass and went on forever. There would be huge amounts of food, as many as eight or nine courses; the well-to-do had Chilean wines. The women went to great efforts, adopting the latest food fads from the capital and showing off as much as they could. Everything happened at these lunches—marriages were planned, business transacted, gossip exchanged, politics discussed, all sorts of rumors started. They would last until the early hours of the evening, when the young people went off to the movie theater in the plaza.

"The strangest lunches were given by Don Pedro, whom everyone thought was Arturo's rival in business. Don Pedro was considered very eccentric and not quite respectable; I think most people came to his lunches out of curiosity more than anything else. He was the opposite of Arturo. People called Don Pedro 'the pirate'; he had a great love of the sea, which no one could quite explain; he was short and rather fat and sort of lopsided, with a strange walk and one eye bigger than the other. He swore like a sailor, and he was supposed to be very sharp and ruthless in business. When Arturo got mad at one of his customers, he used to say, 'Go to the pirate and see what you get from him.'

"Nobody knew much about where Don Pedro came from. There were all sorts of rumors—that he had grown up in one of the richest haciendas in the country, that he had studied in Paris, that he had murdered his father and run away, that he was an illegitimate son of the king of Spain by an Argentine actress. He had six sons who were the absolute terror in town.

"Every time a young girl got pregnant, the family would blame it on one of Don Pedro's sons and go to him for money, though he always just swore at them.

"He had a huge house by the plaza that he had built out of several older ones. It had a series of stucco arches across the front which made it look Roman. I think Don Pedro got the idea from a movie. He must have had a dozen servants, among them a Chinese cook and a French one—but his household always seemed on the verge of disaster. The garden was hopelessly overgrown despite the three gardeners, and they kept many birds. These were another of Don Pedro's passions, and he was always having new canaries or parrots brought in from the jungles beyond the mountains. He never kept them in cages, and at his lunches they would always fly around and sometimes did their business in the soup. They also swore, just like him.

"Don Pedro's lunch parties were held only once or twice a year. The food was always very good, and Don Pedro, who loved eating and drinking, always had the best wines. But the lunches were terribly disorganized; the servants (they wore strange blue uniforms like toy soldiers) dropped dishes and tripped over the birds. And Don Pedro shouted and laughed at everything.

"But the oddest thing about the lunches was that his wife was never there. Don Pedro always apologized for her and said she was feeling tired, as if everyone was used to seeing her, though she never once appeared. She didn't belong to the Ladies' Social Club or go to mass, either, though it was rumored the bishop heard her confession in private in the middle of the night. Most people saw her only when she went out for a drive—Don Pedro had a huge black car with a chauffeur—wearing enormous jewels that Don Pedro gave her. I also used to see her standing in the balcony in the early morning, wearing a silk kimono and brushing out her long, reddish-brown hair, which was very pretty.

"Magdalena had been Don Pedro's mistress for many years before he married her, which he did just after the death of their second son.

As someone's mistress she was never part of the respectable circles. After Don Pedro married her, she was invited to the social functions, but she never went. She never even sent her regrets. People resented this and concluded she was either a snob or a madwoman. She was very beautiful, and some said she had been an actress in the capital before he brought her to Pica. Others said she had been a whore. Some young men used to direct traveling salesmen to her house. Her sons used to let them into the house, where they sat in the courtyard until the Chinese cook chased them away with the cleaver.

"In public, Don Pedro and Arturo were supposed to be great enemies. On the street, Arturo, who was so polite to everyone, hardly nodded to Don Pedro, and Don Pedro made jokes about Arturo behind his back. Don Pedro was never invited to our lunches, though we went to his.

"But at night, after dinner, Don Pedro would sometimes come into the house by the back stairs. Arturo made it clear that my presence was not required, so I would greet Don Pedro and leave them. They would sit in Arturo's study and drink brandy and talk business for hours. Sometimes he and Arturo went away on 'business trips' at the same time, but I think they went off somewhere together.

"Magdalena frightened me a little because she reminded me of my mother. But I was fascinated by Don Pedro. To please me Arturo once invited him to dinner when Magdalena was away. I worked very hard on the food because I so wanted to impress Don Pedro. After the meal was over, he said it was the best meal he had ever had in Pica. It was the nicest compliment I had ever had from anyone there."

VIII

DON PEDRO ARRIVED in Pica out of nowhere, not long after Arturo's uncle had died. He came in a long flatbed truck loaded with kerosene stoves. Both the flatbed and the stoves were somewhat of a novelty in Pica in those days, so he attracted a great deal of attention. He sold all the stoves out of a tent he pitched at the edge of town and, when they were all gone, he sold the truck to Arturo for a little cash and a used Ford automobile. Then Don Pedro disappeared.

Two or three months later he was back. He had a new, flashier car and a lot of cash. He bought out a failing business just south of the plaza and set himself up in the same line of work as Arturo's.

Arturo was not happy. He had been in Pica just over two years and was just starting out. Many of his uncle's customers and even some of his partners thought he was too young to take over the business and didn't trust him yet. And Don Pedro seemed to be a sharper trader.

Don Pedro said the car Arturo had sold him had been worthless and let it be known all over town that Arturo was a thief and a shady dealer. He began to build up his agency so that he could match Arturo in every line of business.

Soon, customers were coming to Arturo saying things like "Don Pedro said he could get it for me—" The whole town could feel the tension between them. Sometimes, when Arturo walked into a café, all conversation would suddenly cease. Heads would turn back and forth between him and the corner where Don Pedro sat with a handful of cronies. The same thing happened when they passed each other on the street: People stood still, watching to see what they would do.

They did nothing. Arturo usually nodded stiffly; Don Pedro coughed or adjusted his lapel, his eyes, perhaps because of their uneven size, seemed to drift off into the distance. People noticed that at these times their gait, usually so full of strength and swagger, faltered, as if they were unsure whether they would walk on or turn back the way they came.

Arturo began to have trouble sleeping. His partners looked sullen and began to whisper among themselves. Arturo's mistress complained that he no longer cared about her, that even when they made love he seemed to be going over his inventory.

In fact, both men's businesses were doing well, even prospering. Despite Don Pedro's growing success, Arturo had more orders than ever. Clients smiled and pressed his arm. "We went to see Don Pedro," they said. "He made us a good offer, but we prefer to do business with you. We feel safer with an honest face than with that pirate." Arturo smiled and tried to look calm, but he didn't feel it in his heart.

Meanwhile, other businessmen in town, the ones with only one or two agencies, were closing up shop. "With these two giants walking the streets, nobody pays attention to us anymore." Eventually, they went to Don Pedro and Arturo to sell their agencies.

Nearly a year went by. Arturo's mistress left him to return to her family in the north. Don Pedro could be seen most afternoons in the café, drinking his favorite liqueur hour after hour and making low-voiced comments about "so-called respectable men of business."

Once, in the early hours of the morning, while it was still dark outside, Arturo was awakened by a handful of pebbles thrown against his window. He looked out and saw a dark figure in the street. It was Don Pedro, motioning him to come down.

Arturo dressed quickly, tucked an old pistol in his belt.

"Shh!" said Don Pedro when Arturo came out. "Speak softly. We don't want anyone to see us."

"What do you want, Don Pedro?"

"Do you like to fish?"

"Like to fish? I haven't done any fishing since I was a boy in Italy. What do you mean?"

"I mean, I want you to come fishing with me. Here is my car, all loaded up and ready. You need only bring your clothes. I have a boat and a place on the shore."

Arturo stared at him in astonishment. "How can I do that? Are you crazy? I have a business to manage and so do you."

"Do what I did—leave a note saying you went to the capital on urgent business. It won't bankrupt us to have a day or two to ourselves."

So Arturo agreed, mostly because he couldn't think of anything else to say. But he took the pistol with him.

Don Pedro drove east on the road to Casilda, but turned off before reaching the customs station. They traveled along a rough track over the desert and, just as dawn was breaking, reached the sea.

The pink and gold of the sunrise broke into long streaks over the silver surface of the water. The sand, littered with driftwood and the rubbish of fishing boats and steamers, was a pale yellow band stretching unbroken as far as Arturo could see in both directions. The only sounds were the slow lapping of the waves and the calls of a few ocean birds.

Don Pedro steered northward along the beach until they came to a tiny shack built mostly of gray weathered driftwood and a bit of rusting sheet metal.

"My castle," said Don Pedro. "I bought this and the land a month ago. Someday I will build a real castle here."

Arturo helped him unload the fishing gear, some cans of food, and two cots. Then he followed Don Pedro out to sit on the sand.

"Why do I love the sea?" asked Don Pedro. "Have I ever been a sailor or a fisherman? No, and I wouldn't want to be. I want the sea as a mistress, not a wife.

"There are no roads on the sea. You can go in any direction you want if your boat is seaworthy. The water cares nothing for human beings, and a man—even a big, important man—is as nothing on its surface."

Arturo nodded.

"I can see we are simpatico after all," said Don Pedro, looking at Arturo with his smaller eye. "Let me share my mistress with you."

They spent three days together by the ocean. In the early mornings they rowed out in Don Pedro's little boat and fished until noon. They spent the heat of the day sleeping in the shade of the shack, ate the day's catch for supper, and stayed up late drinking rum by an open fire.

Don Pedro did most of the talking. He told Arturo all about his life before he came to Pica; it was as if he had been a man lost in the desert for years without anyone to talk to.

"I was born on a hacienda north of the capital," he began. "My father was the third son of a wealthy landowner, with more than a thousand peasants on his estate. I don't remember much about my grandfather. He was supposed to be a mean and stingy man; my father never said a good word about him. He had sent my father to the capital to the university, where he was supposed to study law. But my father wanted to be a poet. He wrote long epic poems about the conquistadores and the Incas. Were they any good? I can't say; I can't be objective about them because my father wrote them. But it was because of his poetry that my mother married him.

"My mother was from the capital and had a family in the government then. My father had always dreamed of getting away and living in Europe, and through my mother's family connections, he was made consul in Nice. I was only eight when we sailed away, and it was almost twenty years before I saw my country again.

"My father loved living in France as much as he had imagined he would. My mother did not; she detested it. My father's official duties were light, and he had plenty of time to devote to his poetry and to new habits—drinking, gambling, and mistresses.

"My mother grew ill; she asked to be taken home. She said she would die if she had to stay in Nice. My father was preoccupied. My mother stayed in bed while my father went to the opera or the theater or out walking along the Promenade des Anglais.

"After three years, my mother really did die. A year after that there was a revolution in Yayaku. 'There is nothing like a revolution, to clear the mind,' my father said. But I think he was referring to the French Revolution. He lost his job but he didn't seem to worry. We moved to Paris and took a flat on the Avenue Hoche.

"He got to know a lot of artists, or people who called themselves artists. He referred to them as his 'fellow poets.' They ate his food and pretended to admire his poetry (he wrote only in French by that time). They brought their friends to his parties. There were usually two or three of them staying with us, and when they left, something—silver, the little objects my father liked to collect—often went with them.

"Perhaps some of them were real artists. I'm sure some of them must have been. Or perhaps all artists are like that. But since then I have had very bad feelings about poets and composers, painters and critics. At our house they only seemed to talk and eat.

"By this time, my father was drinking English gin from the time he got out of bed, usually at one or two in the afternoon, until he collapsed at night. Everyone was robbing us more or less openly. The servants, the merchants, my father's friends and mistresses. I was too young to know what to do about it. My father made a big show out of being generous to everyone. But I think he was mostly afraid of being left alone, abandoned, and that if he made people stop stealing from us, they would all go away.

"When the war came, we were living in three rooms in the Rue de l'Estrapade. My mother's money was gone and there had been complaints about the noise. We were living on a pittance from my father's family. The visitors were down to a trickle: only those who were truly starving and didn't mind coming to us in our reduced circumstances. These were my favorites, in a way.

"After the Armistice, we were quite alone. My father spent most of his time in bed. 'Tell our guests I am too ill to come down,' he would say. 'But please tell them to enjoy themselves without me.' No doubt his friends were enjoying themselves, but it was no longer with us, because nobody ever came.

"My father insisted I study law at the University of Paris. Up until then, my education had been anything but practical—I had had strange tutors. Most of them were friends of my father's, artists who taught me about such things as poetry and astrology. I went to the lycée in Nice for a while. And of course I picked up some things from my father's mistresses. But I managed to pass the baccalaureate somehow.

"I made a show of going to classes, but I was really learning something else: how to keep us alive. I've always been a good talker; 'Mesmer,' some of our Paris friends called me. It proved useful in certain lines of business, and I managed with this and by pawning what valuables we had left to keep us from starving.

"At last, it became clear that my father was dying. My grandfather had died some time before, and with his death the small amount the family gave us stopped completely. My uncle ran the hacienda and the family now, and I wrote to him.

"He sent a one-way, third-class steamship ticket to Yayaku and a short note. 'The ticket is for you,' he wrote. 'If you intend to use it, write to me and I will see what can be done for you when you return home. As for my brother, he has been running along the road to hell all his life. I have no wish to impede his progress now.' The ticket came in handy. I cashed it in, and it helped pay for the funeral.

"Only one of my father's old friends came to see him laid to rest—a crazy poet who wore a velvet cape and a broad-brimmed hat.

" 'Cheer up,' he said, after we'd thrown handfuls of dirt on my father's coffin. My father is dead, too, and he left me some money. I've dropped poetry and all those artists and decided to become a millionaire. I'm off to the Amazon to set up a plantation. You,' he said, touching my chin with his silver cane tip, 'you can be my assistant.' So I sold what was left in the flat and went with him.

"I don't know if my poet friend ever became a millionaire because I gave him the slip as soon as we landed in Rio. It took me nearly three years to work my way around the continent to Yayaku. I can't tell you how strange it was hearing people speak Spanish all around me, when I'd spoken it only to my father for so many years.

"I went up to the hacienda. I was tired. My line of work was hard enough in Paris, but it was much worse over here. I was penniless and in rags.

"My uncle was dead too, by then. My cousin was the head of the family. 'It's not good to have a member of my family looking like a beggar,' he said. He gave me 10,000 reales and told me to go away.

"From some business associates in the capital I heard of Pica. 'It is the town of lost souls,' they said. 'It is where the homeless make their home.' So I went there.

"And now I am becoming a rich man! A good story, is it not?"

Arturo nodded. Although he didn't say so, it was a story not too different from his own.

On the last morning, Arturo awoke to find Don Pedro whittling sticks with his knife and sticking them in the sand.

"What are you doing?" Arturo asked.

"Come," said Don Pedro. "There is enough in Pica for both of us. Let us be enemies in public; you can be the respectable businessman, I can be 'the pirate.' But there is no need to fight over anything."

The sticks stood for the agencies. All morning they traded them back and forth, and they came out happy with the bargains they had made. Arturo had even managed to unload one or two of his more troublesome partners.

IX

AT FIRST, ANTONIA told no one that she had met Magdalena, not even Arturo. She stole away to visit her often, two or three times a week. They would talk together in Magdalena's sitting room, which, Antonia imagined, resembled a Chinese boudoir. It was a small room. The walls were covered in a slightly faded lavender brocade. Two enormous couches full of silk pillows embroidered with Chinese motifs faced each other. Between them stood a low table with a glass top. Magdalena had carefully arranged her collection of combs beneath the glass. Her silver hand mirror sat on the table together with a large leather-bound book. The book had a lock and Antonia assumed it was Magdalena's diary. Large vases of dry flowers stood on a dark Oriental rug very much like the ones Antonia had seen at the count's house in Genoa. A bronze Buddha had been placed next to the door as if to guard it.

During their first meetings, it was mostly Antonia who did the talking. Magdalena would sit on the couch with her legs crossed, her patient eyes bright with what looked like unshed tears while Antonia spoke. Magdalena would respond in a low, deep, comforting voice.

"Is it true you met Arturo on the train?" asked Magdalena one day.

"Yes, it is true, but how do you know that?"

"Your Arturo told my Pedro. He also told him it was the most startling thing that had ever happened to him; that until then he did not believe in love at first sight."

Antonia laughed. "I was terrified of our feelings. He followed me for days. And I looked everywhere for him."

"And you married him three weeks later?"

"Two weeks. Yes, two weeks—that is also true."

"And you came here right after the wedding without him?"

"Yes, he needed to settle a few things in Italy, but he was worried about the war. He said it would be easier for a single man to get out later than for a man and a woman. I don't quite know how I got the nerve to do it. But I had such faith in him, and I knew he would never let me down."

"But married in two weeks! How romantic."

"It might seem that way, but it didn't feel that way at the time. Everything, including Pica, was different from what I had imagined. While I was waiting all that time, there were moments when I was afraid I had forgotten what he looked like. I had only a few pictures of him, and I looked at them over and over. Sometimes it was Toma's confidence that kept me believing. Everyone, including Arturo's partners, was so suspicious of me. Strangely, though, I enjoyed my time alone in Pica. For the first time in my life I could do what I wanted. I don't know, it was as if all my life I had been waiting for a time when I could be truly free. When Arturo returned, we both felt a little bit like strangers. Neither one of us knew what to expect.

"Changing his house around! Only when he arrived did I realize it might shock him. But if he was uncomfortable about it, he never let me know. I guess he thought there were more important things for us to worry about. The night he arrived, he said half teasingly, 'You are like a stranger I very much want to know.' "

"Coming to Pica changed my life, too," said Magdalena. "But in the opposite way. I had been free all my life. I had known many men. But Pedro was different. When he came to see me, it was something wonderful. Like a storm he swept me and I was all his. Then he would leave, I never knew for how long. There were no letters in between. When he came back it was as if he had never left. The storm of happiness again! While he was gone, I worked hard at being an actress. I was busy, but I was always waiting for him. I wanted him to be the one who knocked at my dressing room after my performances. I would pretend he was sitting in the audience.

"Once he went away for a very long time. I really thought I would never see him again. I asked everyone I knew, but no one had heard of him. I refused to go on tour with my company for fear that he might come and not find me.

"Then one day, I will never forget the date—it was the tenth of September—I walked into my dressing room after a performance and there was Pedro standing with his arms open. '*Peliroja*,' he yelled. That was his nickname for me, for my red hair. I fell into his arms. We held each other for a long time. I was so happy. I started to cry and couldn't stop. He then led me to the little table where I kept my combs, and there he had placed two tickets. 'We are going,' he said, 'on vacation.'

"I was in the middle of a play. I had an important role. I just left. For me it was an enormous chance; I knew my company would never take me back again. I left without even packing a suitcase. He took me to the south of Chile. We stayed in an isolated cottage overlooking a lake. I was surprised at how much I liked keeping house with him. Pedro would catch fish; he had a knack for it. We would grill them in a little fire he made outside. I used to say the fish asked him to catch them. 'Only the lady fishes,' he would reply.

"Looking back, it seems strange that we never spoke of the future.

"When the time came to go back, the idea of leaving him was impossible to bear. Also, I thought I was pregnant. I had been pregnant before, and never felt any love for the child I had decided not to have. But his unborn child clung to me, and I to the child.

"So, when he wanted to bring me to Pica, I accepted. I said good-bye to my friends in the theater. They thought I was somewhat mad to give up what I had worked so hard for, but I yearned for children, many of them, and Pedro and a real home all my own."

"And how was it when you got to Pica?" asked Antonia.

"My life was completely changed, as yours was. Suddenly, I had to keep a large house and manage servants. People stared at me on the street. Even the servants were disgruntled at working for someone they considered just a mistress. Pedro had his business to worry about, his life away from me. He became a stranger. I laugh now, but when he left for the office the first morning, I didn't know what to do until he came back. For a long time my day began when he came home from the office.

"This business of us not being married—I even got a letter from the bishop's mother: 'With your fat belly,' she wrote, 'I would be embarrassed to be seen in public. Your child will be a bastard; I will see to it that my son doesn't baptize him.' How vulgar, I thought. What must the others be like? Pedro taught me the advantage in their disapproval. I could stay home and not go to those dreary canasta parties. It seemed better to be a mistress than a wife, and Pedro liked it that way, too."

"Why did you marry later?"

"After the death of our second child, Don Pedro's lawyer came from Montana de Plata. He was worried about the legal status of our children. The laws of Yayaku didn't protect mistresses or illegitimate children, and if something happened to Pedro we would be in a very difficult position. So we did it. We just went to an old priest Pedro knew, who made me a wedding band out of a jasmine branch. He had us married in a few minutes. I don't know how people found out, but the next day I was invited to join the canasta club. I never even answered their invitation."

"A wise decision," said Antonia. They both laughed.

Another afternoon, Magdalena asked, "And how is your Arturo?"

"Oh, he is well," answered Antonia.

"Tell me how your are days together."

"Well, he goes off in the early morning."

"Yes? And after the morning?" Magdalena asked with a small smile.

"Well, he usually closes down his business at noon. Then he comes home and we eat together in the courtyard, under the jacaranda, alone. Sometimes it reminds me of when we first got to know each other."

"And what do you talk about?"

"At first I tried to ask him about his business. It is so important to him. Often his eyes drift away from mine, and I know he is back at his office, going over his ledgers or his inventories. The body is there, but he isn't. It's important to me to hold on to something that is important to him, something that would help me understand who he is. But he doesn't like to discuss his business with me."

"Men never do. Isn't it silly of them? But you must have persisted."

"Yes, at first I made some little suggestions—I was worried about how disorganized everything looked in the office and in the warehouse. 'How can you manage with everything falling over everything else?' I asked. 'What would you say about me if I kept your house like that?'

"But he always said things were better that way. 'It keeps my partners at bay,' he said. 'Everything is in order, but only in my head. It is safer that way.'

"We talk mostly of inconsequential things. Sometimes I talk about the things I want to do to the house, sometimes I complain about the servants or how hard it is to get things in Pica. But that is not what is on my mind."

"What is on your mind?"

"I try to imagine—I spend hours and hours at it—I try to imagine what he thinks of me."

"And what do you imagine?"

"Nothing. That is just it. I come up with nothing."

"Shall I try to imagine for you?"

"Please, if you think you can."

Magdalena leaned back on her cushion and pulled her legs up under her. She closed her eyes and began to speak.

"He loves you very much, even more than when you were first married. It is a rare passion he has for you, one that goes deep, like the roots of a tree in the desert, roots that drink rivers that are buried under the sand. But you also frighten him. You are strange, you are different. People—the simple people in this town—find you mysterious. You attract attention. You are not dried up like them. You are full of fire and dark waters.

"Arturo thinks: 'They watch her moves, they copy her clothes, the way she wears her hair. They wonder what she will do next.' He thinks: 'I have married a woman of style, a woman of fashion beyond fashion.' He thinks: 'I have married an original.'

"But he also thinks this: 'On the other hand, she is a nuisance. It didn't take long for her to offend almost everyone. She won't take advice. She won't take my advice and join the Ladies' Club. She acts as if she doesn't care about anyone else in town.' It isn't his fault, my dear Antonia, that the unimaginative ladies of this dry place can find only such topics of conversation as servants, children, and other people's indiscretions. It isn't his fault that they spend the whole time devouring little sweet cakes, or that they giggle when they mention your Arturo's youthful follies.

"Listen, Antonia, to these thoughts. He thinks: 'I have a jewel, but one without a proper setting. I want my jewel to shine and stay fixed and secure at the same time. What is the right setting for this rare jewel? What is she missing?' "

"But what is the setting, Magdalena? What is it?"

"Romance, intrigue, a gentle, delectable tragedy wrapped in sweetness. Something that will pull you away and then back into his arms again, so that he can hold you even tighter than before."

X

IT WAS DON PEDRO who brought up Antonia when they had dinner one evening.

"Your beautiful wife has made quite an impression," he said.

"Yes, I am afraid she has."

"You don't seem entirely pleased, Don Arturo."

"Well, it is not entirely as I expected," said Arturo, turning slightly away from Don Pedro and glancing toward the door.

"Go on, Don Arturo, tell me what you expected."

"In Italy, she seemed different from how she seems now."

"You mean she has changed?"

"Not exactly. She was such a quiet, shy girl when I met her. She was a fragile thing, desperate for some kind of strength. When I held her, she seemed to reach right inside me for something to hold on to. She was terrified when I made her leave Pica before me; I had to force her. But, when I returned—"

"She had found her own strength."

"Yes, and her own will. I worry that this place is too small for her, that all of us here are too small for her. Every day I can see her growing bored. I wanted someone to raise my family. Now I am afraid she will break away before we have a chance."

Don Pedro lit the cigar he had been holding in his mouth. "Tell me, my friend," he said after he had filled the air around him with a blue haze, "tell me what you want in a woman. Do you want a rose?"

"What do you mean?"

"A rose is a beautiful, gentle thing. It hasn't much strength, but it smells sweet. It blooms for a day or two, then fades away, leaving its bitter fruit. That's all. Is this what you expected from Antonia?"

"Well, not exactly."

"This is what you are telling me, though. To love a woman, particularly a woman like Antonia, you must also love surprises. Did I ever tell you my wife surprised me?"

"No."

"When I met her—it was before I even came to Pica—she was an actress in the capital. She was a great romantic actress, she was even becoming famous. On stage she was full of passion, she was a storm that tossed the other actors around like little rowboats and swept over the audience with a hot and relentless force. 'What must it be to possess such a woman!' I thought. 'What ecstasy to make love to such a woman.'

"Of course, she had admirers, most of them far handsomer and richer than I was then. But I made her conquest a particular adventure, and once I had had her (and she didn't disappoint me) I left her.

"I came here, I began to prosper and grow rich. I became established. But then I grew bored. The women of this desert place were tiresome. I longed for that thick, humid love—that love like the air before a hurricane. And I wanted something else. I wanted to startle the simple people of Pica, to show them a woman who was not afraid to be the wife of a pirate. I wanted her to walk beside me in these narrow streets like a panther. I wanted to stun you all with her beauty and her wildness, which only I could hold in check.

"So I went back to the capital and brought her back here. I built her this grand house in the middle of town, a stage for her to play out her greatest roles. But no sooner had she moved in, than she lost her taste for dramatic acting. She grew into something sweet, gentle, and shy. She seemed to want to do nothing but produce children and whisper to her secret friends in her private room. And when she had borne half a dozen of my children, I married her. What could I do? Throw her out because she no longer fit my dreams of what she should be?

"No, my friend. I grew to like her surprises, to be thankful for them. A good woman is like a good piece of music. She changes without your noticing it; she brings out new melodies, plays unexpected harmonies. There is no end to her surprises. And if you are lucky, you will learn to listen and find songs inside yourself you never knew existed.

"I think Antonia is such a woman."

• • •

"ALL THAT first year in Pica," Antonia told the count, "I felt Arturo was searching for something, something for me. Something to show that the gossip and raised eyebrows didn't matter to him. Something to show me that he loved me for being different from the others."

"And did he find it?"

"He found one thing."

"And what was that?"

"He remembered what I said in Genoa—that my piano was more important to me than anything else. There were only two pianos in Pica then. One was the old battered upright in the opera house; the other belonged to the bishop's mother. He knew the ladies of the town craved any kind of diversion, and playing the piano was something I did really well.

"He didn't say anything to me, but after much searching, he located a suitable instrument—a huge concert-sized Bosendorfer—in La Paz.

"It was too big for the little train that went over the mountains, so he had to have it carried by mules over the mud-track roads through the valleys. It took weeks.

"When it finally reached town, the crate was battered and covered with dirt. He tried to keep it a secret by sending me out to the cathedral when it arrived. But it created such a commotion in the street that I ran out to see what it was. It took six of the biggest warehousemen to hoist it up our stairs. It looked magnificent when it was uncrated— much bigger than my piano in Artemisia. And what beautiful inlay on the keyboard. But it was such a disappointment when I tried to play it! Half the keys made no sound at all, and the rest were so out of tune it was painful. It was infested with moths that had eaten all the felt, and soon they were all over the house. It took months to get rid of them.

"Arturo finally had to send all the way to the capital for a tuner who came down and spent nearly a month with us working on the piano. He was a big fat man who liked to wear dignified clothes like a lawyer, but he soon had to take off his black coat and roll up his sleeves. His arms were covered in filth to his elbows in no time, and his shirt was drenched in sweat.

"How he yelled at us when he saw the way things were inside! He called us criminals for neglecting such an instrument before we could explain how we had got it. He worked, and worked, and drove us all crazy with his pounding on the keys from morning to night. Then he bored us to death at dinner talking about all the fine pianos he had worked on in the capital.

"But in the end, the piano was put right. Such an instrument! It was almost a terror to play, the sound was so big and full! They used to tell me you could hear it in the cathedral.

"I spent days and days just practicing. I can't tell you what it was like—like coming home and finding everyone rich, and happy, and younger and more beautiful than you remembered them. I lost myself in the old music just as I had when I was a girl.

"Right away, Arturo wanted to have a concert. I was terrified of that, of course. I hadn't played in front of people since I was a girl at school, and the only person I felt comfortable playing for was Papa. But Arturo insisted. He said it was his 'payment' for going to all the trouble over the piano. I knew he wanted me to do it for other reasons—to make up for not going to the canasta parties or baking cakes for the bishop, a way for me to be different without offending anyone. He thought there should be concerts every week—on Thursday afternoons. It was to be my setting. So I agreed to have one. 'If they don't enjoy it,' he said, 'you don't have to do it again.' "

"And did they enjoy it?"

"Well, not exactly. Arturo should have known. He insisted on inviting practically the whole town, even people I hardly knew. We had never had so many people in the house before. The ladies looked around at my Indian things and were shocked. 'But we thought you were rich!' they said.

"I was so worried over it all. We didn't have enough things, so nothing matched. I used some silver and crystal from home which contrasted with the local things. 'Nobody will notice,' Arturo said. Of course, he was right. That was the problem.

"The playing went well. I played some Chopin and a Mozart sonata that I had known for year, a firm, solid piece—almost a march. It reminded me of Mama—of her walk, which was my favorite thing about her."

"So they did like it."

"Well, as I said, not exactly. I think most of the ladies weren't used to sitting still without talking for long except at mass. And they certainly weren't used to Chopin and Mozart. They tittered and scraped their chairs on the floor. And of course, most of the men were bored to tears. They coughed and lit up cigars and stared up at the ceiling as if they wished they could float out through the roof."

"Didn't anyone appreciate your music?"

"Well, yes, one person did. And he really saved the whole thing for me. But it caused no end of trouble later on."

"Who was that?"

"His name was José Martín. He was Captain Martín then, the big heartthrob of the garrison, the dashing mulatto. When I stopped playing, everyone just sat for a moment looking half asleep. Then Captain Martín jumped out of his chair and shouted: 'Bravo, bravo Signora Rontella!' He shouted, just as if he were at the opera. So, of course, everyone stood up and started clapping, too.

"Captain Martín came over to me and took both my hands in his. 'Allow me,' he said, 'to kiss the instrument of so much beauty. I have never been so moved by anything as by your playing.' And it was true, I saw tears in his eyes! 'You must promise to give us all such pleasure often!' And he kissed my hands again. The guests had their mouths open, and they all rushed up to say that I had to give more concerts, a concert every week. They wouldn't let go of me until I agreed. Such a nuisance! I wished I had played the wrong notes!

"But Arturo was pleased. When everyone had gone, he took me into his arms and told me how proud he was. But he didn't know what trouble he had started! With Captain Martín, I mean."

XI

BY THE TIME José Martín entered the National Military Academy, he had already acquired his aura. He had had it, in fact, since his first year at school.

It was something about him that people noticed, but of which they were never fully conscious. Even when people praised him, which both his teachers and his fellow students often did, they never spoke directly of the aura, only of its effects.

The aura José Martín had was difficult to describe precisely. Part of it was his self-confidence. He seemed always absolutely sure of himself, but this did not mean he bragged or boasted; he did neither. It did not mean that he always knew the answers to his teachers' questions, though, being an exceptionally bright and hardworking student, he usually did. The aura had a calm, quiet quality about it; it was in his eyes, which were clear and always unflinching, and in his voice, which was full, hard, and commanding without ever being loud or harsh.

In class, when asked a question to which he did not know the answer, José Martín never squirmed or made excuses. He answered, simply and clearly: "I do not know, Sir." His teachers, after they understood that he was not merely being insolent, dropped the cutting, sardonic manner they assumed when faced with ignorance. They accepted his answers as statements of fact, forgave him without saying so, and moved on. His manner was so direct, so utterly lacking in trepidation, that he gained the respect of the entire staff, from the rector to the lowest sweeper. His teachers lavished praise and honor on him. He received this homage with cool poise, with the smallest polite smile. Even the most ambitious of his classmates were unable to be jealous of him.

"Martín has an inner light," said the rector, and selected him for the priesthood. On his graduation, José could have claimed the highest scholarship to the Jesuit university, but he had his own plans and instead chose the military academy. The rector, who believed that any decision José made could not be wrong, acquiesced with a fatherly smile and a pat on José's forearm.

At the academy the talk was of honor and control. In those days, most of the instructors were still retired French officers, stiff, straight-backed men with bristling white mustaches. They spoke of the Third Republic with contempt and of the Dreyfus affair as if it had happened the week before. "The facts of the case show that the Jew was no soldier," said one of them. "Had he been, he would not have protested his sentence, particularly if he were innocent. Like a politician, he confused justice with honor. For a true soldier, honor comes first, second, and third."

The commandant, a Yayakuan, spoke of the academy as purgatory. "You enter this river of fire," he said, "as naked as when you entered this world. No prayer from high places can help you. Your mother's money, your father's position, are burned away. Your childhood, soft or hard as it may have been, is burned away. Your ambitions, your love for the easy life, your weakness for wine and women, are burned away. Only then, if anything remains, can you raise to join the elect.

"Order, obedience, and authority: we observe these three," said the commandant. "But the greatest of these is order. Our fatherland lies in the darkness of politics, corruption, and self-interest, in the night of poverty and backwardness. Order is the light we must strive toward."

In the academy José Martín's aura was noticed again. He was singled out for special training and assignments and had meetings alone with the commandant.

One hot August afternoon, as the cadets stood at attention on the dusty parade ground, three men passed in front of the rows of the dark green uniforms. One was the commandant, one was a young officer, and the third was General Salas himself.

The sun gleamed on the gold braid on the general's shoulder, and glinted on the medals on his chest as he moved. The general's walk had an irregularity about it, as if he were slightly lame but tried hard not to show it. It was only in contrast to the stiff gait of the younger men on either side of him that it was noticeable at all. With each step, the general's head had a tiny extra bounce like the head of a thistle springing back against the wind.

The three men walked slowly without stopping until they came to José Martín. Here the commandant stopped, and, without speaking, turned his head toward the general a few degrees, as if to say, "This is the one." The general stepped up to José so close that he could hear the rasps in the general's breath. The general tilted his head back so that the sunlight broke through the shadow under the black visor, and José could see his pale green eyes for the first time.

The general's thin, wrinkled lips pressed together in what could have been a suppressed frown or a smile. He reached out his hand and laid it along José's neck for a moment. Then he abruptly dropped his arm and turned away.

The three soldiers moved on down the row, and a few minutes later the general and his adjutant left the academy. But the effects of the visit were powerful and lasting. For the rest of his time at the academy, José Martín was known as "the one who was touched."

XII

"TELL ME ABOUT this Captain Martín," said the count. "Antonia, are you blushing? Was this a real romance, after all?"

"No, it was silly. I just put my foot in the stew over that one."

"Did you? Did you fall in love with him?"

"No, no. I told you. He fell in love with me. I let him fall in love with me."

"You encouraged his affections?"

"No, that is, I didn't intend to. I was so young. I didn't know how to handle it."

"Tell me how it happened."

"Oh! it's embarrassing! What can I say?"

"Come, now," said the count, "you brought it up. Now you must pay."

"I suppose."

"How did you meet him?"

"I am not sure. I used to see him on the street. Someone must have pointed him out to me at some point, because I knew who he was, and he used to nod when we passed each other. He gave me a look—all the men did, but this was different—a look like he wanted to eat me up. A hungry look. It was odd, because otherwise he was so self-contained, so confident. He had a kind of reputation in town, people held him in awe. It was said that he was a protégé of General Salas. Great things were expected of him. You treated him with a kind of respect, more than he would have gotten because of his age and position. You treated him better than that because everyone thought he would be important one day. You wanted to be able to say you were his friend. Even Arturo treated him that way, and usually he didn't have much to do with the army men."

"So, how did you get to know him?"

"He kept coming to those recitals I gave. He came with the commandant and his wife the first few times. It's funny because I think he really appreciated the music. I think he might have been the only one there who did, who felt it deeply, I think. Sometimes I was sure I saw tears in his eyes."

"Maybe it was just his infatuation."

"That might have been part of it, but there was more to it than that. Perhaps the infatuation and the music were all mixed up together. That was how it seemed at the time.

"He knew nothing about music, or about much else besides the army and the basic things he learned in grammar school. He always talked about how ignorant he was, but he was, you know, very intelligent. Not quick, not showy, but in a profound way. He grasped things deep inside. And he exuded power. It is hard to describe, but he was someone who could make people do things just by wanting them to.

"He was very quiet, particularly for a Yayakuan man, and aloof. Sometimes he would talk to me after the recitals. Not much, at first, just to compliment my playing. But I could tell he was holding back, waiting for the moment when he could say more.

"But I didn't think anything about it. I must have been flattered or perhaps a bit lonely. It seemed so innocent to me. I was thinking of

Mama and how she got away with so much more than that, and it wasn't innocent at all. How was I to know people would start gossiping?"

ONE DAY, Don Pedro saw Captain Martín crossing the plaza. "Hey, my fine Captain!" he called. "I see you so little these days! There are rumors that you have fallen in love!"

Captain Martín colored and turned his back without speaking. Don Pedro laughed.

When they next met, Captain Martín spoke angrily in a low voice. "Where did you hear rumors that I am in love? Who said something to you?"

"No one," answered Don Pedro. "Simply a guess. But your reaction confirmed it. If it had been a matter of an affair, a flirtation, a dalliance, you would have stopped to boast, to joke about your lover. But you went on in silence. This points to the involvement of the heart." Captain Martín frowned.

"Now it only remains to determine the object of your affection. Is she married, perhaps? Ah, I see that she is! Is it the prefect's wife?"

Captain Martín spat on the ground.

"No? Not to your taste, no doubt. Perhaps it is that delectable young thing, Antonia, the wife of the eminent Arturo Rontella? Is it she you pant after, as a hare after water?"

The captain turned abruptly and stalked off in the opposite direction. Don Pedro continued on his way, smiling to himself.

After that, Captain Martín tried to stay away from Antonia. But for the first time in his life he discovered something he could not will himself to do. It became necessary for him to talk with her each day, to see her, and, if not to see her, to see or touch something she had touched.

As the depth of his obsession became clearer to him, his methods became more furtive. He would sneak out at night and watch her windows from across the plaza. From the shadows of the market portals he would watch her cross the street, then would match her steps exactly.

He pestered and bribed the laundress to steal some of Antonia's clothes. After many delays and hesitations, the laundress supplied him with a single stocking, perhaps thinking that this would be less likely to be missed. Captain Martín hung the stocking in his closet like an image in a secret shrine. Sometimes he would speak to it, saying the things he had never dared to say to Antonia herself. Occasionally he would stroke the silk, imagining it filled with her ankle or thigh.

She invaded his thoughts like a disease; he could not shut her out from his mind. He lay awake at night thinking of her. When he slept, she came into his dreams. And when he awoke in the morning, he was conscious of her before the light of the day.

He knew that she possessed him as surely as if she had been a poison. And he knew there was only one antidote; he must possess her, as totally and completely as she possessed him. He had to meld her mind and body into his, to drink in her thoughts, her dreams, the secrets that he could sense in her music. He had to feel her hair, the warmth of her flesh, the blood coursing through her veins, the silent working of her brain.

A colder part of him realized that all this was impossible and dangerous. Try as he might, he could detect no sign of passion in her attitude toward him, only a mild affection. It made him angry sometimes when she seemed so indifferent to his feelings. Was it possible that she could be so unaware? Or was she simply mocking him, teasing him? There were times when his feeling was so strong and so confused that he wanted to tear her apart.

The icy part of him spoke up: She is only a woman, this part reminded him, a rich, spoiled girl married to a rich and powerful man. It is dangerous and stupid and weak of you to let her affect you like this. You are a man with a future, a future in which such sentimental absurdities have no place. If you must possess her, do so. But don't let her possess you in return.

But the voice grew too weak. When he was with her, he found himself steadily more tongue-tied, more awkward, more ill-tempered. At last even she began to be aware of the powers moving beneath the surface—or perhaps of the gossip that was at that point circulating in the town—and began to turn away from his path in the street. It made him more furious, more desperate, than ever.

Antonia had heard things about the captain that made her feel different about him. There were stories that he had made several Indian girls pregnant, and the "visits to relatives" of several young women of good families were also attributed to him. There was nothing unusual about this gossip, but she had also overheard two old women in town speaking about an outrageous affair he was having with the wife of a prominent man in town. "They say he is mad about her!" said one of the women. "And such a man, when overwhelmed by such passion, no woman—not even the most virtuous one—can resist." The other woman sighed, but when they noticed Antonia listening, they broke off and scurried away.

Not long after this, when Antonia went to visit Magdalena, she saw a dark form moving quickly toward her down the narrow alley leading to Magdalena's back door. Since there was no room for two people to pass Antonia quickly backed out to the street, her heart pounding. Standing in the sunlight, she was shocked to see Captain Martín emerging from the alley. He gave her a look that seemed to her to be one of absolute loathing, and turned away without speaking.

What was he doing with Magdalena? she wondered. What did they have to say to each other? Could Magdalena be the married woman with whom Captain Martín was passionately in love? It seemed impossible, but why else would he be visiting Magdalena and leaving through the back door?

Antonia did not try to find out. She went home and avoided going near Magdalena's house for several days. From time to time she caught Captain Martín's malevolent (she thought) gaze as he watched her from a dark doorway or alley. She began to lose sleep. He must know I have guessed his secret! she thought. What might he do to me if he fears I will reveal it?

After a week had passed, one of Magdalena's sons arrived at Antonia's house with a note. "You must come to me at once!" the note said.

Reluctantly, Antonia crossed the plaza, squeezed through the narrow alleyway, and found her way to Magdalena's room, where Magdalena was frowning; Antonia had never seen her look so angry.

"Antonia!" she said sharply from the cushion on which she was seated. "Please sit down. I have to have a talk with you."

Antonia did as she was told. Magdalena tilted back her head, passed both hands over her forehead, and closed her eyes. She remained in that position for several moments while Antonia tried to imagine what she was going to say to her.

"Antonia, I am very disappointed with you," Magdalena began at last. "I had thought you were a woman with tact, honor, and sophistication. But now I find you behaving like a flirtatious little fool."

"What, *por Dios*, do you mean?"

"You have allowed someone to fall in love with you. And not just in love, but passionately, dangerously in love! In love up to the eyebrows! Oh, Antonia, how could you be so careless?"

"I still don't know what you mean, Magdalena," said Antonia, truly confused.

"Oh, Antonia, the rumors are all over Pica! That Captain Martín is in love with you—only the rumors are worse: They say you are having an affair together! If it were so, perhaps the poor boy could get some sleep! You are destroying him, and he has such a future ahead of him."

Antonia was too astonished to speak. So it was she the old ladies were gossiping about! It was she with whom Captain Martín was in love! Now that she knew it, she could see it all plainly. What had prevented her from seeing it?

"Fortunately," Magdalena went on, "Arturo knows nothing about it. So far, it's just ladies' talk and doesn't amount to much. But you must do exactly as I say. Everything will be all right, then, and I'll forgive you for this. But you must be obedient.

"It's all arranged for Captain Martín to be transferred to a new post. He will be told in two or three days. But in the meantime, you must break off this love affair—"

"But there is no love affair."

"Yes, there is, but it's only one-sided. He will never forgive you, he will never forgive the world, if he thinks all this meant nothing to you. And, I'm afraid he may not leave you alone. He is a man of great passion who keeps everything inside. Who knows what kind of explosion may result!

"Here is what you must do: Send a message to him to meet you at night in the cathedral—in the dark seats at the side near the Chapel of the Virgin. You must hint that it involves an affair of the heart. Wear a simple dress that is pale in color—nothing bright or shiny. And no jewelry—maybe a locket or a brooch only and certainly your wedding ring. Let your hair be just a bit untidy, to give you a distracted look.

"Make sure no one sees you go to the cathedral. There will be a full moon next week. Make sure that you sit so that the moonlight falls across your face—it should make you look sickly. Sigh softly when he arrives, but by no means let him touch you or take your hand.

"You must tell him how deeply in love you are with him, how you think of him all the time. Then, you must say that you are frightened, that you don't dare see him anymore or you will be afraid that he will sweep you away. Fall on your knees if you think it will be convincing—it is important that he believe you absolutely.

"Beg him to forgive you, but say that you must never see him again. Say something like 'Sir, such passion as ours is not for this earth! We must break away before we are burned to cinders. I pray to God that you will forgive me, but we must never set eyes on each other again. Allow me to depart from you this night forever. Adieu! Adieu!' You may look into his eyes at this point, but don't linger. Turn your face away as soon as his eyes soften.

"Then you must give the slightest sob and turn and walk out of the cathedral without looking back. When he is transferred a day or two later, he will think it fate. He will keep his memory of you very fondly!

"Now, here, sit down with this paper and write what I tell you. When you are finished, one of my boys will take it to the captain. Then none of those old gossiping hens will think it came from you."

Antonia did not like Magdalena's scheme at all, and liked even less the coy, sentimental, flowery note Magdalena dictated to her. But she was too flustered to know what else to do.

The following evening, she dressed more or less as Magdalena had told her, told Arturo she had to attend to an errand, and went to the cathedral. She found a beam of moonlight and sat down to wait for the captain. It was very dark in the cathedral, which was lit only by a cluster of fluttering candles near the altar. She could see through the shadows the rough, bare concrete ribs of the building which had never been covered with the marble and gold leaf intended for them.

She waited for more than an hour. Then a small voice whispered in her ear so suddenly that she jumped up with fright. It was a small boy with a note which he pressed into her hand and then ran out into the night.

Señora [the note which seemed to have been written in a rush said],
  I regret that I am unable to meet you tonight as you asked. My duties

prevent me from doing so. Also it might not be proper for a young, single man such as myself to meet an older, married woman under such circumstances. It might lead to gossip.

> *Respectfully,*
> *José Martín*

ONLY MANY YEARS LATER did Antonia learn that on the way to meet her in the cathedral, Captain Martín had been intercepted by Don Pedro. "If you go to the cathedral tonight, I will see that you never rise above the rank of captain."

That afternoon, the commandant had informed Captain Martín of his transfer to a post in the north. After writing the note to Antonia, Captain Martín visited a house at the edge of town overlooking the empty desert. He chose, and paid for the evening, a tall, dusky beauty from the capital for, as the procuress put it, "a little rest."

After an hour, when it became clear that the captain would not be able to perform, the girl began to laugh. It was loud, high-pitched, half nervous, with a sharp, grating, mocking edge.

Captain Martín got out of bed. He reached out and struck the girl twice across the mouth. She was not badly hurt, and opened her mouth to shriek. But in the instant before the sound began she caught a glimpse of his face.

She swallowed; all that came out was a terrified whimper. She half rolled, half fell off the bed. On her knees she began to kiss Captain Martín's feet.

Captain Martín ignored her. He looked out the window where, over the desert, green and gold streaks were beginning to form. He could imagine the future forming there, in the sky.

Part Four

Part Four

across your face—it should make you look sickly. Sigh softly when he arrives, but by no means let him touch you or take your hand.

"You must tell him how deeply in love you are with him, how you think of him all the time. Then, you must say that you are frightened, that you don't dare see him anymore or you will be afraid that he will sweep you away. Fall on your knees if you think it will be convincing—it is important that he believe you absolutely.

"Beg him to forgive you, but say that you must never see him again. Say something like 'Sir, such passion as ours is not for this earth! We must break away before we are burned to cinders. I pray to God that you will forgive me, but we must never set eyes on each other again. Allow me to depart from you this night forever. Adieu! Adieu!' You may look into his eyes at this point, but don't linger. Turn your face away as soon as his eyes soften.

"Then you must give the slightest sob and turn and walk out of the cathedral without looking back. When he is transferred a day or two later, he will think it fate. He will keep his memory of you very fondly!

"Now, here, sit down with this paper and write what I tell you. When you are finished, one of my boys will take it to the captain. Then none of those old gossiping hens will think it came from you."

Antonia did not like Magdalena's scheme at all, and liked even less the coy, sentimental, flowery note Magdalena dictated to her. But she was too flustered to know what else to do.

The following evening, she dressed more or less as Magdalena had told her, told Arturo she had to attend to an errand, and went to the cathedral. She found a beam of moonlight and sat down to wait for the captain. It was very dark in the cathedral, which was lit only by a cluster of fluttering candles near the altar. She could see through the shadows the rough, bare concrete ribs of the building which had never been covered with the marble and gold leaf intended for them.

She waited for more than an hour. Then a small voice whispered in her ear so suddenly that she jumped up with fright. It was a small boy with a note which he pressed into her hand and then ran out into the night.

Señora [the note which seemed to have been written in a rush said],
I regret that I am unable to meet you tonight as you asked. My duties

prevent me from doing so. Also it might not be proper for a young, single man such as myself to meet an older, married woman under such circumstances. It might lead to gossip.

Respectfully,
José Martín

ONLY MANY YEARS LATER did Antonia learn that on the way to meet her in the cathedral, Captain Martín had been intercepted by Don Pedro. "If you go to the cathedral tonight, I will see that you never rise above the rank of captain."

That afternoon, the commandant had informed Captain Martín of his transfer to a post in the north. After writing the note to Antonia, Captain Martín visited a house at the edge of town overlooking the empty desert. He chose, and paid for the evening, a tall, dusky beauty from the capital for, as the procuress put it, "a little rest."

After an hour, when it became clear that the captain would not be able to perform, the girl began to laugh. It was loud, high-pitched, half nervous, with a sharp, grating, mocking edge.

Captain Martín got out of bed. He reached out and struck the girl twice across the mouth. She was not badly hurt, and opened her mouth to shriek. But in the instant before the sound began she caught a glimpse of his face.

She swallowed; all that came out was a terrified whimper. She half rolled, half fell off the bed. On her knees she began to kiss Captain Martín's feet.

Captain Martín ignored her. He looked out the window where, over the desert, green and gold streaks were beginning to form. He could imagine the future forming there, in the sky.

I

IN PICA, THE WAR in Europe seemed not to exist; in the countryside, in the mountain villages, even in the haciendas of the north, the war, if it was known at all, was less substantial than a dream. But in Montana de Plata, in a few grand houses west of the Plaza de Armas, the idea that there might be more to come, that all the nations of Europe might be set ablaze, as they had been in the last war, slowly began to form. Some realized that, with the rest of the world at war, Yayaku's position among the nations might change, that the copper, tin, and iron concessions might thrive again, that the languishing rubber plantations beyond the mountains might seem like fields of gold.

The foreigners thought of these things before the Yayakuans themselves. There were many Englishmen still in Montana, and the British newspaper patiently reminded the good people of Yayaku how British money had built the railroads, how British engineers had devised the intricate systems of cog tracks and switchbacks that carried the Indians from their homes in the mountains and down to the coast. They reminded Yayaku how British banks and British engineers had developed the tin mines in the east and carved the new plantations out of the jungles beyond the mountains. What would Yayaku be, they implied, without us?

The British ambassador said the same things to the president of Yayaku when he came to call. The president nodded and smiled, but he was out of sympathy with the British, who seemed to consider utterly ignorant anyone who did not immediately recognize British superiority. The British ambassador was so polite, so correct, that with every word he seemed to be calling the president a savage. In a distant part of his mind, the president made a note to wait until the British were in no position to protest, and then to nationalize the railways.

The president much preferred the French. The current French ambassador, however, was a sour little man who seemed to think his position was some unjust punishment meted out by his hidden enemies in France. He had a shrewish wife who had mortified the president's wife by loudly insulting the Yayakuan National Opera at an official reception for the prima donna. At such gatherings, the president always tried to engage the ambassador with memories of his own student years in Paris. "Oh!" the ambassador would say with a sigh and a crooked smile, "it's nothing like that anymore, nothing at all like that, I'm afraid. You have no idea how everything's come down in the last few years."

The German ambassador rarely appeared in person at the presidential palace. He was a friend of the minister of the interior, a political adversary of the president who stayed in the cabinet to appease the opposition. To the minister (and, the president assumed, to the German ambassador) the war would last for a few weeks or months at the most, and German victory was a foregone conclusion. "Keep in mind the advantages of favoring the victor," the minister whispered in the president's ear. "The time in which they will truly need us is short, and they will remember those who helped in their triumph."

The president, on a vacation trip to Switzerland as a child, had visited a glacier. When he imagined a German triumph, he immediately remembered the impossibly heavy and powerful river of gleaming white ice, and the overwhelming astonishment, wonder, and intense cold and dread he felt while gazing at it.

The American ambassador was a tall, youngish man with thin, light brown hair and round spectacles. He spoke a formal, old-fashioned Catalan, sprinkled with occasional endearing errors in grammar, but, because he knew the president was proud of his command of English, they usually spoke in that language. The president was pleasantly surprised by their intellectual conversations. The ambassador had been a professor at an American university, and sent the president books by Hemingway and Santayana to read.

The American avoided talking directly about the war; with a sad face, he made allusions to the "situation in Europe." He had the seriousness, the president thought, of a precocious child. There were many in the capital who said the American ambassador acted only on the "advice" of the Great Basin Mining Company. The president didn't seem to care about this. After a meeting with the Europeans, he felt tired and irritable, but whenever he met the American, he spent the rest of the day in a comfortable haze of optimism, and went to bed with a smile on his lips.

The president's study faced north. He liked to work there late in the day and watch the twilight fade from its long windows. The east, where Europe lay, seemed wrapped in a thick, oppressive darkness; the west, toward the sea, was full of dying fire. But just over the northern horizon was a glow like the lights of a great distant city seen from a desert. The president would stand at his window watching the glow that seemed to grow stronger and more definite each night, thinking of the Americans.

II

THE FIRST THING everyone in Pica noticed about the Americans was their size. They were big, not only in body. Most of them were a head taller than the average Pican. Some of the older Americans also had huge bellies, as big as pregnant women's, wide hands, and arms thick as boulders.

Everything about them seemed large. They moved with an excess of energy. Even in the hottest weather they swung their arms wide, dripping with sweat. The Pican children imitated the swagger while they walked, which reminded everyone of the cowboys in the American movies. They also wore the cowboys' pointed, impractical boots, and enormous tall hats as well.

When the Americans stood still, they always seemed to have their hands on their hips. The walls of the café shook at their laughter, and they were unable to pay for anything without displaying a large bundle of bills.

A consortium of American companies headed by Great Basin Mining had taken over the copper concession eighty miles east of Pica. The

French had abandoned the mines there twenty years before, when their young engineers had gone home to fight in the war. Important as they had been in the old days, there were few Frenchmen left in Pica, and all of them were elderly.

The first Americans arrived in a strange-looking vehicle no one had seen before and booked an entire hotel. Unlike the French, however, they did not set up houses in town. Only their agent, a Peruvian named Enrique they had brought with them from Montana de Plata, rented a room from an old lady who lived near the cathedral. Meanwhile, the Americans stayed at the hotel, had their meals together without Enrique, and took no interest in the events in town except for the movies. At the movies they put their large feet up on the back of the seats, chewed gum, and made noisy remarks in English. None of them knew more than a few words of Spanish, and they relied on Enrique, whom they called "Hank," for everything.

At the hotel, the Americans would eat only the blandest of food. For breakfast they brought big, bright yellow boxes of something called cornflakes. The Picans who tried it said it looked and tasted like wood shavings. It was rumored that the Americans ate only baby food, and some of the men in town, Don Pedro among them, took to calling them the "baby giants."

After a few weeks, the Americans got into their jeeps and disappeared toward the east. Enrique, who stayed behind, kept himself busy. Arturo and Don Pedro offered him the most generous "commissions" and so they got the lion's share of the American business. Like the Americans themselves, the business was large. Not long after they had left town for the mines, two flatcars of heavy equipment arrived with a contingent of geologists from Montana de Plata, the government quota of "trained nationals." Huge crates containing, it was said, whole houses came not long after, followed by an endless stream of furnishings and equipment. It looked as if the Americans were bringing everything they needed from home, even their bathwater.

The Americans widened and flattened the road to the mines and their trucks carried load after load. This new road, the "Americans' Highway," it came to be called, was for a time a favorite Sunday drive for those Picans with cars. Even Magdalena took the trip out to see the "town with no name" rising up in the desert, the double row of white one-story wooden houses (the ones that had come out of boxes) facing one another across the straight, paved road, the tiny golf course, the club, the school, and the Americans' movie theater, to which the Picans were sometimes invited to attend special films about life in the United States and to incomprehensible amateur theatricals staged by mining officials and their wives.

"It's not a real town," Magdalena told Antonia. "It's a toy out of a box. And in the middle of nothing! Why would they want to live there, when they could have nice houses here in town?"

The American wives and children were never seen in Pica. They never appeared at the cathedral or at the opera, as had their French predecessors. The older children spent most of the year back in their own country at school.

"What do they do there, out in the desert?" Magdalena wondered to Antonia. *"Pobrecitas!* Nobody even knows their names!" And they were too far to gossip about.

Don Pedro recommended one of Magdalena's maids to the managers of the American Club. The maid went out with the first group of local servants; on her weekends off, she would come back to Pica and stay with Magdalena.

"None of them are Catholics," Magdalena told Antonia. "That explains why they never come to the cathedral. They have their own little church and take turns giving the service.

"All their food comes from America in boxes and cans. Everyone drinks American whiskey, the women too. Some of the women smoke cigarettes. They often take their baths standing up. They have their own power generator, so they have electrical refrigerators. They also have washing machines and complain about the dust. But the houses are not all finished, so the other wives and children have not been sent for yet. As a result, there are still many more men than women. Some of the wives, it is said, have abandoned their husbands for other men. It is even said that the younger ones practice free sex.

"The women sit at their club all day playing cards and reading American magazines. They want nothing else but to go back to America. They will be here only three or four years; then they go back. Sometimes in the evenings they have dances and play music. Their music comes from America, too; so do their clothes and furniture. They themselves come from a place in America called Utah which, it is said, is not too different from here, except that everyone speaks English, and you don't have to go so far for a Coca-Cola.''

Arturo and Antonia both were fascinated by the Americans, though for slightly different reasons. Arturo and Don Pedro went to Montana de Plata to visit the American ambassador, who assured them that everything the consortium needed at the new American concession would be purchased from them, not through agencies in the capital. The money the Americans brought was making them both rich. More and more American things were coming to Pica—their records, for example, which had a sly, loping energy about them, like the Americans themselves.

Antonia particularly liked the magazines, whose bright pages were filled with pictures of young, good-looking people who seemed rich and happy, whose white teeth and wide smiles seemed to be the essence of health and contentment. In these magazines, too, Antonia saw pictures of the American "dream homes." Their relaxed, sun-filled rooms made her sigh at the sight of her own home which, despite her best efforts, still seemed dark and tired to her. The kitchens of these homes were filled with bright new machinery that prepared American food in minutes, with gleaming white refrigerators and stoves and with cabinets stocked with shiny pots and mountains of food. The sight of such abundant new things was a revelation to Antonia, a peephole into a clean, modern world over the northern horizon.

After the Americans' town was started, Arturo would sometimes invite some of the Americans over for dinner whenever they stayed at the hotel in town. Despite Antonia's best hopes, these dinners were not a success. Antonia hoped to interest them in some of the local foods, but when she answered, to a suspicious inquiry, that a special dish was llama meat, her guests nearly choked. And the conversation was not easy. Few of the Americans spoke Spanish and even with the company's interpreters to help, there seemed little to say. The Americans seemed embarrassed by questions about their homeland, and they never wanted to talk about the war. They were even more embarrassed when Antonia asked about their impression of Yayaku.

She was disappointed with the American women, the wives of the men who worked for the mining company. They looked nothing like the women in the magazines. They were rather thin, for the most part, and their faces were rarely lit up by the glorious smiles of the magazine pictures, though they did have shy, friendly ones that many of the men seemed to have as well. They also seemed honest, direct, and unpretentious; none of them pretended that they were in Yayaku for anything other than work and, without complaining, they all said they longed for home. Antonia tried to show off her Indian artifacts, but few of the Americans took any interest. One man took her aside, and with his few words of Spanish, told her he could sell her "good stuff" at his company store. Only one or two of the Americans had been out of the United States before; they couldn't imagine living anywhere else. "But didn't you come from somewhere else, in the beginning?" Antonia asked.

The Americans only stared at her in amazement. "A few of us did, or our parents, or our grandparents. But we are Americans now," they answered her. "Once you become an American, all the other places in your past are erased. America is the beginning for you, and those other places no longer matter. If you are an American, only what you are matters, and where you come from is not important." Antonia liked this answer, and it made her dream even more of the great, clean country to the north.

One afternoon another American arrived in Pica. He called himself James M. Coyle, S. J. (for "soft job," he said with the thin smile he wore when he made a joke). Father Coyle came into Arturo's office looking for some parts for his ancient truck, which he had driven from the mission outside La Paz where he had been working. He was visiting his sister, who was married to an engineer at the mining settlement.

The truck was an old one, and the parts had to be ordered from the supply company in Montana de Plata. Father Coyle spent several days in Pica waiting for them to arrive. During that time, he had several conversations with Arturo and with the other men in Pica, who told him there was no high school in Pica. Then Father Coyle went back to Missouri for his third probation. In a year he was back. The Jesuit provincial in Montana had given his permission to open a Jesuit school for boys in Pica.

"FATHER COYLE did not look like a priest," Antonia explained to Count Mora. "He looked like an American. He was very tall and thin, though his shoulders were broad and strong. In those days he had sandy-colored hair that was cut very short, and he wore glasses. He had that lean, open sort of face that American boys have, the sort of face that never really looks old but gets fine little wrinkles around the eyes and mouth, which look like the folds in an old shirt after it has been washed many times. He never dressed like a priest, either. He wore dark pants and a white shirt with a cross pinned over the heart.

"He had the worst temper, I think, of any man I have ever known. It was terrible, and it gave him a lot of sorrow, not just because it was always getting him in trouble with his superiors, but also because he was so ashamed after he got over being angry. Every time he lost his temper, he did penance for days for 'his sins of pride.' But he never got angry without a good reason, as far as I know, and never for himself. And it was like the wrath of God when it came on him.

"The bishop hated him and tried everything he could think of to get rid of Father Coyle. But the bishop was afraid of that terrible temper and also of the fact (which I think he must have known) that Father Coyle was a much better man and priest than he was. They lived so differently—the bishop in his palace with his mother and all those servants, and Father Coyle in a little room with just a cot and a table for his Bible, Saint Ignatius' Exercises, and a few other things. The bishop sometimes gave sermons about the 'folly of pretending to be poor,' and everyone knew whom he was talking about.

"Arturo lent Father Coyle a house he owned at the edge of town for the school. Father Coyle set it up so that the rich people could send their sons only if they paid for a poor boy to come, too. He had six boys at first, including Don Pedro's second oldest. I think the first thing he taught them all was basketball (Father Coyle had played in college in America), and if you went out there in the afternoons, you would sometimes see them running around the hoop in the yard with the ball.

"He was very handsome, and the ladies all fell over him at first and brought him cakes and offered to do things they did for the bishop. But he wouldn't accept them. He tried to get them to do things that they didn't like to do at all, such as helping take care of poor people when they were sick and looking after their own servants when they got pregnant instead of throwing them out. This dampened their enthusiasm right away, which relieved the bishop at first, but there were those among us who really admired Father Coyle and tried to help him.

"Later, when the school got bigger, he had younger priests help him for a year or two at a time before they took their final vows. Sometimes they were from Yayaku, sometimes they were Americans. He was a very gentle man, really, and I used to feel sorry for him because sometimes he seemed very lonely. He played the guitar, sang those slow American songs about cowboys and loneliness and the sadness of poor people. His songs reminded me of my father.

"It's funny how he changed things in Pica. It happened very slowly, but somehow the church improved after Father Coyle came. No wonder the bishop hated him! I remember one time Father Coyle lost his temper over the collection the bishop was taking up from all the well-to-do people to finish the cathedral. Father Coyle shouted something about 'the golden calf' and 'money-changing in the temple' at the bishop in public. Then he brought the sickliest-looking, most ragged children with him to mass. They filled up all the back rows of the cathedral and the men had nowhere to sit. Finally, the bishop broke down and turned the money over to a hospital and a new orphanage.

"He was the kind of American who always seems to be childlike, in the way he looked and the way he was. He was really naive in some matters—Arturo always said he was a 'jesus fool' for thinking that people could be taught to be good, and that this was why Father Coyle would get so angry, when people acted just like people.

"He was very patriotic about his own country, though he went back there only once every six or seven years to see his family. He didn't speak of it quite that way, but you could tell that when he talked about America he thought it was the best country in the world, not just the richest or the most beautiful, but the most noble. His eyes would light up until he looked even more like a child. He was like that even through the war. He hated the war and everything that had to do with it. He said Americans fought wars only when they had to, and that they were forced into this one. He was a great admirer of the American president and said he would never have gotten into a war if he had had any choice at all.

"So before I even had a child, I decided to send our children to America to study. Arturo was not in favor of it at all. He wanted generation after generation of Rontellas living in Yayaku, and he said if we sent our children to America they would never come back. He was right, after all. But I had my heart set on it, and in the end I had my way."

III

IN THE SPRING after Arturo's return, Antonia became pregnant. It was both a happy and a sad time for her. Arturo was delighted and spent as much time with her as he could. Often, he didn't have as much time to stay with her as he would have liked, and Antonia could feel the strain in him while he tried to keep his mind away from his business when he sat with her in the evenings. She felt so strange having a living thing growing inside her, a part of her moving toward a separate life. Some days she woke up full of joy, other times with the darkest misgivings.

They told Toma the news about the baby before anyone else. Toma was delighted. The night after they told him, they found a huge bouquet of flowers on Antonia's pillow from him.

Toma was sure that the baby would be a girl because of the way Antonia walked, although he could not quite explain the change that he saw. He pestered her with all sorts of superstitions. He gave her a maté which tasted like sulfur to give the baby blond hair. He told her not to look in mirrors after dark and to wear a chicken feather between her breasts to make sure she gave good milk. The newspapers were clipped before Antonia could read them; all the pictures of ugly people were cut out, and Toma explained that Antonia should look only at beautiful things. He cut pictures of beautiful babies out of magazines and hung them around the house so the unborn child would have the idea of what looked beautiful. But Antonia didn't think the baby pictures were beautiful. She started taking them down until she felt foolish and let them be.

Arturo was persuaded to wear a dried hibiscus leaf under his lapel to prevent people from looking at Antonia and giving her the evil eye. Toma no longer walked, but moved in little jumps, never taking his eyes off Antonia for very long. In the mornings, Antonia found empty bowls and orange-scented towels within easy reach; when she pressed him, Toma admitted that he was waiting for her to do what all pregnant women do: throw up in the morning.

About a month into her pregnancy, Antonia did begin to feel ill. Her legs swelled up and she had trouble keeping food down. Some days she was so weak she had to stay in bed.

Arturo brought a doctor from La Paz, but he didn't find anything wrong. He simply told her to eat mild food and told Arturo to keep her quiet. "It's all in her mind," the doctor said. "It's like this with some women—it's as if they don't want to be mothers at all. So they get sick. It usually passes when the baby is born. But don't worry too much about it. These reluctant mothers often love their children more than anyone else."

Magdalena sent Antonia a letter about her own children, about how much she loved them, and how that love made up for all the pain they caused her before they came into the world and after.

But Antonia wrote a sour, frightened letter in return. "I grow weak while she [Antonia had decided to believe Toma's prediction] grows strong," she wrote. "My belly swells bigger and bigger while the rest of me melts away. She is eating me from inside."

The idea of being a father made Arturo feel a new burden of responsibility. At nights he stayed awake worrying. He realized how little Antonia knew about his business and worried that if something happened to him, she would not be prepared to look after everything. He knew the time had come for Antonia to share with him his business plans. He had made a substantial amount of money and was planning to invest it in something different. When he heard of a rental building for sale in Montana de Plata, which he thought would be a good investment, he asked Antonia to travel with him to see it. It seemed a rare opportunity; the owner, a wealthy English widow, wanted to return to England. The building was new, in an exclusive part of the city, and was rented to well-to-do tenants. Secretly Arturo was also looking forward to showing off Antonia to his wealthy friends in the capital.

Antonia was so excited that for a few days she did not think of the baby or the house. She spent hours preparing her wardrobe. She knew that the clothes she had brought from Italy were still stylish, and she modeled them for Arturo. "Does it rain there?" she asked teasingly.

"Yes, it does," answered Arturo. "But not hard enough to walk with a roof over one's head," he added as he gently kissed her forehead.

The night before leaving, Antonia found it difficult to sleep. Although she had often seen the little plane that brought the mail, the idea of flying made her nervous. The look on Toma's face when they told him about their trip did not make her feel any better. Arturo, sensing her nervousness, tried to erase her fears.

"What if the engine fails?" asked Antonia.

"Well, then, we would just glide down. The plane is so light that it would land gently in the soft desert," responded Arturo.

"But then, Arturo, who would rescue us?"

"The Yayakuan Army, Antonia. You often wonder why we have such a large army since there are no wars here. Well, they watch for fallen planes. Now get some sleep."

That night, she dreamt of being stranded in the desert with no water or food. When she packed her bag in the morning she secretly included a Thermos of water and two apples.

The pilot of the tiny orange airplane was already warming the engine when Arturo and Antonia arrived at the airport. Before she knew it, Antonia was sitting next to the pilot. It was hot inside the plane and the noise was deafening. "Up, to the clouds," said the pilot. The little plane seemed to obey as they rose slowly but effortlessly. Then the noise diminished and they were floating in the air. Antonia turned to Arturo, who was sitting behind her and looking out the window.

"Look, look, Antonia," he said.

Reluctantly Antonia pressed her head against the window and below she saw the familiar streets and structures of Pica. From the air Pica reminded her of the crèches she had seen in Italy at Christmastime.

From above, the desert looked like cardboard, an infinity of brown sand, its monotony only occasionally broken by the tiny oases at the end of rivers that flowed from the Andes. They flew above the long thin road that went from Pica to the capital.

"See the road, Antonia?" asked Arturo. "Had we gone by car it would have taken us three days."

The plane seemed to have settled into a monotonous glide when it suddenly lost altitude. "Air pocket," the pilot explained when he noticed Antonia's terrified look. Antonia was not consoled. She reached in her pocket for something Toma had given her. It was a bunch of orange feathers tied with string. "Make sure it is out, next to the window," Toma had said. "That way God will see it and let you fly, thinking that you are a bird."

There were many more air pockets and Antonia was beginning to enjoy them. It reminded her of the rides she and Marco had taken with their uncle to the island of the Piglets when the sea was rough. She thought of Marco, of the day when they finally had finished building their boat. "Pray, Antonia," he had said, "pray that it floats." She remembered the look of victory on his face when the little boat bobbed in the waves. Thinking of Marco, Antonia fell asleep.

The pilot woke her, announcing excitedly, "Montana de Plata, Montana de Plata." Looking down she could see a spreading city with neat rows of houses and low buildings. Domes of colonial churches and small masses of green trees were scattered here and there. The city was enveloped in a gray mist, so unlike the dusty white air of the desert. To Antonia, who had never flown before, everything seemed orderly from above. When they began to lose altitude and approached the landing strip, Antonia closed her eyes and did not open them again until she felt the jerk of the plane touching the ground.

As they walked away from the plane, Antonia turned around to look at it once more. It seemed strange to her that something so small could soar so high and float in the air.

"Next time," said Arturo, "you will not need Toma's feathers."

"Oh, yes, I will!" said Antonia teasingly, and pulling out a small feather, she stuck it in his buttonhole.

As they drove to the city, Arturo explained to Antonia that Montana de Plata was named after a mountain of silver that, according to legend, was the sacred mountain of the Incas and was kept hidden by them. It was said to be entirely of rich silver ore. Since the time of the conquistadores, many had lost their lives looking for this mountain. No one had ever understood why the Spaniards, who had settled in this place and had later made it the capital of their empire, had called it such. He added that people thought it was because of their greed. He also told Antonia that no one understood why the Spaniards, who came from a sun-washed country, had chosen to settle in a place where the sun never shone, a place surrounded by eternal grayness. Antonia, who missed the gray days of Artemisia, murmured, "Arturo, it is so nice not to have to squint all day."

"My dear," added Arturo, "it is nice to see your eyes wide open."

They drove through long straight streets bordered with jacaranda trees in full lavender bloom, streets that led to plazas with fountains of sparkling water and pots of bright flowers. Women dressed more fashionably than those of Pica sat on wrought-iron benches watching their children play. The streets were clean, noisier than in Pica. Buses bursting with passengers stopped the traffic to allow the people in and out. Yet there was a calmness in people's faces, no one seemed to rush.

They passed by the National Palace, which stood across the Cathedral in the main square. The palace was a yellowish building that belonged to no discernible architectural style. It resembled a Greek temple, but the columns were too thin and the pediment too massive. There were many wings, and formal French gardens around it. Arturo explained that the palace had burned down and had been restored several times, and that each new president had added a wing. Antonia rather liked it. She imagined that the history of Yayaku, its thirty-four revolutions and eighty governments, was written in the facade.

They arrived at the Grand Hotel Yayaku, which also stood in the main square overlooking the colonial cathedral. The hotel reminded Antonia of the one in Casilda, but it was grander, full of mirrors, and it did not smell like citronella.

A great fuss was made on their arrival. Numerous porters rushed to unload the car and open doors. The manager ran to meet them, made a deep bow, and declared himself "at the loyal service of the distinguished bride of Don Arturo."

He escorted them to what he called the "Suite of the Camelias," named after the national flower of Yayaku. The room was large, painted in soft pink with furniture covered in flowery chintz. It had a large balcony that faced a plaza, and it smelled of fresh flowers. The manager explained that the hotel had been designed and furnished by the British when they came to build the railroads, and that it had recently been refurbished in a manner "faithful to its original." The manager hurried about fluffing pillows and tried to close the drapes. "You must want some privacy," he said as he covered his eyes in a pretense at embarrassment. Finally Arturo had to send him away.

Arturo and Antonia unpacked in silence. Antonia loved seeing her favorite dresses hanging in the huge closet. She walked toward the balcony where Arturo was standing. He moved closer to her, broke off a pretty geranium from one of the many pots, and placed it in her hair. They walked back to the room, and Arturo gently closed the drapes.

The next morning Antonia was up early. When Arturo awoke he found her at the desk looking over the maps of Montana de Plata. They hired a car and a driver who took them through the different neighborhoods of the city. In the morning the city was full of activity. Carts stood on street corners and vendors offered produce, milk, and flowers to neatly dressed housewives followed by uniformed maids carrying baskets. Arturo and Antonia spent the day visiting buildings and vast empty lots. Antonia listened carefully and Arturo made notes in the little pad he always carried. Both Antonia and Arturo were tireless. They visited the building that belonged to the English widow. It stood in a street flanked by large jacaranda trees, and its neatness and sturdy construction reminded Antonia of a little fortress. It was larger than they had expected: thirty rental units, all of them occupied. Arturo explained to her that at the terms offered, the return on their investment would be too low, but that perhaps the widow would consider an arrangement by which they would pay over a few years. "The currency generally devalues here, so if we pay over five years, the last payments would be, in real money, half of what they are now," he said.

Three days later, after several meetings with the widow, the little fortress was theirs and a corporation was established. Antonia was the president, Arturo the chairman. The name of the corporation was A.A.A., the last A for Artemisia.

That night Arturo and Antonia went to the National Club for dinner. They had been invited by Don Demetrio Ribera. "You will like Don Demetrio," Arturo told Antonia. "He comes from an old Peruvian family. His father owned the copper mines and sold them to the Americans for an astronomical amount of money that he then invested in real estate. He owns half of Montana de Plata and God only knows what else. He has seven brothers with wives and children, but he never married himself, although he has broken many hearts. He lives a month with each brother and the other five he travels. He has been everywhere, but loves Italy above all. He can tell you about every town square in every hill town in Tuscany and about every good restaurant in Rome. He speaks perfect Italian. Demetrio would love the chance to show you off; he will make you feel comfortable. His nickname is 'El Condor Pasa,' meaning that like a condor he is a true Yayakuan aristocrat and that he moves from one triumph to another, never committing himself to anything."

"How did you meet him?" asked Antonia.

"We have had many business deals together. Once, about ten years ago, we spent a few days in Paris together. It was my first time in Paris and he showed me everything there was to be seen. We spent so long at the Louvre that I had to soak my feet in saltwater that night. I know you will like him. Just don't fall in love with him, not even a little bit. Remember, I am a very jealous man!"

From the outside the club looked like many of the comfortable old buildings of Montana de Plata. The only feature that made it different was the enormous front door, on which the initials of the club had been carved in dark wood.

Inside was a seemingly endless hallway lined with mirrors. Antonia saw herself and Arturo reflected in what looked like an army of little Arturos and Antonias. "Look how many we are," she said. "When Marco and I were young there was a similar setup of mirrors in a Genoese hotel where my mother and the count used to have lunch. Marco and I would amuse ourselves pretending our reflections were armies." Antonia turned around and saluted him in a military fashion. "My little girl," said Arturo, smiling as he gently squeezed her hand.

At the end of the hallway stood a large marble statue of Diana, obviously a poor copy of another, better proportioned, Diana. A label explained that it was the gift of Don Eustabio de Moreno, founder of the club, patron of the arts and grandson of the Don Reynaldo de Moreno who arrived at Yayaku in 1539 in the service of his majesty the king of Spain. Next to it, a few large overstuffed chairs were placed beside a door that led to a very large room. "I am Demetrio Ribera," said a tall distinguished-looking man who sprinted from one of the chairs to greet Antonia and Arturo. "Here in Montana de Plata we have heard of the lovely young bride of Don Arturo. I see that the rumors this time are well founded. Doña Antonia, you are a treat to my tired eyes, a true Italian beauty. Italy, how I love Italy. When I was young I went there on a vacation and stayed a year. My father had to come and bring me back or I would have never left."

· · ·

Don Demetrio, reminded Antonia of the food in the grand old hotels Donna Dora liked so much. They were served lobster soup, boiled salmon with a caper sauce, and roast veal. They drank excellent wines in great abundance. Antonia noticed that the men did most of the eating. The women ate a few birdlike bites, and then pushed the plates aside, with the exception of Demetrio's sister, who never refused when served.

After the main course, rum cake and cheese and fruit were served with port. The men smoked Cuban cigars and the conversation moved to the war. Demetrio believed the end was near. The Americans, he thought, no longer had a choice; they had to enter the fray.

"Mussolini, *un grand bouffon;* because of him, Italy is the great tragedy of the war."

"What do they say about him in Italy, Antonia? Do you agree with the Italian position?" asked Ismael.

"It must be hard for you, with all your family in Italy," interrupted a woman with a large beauty mark on her cheek. "Have you had any communication with them?"

"We get some letters, but they take so long in arriving, it is very difficult to feel in touch."

"Our archbishop, he has good contacts in the Vatican; if I can be of help let me know," said Demetrio. "I went to school with Fernando, and I play cards with him every Tuesday."

"Tell the truth, Demetrio. Did he really have a child by his mestizo mistress?" asked a woman who covered her mouth with her hands as she laughed.

"Who knows, who knows? Remember, Felicia, we were all young once."

"That archbishop!" said Josefa. "So aristocratic. I don't think he ever leaves his palace. Yayaku needs someone who cares more for the poor. I don't trust him; there are too many rumors about him. The mestizo mistress is just one of them. I hear he goes on trips and takes off his habit. I hear he travels with female companions. His politics are all wrong; he should be more careful about sidling up to the rich. He is hurting the church. The young priests don't listen to him."

"Nonsense," said Don Demetrio. "He is doing just what he should do. Don't forget, the church owns much of Yayaku, and we don't quite want that changed."

IT WAS EARLY and the club was still empty. As Don Demetrio went to fetch a waiter, Antonia looked around the room. It was large and dimly lit by enormous crystal chandeliers. The walls were covered with dusty paintings and many large mirrors in gilded baroque frames. The furniture, which did not seem to belong to any particular style, was bulky and covered in deep-red velvet. It reminded Antonia of Lina's furniture, local craftsmen's interpretation of European styles. Here though, they looked friendlier and more comfortable. Large bouquets of bougainvilleas stood on top of pedestals. Their dark-fuchsia color matched the velvet that covered the couches, and their delicate scent blended with the ancient odor of countless cigars.

Don Demetrio returned, followed by a waiter carrying a silver tray holding a bottle of Dom Pérignon and three elaborate crystal champagne glasses. "Let's toast love," he said. "The kind of love that makes oceans meet: Antonia the Atlantic, Arturo the Pacific. *La confluence des amours.*" Antonia was aware that as people began to arrive they all nodded to Don Demetrio, but that it was she they were obviously interested in. It gave her an uncomfortable feeling, softened by the obvious pride on Arturo's face.

"I have invited a few friends to meet you," said Don Demetrio. "I think you will enjoy talking to them. They all share a great passion for Italy."

They were seated around a table set with so much silver and crystal that Antonia wondered uneasily how long dinner would last. She could see Arturo at the other end of the table listening intently to a large woman who was using her hands in a manner calculated to display her abundant rings. He was smiling and obviously enjoying himself. As she looked around the table Antonia noticed how carefully groomed everyone was. These women were not dressed in local copies of clothes from European magazines. They wore carefully selected, mostly Italian clothes, with ostentatious baroque jewels. The men wore well-cut suits with wide lapels, and had combed back their hair with a lotion what made the hair slick and shiny. They reminded her of Rodolfo Valentino with darker complexions.

Demetrio, sensing Antonia's nervousness, began the conversation. He talked about his trips to Genoa, and about the Genoese painters. She felt she was talking to the count; he had the same calm manner, but unlike the count who was modest about his knowledge, Don Demetrio seemed too eager to establish his intellectual credentials. He also had the terrible habit of dropping French words into the conversation.

"That Cambiasso, the lines, he is the best of draftsmen. Castiglione—no one understood the Bible better than him. Those scenes of the Journey: You can almost sense the tension; even the tiniest of animals seem desperate to escape. We bought a Castiglione for our national museum. One of these days Yayaku will have a fine collection."

"Crazy," said the gentleman to Antonia's left as he pushed aside the capers that had been sprinkled on the salmon. "We can't even take care of our national treasures; thousands of Inca artifacts to be excavated, colonial churches to be restored, and we spend our money on an obscure Genoese drawing!"

"Oh, no, my dear Ismael," said Don Demetrio, "we have a duty to show our people the art of other civilizations—*notre devoir civilisatrice.*"

"Fine, fine, but then let's swap. Give them some of our Inca things in exchange for some of their things."

"That is a good idea," said Antonia. "In Italy we know so little about the Incas. I had been to many museums but had never seen anything from your culture."

"Who is your favorite artist, Doña Antonia?" asked Ismael.

"I don't really know. I have many favorites, but if I had to pick one, I think it would be Piero. *The Flagellation*: What a mysterious painting! No one really knows what Piero was trying to do. Once I spent a week looking at the Pieros in Arezzo, San Sepulcro, Urbino. I would love to go back to see them.

"When I went to school," added Antonia, "in the chapel there was a copy of Piero's Madonna. I thought she was the most beautiful woman I had ever seen. I used to daydream that I would look like her when I grew up. We were not allowed movie magazines in school, so we had to make do with virgins and saints."

"I think your fantasies worked a little," said Don Demetrio. "I see in your face a combination of Bellini and Botticelli Madonnas. *Le visage exquis.*"

"Did Cambiasso or Castiglione do a Madonna?" whispered a nervous young woman, who seemed intent on flirting with Don Demetrio.

When there was no answer, her husband, who was looking at her

distractedly, broke in. "Ah, no, my dear Demetrio, you stay wi
Piero and your Genoese, I prefer the Venetians. There is nothi
Tiepolo, Bellini, or Giorgione. I have spent hours in front of *Th
pest*. The light—they knew just how to handle it. And then
Veronese, a giant, a giant. For us from these dry places Venice is
fascinating. Here we fight for a bucket of water, and there, a wh
is built on it. We spend three weeks every year there. My wife,
loves Italian fashions, so while I admire my *Tempest* she goes
crazy in the stores. At night we go to the opera. The perfect vac

"Ah, Miguel. You forgot the food, the pastas, the perfect pr
and melone, the calamari, the great Barolos. The Italians know
live," said Demetrio, gesturing grandly.

"The last trip," said Josefa, "we went to visit the Villa Malc
so balanced, so spare. When I got back to Montana de Plata eve
looked lopsided, and I couldn't stand the clutter in my house.
rid of some of it. My mother-in-law thought we had gone crazy
she found out that we had done away with her father's coloni
turned-bar, she called us 'traitors to our heritage.' "

"For me Florence is best," said the woman sitting next to
She spoke very fast, as if in a great rush. "We married peopl
have the time Demetrio has had to spend in Italy. So we hav
content with visiting the most well-known places. But how can
anything better than Fra Angelico, the simplicity, the purity,
mystic! What do you think, Antonia?"

"It is hard not to agree," responded Antonia.

"Excuse me for changing the topic," said a statuesque elde
whom Antonia imagined to be Don Demetrio's sister, for she
same way of gesturing with her hands as if delivering a lectu
Corequenque you have to see, our own wonder of the world.
be your first vacation with Arturo. We will arrange for a good

"I have read about Corequenque, and Arturo has promised
me," answered Antonia. "I would also like to see the great
churches in Cuzco, those altars made of gold and mirrors,
madonnas with Indian faces. I imagine that the native womer
make wonderful madonnas, with their high cheekbones and
eyes, faces so full of mystery and suffering."

Half a dozen waiters in impeccable uniforms served dinn
enormous silver trays. The menu, which had been carefully pla

"Naughty! The two of you," said Felicia. "I know that is not just cards you two play together."

At the other end of the table Antonia could hear Arturo enthusiastically discussing Father Coyle's plans for a school in Pica. "Send him to us," the woman on his right was saying. "We have terrible schools in Montana de Plata. I wish we did not have to send our children to school abroad so young."

Before Antonia knew it, dinner was over. On the way back to their hotel, Antonia told Arturo, "I never thought I would hear the name Castiglione in Yayaku and tonight I did. I liked Demetrio and his friends. I would even play canasta with those women in order to get to know them better. Tell me more about them, Arturo; they are so different from the people I have met in Pica, all this talk about art, about Italy, about the war."

"These, Antonia, are the old families of Yayaku. Families that have been here for many generations, families that run Yayaku. I don't know them very well myself. I know Demetrio best. The others I met through him. They stick together, they travel together, they marry one another. You will notice that the newspaper here in Montana de Plata is constantly writing about their parties, their outfits, their engagements and marriages. They are the local version of the Savoias in Italy. It is not easy to break into their world. We are their contacts in the provinces. They will always be friendly, but only up to a point. They protect their territory. One thing, though, they are all crazy about Italy, and we Italians are the only non-Yayakuans they will do business with."

"Where did their families originally come from, Arturo? They look almost Spanish but not quite."

"Their ancestors were the Spaniards who came to conquer Yayaku. The men brought no women, so they soon intermarried with the Indian women, thus the name mestizo."

"What a wonderful evening, Arturo!"

"You were wonderful, my dear," said Arturo. "I love to show you off. You charmed them all."

"Thank you, Arturo, but it's you I want to charm," she said, and leaned over to turn off the lights.

As she went to sleep Antonia thought about Piero's pregnant Madonna. Her belly was so big, she could not fasten her dress. Antonia wondered how it would feel when her pregnancy got to that stage. She touched her own belly which was beginning to swell, and tried to picture what her child would look like, but only the features of the Madonna came to mind.

Back in Pica, Antonia's mind frequently wandered to thoughts of Montana de Plata. She told Magdalena about the dinner at the club, about the real estate. "Good for Arturo," said Magdalena, "he has found a way to interest you."

"I know what you are saying," answered Antonia. "I will be kinder about Pica."

Two weeks later, they returned to finalize the sale. It was a busy but special trip. While Arturo attended to other business, Antonia spent many hours with the manager. She saw how he kept the books, and met with him and the tenants to plan improvements. Sometimes she went to Arturo's meetings. As in Pica, people in Montana de Plata were not accustomed to a woman making business decisions, so they were reticent with her. But Antonia was used to such awkward reactions and responded calmly and self-assuredly.

They were invited to visit Demetrio's friends with their large families and rambling houses, and went with them to a bullfight and the horse races. They had dinner with Demetrio several times. More and more he reminded Antonia of the count. "There is a man, a friend of Arturo's," she wrote to the count, "who knows almost as much about art as you do. When I am with him I have to think hard about all the things you taught me."

They went to a little restaurant run by a Swiss couple, where they had long dinners over a bottle of wine. The owners, who had known Arturo during his days as a bachelor, made his favorite dishes. "So happy, so happy for our Arturo to have found a good and pretty Italian wife. You should always stick to your own," the wife would say in her heavy Swiss accent as she served their dinner. Antonia liked living in the hotel, without servants to supervise or meals to plan. Unlike their social life in Pica, here Antonia did not feel she had "obligations." If anything it was Arturo who, often tired at the end of the day, suggested they stay in.

IV

IN THE MIDST of this, the letters began to arrive from Italy and from Buenos Aires. Marco's letter began

Congratulate me! I am to be married! I hope you will be as happy as I am about it, though with the way things are, and you having a baby, I suppose you won't be able to come here for the wedding.

But that is the only thing I am unhappy about! She is a wonderful girl, so kind and so beautiful! Her name is Flora, and she is Señor Parodi's own niece, imagine. He said I needed someone to settle me down, and he was probably right. He has even lent me money to buy us a new house, in one of the best neighborhoods. Flora is already hard at work getting it ready. I am so lucky! I can't believe how lucky I am!

Has Mama written to you? I know she is still mad at you, but if you write to her, could you please explain about my wedding and how I can't send her as much money as she is used to? She is so extravagant! How can she expect me to support all that extravagance, particularly with things the way they are? You can explain it better than I. Please try to, anyway, and I will love you for it.

I have to go now to meet my sweet Flora. Think of me, little Antonia.

Love,
Marco

• • •

My dear Antonia,
I want to warn you that my letters may not arrive as regularly as they did in the past. The good monsignor has consented to be my post-

man, and everything will have to go through Rome. Keeping things from the censor's tireless eyes is my object. It will allow me to send the truth instead of the ridiculous garbage we are being fed by the newspapers.

I have some bad news in this letter. It's about your friend Elsa Gassendi. Her father's mother, it turns out, was Jewish. Nobody knew, or rather somebody knew, because someone denounced him. He's lost his job at the hospital and so has Elsa, and her brother has been sent home from school. For now they are all living in the villa in Artemisia, and are not too badly off as yet. One wishes one could know that this is the worst they will have to endure.

Of course, everyone is angry about it, but nobody dares do anything. I have been down once or twice to see if there is any chance of getting them out of Italy, but with this war, I am not sure that would do much good. Still, one must hope for the best for them.

War, war, war! That is all one hears about these days. Still, Italy is out of it so far, but how long can that last? I was all prepared to depart the stage, but now I'm determined to stay through until this awful act is over. At least I will have the satisfaction of telling the playwright what I think of the ending.

In case your mother has kept her promise and isn't writing to you she is well. In fact, she seems to be doing better than any of us. She has struck up an "acquaintance" with a minor officer at the supply depot, and I imagine her cellar is filling up with provisions in case things get as bad as some people expect. Your mother is an endlessly resourceful woman, and there is absolutely no reason to worry about her. In the meantime, I hear from Signor Ravecca at the bank that she is giving the most notorious parties. Dozens of guests in the most elegant evening clothes and the flashiest cars. Nobody seems to know who they are, but the good signore says they are clearly people of importance. What is she up to, he wonders. I expect that this is another form of laying up goods for the lean years.

I have been to see her once or twice. She complains bitterly about you going away, not that that need concern you. To me, it simply means that she misses you. She is not quite as hard a person as you think, though I know that will be hard for you to see just now.

I expect you've heard the really good news, that Marco is to be married. He wrote me to tell me and to ask me for a loan to help furnish his new house (he says he's been sending your mother every spare penny). I sent him what I could as a wedding gift, though of course you can't get much out these days.

I must get this letter off to the monsignor before I tear it up again and leave you with no news at all. Please write me your good news to the address I give above, and it should reach me eventually.

> *My deepest affection,*
> *Emilio*

• • •

Dear Count Mora,

It is good to hear that you are well, at least, in the midst of all the uncertainty that surrounds you. I have made the arrangements you suggested, and funds will be regularly deposited for Donna Dora's use as need be. (Please say no more about helping, you have done enough of that already.) If this link is cut off for any reason, my brother has access to further sources in Genoa in my name. I'm sure it won't be necessary to caution you not to tell him they are for the benefit of my mother-in-law, if you need to, say you are smuggling them out for my benefit. He has my instructions to use these sources in this way.

I have also deposited money to cover the loan you made to Antonia's brother, Marco. I share your concern about this marriage; he made an application to me (without telling Antonia) for an even larger sum. If I wasn't so busy myself, I'd make the trip to Argentina to look into the thing. As it is, I have asked a business associate of mine in Buenos Aires to see what he can find out. (Please, nothing to Antonia about this; her only concern at the moment is that she won't be able to attend the ceremony.)

Thank you, again, for the news of my father. I have his letters from time to time, but it is good to hear from someone else that he is well. It still breaks my heart that I wasn't able to be there when my mother died. Yes, it is true what my father says about the baby, although it surprises me Antonia herself hasn't written about it. She is getting quite big now. You can imagine what it means to a man of my age to be awaiting his first child! Joy doesn't begin to describe it!

She is still full of surprises. It was a surprise (a pleasant one) to find her in such control when I finally arrived in Pica. I was so very worried about her, and there she was, in a big house, the house transformed, full of life and color and Antonia looking more beautiful than ever. She helps with my business decisions, and not only enjoys it, but seems to have a natural talent for it. The baby will, I hope, complete the picture; I had been so worried that Antonia is too remarkable for such an unremarkable place as Pica.

Keep well, my friend. With God's help, we will be together in Italy again before too long.

Arturo Rontella

• • •

Dear Count,

I know it was nasty of me to keep the news from you. I felt guilty, I guess, being so happy after leaving you alone. It's so unfair that you are left behind with so many worries when you have done so much for me. I only hope that I can make it up to you after all these bad times are over.

Since Italy came into the war, almost our only news of home is the broadcasts from the British radio. And such news they bring! It is an English girl who reads the reports, in a clear, sharp Spanish. It breaks our hearts to listen to her speak so calmly and so correctly of how bombs are falling on her home! We feel as if she were speaking to us as friends, and were hiding her true feelings so as to spare us the pain they would cause us. She has become quite a heroine now. All the talk in town is for the Allies, and how brave they are to stand up to these terrible invasions. The talk of the Italians, lately, has not been good. People have even said bad things in Arturo's hearing, but he is very proud and good and refuses to give up his citizenship (as the prefect has been urging him) or to say anything bad against our country. But I can see how it hurts him.

The good news is that I have become a real businesswoman. Arturo and I have bought an apartment building together in Montana de Plata. We call it our "little fortress." I am his partner, and the president of a new company. Can you imagine that I am now learning about balance sheets, mortgages, depreciation, all of the things real business people know? Our building manager has never had a woman boss before. He doesn't quite know what to make of me, but I think he is beginning to take me seriously.

No, Mama still has not written, so I am doubly grateful for your news of her. Even after all the things she has done, I still worry for her

ment on the baby. "Arturo must be so happy," one of them said
her. Antonia smiled back, hating her, hating all the women and their
bands who were giving Arturo such pain. And he himself remained
nt, cut off from her, even in his tender moments, which grew more
quent as the birth grew nearer. She could only watch as the lines in
face grew stiffer and stiffer, as if freezing in anger.

"He's too good a man," Magdalena said to Antonia. "That's what
n Pedro says. It's not that he couldn't do to them what they are
ng to him. It's that he would suffer for it, because he understands
at he is doing. Don Pedro says bad men are not bad by what they
Good men do some bad things. Everyone does. But the good men
w it, sooner or later.

"The bad men fool themselves. They think, 'I'm doing the right
ng. I am justified. I am only looking after my own. I have no other
ice. I am only doing what everyone else does.' So they go on doing
se things, and they sleep well at night, thinking to themselves that
y are good men.

"Arturo, Don Pedro says, can't fool himself like his partners. You
uld hear what they say behind his back! That he has cheated them,
t he is always holding things over them, that he won't forget their
e mistakes. They say he is a little tyrant, that they will get even with
. They've even gone to Don Pedro, thinking that he is Arturo's
my, asking for help. 'We're only trying to steal back what he has
en from us,' they say.

"Poor Arturo! It is so sad, my dear Antonia. Do you think King
r would have been happier if he hadn't been so fond of flattery?
his daughters would have hated him even more for disbelieving
r lies. They would have plotted against him even more, and the
r king! He would have known they were doing it! And he would
e had to kill them, while feeling all the sorrow of killing his own
ghters. The king would have been like Arturo with his partners."

After several weeks, an uneasy peace was formed. A new partner,
io, was brought in. Arturo kept control of the company with a bare
-one percent. The partners increased their shares slightly, and kept
nt, waiting for another chance.

Not long after this truce, two new kinds of letters began to arrive in
ro's box at the post office. One kind, which he immediately burned

as well as for you and the others I have left behind. Plea
often, so that I can hear your words in my mind, and the
me as they always have.

With a
Antonia

JUST AFTER THE WAR began, Arturo's agent Carlo died.
her widow's weeds, was inconsolable over being unable
Italy. She had to settle for the forlorn little cemetery at th
swept with the dust of the desert, and she wept so har
if she were trying to bring the dry earth to life.

There was a battle among Arturo's partners over t
owned in the business. Carlo had been Arturo's frienc
had kept the other partners at bay. Now the resentments
came to the surface.

The partners would lock themselves up in Arturo's
far into the night. Arturo came home exhausted and pal
down look. He ate hardly anything, and complained
again. Antonia would try to talk to him, but he pushed
not something a woman in your condition should think
When she pressed he would say, "I had a dissatisfie
"The tax men are at it again." At first Antonia believe
ually came to realize that this was a more serious prol

"Those are problems our men are used to," Mago
they talked about it. "Those are little problems. This
ger. It's Arturo's partners who are causing it, accord
Pedro says."

The partners' wives would smile at Antonia in the

after reading, was written in large, awkward handwriting on cheap paper. They were letters of few sentences, letters of warning. Mostly they spoke of Antonia, saying in the most graphic terms of her infidelities with Captain Martín, with "that maniac Indian who follows her everywhere." They urged him to wonder if Antonia's baby would arrive with mestizo skin. Despite the crudeness of the penmanship, Arturo thought he recognized the handwriting of his partners' wives.

The other letters were equally disturbing. They were addressed to Antonia in greenish-blue ink on heavy, violet paper. Arturo, from the letter she wrote him before he was married, recognized the handwriting as Dora's.

Arturo put these letters in a drawer in his desk. There were a lot of them, and the drawer was soon almost full.

At home Arturo was almost cheerful again, and Antonia thought the crisis was over. She told him that Magdalena had told her about his partners, and even persuaded him to talk to her about his business.

Arturo's business was not a solid thing, not something you could put your hands on, like a racehorse, or your feet into, like a field of grain.

He owned no factory, no copper mine, no vast hacienda. Not even, like the British, a railroad. The things in his warehouse were not objects he had made, or caused others to make, or (sometimes) even things he owned.

The Yayakuans—the poorest campesinos and the great landowners alike—couldn't understand it. They still lived in the dream of the Inca and the conquistador: Wealth and power are in the earth. To them, Arturo seemed to take gold out of the air.

"It is something only a stranger could see," Arturo told Antonia. "Yayakuans are so earthbound; to them silver in the ground is wealth, cattle on the prairie is wealth. They don't see that money comes from moving such things from one place to another. Only foreigners could see that here and, I might add, only a certain kind of foreigner. It might have been anyone, but it happened to be me."

His business was a fleet of paper, he told Antonia, tiny ships full of words. The papers said "A trainload of cow skins in March," "A hundred tons of copper ore in July." The papers moved from here to there, from a mine in the eastern mountains, or a hacienda in the north, sometimes by way of the capital. They sailed into the harbor of Arturo's desk for a week or a month. Then they were off somewhere else, to America or Japan. As often as not, Arturo never saw skins or copper ore himself, only the papers.

Other papers sailed the other way: licenses, "exclusive rights to sell United Oil products in the province of Pica," or "exclusive dealership for Ford automobiles for the southern region of Yayaku." These papers were not things, or the right to own things, but for the right to buy them and sell them again. "This is what I do," said Arturo. "It is not so very complicated. I buy whatever I can sell wherever I can. That's all."

All of these papers, his fleet, the source of all his wealth, sailed in a sea of voices. The voices were those of customs agents, subministers, deputy ambassadors for trade, official and unofficial, keepers of seals and signatures and handshakes, men whose favorable words kept his ships afloat and whose curses could send them straight to the bottom. Sometimes the sea was calm and the sailing was smooth. At other times the sea was trouble, and Arturo worried for his little paper ships as much as his ancestors had in the time of the Dorias.

The voices took much tending. Some of them, the softer ones, needed bribes. The American accents were interested mainly in handsome profits. But the trickier voices needed other things, things that they rarely mentioned by name: special favors and reassurances, and a visit from a deputy ambassador at a particular time, certain rare kinds of flattery. Arturo was good at the tending; so was Don Pedro, and both of them prospered.

"That is why Don Pedro and I go to the capital," he told Antonia. "To sit around a table with men like myself. These men give themselves names that sound like those of learned academies, or secret societies: The Circle of Cotton, The Institute of Ore, The Society of Leather. Like the old merchants, the ones with ships of wood, we talk about the weather and the sea and send offerings to emissaries to smooth the passage. We are almost all foreigners, mostly Italian like me. We are strangers even though some of us have lived in Yayaku for a generation."

Lately, the weather was troubling. There were new voices in the wind, voices promising tempests.

Among the many political parties that, Arturo explained to Antonia, "infested" the nation, there was one whose long, complicated name had been shortened to "the Wing." For more than sixty years, the Wing had taken up a handful of seats in the National Assembly and made noises out of proportion to their numbers about wealth, land, and the natural rights of people. As the Assembly was nearly without power, the Wing had meant little and had accomplished little most of that time. Then, a generation earlier, a foolish president had outlawed the Wing as subversive and had thrown many of its prominent members into prison.

This was a grave error. Small and weak, the Wing had grown quickly in the dark, its now secret members multiplying faster than mushrooms after the rain. And in the imagination of its adversaries, the Wing had grown even faster. Any amount of intrigues and sabotages were attributed to it; any number of prominent men were rumored to belong secretly to its ranks. The more it was suppressed, the more it seemed to grow. In the cafés in the capital, in the village squares, there was talk of the "shadow of the Wing" which, Arturo told Antonia, seemed to expand every year.

Antonia had a new project in mind. It was to build a house. She waited for the right moment to bring it up to Arturo. One day when he asked her which room would be appropriate for the baby, she decided to bring it up.

"We will need a new house soon with a family coming," she said.

"Why?" said Arturo, smiling at her. "We already have the biggest in town. We won't need any more room unless you give birth to an army."

"But this house is awkward and old-fashioned, and it isn't safe for children. Think of all the places they can fall into! And there is no place for them to play except the street and those dusty courtyards."

"Many children were born and raised in this house."

"But that was when children were kept chained like monkeys. I don't want my children to grow up like that. I want them to be free in their own house."

"Well, then, what kind of house do you want?"

Antonia brought him an American magazine. The house in the pictures she showed him was only one story, with a tile roof, and spread out a little like an old hacienda. And it was surrounded by a beautiful garden which came up right to the windows and the doorways.

"But we could never have a garden like that," Arturo said.

"But why not?"

"It is too dry here."

"But there is a garden in the plaza."

"Yes, but it has to be watered."

"Well, our garden could be watered, too."

It happened that the garden was built even before the house. Antonia chose a lot that Arturo owned east of the cathedral. "Why would anyone want to live so far out of town when they have a house right on the plaza?" people asked, and shook their heads again at the strange woman Arturo had married.

Antonia had a wall built around the lot and, in the last few months before Mariana was born, spent much of her waking hours there, planting her garden where no one from the town could see her.

VI

Dearest Sister,

I hope you will allow me the honor to call you that, my dearest sister, even though I have never had the privilege to meet you. Marco spoke of you with such sweetness I feel you are my sister. And now I must write to you as a stranger, with such a sorrow! My eyes are burning with the tears of what I must tell you!

Dear sister, dear, sweet Antonia whom I feel so close to, in spite of the distance that so cruelly separates us! Oh, life is so hard and so harsh! Our Marco, our sweet, beautiful Marco is dead! It is so sudden and swift I cannot believe it! I lie on my pillow and weep for hour after hour! I am inconsolable, as I know you will be when you read my sad sorrowful letter.

But I must drag myself from my anguish and heartbreak to write to you of such shameful things! He died so quickly—at least there was one

blessing because his pain was so short. They say it was typhoid and they had to bury him in quicklime right away. And there was no time to make provisions. And now the bills come every day! There is no money even to pay for the funeral!

Dear sister, I beg you, I implore you before the Virgin and Jesus to forgive me, but I must have money to pay all these bills! The creditors are threatening to throw me out into the street, me, when I am so weak with sorrow I can hardly stand! Please, dear sister, in Marco's memory you must send me [here was mentioned a sum that made Antonia gasp] *as soon as you can. It would shame me too much if your husband knew; I would prefer it if you didn't mention my request to him. It is bad enough that I must ask my poor husband's sister.*

Yours in sorrow,
Flora di Credi

. . .

My dear Arturo,

I expect by now the terrible and unexpected news of Marco's death has reached you. It is a heavy blow for me, as he was the closest thing to a son that I will ever have, a blow made heavier for it was I who urged him to go to Argentina. Can I forgive myself? How is it that one's best intentions can go so wrong?

I have written separately to Antonia, knowing that she will find no greater comfort than you will give her. I am writing to you about another unpleasant aspect of this tragic affair. The news of Marco's death came in the form of a rather distasteful letter from his young widow. In it, she said she was deeply in debt, and begged me for money, claiming she had no one to turn to. The amount she asked for was shockingly large. I'm afraid I had to dip into your special account to cover it.

There is something in this sad business that wobbles on three legs. I cannot believe that Marco sank so far in such a short time as to leave his widow in such a state. Is there some way that the matter can be discreetly looked into? Please forgive me for intruding my suspicions on your mourning, but I fear that I may have sent Marco into a den of wolves.

All is well as can be expected here. I look forward to hearing the good news—that of the birth of your child.

Yours with regret,
Emilio Mora

• • •

Dear Count Mora,

Thank you for your letter. Yes, the news had reached us by telegram from Marco's agent about a month ago, and it has been hard on us both, particularly with Antonia's condition. There is always a feeling of guilt at such times, that Antonia feels as well as you do, but whatever hap-pened must have had more to do with Marco and his fate than with either of you. Although I have never met Antonia's brother, I feel sure that your intentions could only have been good and wise. There are some situations when even the best of intentions can only go awry.

I, too, have received a letter from the widow asking for a large sum to cover Marco's debts. She begged me not to shame Marco's memory by telling Antonia. At the same time, Antonia came to me asking for a large sum to send her mother. Since I knew Donna Dora was provided for, I pressed her and she showed me the letter the widow had sent her. From the three of us, she has asked for a small fortune.

I don't know what to say about this sad matter except your suspicions seem to be justified. My associate in Buenos Aires reports that no business is in thriving health there, but that Rodolfo di Credi's holdings seem perfectly secure as far as he is able to tell. No word of any bankruptcy or liquidation. He also has not heard anything of Marco's marriage, or of his death, or even of any outbreak of typhus.

It is enormously frustrating not to be able to do more. Even if it were possible for me leave Antonia, relations between our two countries are not good these days and travel between them is not easy. So it must remain a mystery for the time being. Please let me know if you hear anything new from the widow. Our last letter (after we had sent the money) came back to us.

Yes, we have been receiving letters from Donna Dora, just in the last two months or so. I haven't passed them on to Antonia as yet, or even told her that they have arrived. I am waiting for a happier time.

Yours,
Arturo Rontella

ANTONIA WAS very quiet after reading the letter that said Marco was dead. She went up to a low-ceilinged room at the top of the house, on a little half floor between the main floor and the roof over the servant's rooms. It was there she kept her trunks from Italy. She had hardly looked at the things in the trunks since she arrived in Pica and had slowly made another kind of life. She didn't want to be reminded of her old life, the life that had included Marco.

She had a few photographs of him in her room and the letters he had sent from Buenos Aires, but in these trunks she could find nothing more. She remembered other things—a few birthday gifts of jewelry, some shells they had collected together, a cigarette holder he had sent her from school and which she had never used. But none of it was to be found in the trunks. In her haste to leave home, they must have been left behind.

She spent a long time in the room sitting on one of the Frenchwoman's couches, which she had had Toma drag out of the living room. It was odd about things, she thought, things that contained memories. To anyone else, even to Dora, those little objects that held memories of Marco meant nothing. They were important only to her, and now she had lost them, and almost everything else about him. It was as when her father died, far off in a place she had never seen, with no goodbyes, no last messages, just a letter from a stranger.

She came down for a silent dinner with Arturo, who understood her well enough to speak no more than was necessary. Then she went to bed but didn't sleep. After dark and before Arturo came in she put on some clothes and slipped out of the house. She walked by the back alleys where she couldn't be seen out to the garden, which waited, behind its brick wall, for another new life to begin.

She let herself in. She looked up and noticed that the stars were coming out. From the tap set up to water the garden, she filled a pail of water and sat to watch as the stars slowly covered the surface of the water with their reflection.

An hour or two later, the gate opened again, and Arturo came up behind her. She didn't look up. Crouching there with the moonlight on her swelling belly, she looked like a stone goddess of fertility from the ruins of Corequenque.

"It ought to be the sea," Antonia said in a very quiet voice when she saw Arturo. "It ought to be the Mediterranean. But it was the best I could do."

Two weeks after this, their daughter was born. The labor was not difficult, but it was long and tiring. It began in the very early morning. Arturo awoke, went out for the midwife, and waited. When, by midday, the baby hadn't come, and the midwife waved him away from the room, he went to the office. He worked fitfully while watching from the one narrow window for Toma's sign. The sign did not come.

Arturo went home for lunch and found there was no change. He went back to work and came back home for supper. "No change?" he asked Toma. Toma shook his head, and something fell out of his hands onto the floor. Before Toma could grab it again, Arturo picked it up. It was a tiny bundle of what looked like twigs, straw, and hair.

"Well," Arturo said, handing the bundle back to Toma, who stood with his eyes on his feet. "I suppose it can do no harm."

At last, just after sunset, the baby was born. Arturo heard its cries and burst into the room. The midwife, holding the shriveled, glistening bundle in her arms, gave him a fierce look, but he came into the room anyway. Antonia looked up from the bed with the weary look he had come to know. "At least it is over," she said, trying to smile. "Or is it just beginning?"

"It's a wonderful beginning," said Arturo. "I have the two most beautiful women ever," and he knelt close to the bed to hold Antonia. He had tears in his eyes. Antonia wiped them gently, and felt her own tears melting with his. They held each other for a long time. They both knew that a new bond held them to each other.

Arturo rose and moved toward the crib. He peered at the baby excitedly. "Why is she so small?" he asked the midwife. "Is she breathing all right?" "How often does she have to eat?" Finally Antonia sent him to fetch Toma. As Arturo opened the door to call him, Toma nearly stumbled to the floor. "So pretty, so pretty," Toma said, bobbing joyfully. He and Arturo stood by the crib contemplating the baby in silence as Antonia fell asleep.

Arturo spent the next day spreading the happy news. He sent telegrams to the count and Dora, to his family and Signor Ravecca. He went to see Don Pedro, who gave him a glass of brandy and toasted "the new dynasty." He even called the bishop and ended up talking to his mother. "I will pray that the Lord gives your daughter the divine call and that someday she will be a Mother Superior," the bishop's mother said.

He ran back and forth to tell Antonia everyone's reactions, and stopped several times at the flower shop until they ran out of roses. He gave his employees the day off, and wine to take home.

At the end of the day he was so tired he fell asleep with his clothes on.

MAGDALENA WAS the first visitor. She arrived holding a large package tied with pink satin ribbons. She placed the package in Antonia's lap and made her way to the crib.

"Antonia, Antonia!" she said excitedly. "Come here and look. Your baby has a mark on the right side of her mouth. Do you know what that means? It means your child will be lucky in love!"

Antonia smiled as she unwrapped her present. The paper fell away to reveal a somewhat lumpy and unevenly stitched baby's blanket. Antonia gaped, but then realized that the work must have been Magdalena's own, and set her face into a look of delight. "How lovely, Magdalena," she said softly. "Thank you."

"I don't know about it being lovely," she said, "but I made it myself," responded Magdalena. "I never made one for my own children, but I wanted something special for your baby." Antonia lifted the baby from the crib and, wrapping her in the blanket, placed her in Magdalena's arms.

The baby was named Mariana after Arturo's mother. For days after she was born, the house was filled with all the people of Pica. Antonia was given an endless stream of advice. She was told to put a red ribbon on the baby to ward off the evil eye, and warned not to take her out of the house for at least two months because the air was too harsh. She should eat liver so that the baby would never get hepatitis; she was told to wrap the baby's legs together so that they would stay straight. Finally Antonia could stand it no more and refused to see anyone.

Arturo was gentle with Antonia. He knew the pressures on her, and he thought of ways to make her relax. He encouraged her to play the piano, gave her a pearl necklace he especially ordered from Montana de Plata, made an effort to come home early. He made thousands of plans for Mariana. During the day he would sneak out of the office to see his daughter.

Antonia shocked the town again by refusing to have her baptized in the cathedral by the bishop, and preferred to do without the big ceremony everyone was expecting. Arturo agreed with her. They went out alone to a little village church north of Pica, and Father Coyle performed the rites. Antonia liked the loping way the Latin came out of his mouth, without any of the extra flourishes of the bishop. This was a ceremony for God, she thought, not for the assembly in the cathedral or the bishop's own mother.

Mariana was a fat, round, good-natured baby who learned to smile and laugh almost immediately and rarely cried. Antonia loved her so deeply that it frightened her. She watched the baby for hours as Mariana lay in her crib, stared at the baby's wide-open, deep-blue eyes and waving hands, which seemed to want to take in everything.

But Antonia's sadness did not leave her after Mariana was born. She seemed quieter, more withdrawn than ever. Arturo, thinking she was still tired, hired a nurse for the baby. The nurse was a large, bossy woman who reminded Antonia of Eliana. She let Antonia see the baby for only an hour or two each day, and insisted that Antonia stay in bed until noon "in order to get some rest." But it was something else that was troubling Antonia.

She spent more time in the walled garden at the edge of town. She would leave the baby with the nurse and go out in the morning and work in the garden, sometimes until late afternoon. Workmen had begun to lay the foundations for the house—a long, sprawling, L-shaped building very much like the one Antonia had pointed out in the magazine. The flowers and the shrubbery, much of it carefully imported from hundreds of miles away, were beginning to take root and flourish under Antonia's constant care.

A few days after the baby was born, a note arrived from Magdalena. The note said: "I am sending someone to you. Do not worry when she will arrive; she will pick the best time herself. She is a wise woman, one of the wisest I know, and she will know what to ask you and what to say."

Antonia was surprised. Why, she wondered, had Magdalena sent her a note instead of telling her? Before she had the time to ask her friend, Toma came to tell her there was someone waiting for her.

"There's a woman here who wants to see you," he said in a small voice and a frightened face.

"Take her to the room with the balcony and I'll come to her," Antonia said.

"But Señora!" said Toma, looking alarmed.

"It's all right, Toma, I'm expecting her," Antonia said, and she began to get dressed.

The woman in the front room did look strange. She was thin and her face was dark and very deeply lined, lines that suggested her life had not been full of sweetness. Her hair was long, half black and half gray, and worn loose and straggling over her shoulders. She was dressed in layers of woolen cloaks although the weather was not cold.

"Magdalena sent you?" Antonia asked with some hesitation. The woman looked familiar.

"She did," answered the woman in a thick, rich voice. "She said you might need me." The woman did not smile, and she did not sit down when Antonia offered her a chair. Antonia, with a start, realized how she knew her. She was the woman with the fierce expression who had stood in the crowd outside the balcony when Arturo came back to Pica from Italy.

"Magdalena is one of my closest friends here," said Antonia. "But I am not quite sure why she has sent you, or why she thinks I might need you."

"Magdalena is never wrong about these things," said the woman without any emotion in her voice. "If she sent me to you, then there is something you need."

There was a long silence and Antonia sat down. The woman remained standing.

"What is it?" Antonia said finally. "What is it that you do for people? What is it that Magdalena thinks you might do for me?"

"That is a hard thing for me to say, to you, a foreign woman," said the woman. "I can do some things for some people, some for others. There are those who come to me with problems with the idea that there is something wrong or out of place in their lives. I know certain things—certain old things from the past, from the time of the conquistadores. There are those who say I am in touch with things—some call them forces, some call them spirits—that belong to this place. There are some who think I can bring these things back into balance with the world."

"I am not sure what all of this has to do with me."

"Perhaps nothing. Perhaps nothing at all."

There was another long silence. The woman showed no sign of leaving.

"There are people who come here—foreigners," the woman said, "who don't feel as if it is their home. They are like the flowers in the plaza, delicate, brought from far away, and unable to survive here without special care. If the flowers in the plaza are not watered, they wither away. Some of the foreigners who come here feel the same way.

"It is as if they were flowers themselves, fragile, unable to put roots in the soil. It is not easy to make them a part of this place, which, after all, is not their real home. There are things that can be done for these people, to help them belong here."

"What sort of things?"

"There are certain herbs, certain ceremonies that, it is said, can help this unbalance of a person away from home."

"Can you do these things?"

"There are those who say so."

Antonia stood up. She crossed the room in front of the woman and went to the window overlooking the plaza. "What must one do?" she asked, "to have these ceremonies performed?"

"She must give up many things. She must give up the thought of living anywhere else on earth. Once the ceremonies have been performed, they cannot be undone. She will be tough as the toughest desert plant. She will thrive in the desert. But if she leaves, even to live in the place of her birth, she will grow weaker than before and waste away like a plant once it has been uprooted. It is a price that must be paid."

Antonia turned and looked at the woman. "I would like you to do these ceremonies," she said.

The woman opened her cloak. Tied around her body were dozens of tiny bags and bundles. She began detaching some of these, and pulling them open with her long, thin fingers.

After the woman left, Toma came into the room with the same look of fear he had had when the woman had arrived. Antonia smiled. "What is wrong, Toma? The woman was a friend of my friend. She did nothing bad and now she is gone."

Toma looked down at the floor. "It is nothing, Señora." He started to leave.

"Wait a moment," Antonia said. "You know something about this woman, don't you? What is it?"

"It is nothing, really, Señora."

"Please tell me what you know, Toma. It is important that I know."

Toma looked up at her. "Long ago, when Señor Rontella first came to Pica," he said, "this woman came to live with him."

Antonia stared at him. "And what happened, Toma?"

"One day, Señor Rontella sent her away. People were worried about it. They said she was a witch who would put a curse on any woman who married him."

The next day, Antonia went to visit Magdalena. The little door to the alley was shut, and one of Magdalena's sons answered the knock. "My mother is asleep," he said to her.

"I would like to wait," said Antonia.

The boy took her up to Magdalena's sitting room. The curtains were open, letting the sunlight through a window overlooking a back alley. In the sun the room looked dusty, and the bronze Buddha looked too shiny.

After a few minutes Magdalena came into the room, wearing a beautifully embroidered silk kimono. Without saying a word, she lit the Chinese oil lamp, drew the curtains, and sat down. The room was at once filled with its usual atmosphere.

"What brings you here, Antonia?" Magdalena said, smiling sadly.

"You sent a woman to put a curse on me!"

"You mean Lara? But she is a good woman. Why should she put a curse on you, particularly since I asked her to go to you as my friend?"

"Toma told me that she used to be Arturo's mistress! That she promised to put a curse on anyone who married him! How could you do such a thing to me?"

"Antonia," said Magdalena, frowning and drawing her legs, encased in silk pants like those of a harem girl, under her on the couch and holding her ankles with her hands. "That was years and years ago. Before I was even in Pica. And Lara says she has forgotten all about that, that it means nothing to her, that she has more important things to fill her mind. She likes you, admires you. She told me so herself. Antonia, do you really think I would send an evil woman to you? One who would put a curse on you?"

"No, I didn't. But now I don't know. How do you know this Lara wasn't lying to you about not hating me?"

"I don't know, but I feel it to be so. I feel such things, Antonia. I feel I couldn't do anything to harm you even without meaning to. Please, Antonia, understand the real reason why I did it. Lara has helped me in difficult times; I thought she could help you too."

Antonia was silent for a moment, thinking. "Whatever happened, you only meant good. But please, don't send me any more witches or spells in the future. I don't need them, and they only worry me."

Magdalena nodded solemnly. "God forgive me for saying this, Antonia, but your husband was quite a ladies' man before you were married, but I'm sure that's all over now. He loves you and he is the kind of man who, once married, stays so forever because he waited so long."

In trying to unravel her mixed feelings about Lara, Antonia could not quite decide what it was that upset her the most: the fear that a curse might have been put on her, or her jealousy at the thought that Arturo could have loved Lara.

A FEW DAYS LATER, Antonia went out to see Father Coyle. She found him in the back of the school, working in a little vegetable garden he kept there. "Señora Rontella, it is good to see you," he said, rubbing his hands free of dirt. "Would you like something to drink? Come and sit here in the shade."

Antonia sat on a wooden camp stool under an old jacaranda tree at the edge of the garden and Father Coyle brought her some lemonade.

"Please forgive the appearance of my little garden," he said. "I don't have much time to work on it, and I keep insisting on trying to grow things from home. It's really too dry for them here."

Antonia thought for a moment of her own garden, watered every day just to produce flowers. "It looks like a fine garden to me," she said.

"Thank you, and how is your Mariana? I haven't seen her since the baptism."

"She is fine. I was just thinking that it was a shame that you only teach boys. I would like to have my daughter go to a good school when the time comes."

"Well," said Father Coyle, with his large childlike smile. "Now that you and I are both putting down roots here, we will have plenty of time to talk about what the possibilities are."

Antonia smiled and nodded.

"It's funny, isn't it?" Father Coyle went on, "how you can come hundreds and hundreds of miles from the place you were born and find your home there. And you know, somehow that is your home. I suppose it's one of God's ways of telling you that He does have a plan for your life, after all."

"Do you really feel that way, Father?"

"Yes, I do. Don't you?"

"I suppose. Yes, I do feel a plan to it sometimes, though it is hard to grasp."

VII

AFTER HER VISIT with Father Coyle, Antonia began to feel stronger. As she became more of her old self, she began to notice that she no longer ran her own house. When she wanted to get up before noon, the nurse objected; when she wanted to see the baby, the nurse put up an argument. Opposing this large and relentlessly cheerful and charitable woman took all of Antonia's energy; she found herself getting headaches from having to repeat her wishes so often before they were obeyed.

"I didn't get married and come two thousand miles for this," she thought. "This woman is worse than a mother-in-law."

She brought up the problem of the nurse with Arturo over dinner, but he seemed distracted and begged her to keep the nurse on for a while longer, until she felt stronger.

"But I feel stronger already!" she protested.

"Yes, but won't you need some help while the baby is small?"

"This woman is no help at all! All she cares about is giving me orders! She doesn't even let me out of bed, and she acts as if Mariana were her own little doll, not my baby at all."

"Well, put up with it for a while longer," Arturo said with a sigh. "If it still doesn't work out, we'll try something else."

In order to escape from the nurse, Antonia's visits to Magdalena became more frequent. One afternoon she found Magdalena in her room surrounded by her younger children. They were looking at a small faded photograph of Magdalena's father.

"Look, look," Luis was saying, "he has the same nose as little Pedro."

"No, my nose is like my father's," answered Pedro without hesitation.

"He was bald," said the youngest. "That means that we will all be bald too. Look how thin Pedro's hair already is."

"That's unkind," said Magdalena. "Besides, bald men are very elegant, especially if they grow a thick beard."

"What color were his eyes, Mother?" asked José shyly.

"I wish I knew," replied Magdalena. "You see, my children, I never met either of my parents. They died when I was very young, too young to remember them." The children, sensing her sadness, moved closer to her, and the smallest one sat in her lap.

There was a long silence.

Little Pedro noticed Antonia, who had been standing by the door watching them. He ran to her and asked her to join them. He took the picture from his mother's hands and showed it to Antonia.

"Can you tell us who looks more like him, Doña Antonia?"

Antonia studied the faded photograph. "I don't know about the features," replied Antonia, "but I can tell that he was a kind and strong man, and in that way you all resemble him."

Magdalena silently took back the picture. With a little key that she kept under one of her combs, she opened her diary and carefully placed the picture inside it.

"Now, children," she said, "it's time for your hot chocolate and your homework. We will continue this another day."

One by one they kissed their mother on her forehead and left the room.

Antonia and Magdalena sat in silence for a long moment.

Finally Antonia spoke up. "Tell me about your parents, Magdalena."

"I know very little, and every time I have tried to find out more about them, I run into dead ends," Magdalena said sadly.

After a silence, she continued.

"The little that I know was told to me by the people who raised me. I don't think they knew much themselves. This picture is the only thing of his I ever had. Of my mother I know even less. I know she died in childbirth, and that she was very young and very beautiful.

"My father was an English archaeologist. He came to Yayaku with the first Anglo-American survey of Corequenque. There he fell in love with the daughter of one of the Indians who served as his guide. He was already gone when she discovered she was pregnant. Her family thought it was a curse from the gods to have a child with foreign blood. My own grandparents were afraid the curse would bring them more disaster if I stayed with them. So I was raised by two unmarried aunts who gave me their last name, a roof, and not much attention or love.

"When I was a child, I would make up little plays about my parents. My father would be a handsome red-haired man who arrived in a galleon, my mother an Indian princess. I had them meet each other in thousands of ways. In school I never paid attention to what the teachers were saying. I had my little dream world. When theater troupes came to town, I would sneak into the theater through the back door and watch the rehearsals. By the time I was fifteen they offered me a job. I went with them. I never thought of telling my aunts. I don't think they looked very hard for me. Later I was told that they had managed to get some money from the Anglo-American expedition to bring me up. I think they were just as happy to keep the money."

"Your story is similar to mine," said Antonia.

"My father lived in Argentina. He came home only once a year. My mother was always too busy with her own life and we saw little of her. She trained us to stay out of her way. We had a servant, Eliana, who organized our lives the best she could, and when we were very young we were sent to boarding schools.

"My father's visits were short, and while he was home, my mother played at being the perfect mother. Everything functioned like a real family. She even got up to have breakfast! My father spoiled us. He told us wonderful stories about the gauchos in Argentina, he took us on long walks to pick chestnuts, and out for cakes and candies. When he left, life was unbearable. My brother and I would make up stories about him. I think we confused the stories we made up with the ones of the gauchos he told us. We were always preparing ourselves to run away to Argentina to be with him. I don't understand why he didn't take us with him. I wish he had.

"The most important person in my childhood was someone who was not even related to us, a man who made it his mission to make us happy.

"He had been one of my mother's many lovers. When their affair ended, he managed to continue to be part of our lives. I think Mother was relieved to have him do her job. I don't know how he did it, but he even acquired father's permission to look after us.

"He still writes to me. One day I will read you some of his letters."

It was getting late. Magdalena and Antonia did not notice that they were sitting in the dark. A servant came in and turned on the light.

"I must go," said Antonia.

"Think," replied Magdalena, "now we have our own little families. How very lucky we are."

On her way back home, Antonia thought of the afternoon, of Magdalena surrounded by her children. How warm and close they were to one another. She rushed home to Arturo and Mariana. When she reached the house she was out of breath and smiled to realize that she had been running.

At home, however, the problems with the nurse never seemed to stop. The nurse ordered the baby's room moved from the one next to Antonia's to the room next to her own. The nurse refused to let Toma touch the baby. The nurse ordered special food for herself to be sent to her room. Antonia found herself spending most of her days countermanding the nurse's orders.

The nurse refused to raise her voice at Antonia and insisted on treating her like a sick child. *"Pobrecita!"* she would say, smiling indulgently when Antonia shrieked at her. "Such a temper you have! You must go right to bed, you are so tired. I will have the girl bring you up some tea. No, no, I won't have any argument at all. Straight to bed, my little mother goose. I will look after everything for you, my dear. A girl with your delicate health shouldn't try to overdo things."

One morning things came to a head. Antonia woke up to find out that neither the nurse nor the baby was in the house. "She took the

baby to the doctor in Casilda," Toma told Antonia. "She said the baby was too thin, wanted her doctor to look at it."

Antonia, thinking of the drunken old doctor in Casilda, flew into a fury. She went immediately to Arturo's office and demanded to see him. His secretary explained that Arturo was at the train station, but Antonia insisted on waiting in his office. Arturo's secretary, who was used to Antonia's visits, said nothing and let her in.

Antonia sat down in one of the chairs opposite the desk to wait. The desk was, as usual, covered with papers, but it was a rectangle of violet which called her attention. She picked it up.

An hour later, Arturo returned to find her in tears. "Why didn't you tell me about my mother's letters?" she said. "This one must have been here for days, and she has written dozens."

Arturo opened a drawer. "Here are the others," he said. "But why didn't you give them to me before?" cried Antonia. "Why did you hide them from me?"

"Because I knew they would upset you just as they have. I was keeping them for you until the right moment."

Antonia and Arturo went home together, taking the letters with them. Antonia shut herself up in her room and didn't even notice when the nurse brought the baby home.

Dora's letters were very strange. Antonia had received very few letters from her mother when she was a child, and these were always as short as possible, no more than a few lines, and held strictly to business: "I will send the car to your school on Tuesday. Please be sure to come home. Dora."

These letters were different. They had no dates, greetings, endings, or margins. They were all exactly two sheets long, and every inch of both sides was covered with her tiny, precise handwriting. They began without introduction and ended abruptly at the end of the second side of the second sheet, sometimes in the middle of a sentence. Occasionally the next letter picked up the theme, but more often it went off on another subject altogether.

Antonia had the impression that Dora was simply writing down whatever came into her mind, without making any attempt to sort it out or even thinking much about who she was writing to.

As clearly as Antonia could make out from the postmarks, the first letters were mostly reproaches. "How could I have given birth to such

children!'' one of them began. "Some evil witch must have stolen my babies and left snakes in their place! Now, when I am old, and no use to them, they abandon me without defenses in this terrible time, when I have fools and enemies on every side.''

In other letters, she wrote to Antonia using a tone she had never used when speaking to her, giving her the benefit of her peculiar advice, almost as if she were a friend. "I hope, Antonia, that you have the sense not to have any children. All the work and sacrifice, all the damage to one's body and then nothing but ingratitude.''

Besides, if you have children in that part of the world, they will be born with all kind of curses. I have heard there are sorcerers and witches there who can lay curses on people. I read the story of one poor child born with three eyes, and another with no feet. You see, Antonia, you don't realize it, but your husband is a powerful man. In order to get to be powerful, powerful enemies are made, and those enemies are the ones that will hire the sorcerers. You can find one in any marketplace, I am told, who would curse a whole family for a few coins. Perhaps you should find one yourself to rid yourself of your husband's mistresses. Don't fool your-self that he doesn't have any! Remember, I know men are . . .

I was looking at the picture of you, Antonia, one taken just before you married that man. If I were you, I would wear my skirts very long; your legs are less than perfect. When Arturo was around me, he kept on looking at my legs, so I could see he was attracted by that feature. Grow up, Antonia, learn a few things to keep your man, or you will be left with an empty bed every night . . .

Those friends of yours, the ones who fixed your marriage for you, they tell me that your father's business is doing badly; they heard it through some banking contact, and can't keep from telling me, the gossips that they are. I don't believe it for a second. Your brother had just learned some sharp tricks to snatch money away from his own mother on the side. Or perhaps he has some woman. I have the feeling that he has a woman, one of those who knows exactly how to get money out of a man. A greedy woman, who will be the death of me . . .

Watch out for that husband of yours, Antonia. He strikes me as someone who has funny business practices. You must be careful of him. Wake up so that you don't find yourself in the street someday. I always

baby to the doctor in Casilda," Toma told Antonia. "She said the baby was too thin, wanted her doctor to look at it."

Antonia, thinking of the drunken old doctor in Casilda, flew into a fury. She went immediately to Arturo's office and demanded to see him. His secretary explained that Arturo was at the train station, but Antonia insisted on waiting in his office. Arturo's secretary, who was used to Antonia's visits, said nothing and let her in.

Antonia sat down in one of the chairs opposite the desk to wait. The desk was, as usual, covered with papers, but it was a rectangle of violet which called her attention. She picked it up.

An hour later, Arturo returned to find her in tears. "Why didn't you tell me about my mother's letters?" she said. "This one must have been here for days, and she has written dozens."

Arturo opened a drawer. "Here are the others," he said. "But why didn't you give them to me before?" cried Antonia. "Why did you hide them from me?"

"Because I knew they would upset you just as they have. I was keeping them for you until the right moment."

Antonia and Arturo went home together, taking the letters with them. Antonia shut herself up in her room and didn't even notice when the nurse brought the baby home.

Dora's letters were very strange. Antonia had received very few letters from her mother when she was a child, and these were always as short as possible, no more than a few lines, and held strictly to business: "I will send the car to your school on Tuesday. Please be sure to come home. Dora."

These letters were different. They had no dates, greetings, endings, or margins. They were all exactly two sheets long, and every inch of both sides was covered with her tiny, precise handwriting. They began without introduction and ended abruptly at the end of the second side of the second sheet, sometimes in the middle of a sentence. Occasionally the next letter picked up the theme, but more often it went off on another subject altogether.

Antonia had the impression that Dora was simply writing down whatever came into her mind, without making any attempt to sort it out or even thinking much about who she was writing to.

As clearly as Antonia could make out from the postmarks, the first letters were mostly reproaches. "How could I have given birth to such

children!'' one of them began. ''Some evil witch must have stolen my babies and left snakes in their place! Now, when I am old, and no use to them, they abandon me without defenses in this terrible time, when I have fools and enemies on every side.''

In other letters, she wrote to Antonia using a tone she had never used when speaking to her, giving her the benefit of her peculiar advice, almost as if she were a friend. ''I hope, Antonia, that you have the sense not to have any children. All the work and sacrifice, all the damage to one's body and then nothing but ingratitude.''

Besides, if you have children in that part of the world, they will be born with all kind of curses. I have heard there are sorcerers and witches there who can lay curses on people. I read the story of one poor child born with three eyes, and another with no feet. You see, Antonia, you don't realize it, but your husband is a powerful man. In order to get to be powerful, powerful enemies are made, and those enemies are the ones that will hire the sorcerers. You can find one in any marketplace, I am told, who would curse a whole family for a few coins. Perhaps you should find one yourself to rid yourself of your husband's mistresses. Don't fool yourself that he doesn't have any! Remember, I know men are . . .

I was looking at the picture of you, Antonia, one taken just before you married that man. If I were you, I would wear my skirts very long; your legs are less than perfect. When Arturo was around me, he kept on looking at my legs, so I could see he was attracted by that feature. Grow up, Antonia, learn a few things to keep your man, or you will be left with an empty bed every night . . .

Those friends of yours, the ones who fixed your marriage for you, they tell me that your father's business is doing badly; they heard it through some banking contact, and can't keep from telling me, the gossips that they are. I don't believe it for a second. Your brother had just learned some sharp tricks to snatch money away from his own mother on the side. Or perhaps he has some woman. I have the feeling that he has a woman, one of those who knows exactly how to get money out of a man. A greedy woman, who will be the death of me . . .

Watch out for that husband of yours, Antonia. He strikes me as someone who has funny business practices. You must be careful of him. Wake up so that you don't find yourself in the street someday. I always

baby to the doctor in Casilda," Toma told Antonia. "She said the baby was too thin, wanted her doctor to look at it."

Antonia, thinking of the drunken old doctor in Casilda, flew into a fury. She went immediately to Arturo's office and demanded to see him. His secretary explained that Arturo was at the train station, but Antonia insisted on waiting in his office. Arturo's secretary, who was used to Antonia's visits, said nothing and let her in.

Antonia sat down in one of the chairs opposite the desk to wait. The desk was, as usual, covered with papers, but it was a rectangle of violet which called her attention. She picked it up.

An hour later, Arturo returned to find her in tears. "Why didn't you tell me about my mother's letters?" she said. "This one must have been here for days, and she has written dozens."

Arturo opened a drawer. "Here are the others," he said. "But why didn't you give them to me before?" cried Antonia. "Why did you hide them from me?"

"Because I knew they would upset you just as they have. I was keeping them for you until the right moment."

Antonia and Arturo went home together, taking the letters with them. Antonia shut herself up in her room and didn't even notice when the nurse brought the baby home.

Dora's letters were very strange. Antonia had received very few letters from her mother when she was a child, and these were always as short as possible, no more than a few lines, and held strictly to business: "I will send the car to your school on Tuesday. Please be sure to come home. Dora."

These letters were different. They had no dates, greetings, endings, or margins. They were all exactly two sheets long, and every inch of both sides was covered with her tiny, precise handwriting. They began without introduction and ended abruptly at the end of the second side of the second sheet, sometimes in the middle of a sentence. Occasionally the next letter picked up the theme, but more often it went off on another subject altogether.

Antonia had the impression that Dora was simply writing down whatever came into her mind, without making any attempt to sort it out or even thinking much about who she was writing to.

As clearly as Antonia could make out from the postmarks, the first letters were mostly reproaches. "How could I have given birth to such

children!'' one of them began. "Some evil witch must have stolen my babies and left snakes in their place! Now, when I am old, and no use to them, they abandon me without defenses in this terrible time, when I have fools and enemies on every side.''

In other letters, she wrote to Antonia using a tone she had never used when speaking to her, giving her the benefit of her peculiar advice, almost as if she were a friend. "I hope, Antonia, that you have the sense not to have any children. All the work and sacrifice, all the damage to one's body and then nothing but ingratitude.''

Besides, if you have children in that part of the world, they will be born with all kind of curses. I have heard there are sorcerers and witches there who can lay curses on people. I read the story of one poor child born with three eyes, and another with no feet. You see, Antonia, you don't realize it, but your husband is a powerful man. In order to get to be powerful, powerful enemies are made, and those enemies are the ones that will hire the sorcerers. You can find one in any marketplace, I am told, who would curse a whole family for a few coins. Perhaps you should find one yourself to rid yourself of your husband's mistresses. Don't fool yourself that he doesn't have any! Remember, I know men are . . .

I was looking at the picture of you, Antonia, one taken just before you married that man. If I were you, I would wear my skirts very long; your legs are less than perfect. When Arturo was around me, he kept on looking at my legs, so I could see he was attracted by that feature. Grow up, Antonia, learn a few things to keep your man, or you will be left with an empty bed every night . . .

Those friends of yours, the ones who fixed your marriage for you, they tell me that your father's business is doing badly; they heard it through some banking contact, and can't keep from telling me, the gossips that they are. I don't believe it for a second. Your brother had just learned some sharp tricks to snatch money away from his own mother on the side. Or perhaps he has some woman. I have the feeling that he has a woman, one of those who knows exactly how to get money out of a man. A greedy woman, who will be the death of me . . .

Watch out for that husband of yours, Antonia. He strikes me as someone who has funny business practices. You must be careful of him. Wake up so that you don't find yourself in the street someday. I always

protected myself from your father; all the jewels I had him give me will protect me now from that snake I was given for a son . . .

I saw the count the other day. We both fear for you, for different reasons, of course. That silly baby has no idea of the world you live in; he only worries about the war. I worry about your incompetence to run your life. I showed him the reading I am doing on witches and what they can do to you. He thinks it's all nonsense, and tells me I would do better just by saying a few prayers. That old hypocrite! Just imagine he wants me to turn religious. By the way, he doesn't look too good. Maybe it's because he does not have a woman and is stuck with his old wife. Maybe he misses you. At times I think he had a liking for you, and that there was another reason for his playing "Papa" to you . . .

Someday I hope you will know how it feels to be a poor old woman abandoned by her children in the middle of such bad times! Your brother—I hardly hear from him and get no money. And our relatives— no one helps me. My sisters have their daughters at home; they are young enough to climb the hills to do errands but they turn their backs on me. Their sons have gone to war; they deserve the worries. My brother, too, turns away, after all I did for him when he was poor and I was rich . . .

I ran into the count again. He was on his way to sell some family heirloom. That lazy man! He has never done a thing in his life; that job of his is just paper-pushing. Of course, now even I have to sell my treasures for whatever I can get, no husband, no children to help, and now this war . . .

The day will come, Antonia, when you will find other men attractive. Your Arturo won't be the sun forever; remember, I have met him, and he is already old. It's quite an art to make yourself attractive to men. If you were here, I could teach you, but then again, why give you my secrets when you do so little for me?

VIII

AT THE END OF THAT YEAR, America entered the war. Early in the next year Yayaku entered it on the side of the Allies. In practical terms, this meant little. Yayaku sent no troops overseas, and the involvement of the Yayakuan military consisted of helping the Americans patrol the coast for "hostile vessels." But the German, Japanese, and Italian embassies were closed down, and contact with Europe became even more difficult. Italy was no longer simply on the other side of the ocean; it was also on the other side of the war.

The count's letters continued to arrive through the monsignor and so did the violet letters from Dora, postmarked Vatican City, though how she got them there, Antonia never knew. Arturo, who knew that it still upset her, joked about them and called them "Dora's epistles," but he still hid them for a day or two before giving them to her. The letters continued as before, several months behind events.

How terrifying to hear your news, a grandchild of mine to be born in that part of the world, to a mother who is so ignorant that she won't know what end to feed. You poor thing, remember this is the time when men begin to look for another woman. Rub some olive oil on your stomach every day. It will help with the stretch marks. Keep your husband away while you are pregnant; believe me, it is not worth the trouble until after the baby is born.

I hope you can avoid having another. There are ways, but I'd have to show you. In the meantime, there are things you can put in his food to make him leave you alone. Ask some old woman out there, one is bound to know.

Your worthless brother has turned out just as I expected; an idiot for a woman. I have just received a sobbing letter from someone who claims to be his widow! There is something in this that doesn't smell like a rose. She asked for a ridiculous amount to pay for the funeral! Of course, I did not send the little saucebox a thing. And in the meantime, no one tells me he is dead, and the money still comes from your father's business, though the sums are not enough to feed the cat these days. Something is bent in this business. If I could get over there, I could smoke it out, but there's no chance of that now.

Mariana? Where did you and that husband of yours find that name? The count thinks it's proper Spanish and Italian, but I think it's an insult to a family with all those beautiful names. I am sure it was you, Antonia, who would not call my granddaughter Dora; I was so much hoping you would, and Arturo would not have objected. After all, you will have learned how to control him by now.

The poor girl, growing up with an inexperienced mother in a country filled with witches and llamas and the likes of that Toma. I cannot make myself wish you well, except that by having a child you will control Arturo better. If you were here, the competition would be tougher, with all the young men off in the army. What color eyes does she have?

I did tell our relatives about the event. However, I did not allow them to congratulate me. They are knitting away—a most primitive way of showing their ignorance. By the time the garments arrive, they will be too small.

I have no gift. My gift is to keep the house up. It takes up all of my strength. This is a true monument for us to keep. If my granddaughter has any sense, she will come to live here. I am surprised that Arturo was not disappointed you had a girl. I thought he would want a real heir, but, of course, it is very clever of you to have a girl. You know what I mean.

I hope you will now take my advice and not have any more children, or your body will degenerate. It took me so long to get back in shape after having you and Marco, and it cost me so much money and so many trips to Paris. You over there have no chance; not that you had much of a body to begin with. Do nurse the baby. Your breasts are too small, and that way they will be fuller, at least for a while.

• • •

My dear Antonia,

I am glad (if that is the word) that Arturo has decided to give you Dora's letters at last. He was perhaps right to hold them until you were strong enough to read them, but it would have been wrong of him to hold them longer.

But I must be stern with you: You must not let her letters upset you so much. She plays on one's conscience as an old violin; she knows just the right turns to bring out what she wants to hear. Perhaps it is because she has so little conscience herself.

There was, of course, nothing else you could do but leave her. You had to build your own life, and you could never have done that in her shadow. There is no need to worry about her for now; she is well provided for financially, no matter what she might be telling you. She is, in short, perfectly fine, though you must keep in mind that her way of being fine is different from most. She will always thrive in situations that you or I would find intolerable—how lucky she is in these times—though she will, I think, play the martyr for some time to come. By now you must understand that she is an actress, that she has a sense of drama that is, at times, overwhelming.

I still find myself thinking of the real tragedy—Marco, I mean. In the end I think it is no one's fault; I mourn for all of us. I am not able to tell exactly how your mother feels about it. What she says changes; someone put a curse on him, she says sometimes (her head seems to be filled with ideas of witchcraft these days). Or, she says, it must have been a woman, or he was weak, or it would have happened during the war if he had stayed. Often she seems to think he is not dead at all, that it is a ruse to cheat her out of her money. Beneath it all, I feel she must feel a deep sadness, but so deep that no one can see it.

I have taken a little trip to Milano to go to La Scala. How remarkable how things go on despite everything! A bit like your mother, I suppose, but the music always makes me think of you.

With my love,
Emilio

· · ·

Dear Count,

Thank you for your kind words. As always, they are a help to me, and I pray every day for your letters to come through to me.

I have begun to write to my mother, though, as when I talked with her at home, I so often find I have little to say. My letters are always so much shorter than hers! I can't bring myself to answer her letters very directly, and she always writes what she feels, but as if I had never written her at all. So I just act the good daughter, and send her little stories about the baby and sound happy for her. This, perhaps, is not really what she wants to hear, just as hers are not what I want to hear. So we are like two people talking in a storm, neither able to hear what the other has to say but still going on and on in the wind.

Mariana is well, standing up on her own and talking more and more—Italian words and some Spanish and that strange language babies have for their own. How odd it is that I understand her! How strange and wonderful and frightening it is to be a mother! It changes everything, having someone who needs so much. You can no longer think so much about yourself, and I thank her for that every day.

She is such a happy baby. Watching her laugh and smile, one could almost believe that the world is a good place. Perhaps Arturo was like this when he was a child; I can't imagine I ever was. (Marco was like that sometimes, although it was a fiercer kind of happiness, a shriller laughter, a kind of joy despite the world.)

I wish Arturo seemed happier these days. He complains about his indigestion and things; I know something is wrong, but he won't tell me what it is. He smiles and acts jolly, but I don't believe him. Is this the way it is with men, with men in the world? Sometimes I think it must be. But surely there is something I could do to help?

The piano sits, I'm afraid, gathering dust. My free hours I spend working on plans for the house; sometimes it feels sad building a new place to live when so many homes are burning in the world. But it gives my mind something to chew on. Arturo has bought us a new record player and some records from America. In the evenings, when the electricity is running, I listen to the songs from the operas we loved together, from The Magic Flute *and* Don Giovanni. *Isn't it odd to be listening to German operas these days?*

Write me of my mother. I want to know how she really is.

> *With all my love,*
> *Antonia*

• • •

Dear Count Mora,

I'm afraid the investigation in Buenos Aires turned up nothing, worse than nothing. My friend says there have been no reports of my brother-

in-law's death, or even of his marriage. His agent seems to still be doing
business in his name. It is all very mysterious, and this situation with
the war will, I'm afraid, prevent me from finding out much more for
some time. If news finds its way to you somehow, please let me know.

Thank you for all your good works at home. May you keep well.

Sincerely,

Arturo Rontella

WORK ON THE HOUSE at the edge of town continued, in fits and starts,
when the building materials were available. The garden was already
beautiful. It was American style: that is, it was like the gardens in the
American magazines Antonia saw. That meant that the roses, dahlias,
and irises were not arranged in neat rows, but flowed gently around the
garden, hiding the corners of the walls and spilling out over the edges
of the lawn. It was the opposite of Donna Dora's formal garden in
Artemisia.

Antonia still spent time in the garden, more to keep the workmen
from damaging it than to do any real work—Toma was gradually taking
that over for her. It surprised her to see him take to the work with such
delight and competence, when he had so little experience of growing
things. He did complain about the uneven rows, which were difficult to
weed.

Sometimes Antonia and Arturo would walk there in the evenings
together.

"Do you think you made a good bargain?" she asked Arturo one
evening.

"What? With my partners? Of course not!" Arturo said, laughing.

"No, that's not what I meant. I meant with me."

"I can answer that in two ways: no and no."

"What do you mean?"

"I mean no if you are asking if I got what I expected. I didn't, but
I also mean no because what I was doing in marrying you was not a
bargain."

"What was it then?" Antonia asked, smiling. "A gamble?"

"No, you little idiot!" said Arturo with a trace of annoyance. "It
wasn't a business proposition. I was not looking for a profit or calcu-
lating a loss. It had nothing to do with that."

"I see," said Antonia. "It was like a fling, an adventure."

"No, it wasn't like that either."

"What, then?"

"Do you remember the house in Nervi? Where we used to meet? When I first saw you in that house, I knew we had to marry."

"As if it were fate?"

"No, I don't believe in fate. I am not that kind of romantic, and I am more selfish than that. It was a house I never managed to finish. Do you know why? Because I couldn't imagine it finished. At a certain point, my imagination ran out. It was like a game you play while making up the rules, and suddenly inspiration fails you, or the whole thing seems foolish. When I met you, I thought up to now I have been a boy, playing boy's games. With you, I have to be grown up. I can't make up the rules anymore. I have to go from one life into another.

"Don't misunderstand me. I don't always like this new life. Wouldn't anyone like to be a child forever? Wouldn't it be wonderful if the game could go on forever? But I knew I had to move into that other place, and I was too afraid to go alone. So I married you. As I said, I was being rather selfish."

Antonia said nothing for a moment. "I think I understand you," she said, finally. They walked out of the garden into the empty rooms of the unfinished house, passing through the walls that were no more than hollow wooden frames, and then they walked home.

THE ALLIES invaded Sicily. The radio reports were very confused. There were reports that the leader had been overthrown, that Italy had surrendered. But soon it became clear that the end of the war for Italy would not be an easy one.

My dear Antonia,

Such confused times we are living in! One day it looks as if we might shake off all this madness, the next, those men (I can't say their names) are everywhere. Those in power make their confused arrangements, and in the meantime the only thing not in short supply are rumors.

Waiting in line for a few supplies today, I found myself thinking of you, about the day you and Marco arrived at my doorstep with two boxes and a few belongings and told me you were moving in with me. It was not long after I met your mother. I remember Marco saying he wanted me for a father. How I wish I could have granted his wish!

The monsignor has been trying to persuade me to leave the city. He says there will be bombing here soon. How can I say that I would rather face that than my wife in the country with no one to distract me from her face?

I don't wish to sadden you, but I have made some arrangements. Should I die, the two drawings by Cambiasso go to you as well as the tiny Domenico Piola and the two Castigliones. They are my favorites, and I want them for you.

Reading over what I have just written, it sounds absurd. How ridiculous to be thinking of paintings! I probably should sell them while they still might bring more than a lump of sugar. But the thought that I might leave something behind for you comforts me. I like to think of your children looking at them. They will help you explain our afternoons at the museums and the beautiful things you helped me, a stale old man, appreciate again with the freshness of your thoughts and eyes to appreciate.

I wish Marco had had your strength. I guess Dora was too much for a son. I remember the day she told me I should find a woman for him, or, she said, he might become a "sissy." He was only thirteen. I think she found a woman for him herself. One day she took him on a two-day trip, and he never looked the same after that. That must be hard for a son. On the other hand, it is all my speculation. I think very much about how I could have helped him. I should have been more aware, I should have thought of something to say the day we took him to the boat and he left. He was so young. I ramble on and on. You must forgive me.

No news from Artemisia, though if your mother was unwell, I would have heard, I'm sure.

With all my love,
Emilio

•   •   •

Antonia,

Such suffering you have abandoned your mother to, your mother who never let you go hungry for a day in your life. You have no idea what it is like to live here now. Today I went into the hills. My back was hurting, and I have a cold. But, you see, my daughter, I had no food, so after hours of walking in the cold and in the rain, I went to the house of a peasant I know. I traded a beautiful bowl—Sèvres, something I found in Paris years ago, a real treasure—for a little oil, some horrible dried meat and tomatoes, and some wormy flour. So you see how things have become; food is worth almost any price.

One of his sons helped me back part of the way, but then he got scared when we heard the bombs falling in the distance toward Genoa. So I walked the rest of the way home; got home late at night. I was too tired to eat, too frightened to sleep, listening to death rolling through the sky.

In the night, many houses around me were bombed. Ours was saved, but the shaking and the horror! I don't know how much longer I will last, and there is no one here to bury me.

$$\bullet \quad \bullet \quad \bullet$$

My dear Antonia,

I am still well, as is your mother (I will write of her more below).

Things are more confusing than ever, what with the bombing and the Allies taking so long to come north. There is no news, only what one can see with one's own eyes, and the rumors. The mountains, they say, are full of partisans and the British soldiers who have gotten lost behind the lines.

The Germans run everything now, along with a few who still call themselves Fascist. (No one knows who is a Fascist these days; the tally seems to change every hour.) The Germans are very ill-tempered; they blame us for everything. Despite it all, I can feel sorry for them. We all know it is over for them; they are like mad dogs waiting for the bullet, lashing out at everything.

My friends are urging me to leave the city, to go to my villa. But I would rather put up with the bombs than with my wife.

Your mother is perfectly well, even in luxury by our present standards. She has made friends with the new commanders of the supply depot, and seems to lack nothing for now, even though the money is no longer getting through. She has, as you know, a remarkable talent for survival. I rejoice in it, although there are mutters in the village. They say her brother, Roberto, and his sons are with the partisans, and everyone is afraid she will betray them with her new German friends.

We are all forced to give up some of our treasures. But the end to this nightmare does not seem so far off now. I look forward to the day of peace and your return. We will, of course, walk in the chestnut woods; you tell me how much you miss our green forests in your home in the desert. I am glad your garden is going well. I looked up Yayaku in a botany book, and there are beautiful things that grow there, even in the desert.

Send me news of your daughter. Bring her to me before she grows too old.

With all my love for now,
Emilio

• • •

Antonia,

My house, my beautiful house, now occupied by ruthless, filthy soldiers, and me in the maid's room while you sit in comfort in your South American paradise. They have taken all the food I had left, and there is no heat in my part of the house.

You won't hear from the count very soon. They have blown up his house with bombs! He had gone out for a walk, so it is a miracle that he wasn't blown up too! He has gone off to his villa, they say, to stay with his poor little wife.

I am so cold, and will not last long. How lucky for you that you will never see me again! You will not have to hear my voice tell you how it was when you abandoned me!

• • •

My dear Antonia,

The worst of it seems to be over now that the Americans are here. A surprise to see that they are mostly African! Some people thought they were Ethiopians taking revenge at first, but now everyone seems to have adopted them, and hordes of ragged children follow them everywhere, looking for the candy they sometimes give out. And, of course, the women are falling into their arms.

Such celebrations! When the Americans carried the relics of Columbus down from their hiding place in the mountains and took them to the cathedral we knew that it was over at last.

The bad times are not over, of course. In the mountains and in *the north, the fighting goes on. So much of the city is in ruins, and the shortages are terribly severe. Hundreds of people are out of their homes, and there is much confusion everywhere.*

Your mother seems better off than anyone. The Americans occupied her villa, but she refused to leave. So she is in Eliana's room. In spite of her constant complaints, I think she dominates the situation, with those black American soldiers at her feet as if she were the queen of Sheba at her court. Her brother and his whole family have disappeared. No one seems to know what happened to them, whether they were betrayed to the Germans or the Fascists or whether they simply ran off. There are squatters in their house, from what I hear.

Dora seems to have plenty of food. The other day, in a strange mood of generosity, she sent me some coffee. Perhaps it is a sign. It can't be long now, we all pray, before we hear that the war is over.

With love,
Emilio

IX

IN THE LAST WEEKS of the war, Antonia and Arturo moved into their house. Antonia refused to bring things from the old house that "weren't right" for the new one, so the furnishings were sparse: the Indian hangings, the old silver, and the newest things from the old house. Although the rooms were bare, the large windows looked out into the garden, which was full of life and color, brighter than any rug or hanging she could imagine.

Toma and Arturo wanted to give a Sunday luncheon to celebrate the new house. "It's not time, it's not ready," she said. "Besides, the end of the war should be our next celebration. We should wait for that."

But Antonia did ask Father Coyle to visit her. They sat on the terrace, looking out into the walled yard, in the shade of the overhanging roof.

"After the war, Father," Antonia said, "will you still be willing to help me start a girls' school?"

"It would be a pleasure to help you. I sense in your voice that you have some specific ideas in mind."

"I want the girls' school to be like the one you have started for the boys. Arturo will help us bring some nuns from Italy who are willing to come. The archbishop in Montana de Plata is willing to use his influence. I don't want my daughter to have an education inferior to what you give the boys."

"Why do you think that is important?"

"Aren't girls important? Why should they learn less than boys, who won't be as smart as they are in any case?"

"There are those who think differently. They would say a good education is lost on someone who is only going to be a wife and mother."

"Do they say that in your country?"

"Some do."

"And the women, do they put up with bad education?"

"No, not always."

"Then why should my girl have less than those American women? I want her to study here and when she has learned as much as she can in Pica I'll send her to America to school."

"Why America?"

"Because in America, as you are always telling me, Father Coyle, people are taught to be free."

"If that is your wish, I will see what I can do to help you."

X

THE END OF THE WAR in Europe, when it came, was almost an anticlimax, it had been expected so long. The bells rang in the cathedral, the bishop gave a special service of thanksgiving, and the Americans came to town to celebrate. The bands in the bars played "The Star-Spangled Banner," "God Save the Queen," and the "Marseillaise" over and over.

A bigger shock was news of the great bomb the Americans dropped on Japan. The Americans seemed happy, but Antonia listened to the news with horror.

"What does it mean, that the Americans have such a power of destruction?" she asked Father Coyle.

"I hope and pray it means only that the Americans will hold the peace. What can war mean with such weapons? When men see this, they can only lay down their arms."

More news came from Europe, and pictures in the magazines, and the full horror of what had happened was known even in Pica. There were the death camps, the burned-out cities, the tens of thousands of lost and homeless people wandering across a map whose lines were melting and changing.

The letters from Dora had ceased. The letters from the count tried to be cheerful in tone, but said little, and there was an underlying melancholy that disturbed Antonia.

"Do you think the time has arrived for us to go back?" she said to Arturo.

"To Italy? It's not the right time," he answered, and sighed. The sigh, so uncharacteristic of Arturo, shook Antonia like cold wind. She looked at his face. It was thin; he looked tired, worn out. She thought about his ailments, the shortness of breath, the headaches, the days now when he had trouble getting out of bed.

She looked from the terrace, where they were sitting, out into the garden, where Mariana was playing on the grass. Such a cheerful child, she thought, so full of good things. She wished she could make the walls higher to shut out the difficult world from her child.

The war's end did not keep the good times in Yayaku. The Americans and Europeans once again looked at its mines and resources as just one among many, and soon found more profit in other countries, places that had been only temporarily shut away by the war.

The economy faltered. There was a coup in the capital, and General Salas became the head of state, José Martín, so the rumors went, by his side. But prosperity did not follow. The early years of General Salas's dictatorship came to be called the "thundering silence." It was a time when great things happened, but silently, almost stealthily, as if a great, noiseless tide came up in the night, sweeping away one Yayaku and leaving another in its place.

The newspapers of Montana de Plata were not censored, exactly, but they were full of good news—glowing reports of the latest "modernization." The city was changing. Old colonial houses were scheduled to be razed. Banks and new government buildings in glass and stone were to be built in the Alameda. New houses were beginning to be built in places such as Alhambra or Florida, in the outskirts of the city. These new mansions were known as California houses. Unlike the stiff, secretive old Spanish houses of their grandparents, these Yayakuans' new houses, usually one or two stories and painted in shades of coral or sand, stretched lazily, like sleeping cats, among the hills above the old city, swimming pools and tropical gardens at their side. Lured by the city, the Indians and mestizos were starting to pour out of their mountain villages, fleeing their tenant plots on the old estates, and escaping from the dusty provincial towns. Their squatters' huts of tin and cardboard stretched for miles along the river banks, and in the evening the smoke of their cooking fires mingled with the haze of fumes from new automobiles climbing the hills to the east.

Arturo knew that he had to adapt to new methods of doing business. The inner circles of government had changed and new contacts had to be made. His partners were no longer a help, but their ambitions and salaries were a burden. His attention was devoted more and more to the investments outside his business.

Arturo came home every day looking very tired. Antonia worried, but was reluctant to mention how tired he looked. Instead, she looked for ways to spend as much time as possible with him. In the evenings, she would walk to meet him halfway on his way home.

One afternoon, he was late. She paced the sidewalk impatiently. When she finally saw him in the distance, she panicked. His walk seemed slow and painful. She ran toward him. Gently, he embraced her. When she looked up to see his face, her self-control gave away.

"What happened today, Arturo?" she asked. "You look so tired."

"I don't feel well. This afternoon when I was visiting the warehouse I was bit by something in the back of my neck. It itches and feels hot," he said, as they continued to walk.

Before they reached home, Arturo said, "The itching is getting unbearable. My stomach feels strange. I need the attention of my own little nurse."

At home, Antonia rubbed his inflamed skin with alcohol and covered it with a cool towel. She left him resting in bed and went to Mariana's room, where she sat for a few minutes caressing her baby's soft skin. Antonia was looking at her baby intently, trying to determine whom Mariana resembled. Arturo thought she looked just like his mother, with her high forehead and her big slanting blue eyes. Antonia secretly feared that she would look like Dora. She had always found her mother hard and unfeminine, and had hated her eyes.

As she continued her search for traces of Dora in little Mariana's face, she heard Arturo call her. "Feel my forehead," he said. "I think I have a fever."

Antonia gently touched Arturo. "We better call Dr. Sánchez and have him take a look at you," she said.

"If that's what my nurse thinks, then we will," said Arturo.

It was some time before Antonia got through to the doctor. It was late in the evening and the operator at the phone company must have been sleeping, as he often did. By the time she reached the doctor, Arturo had already sent Toma to fetch him.

Dr. Sánchez arrived shortly. He was still wearing his pajama shirt, and had slipped on some pants that had holes patched in various colors.

At night his usual unkempt appearance of a confirmed bachelor seemed worse.

In his crusty voice he asked Antonia, "What's wrong this time?"

"It's not me, it's Arturo," Antonia said. She explained Arturo's complaint as she escorted the doctor to the bedroom.

"Arturo!" exclaimed the doctor. He walked to the bed. "What is it, Señor Rontella? I just delivered you a beautiful baby who is getting all of your wife's attention, so you get yourself bit by an insect in order to steal the attention back to you?"

He took his bent glasses out of his pocket and examined the bite. Antonia detected a sudden look of panic. "Call Toma," he said. "I need some medication. Give Arturo some warm water to quench his thirst and get some wet towels. Let's see if we can keep the fever down."

Toma arrived a few minutes later. He was not alone. With him were the other doctor from Pica and the pharmacist. The two doctors and the pharmacist consulted for a few minutes.

"What is it, what is it? Tell me, tell me," said Antonia in a shaky voice.

"Calm, calm, Antonia," said Arturo. "An old horse like me can surely fight a little insect."

Antonia sat next to her husband. Arturo squeezed her hand and said, "I'll be all right, Antonia. You will make me all right. Remember what we decided the other day? We are an unbeatable pair."

Antonia kissed his forehead, which was burning and wet. "I love you, Arturo," she said.

The pharmacist went to get some medication, and the two doctors helped Antonia with the cool towels. Arturo felt hotter every minute.

"Hold my hand," he asked Antonia. At times it was so hot that she had to let it go.

Arturo began to shiver and to utter meaningless sentences. "Antonia, war, Mariana, Montana de Plata, safe box, Toma."

"Where's the medication?" Antonia asked. "Why aren't they back yet?" She broke into tears.

Dr. Sánchez grabbed her arm and led her out of the room. "The pharmacist is going to bring a medicine. It has sulfa in it. It's new; I think it might help. In the meantime, we have to try to keep the fever down, and you have to help. Be calm, Antonia, we are doing all we can," he added and patted her gently on the arm.

By the time the pharmacist returned, Arturo's convulsions were such that the four of them had to hold him to administer the medicine. He was moaning and he seemed in terrible pain. Antonia couldn't control her sobbing.

Toma, standing by the window, pointed outside. Antonia followed his gaze. In the courtyard Lara was kneeling and shaking something that looked like a rattle.

"Out, out, who let you in? Out, out," screamed Antonia. "You are here to kill my husband." She opened the window and threw one of the towels she was holding at Lara.

"It's not her fault," said Toma. "I asked her to come. The last time she was here she made things better for you. Now she will make things better for Don Arturo."

Magdalena arrived and made Antonia drink something. She could not hold it down. She held her friend's hand tightly. "Pray," said Magdalena. "You must ask God for his compassion."

Outside the crowd was getting larger. In the still of the night the neighbors had heard Arturo's desperate sounds. Antonia could hear them murmur "Bishopi, bishopi."

"Toma, Toma," she yelled, "tell them I don't want the bishop."

Later, she learned that "bishopi" was the name of the spider that had bitten Arturo.

Antonia paced back and forth. She looked at the three men, searching for a sign of hope. There was none. In her panic she did not know what to do. Ordering the maid to stay with Mariana, she ran to the room where she kept her trunks from Italy. She threw everything in the air until she found the Bible the count had given her the day of her First Communion. She ran downstairs and began to read it aloud to herself, little sentences from here and there. It made no sense. She went back to the bedroom and knelt at the end of the bed, her head buried in her hands.

Arturo's moaning became more sporadic, softer, like a long continuous lament. He began to breathe loudly. The crowd outside grew silent. She overheard one of the doctors say, "No more wet towels."

"Is he well?" she asked. There was no answer.

Antonia rose and moved close to Arturo. She sat next to him, placed her hand on his forehead. It felt cooler. "Arturo, Arturo," she whispered as she fixed the sheets around him. Antonia stayed there for a long time. Finally the doctor took her hand and helped her get up.

"He looks so tired," she told the doctor.

"He is resting now," the doctor answered.

XI

WHEN SHE THOUGHT about it later, all she could remember about the days that followed Arturo's death were disconnected episodes, like parts of a nightmare, a nightmare that you can never forget. There were people hugging her, telling her to be strong, uttering to each other *"Pobrecita."* There were Magdalena and Don Pedro running her house, forcing her to eat. There were papers to sign. There was Arturo, in the blue suit he had worn for their wedding, in a wooden box lined in shiny white silk. There was the newspaper with his picture on the front page. PREMATURE DEATH OF PICA'S LEADING BUSINESSMAN, it said.

There was her bed that was moved to Mariana's room. There was the smell of the lilies, the flowers of the dead. There was Toma, who followed her everywhere, just as he had when they first arrived in Pica. There was Mariana, who did not know what had happened. There was no Arturo, just his clothes in the closet, and the empty chair where he had always sat. There was Father Coyle, telling her to be brave, and the bishop, telling her "it was the will of God."

There were the pills the doctor gave her to make her sleep. There was the little cemetery where they took Arturo and left him near Lina's husband. There was the letter from Captain Martín, offering help, telling her he was her "loyal servant." There were those brief instants when she forgot that all this had happened.

No one seemed to be of help to Antonia. Slowly people began to leave her alone. Only Magdalena came every day, although, she, too, did not know how to help her friend.

Antonia spent most of each day in the garden close to the large orange tree. She held the count's Bible in her lap, though she rarely opened it. At times she would get up and absentmindedly pick up an orange for Mariana. She found it difficult to play with her child; it was Toma who would come every chance he had and tried to amuse Mariana. Antonia hugged her constantly; and when she saw in her traces of Arturo's deep brown eyes, his extraordinarily long fingers, tears filled her eyes. Mariana was uttering her first words; occasionally Antonia would decipher "Mommy" or "Toma" in the confusion of the child's gibberish.

She could not abide the servants asking for guidance and told Toma to make up the menus and order the provisions. At the table she moved the food from one corner of the plate to the other. It was only when Toma stared at her that she would place a tiny bite into her mouth. She wore no black like the other widows in Pica. Every morning she slipped on the dress she had worn the day Arturo died.

On her way back from the market, Magdalena would stop to see Antonia every morning. She would bring some flowers or a special fruit. Together they would read the many letters of condolence that arrived in the morning mail. Antonia discovered dimensions to Arturo's life that she had not known. "Paid for my son to go to school," "lent us money so that we could stay in business," "visited my husband every day during his illness," "arranged for my daughter to go to Montana de Plata to continue her education." At times the letters came with gifts: a small yellow and blue canary for Mariana, a special cake made of rice flour and rose water. Some of the letters begged Antonia to stay in Pica and offered their help. "We will watch that no one ever hurts you," someone wrote. Others went so far as to describe Arturo as "the saint of Pica." Antonia made a special packet of all these letters and kept them next to her bed.

Every night, after she tucked in Mariana, she waited at the side of Mariana's bed until Magdalena and Don Pedro came for their evening visit. She would greet them at the door and usher them to the living room where she sat close to Magdalena. Don Pedro sat across from them. He looked older, his hair seemed whiter. Instead of drinking his habitual Cognac, he complained of indigestion and asked for Fernet Branca.

It was invariably Magdalena who started the conversation. She told them about her day, her troubles with the servants, the children's homework and their small adventures. Antonia listened intently, though she rarely responded. Then Don Pedro would recount his day. He tried to talk about things that would interest Antonia. Sometimes he would read from the local newspaper, or retell an old anecdote. He was careful not to bring Arturo into his monologues, because he could not bear the sorrow he saw in Antonia's eyes, and because he could not bear his own. And yet he spoke as if Arturo was there, too, as if Don Pedro were waiting for Arturo's calm and gentle response. Magdalena watched Antonia closely. At times the three of them found one another staring at the pack of Inca's cigarettes Arturo had left on top on the radio; remembering his ritual evening smoke.

A MONTH AFTER Arturo's death, at the insistence of Don Pedro and Magdalena, Antonia went to the customary memorial mass at the cathedral. Antonia agreed to go only after Don Pedro promised that Father Coyle and not the bishop would say the mass. It had taken a lot of negotiation, principally with the bishop's mother, but, since Don Pedro disliked the bishop as much as Antonia did, making the arrangements had given him some pleasure.

The cathedral was so crowded when Antonia arrived that it was difficult for her to make her way to the front; Father Coyle, who was waiting at the door when she arrived, escorted her. Everyone stared at her in silence as she walked along the aisle. She was dressed in the black dress Magdalena had made for the occasion and held Mariana in her arms. The child's blond hair shone in the sea of black mantillas. Familiar and unfamiliar people offered their condolences and the women kissed her. Their kindness was overwhelming, and for the first time since Arturo's death, Antonia cried. In the front pew she found Magdalena and Don Pedro.

At the mass, which was short, Father Coyle spoke of Arturo in simple words, but his words were really for Antonia. "Arturo was a very special part of Pica," he said. He then told the story of his arrival in Pica, and Arturo's and Antonia's involvement in his school. He said it was God who had sent him to Pica, and had given him a mission, a mission that he had shared with Antonia and had now left in her hands alone. He asked everyone to pray to God to give her the strength to continue, and to raise their child to become an outstanding Yayakuan. "We are all here to tell you both that you are not alone: You have in all of us an enormous extended family," he said. The crowd murmured its agreement.

After the mass, Don Pedro, Magdalena, and Father Coyle rode with Antonia to the cemetery. They drove in silence through a silent town. Though it was midmorning, the stores had shut, and people stood in the street to watch the widow visit her husband's grave for the first time. Antonia thought of the day when she first arrived in Pica and how people had stared at her then. She had been without Arturo that day, too.

As she walked toward the grave, Antonia felt that her legs would hold her no longer and she held Magdalena's arm tightly. She saw only the mass of flowers that covered Arturo's grave. She could not quite understand where she was or what was happening to her. The crowd that had followed her from the church stood in respectful silence. She walked toward Mariana, who was in Father Coyle's arms, and Mariana reached for her. A sense of calm came over her as she caressed her child; it was as if Arturo's strength and warmth had enfolded them. Everyone stood in silence, only the gentle midday breeze, fluttering the bamboo trees, could be heard. Antonia turned to Magdalena, still holding her arm gently, and then turned to face the crowd. "Thank you," she said, "thank you, for being here with us," and she reached out her hand to a woman standing in front.

Everyone gently moved aside to make room for Antonia to leave. An old woman dressed in black made her way forward and gave Antonia a white rose. "God will help you," she said, "just like Don Arturo always helped all of us." There was something special about the way Antonia held herself as she left. Her walk suggested confidence; her sad face had a sense of peace. It was she this time who timidly held out her hand to shake theirs. Often Antonia would think of that morning as the beginning of her realization that she belonged there with the people who were reaching for her, who were willing to give her their friendship because she was Arturo's wife, people who wanted her to fill the void Arturo had left.

• • •

A FEW DAYS later Don Pedro went to Montana de Plata on business, and Magdalena persuaded Antonia to stay with her for a few days. Antonia was given the room next to Magdalena's sitting room, the small nursery where Magdalena's many children had spent the first months of their lives. In marked contrast to Magdalena's sitting room with its profusion of silk pillows, Oriental rugs, and dried flowers, the room was plain, almost monastic, and all white. A large rocking chair looked out onto a jacaranda tree in purple bloom. The light that entered the room had the purple hue of the tree; the room felt calm and cool.

There was so much activity in Magdalena's house that it was impossible not to be part of it. Children yelled, servants ran, doors slammed, music filtered out from the large kitchen. Only during mealtimes, when all the children sat around the table, was there peace. Magdalena sat at the head of the table, and began the meal by saying a long grace that ended with "May God bring success to your father in his business trip and may he return to us soon and in good health." As they ate, Magdalena quietly questioned each child about his schoolwork and other daily activities. Anyone who misbehaved was not served dessert. At times Magdalena would ask Antonia to tell the children about Italy. Once, Antonia told them about a city in Italy built on water, where the streets were canals and the cars were boats. Antonia remembered her trip to Venice with the count and the old lady there who lived with all those cats and Tintorettos. She was the one who had told Antonia that being loved was more important than being in love. How unlikely either possibility had seemed to her then. With Arturo she had learned that the lady had been wrong: Loving Arturo had been as wonderful as being loved by him. She wondered what had happened to the lady, had she been able to survive a third war? The days with the count seemed so unbearably far away. She wished she could close her eyes and imagine him just the way he was. There were moments when she feared she would forget what the count looked like, or Arturo, too.

More and more in her hours alone, Antonia thought how nice it would be to see the count again. She felt a need to talk to him in order to reorient her life. He had always given her the right advice, even from so far. She read his letters over and over again.

One afternoon there was a letter from the count.

Dear Antonia,

I am awake very early this morning. The sun has yet to rise. My tired old body seems to need less sleep all the time.

Last night I dreamed you were back. Aside from the immense happiness it would give me to see you again, I wonder whether it might not be a good idea for you to come for a visit. I imagine what your days must be like, with so many decisions to make, with so much emptiness in your life. Perhaps, if things can be left for a while, a time with us in the place where you grew up might be of help. Some time for yourself to rest a little, a chance for us to spoil you a little.

I realize that I am asking you to make what might seem an irresponsible decision. Wouldn't it be wonderful though, to walk under the chestnut trees before the leaves fall and winter settles in?

Think about it.
Emilio

"Why not?" said Magdalena. "With the airplane you can be there in no time. Leave Mariana with us, treat yourself and give the count a treat; just don't stay too long for we will miss you too much."

"Maybe," replied Antonia, "but not yet."

XII

BACK AT HER HOUSE after her days at Magdalena's, Antonia began to feel her strength coming back. She began to open the mail and read the letters from the manager in Montana de Plata; she wrote back with questions and instructions. She looked at the bank accounts and realized that there were large amounts of money that needed to be invested. She met with Arturo's partners and listened to their offer to buy her part of the business. She consulted with Don Pedro. "One thing at a time," *"piano, piano,"* he would say to her when she showed him the lists she had made of things to do. There were also days when she had a hard time getting out of bed, when she wanted Arturo so much she could hardly bear it.

One evening, Antonia gathered the strength to open the little safe where Arturo had kept his papers. It was full of envelopes. The one on top was marked ANTONIA in his clear, solid writing. Just seeing it made Antonia feel secure. She opened the envelope. In it were lists of precise directions on what to do if he were to die. They referred mainly to business. They listed everything he owned, and how to sell his share of the business in Pica. There were sentences of advice scattered here and there. They read: "Consult with Don Pedro," "Trust the manager in Montana de Plata." At the end, underlined, he had written: "Trust yourself; my love will always be with you."

As she finished reading these lines, Mariana, who was playing nearby, pulled her skirt. Antonia put the papers away and lifted her child to her lap. She held her child tight as her tears fell on the letter and made the words run together. She thought of her child, who would never know her father. She thought of the stories she and Marco had told themselves to make their own father seem real. "You will grow up to feel you knew your father," she said. "I will teach you about him."

That night Antonia had a strange dream. She dreamed of the day she arrived by boat in Casilda. She was watching the shore from the deck. Standing in the distance was Arturo. He seemed very tall and was dressed in the black cape with which the count had shielded her when she was a little girl. He held the cape open, as if waiting for someone to enter inside it. Suddenly he pointed to something next to her. She turned to look. It was Eliana's coffin. She opened it; inside was Arturo. His face looked rested, not at all the way it looked the day he died. She looked up to the place on the shore where Arturo had stood, and standing there enveloped in the huge cape was Mariana.

Dear Antonia,

Arturo's death has, of course, provided you with a perfect excuse never to visit your ailing mother. I ail not physically, but emotionally, from the abandonment I have experienced all my life.

Now that you are a rich widow, you are a sitting target for fortune

hunters. They move at the moment of grief and offer their support. The aim, however, is only money. In your case, being naive and ordinary-looking with a body ruined by a pregnancy, you will attract the worst of the worst.

Be wise, and keep it for yourself. You don't need a husband, you need a lover. Sell everything and get out of that miserable part of the world. The count is probably telling you the same. I am sure he wants you here to have company in his old age. I see him now and then. He is like a lonely wolf, wrapped in his cape. They say he has sold almost everything. His wife died, so now he doesn't even have the pleasure of planning how to stay away from her.

I have closed off most of the house, and live only on the first floor. It is too painful to see what those foreign beasts did to it. I just concentrate on the garden which, as always, looks beautiful.

Are you teaching that daughter of yours Italian? I do hope she looks like Arturo.

I have heard that widows wear black forever in Yayaku. Is that true? If so you are lucky. Black will make you look thinner.

I have some more advice for you, but why bother since I know you don't listen to me?

Your mother

•   •   •

Dear Count Mora,

You are right; the time has arrived for me to go back to Artemisia. This will be a short visit; I still have many matters to organize here, but I must treat myself to a visit with you. I don't even want to think how it will be to see Dora again.

Even after Arturo's death, the tone of her letters has not softened. Her concerns for me seem to be mostly financial. She says she is worried I will become another Marco and "squander my widow's trove away"!

I will be flying this time. Mariana is too young to make the trip. She will stay here with my friend Magdalena and under the watchful eye of my faithful Toma.

Would you meet me at the airport in Milano? I would like to stay there a few days to revitalize my wardrobe and to arrive in Artemisia rested. We can go together to see The Last Supper, *and spend a few hours at the Poldi Pezzoli. Perhaps we could go to La Scala. How I would love to hear an opera!* Porcinis *will be in season, and I can't wait to have a few roasted ones.*

Above all, I can't wait to see you.

Love,
Antonia

. . .

Dear Antonia,

I anticipate your arrival with great happiness. My heart hurts for you having to make the trip alone, but I will be at the airport waiting for you. I do have tickets for La Bohème, *and the* porcini *are in abundance this year. I remember how I taught you and Marco to like them. It took some doing. You can have them every day!*

I must prepare you, for you will find much has changed. The war has left many scars, not only physical but psychological ones. I have not seen your mother since you wrote of your arrival. I can only tell you that in her own way she must be happy to be able to see you again. Signor Ravecca at the bank told me she asked for money to paint the house. So, you see, she is preparing, too.

Your news reassures me. I am happy you are coping with the business decisions you have to make and that you are able to draw strength from your young daughter. My frustration is that I can be of so little help to you.

Hurry back, my dear Antonia.

With love,
Emilio

XIII

ANTONIA WENT BACK to Italy alone. She started her trip from the airport at the capital this time, on an airplane that zigzagged up the continent, then jumped the ocean to Europe.

The changes frightened her. Whole blocks had disappeared in the bombing, though already new blocks of apartments were going up in their place. Signs of the king and the leader had vanished, and there was a new strange feeling over everything, a sense that the dead had been buried. The talk was of new parties and new constitutions, of a new Europe. The atmosphere was part joy, part fear.

The count met her at the new airport. He carried two canes and had a young nurse with him. "Antonia, Antonia," he said, smiling so hard it seemed as if his wrinkled face would crumble away. "It was worth all those years of waiting through the war just for this."

Antonia choked with emotion and could not bring herself to say anything. She put her arms around the count the way she had done so often as a child and could not make herself stop crying. They sat in the back of the car in silence as the young nurse drove them home.

His new apartment, in one of the recently built apartment blocks, seemed stark and empty compared with what Antonia remembered. Just a few familiar paintings recalled the old days.

"I sold my villa and almost everything in it after my wife died," he said. "All that weight of the past—I had to throw it off. I had to grow light enough to float off the earth; I didn't want to sink in it anymore. So many things I had! The memories clinging to them made them seem even heavier.

"The flat on the Via Malpensa, of course, went in the war. One afternoon I went out for a walk, and the bombardment started. When

I reached home, the house had crumbled to the ground. It was odd that I felt not sad but elated. Perhaps that's what one ought to feel when one lives so long past one's time.

"It is so good to look at you. You are a woman now, I can see, not that frightened little girl I sent off to the New World long ago. The experience looks good on your face, like the gentle weathering on a great palazzo.

"It saddens me enormously to be the one to tell you so much bad news, the news I did not have the heart to write. No one knows what became of your good friend Elsa and her family. They simply disappeared. I hope that they managed to escape the country, but it is hard to tell. So many disappeared during the war; they were scattered like so many leaves. Your uncle's family, too, vanished without a trace not long after the invasion. His sons were with the partisans, they said.

"You will find your mother much changed. I still see her, though only every few months or so. Though she is changed, she is still Donna Dora. I can only imagine how much suffering her letters must have caused you. You must be kind, for Dora knows no other way. Deep down in that heart of hers, which is so hard to see, she is your mother and she loves you."

The count was silent for a long time. Antonia inspected his face closely. The lines in his face were deeper than she remembered, and there were more of them. His eyes had a distant, sad look. Finally, the count broke the silence.

"My dear Antonia, the saddest for all of us is what happened to our Marco. I wonder if we will ever know the truth. I will never forget the day he left, so young, so full of dreams. Marco had no idea what to expect, he was so unprepared. I live with such guilt. I should have done something to stop him, or I should have gone with him. But I felt so unprepared myself. I had spent too much of my life with books, in libraries, pursuing intellectual concerns. The world of business was strange to me. I never thought that simply my presence could have been of help to him. Perhaps I could have tried to find someone there to help him. How hard it must have been to get off that boat, not knowing the language, being met by strangers. Not that it was easier for you, my dear Antonia, but you had Arturo to wait for. Marco had no one. And Dora constantly asking for more money. I can only imagine what kind of letters she wrote to him. I did not get too many letters myself, and the few that I got were confused, as if he felt inadequate, apologizing for not being able to help his mother with her financial problems. I talked to Dora, imploring her to be kind to him. I guess, as usual, she did not listen. I wrote long letters to him; I tried to tell him that Dora was all right, that I had seen to that. I still remember the day, so long ago, when I took you two for ice cream, just after I had met your mother. What beautiful children you were, what need for love you had. When things were over between your mother and me, I prayed to God that I would not lose you, too. It was more important to me than losing Dora. I remember watching the two of you build that boat, your ship of dreams. You were both going to sail away to be with your father. You both did sail away, you to come back a grown woman, capable of overcoming a tragedy, Marco to disappear. Often in the afternoon when I watch the ships I close my eyes and pretend Marco is arriving. I try to imagine how he would look as a grown man: tall and straight, with those blond curls of his. Those tales about his wife, who could have fabricated them? Did he really marry? Was the woman real? And then the war, the cruel war. I wonder, had he stayed, would he have died in the war like so many? I would have preferred that end for him. Marco with his clothes always a bit too small, and his dangling arms, as if they always grew before the rest of his body. He was a son to me, and I was a very poor father."

"You must not say that. Marco had no choice. It was in Papa's will that he had to go. It's Papa I blame for leaving everything in such a mess, for not taking Marco with him before. If Arturo had not died, he had promised me to go and look for Marco after the war. Maybe someday I will. I dream sometimes of finding Marco with a wife and many children, singing gaucho songs. Other times I despair, thinking of him dead, buried in some little cemetery like Arturo. I don't believe the letters, either. Whatever happened, I want you to promise me before I leave that you will never blame yourself. You were the most wonderful thing in both our lives. Every happy memory I have of my life before Arturo is a memory you made for me."

ANOTHER SUNNY DAY, when the count seemed in a more relaxed mood, he took Antonia to lunch at his favorite hotel in Genoa. Sitting on the terrace drinking his coffee, he cleared his throat the way he did when he was about to tell a long story.

"Did I tell you of Dora's story at the end of the war? No? Well, you will probably hear many versions if it, but I have it from Signor Ravecca, who was there all the time. It is a curious story, and I'd rather have you hear it from me.

"You know she took up with the Germans after they occupied the supply station. I don't think she really cared for them; she was never much of a supporter of the Fascists. I think it was, as always, just a matter of survival.

"There was one captain who was her particular favorite, a blond young man who spoke a little Italian. They used to dine at her house in the evenings, with the curtains open and the lights full on, while everyone else in town, who were close to starving, looked on.

"For this, people hated her even more than before, of course. There were not a few who would have gladly strangled her. Her brother was connected with the partisans, you see, and they were afraid she would betray him to the Germans. And then, there were rumors that she was really spying for her brother, not on the Germans' side at all.

"It was a bad time, everything topsy-turvy. No one knew whom to trust, and the Germans distrusted everyone. Later they acted like wild beasts caught in a trap, lashing out at everything. It was all you could do to stay out of their way. Still, Signor Ravecca said, things in Artemisia were not so bad. I don't know why, but he seems to think that Donna Dora had something to do with this.

"Then the bombing started. In Artemisia, the Americans seemed to be trying to hit the railroad bridge at first, but they never managed it. The church they hit first, then the Grande Hotel Artemisia, then all the houses south of your villa. It was extraordinary; the bombs took away everything right up to the edge of your garden, then they stopped.

"One clear night, the people heard the planes again and the crash of the bombs. This time the Americans seemed to have hit what they were aiming for: the entire supply depot was in flames, including the barracks. Half the town, Signor Ravecca said, stood outside until dawn (Dora was nowhere to be seen) watching for some sign of life, but there was none. At dawn they went back to bed. That was the end of the Germans in Artemisia.

"No one is quite sure how Dora survived until the Americans came. No one saw much of her, and by then there was not much I could do

for her. But she did survive. The Americans came with orders to do something with the supply depot. They were black, just like the ones who came here.

"There was nothing left of the depot by then except ruins. So they sent someone up to tell Dora she had to leave, that they needed her house for their headquarters. But she refused to go. Finally, the sergeant had to go to her. He was a big black man, a singer who had studied opera in an American conservatory and knew Italian well. He went up to talk to Dora, but in the end she stayed and the sergeant and his staff moved in with her. Soon it was he you could see dining with Dora with all the lights on. Some nights he would play on your piano, sing Puccini arias, or those strong, sad songs that American Negroes sing. He had a beautiful baritone, Signor Ravecca said, that could have filled Saint Peter's in Rome with ease. Some nights, when he sang, the town would gather in your mother's garden to listen to him.

"The sergeant was a good, friendly, kind young man. There was not much for him to do in Artemisia (his superiors still hadn't got it quite clear that the depot was useless), so he put his men to work to straighten out the mess left in Artemisia by the war. Signor Ravecca, whom the Americans made the mayor, knew the sergeant well and liked him very much. I met him once, too, when he came to Genoa to see the house where Verdi lived. (He was mad for Italian opera, and was furious that the Allies had bombed La Scala.) I don't think he had any evil motive at all in letting Dora stay in the villa. He just believed her when she said she was a poor widow with no place to go. He had his soldiers call her "Contessa" (which must have amused her no end), and they treated her like a queen.

"I don't think there was anything—carnal—between them. To tell the truth, I had the impression the sergeant wasn't particularly interested in women. But of course, the good people of Artemisia thought there had to be, Donna Dora being Donna Dora. For some of them, it was too much; she had rubbed it into their faces for too long. So they complained to the American authorities.

"They must have had no idea that it would get the sergeant into trouble. They only wanted to thwart Donna Dora for a change; they were tired of seeing her always so much better off than they were. They didn't understand how the pulse against what they called 'fraternization' would hurt him, that the black American soldiers were treated differently from the white soldiers, particularly when it came to relations with Italian women.

"But it was the sergeant who was arrested by the military police, and hauled away for trial. The people felt guilty about that; they hadn't had anything against this poor American, but then it was too late.

"Signor Ravecca had to go to the trial as a witness, so he saw Dora's great performance. It was, from what he said, her greatest.

"Those who spoke against the sergeant at the court martial claimed that he had used his official position 'to seduce and take advantage of a young Italian woman.' Then Dora came into the courtroom. Signor Ravecca said he did not recognize her. She was dressed in the costume of an old peasant woman, a black dress covering her legs, heavy black shoes, and a black shawl over her head. She had made herself look ancient. Signor Ravecca said that he forgave her everything she had done when he saw that. He knew that this was a kind of supreme sacrifice for her, that she could only have done it selflessly to help the sergeant who had helped her.

"She spoke to the court in the voice of an old lady of Liguria. She thanked the Americans for sending such a 'good, kind man' to Artemisia. She said she was an old woman whose husband was dead, whose children had abandoned her; and she dipped her head, as if to hide her tears. And 'that great, kind American,' she said, meaning the sergeant, 'had saved her from starving, from throwing herself into the sea of despair.'

"Then she looked up into the eyes of the judges. 'I thank the Lord Jesus,' she said, 'for sending such good Americans to help our poor, old people, abandoned to these hard times by their own families.'

"Of course the sergeant was let off immediately, and the military judges even thanked Dora for speaking for him. I think he still writes to her."

XIV

THAT NIGHT ANTONIA had trouble sleeping, thinking about the war, about all the suffering it had inflicted, and how far from it all she had been. She also thought about Arturo, about the day he left her on the boat in Genoa, how she had left alone and returned alone.

When she finally did fall asleep, she dreamed about the war. She saw explosions and fires and soldiers dying in the desert. She saw people dying together, people who had never had anything else in common, making one great scream that couldn't be heard because the scream of the flames around them was even louder. She saw quieter deaths—of disease, starvation, sadness. She saw huge cities of hollow shells that had once been buildings. She saw all the things that had happened while she was away in Pica, things that she had only been able to imagine.

On the third day, Antonia got ready to go to Artemisia.

"Do you think she got my letter?" she asked the count. "It's been months since I've heard anything from her."

"I know she's expecting you, because she told me she was. Whether that means you should expect anything from her is another matter. But there is no point in worrying about it, either way, of course."

Antonia sighed. "I know that."

THE SIGHT of Artemisia shocked her even more than she expected. The bombing had done more than even the count had described. Not only the Grande Hotel Artemisia was gone, but also the station and two of the pastel villas. All that was left of the supply depot was a few steel girders in the sand. The foundation was gone—carted off by the Germans, she learned later, as scrap metal. And as for the church, scaffolding over the facade prevented it from collapsing into the crater behind it. The entire district south of her mother's villa was gone. The rubble had already been cleared away, so there was nothing to show that there had been houses except a few stray bricks and a pipe sticking up here and there from the ground.

As she climbed the hill, she could see how Dora's villa had suffered. Though it was still standing, it had a tired, grim look, like that of a survivor at the end of a long battle. The garden was little more than a plot of packed earth, with one half-dead palm standing in it. The south side of the house, next to the bombed-out district, was covered with pockmarks and scars from the flames. Across the road, Roberto's house looked empty. A rusting bedstead stood outside the door.

When Antonia knocked, the door opened almost immediately. Dora was standing there. She neither smiled nor spoke, simply held open the door so Antonia could walk in.

"Hello, Mother," Antonia said.

Dora simply shrugged, as if to say, "So, you are back." Antonia looked at her. She was much smaller than she remembered. Her hair was gray, and tied up tightly in the back. Her clothes were simple, almost severe, pale in color, but, as Antonia could see, beautifully made. And the skirt of her dress was cut short enough to show her legs, which were as lovely as ever. She wore no makeup. Her face resembled the outside of her villa: worn, a bit tired, but still strong and determined.

Antonia was overcome by an intense feeling of sadness, yet she could not cry or make herself say anything. She wanted to get close to her mother but her feet could not move. She looked for changes in Dora but saw only the same Dora, in control. She could not tell if her mother was happy to see her.

Antonia followed her to the parlor, the one in which Dora had met Arturo before the war. Antonia was shocked by the interior of the house. The marble floor of the hall was cracked, scarred, and badly stained. A few pieces of familiar furniture were still there. In one corner two chairs had been placed near a window. Dora moved toward those chairs and took a book that had been placed on a small table next to them. "Read the places I have marked," Dora said. "I want to hear the language they speak in the places my husband and children abandoned me for."

It was a copy of *Martín Fierro*.

Antonia began to read in Spanish.

"Stop," said Dora. "Now that you know the language, translate it for me."

Antonia did the best she could, translating into Italian the passages Dora had marked in pencil.

"All these years," Dora said when Antonia finished, "all these years I wanted to know what he wrote."

There was a long silence. Dora sat looking out into clouds full of rain. Antonia caught sight of her old piano. She stood up and moved close to it. Her hands caressed the old keys. Much of the ivory was gone, and the instrument was so out of tune that Antonia winced. On the stand there was the sheet of a Schubert minuet, one she had loved as a child and had not played for years. She started to play, ignoring the keys that no longer produced sound. She began to enjoy herself. Her memory jumped with almost every note: First Madame de Cranne's voice told her to move more slowly; next the count was beside her; finally, her father was in the room, nodding and smiling. Then she heard Dora's cough, the cough that as a child told her it was time to stop playing.

Antonia stood up and walked to the kitchen where she made tea from what she could find. She and her mother sat together, still talking very little, as the parlor grew dark. Antonia noticed how cold the room was, but Dora didn't seem to mind.

"Mother," Antonia said, "wouldn't you like someone to come up from the village to look after you?"

"I've managed on my own for all these years," Dora said with a frown.

"I know. We could get someone to come up in the mornings. She wouldn't have to live here. She could make sure you were all right, and she'd be a little companionship for you when I go back."

Dora said nothing, but Antonia thought she looked a little less grim, a little more contented. Antonia smiled at her for a moment, and stood up to turn on the lights, and to leave. "I will be away for a few days," said Dora. Antonia knew nothing had really changed.

ANTONIA TURNED down the count's invitation to stay longer, to come back to live in Artemisia. Dora remained silent. The count knew the time for her departure was near, but he wanted Antonia to feel completely ready. It hurt him to think of her going alone, to face that place that she never really liked. But she was determined to go back and run Arturo's business.

She talked about the school she was starting for her daughter, and laughed about it. She was going to have to do much of the work herself. She had gone to visit the Americans at the mine, and persuaded them to contribute materials and money. Arturo had donated the land. Nuns came from Italy to teach in Pica. But when they arrived, it turned out they were from a nursing order, used to caring for the terminally ill, and they knew no Spanish. They were also extremely timid and unused to the dry, hot air of Pica. Antonia said that they spent much of their time shut away in the little dormitory Antonia had built for them.

She told the count that she had wanted to buy a place by the ocean near Pica and build a stone house there, just one room. She would go out there herself, or take her friend Magdalena with her. She said she wanted to be with Arturo so much that it hurt, and that she had to learn to be alone.

"Don't you get lonely out there?" asked the count.

"No," she said. "Not anymore. I have my whole life to keep me company there."

"Have you reconciled with your mother?" the count asked quietly.

"I am not sure 'reconciled' is the right word," she responded. "As we grow older, my mother and I are more alike.

"Everyone seems to me to be two people," she said. "There is an everyday person on the outside, and a private person on the inside. Sometimes I think I'm my mother inside out."

The count tapped his cane on the ground. He wasn't sure exactly what she meant. Dora always struck him as a very selfish person, and Antonia didn't seem that way at all to him. Perhaps she meant that the outrageous Antonia was all on the inside, that she was far less conventional than she seemed. He thought that there might have been some truth to that.

One day, while walking in the woods, he asked her if she had any happy memories of Dora.

"I have a few," said Antonia. "Curiously, those were the ones that I think about most often. It is as if time had scratched away the bad ones."

"Will you tell me about a happy one, Antonia? At my age I prefer remembering the happy ones."

The count sat on a bench under a huge oak tree. Antonia sat close to him and held his hand gently, the way she had when she was a little girl.

"I remember my twelfth birthday. My mother was up and dressed for the city when I came down for breakfast, something most unusual.

" 'I do not have a birthday present chosen for you, Antonia,' Dora said without smiling. 'You are old enough now, I think, to choose your own. Tell the nuns I will pick you up at four today. We should have time to find your gift before we go to the Excelsior for dinner.'

"I could think of nothing else but my mother's promise during school, knowing that her promises did not always come true but hoping that this one would. But at four, as I stood, as usual, slightly apart from my clamoring classmates around the steps of the convent, my mother's car drew up.

"This particular car was one of the grandest my mother ever had. It was swift and nearly silent, long and low to the ground—caramel-colored, with deep-blue leather upholstery and flashing touches of chrome along the fenders and running boards. The seats were deep and the windows high under the roof, so that the occupants were bathed in a shadow of importance.

"The babble around us ceased as fifty pairs of eyes turned toward my mother's driver, elegant for once in a pearl-gray uniform, opening the passenger door. I trembled as I stepped toward him; the other girls shrank back a little. They had never been so close to my notorious mother before.

"I dropped my book bag twice before I climbed into the car, but, remarkably, my mother pretended not to notice my clumsiness. She was dressed in a tight-fitting dress in the same color as the driver's uniform. She wore a collar and hat of snowy feathers that looked like a cluster of clouds around her face.

"She had a pleasant, distant smile on her face, an expression she usually saved for particularly elegant occasions. 'What would you like for your birthday?' she asked. 'A toy, a piece of jewelry, or a new dress?'

"For some reason I couldn't explain why, but I immediately answered, 'A piece of jewelry.' The choice came naturally and almost automatically.

"My mother ordered the driver to a store I had never heard of. We rode in silence, except that she made comments once or twice on my school uniform. 'The only kind of clothes that nuns can think of,' she said, 'are the kind that make you believe women have the bodies of angels.'

"The jewelry store was as remarkable as everything else that day. It had rows of white columns inside, like a temple, and was quieter than a church. The floor was so shiny and slippery beneath my patent-leather shoes that I thought I would never get to the glittering counters that spread into the distance.

"A tall man dressed in black greeted us at the door. He clearly knew my mother well, and treated her with great respect. My mother introduced me. 'Tell Signor Rondo what sort of jewelry you have in mind. And please, Signore, keep in mind the limits of a girl of twelve.'

" 'A bracelet,' I said. I had always wanted a bracelet. My mother had dozens, and I had none, except for one Marco had made me out of seashells. Signor Rondo led me and my mother to a silk-covered couch where we sat while he disappeared into the back of the store. He returned with a blue velvet tray with five bracelets on it.

"I picked up one that had tiny red stones set in little gold beads. It was the most beautiful thing I had ever seen. 'This one,' I said to my mother, who nodded at Signor Rondo.

" 'Good. And, Signore, your regular discount, if you please. I imagine there are not many who bring you as much business as I do.'

"Signor Rondo bowed, took away the tray, and came back with the bracelet in a red leather box stamped with gold designs and two little crowns. It was exactly like the boxes I had seen so often on my mother's dressing table. 'Thank you,' I said to my mother, and Signor Rondo called me *'la bella bambina.'* On the way back to Artemisia I held the little box so tightly that the wrapping was wet by the time we reached the villa.

"Marco, who had taken the train down from Genoa, was already dressed. He ran after me when I rushed up to change for dinner. We opened the box together, and Marco put the bracelet on my wrist. 'You see, Marco, a miracle has happened. Wait for your birthday, you will get what you want, too.'

"Dinner was long and quiet. The Excelsior, which was dark, stiff, and full of gray-haired people, was not the sort of place a child could easily enjoy. It took so long to get dinner, and there were so many courses that both Marco and I were nodding in our seats before dessert. The music made us sleepy, and my mother insisted, as she always did at the Excelsior, that we all stay quiet while the music played.

"My mother also insisted that we each have a glass of champagne with dessert, and I grew so dizzy that I remembered nothing of the ride home. Marco, however, had taken care to count the money my mother paid, and told Eliana that evening that 'with so much money, you could buy groceries for a month.' "

"It is getting cooler," the count said. He stood up and offered her his hand.

WHEN THEY MET again, it was a few days later, after Antonia had been to see Dora.

"I have seen my mother," said Antonia. "Her life has been spent protecting her invention: herself. I think she feels she has succeeded and is happy."

"Well, Antonia, I think you are continuing the tradition and inventing your own self in Pica."

Antonia smiled. He grasped her arm, placing on her some of the weight that his weak legs could no longer hold, and they walked toward the bench under the oak tree. They sat together in comfortable silence. After a while, Antonia kissed the count's cheek and rose to leave.

Antonia knew the time had come for her to go back to Pica. Every day she felt more anxious and a sense of restlessness colored everything she did. More and more her thoughts were directed to her life back there. She wanted to hold Mariana, to get back to her own house, to continue the life she and Arturo had started. These weeks back in Artemisia had strengthened her resolve. She realized that she had left Mariana in Pica as an insurance that she would return. Next time they would come to Italy together, and go home together.

She made all the arrangements for the trip and told no one. The day before she left, she went to say goodbye to her mother.

She found Dora in the garden, sitting in a large rocking chair. It was cool and she had her legs wrapped in a shawl. She wore a large straw hat and her face was looking at a book in her lap.

"Mother," Antonia began.

"I know it, you have come to say goodbye. I saw you yesterday. You did not see me. You were at the bank. The clerk told me you were there to get money to go on a trip," said Dora with her eyes fixed on her book. "You left me once, so there is nothing new about you leaving me again. Go and say no goodbyes. I have heard too many of them in my lifetime."

Dora reached under her chair for a small box wrapped in lavender paper. She handed it to Antonia without looking up. "Take this package with you," she said. Antonia kissed her forehead and walked away. From the sidewalk, when she turned to look at the house once more, she saw Dora standing at the door. The last image of her mother was that of a soldier proudly standing guard. It was a suitable image, Dora guarding her house the way she had always guarded her impenetrable self.

SAYING GOODBYE to the count was more difficult. They had agreed to have dinner that evening. The day seemed endless to Antonia as she thought of how to break the news to him. She went to the restaurant very early and watched him walk in. He looked so old: His movements were slow and painful, his attire worn, his smile tentative.

They sat in silence for a long time, looking at the gray ocean, both waiting for the other to start the conversation. Finally the waiter interrupted to offer them a drink. The count, who had stopped drinking a long time ago, ordered a grappa, and Antonia, who never drank, did the same.

In the end it was the count who broached the subject. "The time has come, dear Antonia, for you to go back; your life is in Pica with your daughter, in the world your Arturo left you, with the strength he left you. Your visit has made me happy. You must believe me when I tell you that is also true for Dora. We no longer have to worry about our Antonia. Go in happiness, my dear. You have made my old age a peaceful one. So, write often, and send many pictures."

At that point his voice broke down; he could say no more. In tears, Antonia reached for his hand across the table. "I wish you could come with me," she said.

"I have thought of that, my dear Antonia, but I am afraid at my age I would be a burden to you. Besides you well know that traveling has always been hard for me. I will be going with you in my thoughts. I will have your letters to look forward to."

Neither the count nor Antonia said much at dinner. The waiters removed the dishes that had been left untouched. It was getting late, and everyone had left the restaurant. The waiter brought the bill and began to turn some of the lights off. The count swallowed the last drop of his grappa and from one of his many pockets he pulled a wrinkled handkerchief and dried Antonia's tears. From another pocket, the one where he kept his mints, he took out a small package, a red velvet box with a white ribbon around it. "Open it," he said to Antonia.

Her hands were shaking as she fumbled with the ribbon. In the box was a pair of emerald earrings, the ones worn by the count's mother in her portrait that Antonia had seen.

"I want you to have them, Antonia. They were given to my great-grandmother by her father on her wedding day. They have always gone to the oldest daughter in the family, so they belong to you, and someday to Mariana. Wear them in joy."

He stood up, walked around the table to where Antonia was sitting, and offered her his arm. "Let's walk home," he said, "there is so much we could say, but tonight words are not suitable."

"Good night. Good night, Father," Antonia said when he left her at the door of her hotel. Antonia realized that she should have called him Father a long time ago. She stood in the darkness and watched the count leave. She felt like running back to him. Instead, she walked slowly to her room. In the long hours before Antonia fell asleep, she thought of the count and of what her life would have been without him.

Before leaving Artemisia, Antonia had one more errand to attend to. Arturo's wish had been to be buried near his family in the little cemetery outside town. Antonia bought a small lot, just big enough for the two of them, under a huge oak tree. She left instructions with Signor Ravecca at the bank. When she died, both their bodies were to be brought back from Pica and buried, under a tombstone made of simple marble, with only their names carved on it. She remembered the trips with her mother and Marco to the cemetery in Genoa, how Dora had made them read the elaborate inscriptions and admire the depressing statuary. She wanted none of that.

XV

THE NEXT DAY Antonia took the train to Genoa. No one saw her to the station. It was the same train she had taken with Arturo so many times. As the train pulled out of the station, she held the package her mother had given her and allowed memories of Arturo to invade her mind. The memories were happy ones, full of his tenderness. She felt a sense of peace. Her hands began to pull the string that held Dora's package together. As the paper unfolded, a note fell out. It was on Dora's purple stationery and smelled of her perfume. "Antonia: When Arturo's house in Artemisia was destroyed during the war, I went there. As I walked through the debris I found a box that contained these photographs. I have saved them for you. I kept one for myself, the one of Arturo at twenty-one. What a handsome man he was! When I die, you shall have that one, too. Your mother."

For a long time she looked at the little box. It had been so carefully wrapped; the paper was so soft and the bow so perfect that Antonia was almost afraid to open it. She looked out the window and saw the olive groves moving past her. She thought of the many olive trees she had planted in her garden in Pica and wondered how much they might have grown in her absence. She felt ready to go back.

Antonia looked at the pictures. On top was a faded photograph of a young boy dressed for his first communion. Looking at it intently, she could see Arturo's features in his child's face: the immense brown eyes set under bushy eyebrows, the large mouth, this time kept firmly tight for the benefit of the photographer, his huge hands holding a large candle. She remembered when Arturo had told her about his first communion. Arturo, who had never liked school, had not attended the catechism classes given to prepare for the day. He knew the priest would not give him communion, but he did not have the heart to tell his parents. So he spent the night in the basement, hoping they would not find him in the morning. It was his mother's tears that got him out and dressed in the "ridiculous" white outfit which belonged to a cousin and was a size too small. As he stood in line with his classmates, ready to receive the communion wafer, the priest skipped him. On the way home there were more tears from his mother. His father punished him and he was not allowed to attend the lunch that had been prepared in his honor. His relatives called him a "heretic." He did not know what it meant, but he had liked the sound of the word. That night when he was in bed and his mother came to say good night, he asked her what "heretic" meant. "A person who has a very personal kind of religion and not that of the church," she answered. Arturo told Antonia he never forgave himself for having ruined the day for his mother and that he never loved her more than for understanding him that day.

There was a picture of Arturo as a young man, dressed in a heavy overcoat, standing beside a heavy-looking young woman. Antonia recognized her as the woman his family had wanted him to marry, a relative who had become a nun. Another one of Arturo in his riding outfit, next to a white horse in the outskirts of Pica. In the back he had written, "To Mother with affection from the Knight of Pica." She smiled, thinking of the day when he had finally returned to Pica and had stood in the balcony with her, waving at the crowd that had come to greet him. The Knight of Pica.

There was a picture of his parents on their wedding day. How Arturo resembled his father! The same posture, the same stance with one foot slightly ahead of the other, the same confident, warm smile. Arturo's eyes were like his mother's, set wide apart, under the same huge forehead.

There was a picture of Arturo's office in Pica; the date was twenty years before his death.

She found several pictures of the house in the plaza. On the back he had written detailed descriptions of the rooms for his mother; he wrote so proudly of those French furnishings she had so quickly disposed of. Antonia felt guilty. Why had he never said anything about the changes? Didn't he like them? Had his taste changed? She would never know.

There were many pictures of Arturo as a young man. In Venice with pigeons in his hands, in front of the Vatican with his mother, in school sitting behind his desk. Antonia looked at them, trying to find clues to the Arturo she didn't know. She still had so many things to ask him.

There was a picture of an unfamiliar woman. It was so faded that it was hard to see her features. All that Antonia could make out was the woman's long black hair, her long thin neck, and the outline of her perfectly oval face. Antonia wondered if she had been someone Arturo had loved. Arturo never said much to her about other women in his life. Once, when she had asked him, he answered, "Before you, no one really mattered, and now, and forever, there is only you."

At the end, Antonia came across the picture of Arturo that had been used by the newspapers on his death. For a moment it seemed to her that Arturo was there sitting next to her. She could no longer hold her tears. When the train finally stopped and it was time to get off, she stayed in her seat. The conductor was obliged to remind her gently that they had arrived in Genoa.

The next day the boat left the harbor and started its long, slow trip to Yayaku. Unlike the other passengers, Antonia did not stay on deck to watch the disappearing cityscape. She sat in her cabin and began to make an album with the pictures of Arturo's youth. She thought of Mariana in Pica and of the day not far off when they would look at the album together. She imagined the questions Mariana would ask, and wondered what answers she would give.

WHEN ANTONIA arrived back in Pica four weeks later, she found an airmail letter from the count, postmarked a week earlier.

Dear Antonia,

I wish I did not have to give you this sad news. Dora died yesterday. She went without suffering, from a stroke in her sleep.

It was Signor Ravecca who found her. She had an appointment with him that morning. When she didn't arrive, he called several times and decided to go to the house. He entered through a window.

Dora had left him a letter to be read on her death. The letter was addressed to me.

I am now in the process of fulfilling her last wishes. She is to be buried tomorrow in the cemetery in Genoa, in a plot she purchased many years ago. Standing in the center of the plot will stand a statue of "the black angel." I have not yet seen the statue, but Dora's letter says it is in storage at the quarry in Pietrasanta. There is to be no epitaph; just her name: Dora di Credi.

She asked that no mass be said, and that the death announcement be printed only after her funeral. So it will be only Signor Ravecca and I who will bid her goodbye.

I saw your mother only once after you left. Two weeks ago, I was sitting on a bench along the boulevard staring out to sea. I must have been distracted for I never saw her arrive. I heard her voice, that deep, cold voice she had sometimes.

"What are you doing here, Emilio?" she asked, staring at me.

"I come here to watch the ships," I answered. "I like watching them go in and come out."

Dora turned back to the water and was silent for a moment. "As far as I am concerned," she said, "the ships only go out. They all sail away and leave me behind."

There was a sadness in her voice.

"What do you come here to see, if not the ships?" I asked. "Does the ocean fascinate you, or the sunbathers?"

She did not turn her head this time.

"I come here often to watch the clouds," she said. "I watch the shadows of the clouds passing over the sand. They are pictures, but I can't quite make them out. They move, they change so fast."

She turned to me again. Her face had melted slightly; it looked very tired and worried. I was surprised by her posture; she no longer sat straight as she always did; her shoulders sagged. "So, you see why I come? I can't make them out. It is as if God writes messages, and then wipes them away before we can read them."

She rose from the bench and walked away. I watched her disappear, moving in that perfect rhythm of hers.

That must have been her way of saying goodbye to me.

Dora with all her confusing messages and her surprises. Dora at the end waiting for messages from God in the clouds and in the sand.

I shall miss her. I shall always thank her for giving you to me.

She left for you this picture of Arturo and everything else she owned. Signor Ravecca and I have taken all the valuables to the bank. We shall see that the house and the garden are maintained until you are ready to make decisions.

Courage, Antonia. Kiss your Mariana for me.

Love,
Emilio

A Note About the Author

Gabriella De Ferrari was born and raised in Peru before moving to the United States, where she earned degrees from St. Louis University, the Fletcher School of Law and Diplomacy, and Harvard University. In Boston, she became Director of the Institute of Contemporary Art, then Curator of the Busch Reisinger Museum at Harvard and Assistant Director of the Fogg Art Museum. Gabriella De Ferrari writes extensively on issues of contemporary art. She divides her time between Connecticut and New York City, where she lives with her two children. *A Cloud on Sand* is her first novel.

A Note on the Type

This book was set in a digitized version of Bodoni, a type face named after Giambattista Bodoni (1740–1813), a celebrated printer and type designer of Rome and Parma. Present-day Bodoni type faces were adapted from the original Bodoni designs and were cut for Monotype machine typesetting in 1911. Bodoni's innovations in type style included a greater degree of contrast in the thick and thin elements of the letters and a sharper and more angular finish of details.

Composed by Creative Graphics, Inc.,
Allentown, Pennsylvania

Printed and bound by The Haddon Craftsmen
Scranton, Pennsylvania

Designed by Anthea Lingeman